MW00790316

NIGHTS OF STEEL AND SHADOW

VOCAB FROM NIGHTS OF IRON AND INK

1. **High fae:** Immortal beings possessing magical powers.
2. **Halflings:** Half fae, half mortal. They do not possess fae's magical powers, but they share their strength, speed, and healing abilities.
3. **Draoistone:** Blue stone that acts as conduit for channeling wild fae magic.
4. **All-Seeing-Eye:** Possesses the ability to see the past, present, and future. It stole Vera's fighting knowledge in exchange for showing her where the godstone would be in the future.
5. **Godstone:** Weapon capable of killing anything, including a God. The Nighters' stole it and are now hiding out with it in the Spirit Lands.
6. **Spirit Lands:** Realm of the dead running parallel to The Lands. Only a pooka can access.
7. **The Rogues:** Halflings that ran away from the Faylands and protect Mayhem from the beasts every full moon.

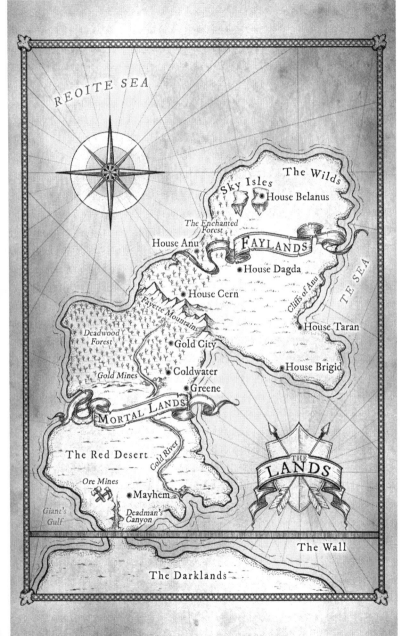

ENCYCLOPEDIA OF BEASTS

Categorized by land, air, and water.

Broken into tiers based on power level: 1-4 with one being the least powerful and four being the most powerful.

AIR BEASTS:

1. Broberie: Appears as a small black bird who moves in locust like swarms to devour dead bodies whole, bones and all. (Tier 1)

2. Flying srphy: Appears as a snake with wings that spits venom. One drop can kill five full grown adults. (Tier 1)

3. Banshee: Appears as a translucent woman in mourning. Wails can burst the eardrum of every living being within a mile radius. (Tier 2)

4. Crua: Appears as a slender figure cloaked in darkness. Controls shadows and uses them as its minions. (Tier 2)

5. Sloaugh: Appears as a skeletal figure in a black shroud. Devours the souls of its victims while it shows them sad memories of their dead ones. (Tier 3)

6. Callitech: Appears as a frozen woman. It freezes its victims, turning them to ice before shattering them. (Tier 3)

7. Fomoire: Appears as a shifting ball of smoke. Turns its victim's greatest nightmare into reality. (Tier 4)

WATER BEASTS:

1. Muckey: Appears as a tiny fish with razor sharp teeth that burrows into its victim's stomach and eats them from the inside out. (Tier 1)

2. Grundylow: Appears as a frog-like creature with fangs that move in schools of hundreds and drag their victims to their death. (Tier 1)

3. Ashray: Appears as a translucent sea ghost that electrocutes its victims to death. (Tier 2)

4. Mermer: Appears as a half humanoid, half fish with fangs and talons. Lures men to their deaths. (Tier 2)

5. Fearga: Appears as a faceless humanoid with excessively wrinkled skin. Dehydrates its victims. (Tier 3)

6. Kelpa: Appears as a shape shifter that shows the victim their greatest desire, luring them into the water's depths to drown. (Tier 3)

7. Treachna: Appears as a three-headed serpent with tentacles capable of controlling currents, capsizing boats, and devouring them whole. (Tier 4)

LAND BEASTS:

1. Corth: Appears as a faceless, armless humanoid that spits acid from a hole in its chest. (Tier 1)

2. Abca: Appears as a short, powerful humanoid made of rock with the power to punch through bone and flesh with a single blow. (Tier 1)

3. Failin: Appears as four times the size of a normal wolf with poisonous, retractable spikes hidden beneath its fur. (Tier 2)

4. Bodah: Appears as a faceless humanoid with long spindly fingers that cast webbing to catch its victims and devour them. (Tier 2)

5. Fets: Appears as the face of their victim, temporarily blindsiding them before killing them. (Tier 3)

6. Dullah: Appears as a headless horseman that carries the spine of its latest victim into battle. (Tier 3)

7. Aibeya: Appears as a female playing the harp. Lulls victims into a false state of calm and sleepiness during which time it carves out their heart and devours it. (Tier 4)

Spirit Beast:

1. Pooka: Appears as a shape-shifting creature that is more spirit than beast. Can travel vast distances in the blink of an eye by hopping between the spirit realm and the realm of the living. (Tier unknown)

PROLOGUE
RONAN

I had walked in darkness for so long, I had forgotten there was light—until her.

Five hundred years ago, I accepted the Enforcer role, knowing I was not only protecting my House, but the Faylands too. I swung my sword with an unwavering conviction that the ends justified the means. But as time progressed, the so-called criminals looked more like desperate mortals. They were no threat.

My confidence dwindled, and the duty I once held as an honor, turned my stomach.

A small piece of me died with every life I took, but I couldn't stop. I had to march on even if I was disgusted by my task.

That's what a good soldier did.

The ink tattooed across my chest was a reminder. I walked in darkness so everyone I loved didn't have to. But how long could I dance with the dark before I became it?

I turned to my battle-mode.

I descended into it more and more to perform my duties; relied on it to shut off my mind and allow my body to do what needed to be done, even if I abhorred it, even as ice crept into my soul.

I started bringing women back as a distraction. Fucking was the only way to make it through the day, the only respite from the deadness inside. For just a few hours, I didn't suffer the unending bleakness of *nothing*.

When a gun had gone off that fateful day, I'd been intrigued. No mortal had ever been so brazen. I was ready to cut them down, until my gaze collided with the most alluring lilac eyes. They shimmered with such fierceness, and such pain.

That wild gaze ripped me from the darkness. It burned away the ice in my bones. My whole body screamed to life.

I didn't know who she was, or what, and I didn't care. I wanted her. I was desperate for her. I needed her blazing passion to keep me warm, to light up my dark world.

The disgust that crossed her features when I offered my hand was expected, so was the fear. It was her fear that stalled me. Others' fear had become as familiar to me as my sword, but I couldn't stand it on her. I didn't want her to be afraid.

Leaving her there, leaving the only thing that had broken through the numbness, was the second most diffi-cult thing I ever had to do, the first burying my mother.

Even though it felt like I was ripping out my own heart, I left. But her eyes—those pain-filled eyes—haunted me day and night. I wanted to eviscerate whoever had stolen their light. It took all my self-control not to hunt her down and demand answers.

When I saw her lying outside the wagon, I thought I was hallucinating. The explosion had left her badly injured, but I'd recognize that beautiful gaze anywhere. I brought her back to my tent to ensure she could heal in safety.

I examined her as she slept, to determine how severe her

injuries were, when I discovered the heavy scarring on her wrists and ankles. I sharpened my blade, preparing to carve open whoever had put them there.

She healed quickly for a halfling. Add to that the lack of a fae brand, and her talons, and I was fascinated. Who was this stunning creature, and why did being in her presence feel so good?

I planned to question her, maybe toy with her a little, before releasing her.

Two words had sealed her fate.

Make me.

If she had been looking, she would have seen my first smile in centuries.

She wasn't afraid.

Vera was mine. She just didn't know it yet.

I knew if I let her go, I would never see her again. I didn't think twice about threatening her life or forcing her into a bargain. I would have killed to keep her.

I had no experience in courting. The females I had been with didn't require it, and I wanted far more than sex from Vera.

The first night, after our disastrous interaction at the river, I returned and used a scrying mirror to ask an old friend for advice. She told me women love gifts. I gave Vera my best dagger the next morning.

She threatened to use it on me.

Next, I gave her silver to buy the finest foods the Mortal Lands had to offer. She bought food that was barely edible and pulled a gun on me. With all those eyes on us in the alley, I had to threaten her, force her to back down. I couldn't have anyone thinking that I had gone soft.

Truthfully, it gave me a perverse thrill. We were locked in a battle of wills and Vera gave it as good as she got. She was strong enough to stand up to me. That was rare.

3

Sensing she needed space, I left, and spent an hour looking for a cloak that was as pretty as her eyes and chains that would be less abrasive on her wrists. She called me disgusting for it, but beneath all the hatred and contempt, I could see her confusion—sense her discomfort. Vera wasn't accustomed to kindness, perhaps even a little fearful of it.

I knew she found me attractive. I could smell her arousal anytime I was near, and I was damn good at sex. Surely, I could win her that way. But no, she fought her attraction as hard as she fought me.

Doubt started to set in.

Kidnapping and forcing her into a bargain didn't lend well to romance, but then she'd open that sassy fucking mouth, and I knew I would take her any way I could. I would have set myself on fire and let her watch me burn just to keep her near.

Gods . . . how she fought me. At every turn. I reveled in her strength, in her fearlessness. With her, I wasn't the feared Enforcer, I was just a man. Slowly, painstakingly, I dismantled the armor around her heart.

The more she let me in, the harder I fell.

As she did, I discovered that beneath her fierceness was a well of pain. She was good at hiding it, but like I told her, the eyes could never deceive half as well as the tongue. It wasn't until we arrived at the Crone's cabin that the pieces came together.

The fury that seized me when she had me forced outside was blinding, and when I heard her scream . . . I had never shifted into my battle-mode so quickly.

The violence I unleashed on that barrier to get to Vera would have toppled cities. The Crone's magic should have shattered under mine. That was my first warning the witch was much more powerful than she let on.

I had heard many awful sounds on the battlefield. Young

soldiers begging for their lives, the last whispered breath before a soul departs the body, the sickening squelch of a blade entering a heart—those noises were deeply unpleasant. But Vera's pain-filled cry, that sound was more wretched than all those combined.

I never wanted to hear it again as long as I lived.

I wasn't prepared for the grisly sight when she collapsed in my arms. The Crone had ripped open her back to the bone. If Vera hadn't needed me, I would have gutted that fucking witch. The mountain of scars ravaging her back told me it had happened many times before.

The Crone had tortured her as a child and was able to harm her again because of me. I would *never* forgive myself for that. I vowed right then, I would protect her at all costs.

Vera would never suffer again.

After I learned she was a dragon, I knew the Faylands wasn't safe. The other Houses would hunt her, if the king didn't add her to his collection of beasts first. I needed her to stay away until I could ensure her safety, but I knew Vera was too willful and stubborn to reason with.

So I looked the woman I would have burned the world down for in the eye and became a monster.

Agony had ripped through my bones at the sight of her tears. But I pushed on, lashing her with words even as my heart cracked open because I'd take her hatred over her suffering any day.

My legs were leaden as I walked away. It only took until I reached the kitchen to realize I couldn't do that to her. I would find another solution, chain her up if I had to.

I rushed back to our room to find Vera and all her belongings gone.

It's for the best. She's safe.

While I had been running back to her, Vera had been poisoning my food.

~

"I made a mistake." Vera's voice cracked. "I was just upset."

A mistake . . .

She was the one who had warned me of the target on my back and had offered my life up to the enemy on a silver platter. She had the audacity to call it a *mistake*?

I couldn't bear the thought of living in this world without her—without those radiant eyes, without that blazing passion, but she didn't hesitate to put my life in peril like it meant nothing.

Like I meant nothing.

My eyes burned. I tore them away.

"I've hurt people. Slaughtered thousands, but you, Vera?" I said, my voice rough. "I could never. Even if the Gods themselves commanded it, I would sooner run a blade through my own chest than see a single drop of your blood spilled."

Even after she confessed her crime before the gallows, all I could think about was how to save her, but I was too weak to do more than beg.

I glanced back, holding her gaze.

"I am not a good man. I know that. Everyone, even my own people, fears me, and for good reason. You were the first who wasn't afraid. The first person to really see me. Not the Enforcer, but Ronan Taran. I didn't feel like a monster when I was with you, but you used me. You made me think —" my breath trembled "—You made me think you cared for me, all the while you were plotting my death. I should have known better. Everyone wants to fuck the monster, but no one wants to love him."

I had foolishly thought she was my reward for all the centuries of turmoil, for all the personal sacrifice. I thought she was my salvation. I could see now that she was my punishment, my damnation.

"Ronan, I lo—"

"Don't," I whispered.

"But it's true."

"No. People don't poison the ones they love. If what you claim is true, you could have disposed of the iron dust at any time, but you kept it. You were always going to use it."

I could understand why she had gotten the iron dust from the Nighters. I had not started our relationship under the best of terms, but I had taken such care to show her what she meant to me.

The night she trusted me enough to sleep in my arms without chains, I was certain I had finally broken through the guard around her heart. I was certain she returned my feelings. But if that were true, she wouldn't have kept the iron dust.

I also understood what I said played a role in her actions. Regardless of my intent, I had been cruel. It wasn't that she had used the iron dust. It was that she had kept it. Whether she was willing to admit it, or not, she hadn't made up her mind about using it. A part of her was okay with my death. A part of her still believed I was a monster.

Vera parted her lips, but I stopped her. "I won't believe a word that comes out of your mouth."

The trust we had worked so hard to gain was shattered.

"I'm sorry," she whispered. "I'm so sorry."

The way she was looking at me, with those big, beautiful tear-filled eyes, took all my strength not to break down and forgive her, but I couldn't.

I had spent centuries alone, hated, and reviled. I had become this *thing* to everyone else, stripped of all humanity. I had no heart, no soul in their eyes. It had been a lonely, sad existence. I'd long lost hope that my life could be anything else.

Then she came, and I found hope again—hope that she would see me, choose me, love me, but she wasn't any different.

I believe Vera cared for me in her own way—she had freed her dragon to save me from the gallows after all—but she thought the worst of me. She could never love me the way I loved her, and as awful and lonely as my life had been, I'd rather have nothing than half her heart.

Still, I didn't have the strength to walk away with her eyes on me.

"I'll need a sword, or a dagger. Whatever you can find is helpful."

She cleared her throat, head bobbing. "Of course."

She left, and I tracked her through the window. When she was far enough away, I pulled the blanket off the bed, covered myself, and slipped from the room.

Vera had made her choice, and it wasn't me.

Now I had to make mine.

1

VERA

One month later

M y timing had to be perfect. Just a second too early or I'd miss my only opportunity to pull this off.

I hid along the train tracks north of Gold City where the train had to wind through the Deadwood Forest on its way to the mountains. The tracks were set on a raised hill with the trees on the left. The area on the right sloped down into a gully.

The forest looked different than before. The black leaves were slowly bleeding into white with the changing of the seasons. It was a stark reminder that we were another month closer to the Blood Moon, and the Nighters were on the loose with a weapon they were going to use to free the beasts.

All because of me. Because I had poisoned Ronan.

It had been thirty-five days, twelve hours, and thirteen minutes since I'd last seen him. Not that I was counting . . .

I'd gone straight to the Faylands after I left Mayhem, determined to protect him, but I had quickly learned how difficult, if not impossible, it was to break into the fae's territory.

There were only two ways in or out—the old mountain pass and the tunnel. The path had been blocked by a rockslide. And the tunnel? I wasn't certain it existed. I had scoured the mountainside for a week trying to find it.

Since I couldn't go to Ronan, I had to bring him to me. I had tried—breaking fae law twelve times.

Some robberies were from the mines. Others were just before the precious metal reached Gold City. All of it was done inconspicuously and in small quantities. Only Ronan knew, and he had not appeared once.

This time, I planned to break the second fae law in an epic way—robbing the fae so big and boldly, he would have no choice but to show up at the scene of my crime.

Laying at a blind curve, just below the train tracks, I had my talons dug into the earth to keep from slipping into the gorge below. My other hand was wrapped around a rope, which was attached to a set of tracks. I had removed the spikes securing them.

If the train ran on schedule, I would see Ronan within the hour. Anxiety and excitement churned in my gut.

I needed to protect him. I wasn't sure how I was going to do that since I could barely protect myself—courtesy of the All-Seeing-Eye—but I could figure that out later. First, I had to see him and make sure he was okay.

I heard the train whistle before I saw the steam billowing in the air. The train wouldn't be visible until the last second, which was what I wanted. The driver couldn't see me too early.

I tracked the train's progress over the winding landscape by its steady chugging. The noise grew louder the nearer it drew. Another loud whistle cut through the air. It was deafening this close. I winced, curling my shoulders forward until it stopped.

The train came into view.

I held my breath, waiting. Just a little closer. A little more . . . Now! I yanked the rope, jerking the section of tracks where it was tied.

Metal screeched and sparks flew as the driver tried to apply the brakes, but the train was approaching too fast. It veered sharply over the rearranged tracks into the gulley. A scream preceded crunching metal and shattering glass. Chunks of dirt and rocks exploded from the earth.

When the debris settled, the front half of the train was derailed, hanging off the hillside, while the rest remained on the tracks.

I slid down and approached the control car, now partially crushed in on itself. The door wouldn't budge. I braced my foot and pulled until the hinges gave way.

The inside of the cab was a mess. Broken glass littered the floor and a harsh scent hung in the air from the brake attempt. There was so much damage, the driver had to be dead.

Wind whistled through the broken windows, flapping a piece of paper above the door. I ripped it off and stared down into a familiar face.

My talons were flexed, fangs bared, and my body posture was rigid, as if I was on the verge of an attack rather than posing. The artist had made me appear violent and frightening or maybe I was the one with a distorted view.

WANTED for questioning in relation to the Mayhem fire. Reward: Five thousand silvers.

This wasn't the first poster I had found. They were plastered across the Mortal Lands.

Boone had covered up the real cause of the fire, but the sneaky bastard had implicated me in the crime. Given I had threatened him with my dragon, it was a bold move but unsurprising. He hadn't become leader of the Rogues by being a pushover.

I was too concerned with Ronan to do anything about it, and to be fair, Boone *had* done as he was told.

There were only faint whispers of a fire-breathing beast. Most of the Mortal Lands was in the dark, believing a fire had destroyed Mayhem.

Crumpling the paper, I discarded it just as icy metal bit into my back. I froze.

"Hands where I can see 'em."

I slowly raised my arms. He inhaled sharply, and I cursed my carelessness. The talons were a dead giveaway.

Thanks to the Crone, I had talons, fangs, and a fire breathing beast inside me.

He patted me down for weapons, and my gun and dagger were confiscated. "I don't know what you did—" the driver sucked in a labored breath "—but they're offering a sweet reward for bringing you in alive."

Speaking of alive . . . How did he survive? His breathing was shallow. He was injured at least.

I tried to twist around to confirm, but the gun pressed deeper. "Face forward. Poster didn't say you had to be whole."

Despite being a terrible fighter at the moment, I liked my odds against an injured mortal. My muscles coiled, readying to strike just as the light inside the car dimmed. My gaze shot to a window.

The sun was setting.

Ice drenched my veins.

How had I not realized the time?

Purple eyes flashed in the darkness of my mind. The dragon stretched its long limbs, gently nudging against its barrier. The nudge quickly turned into a push, then a ramming as it charged its cage.

The beast threw its whole weight against the walls. Cracks splintered up them as horror gripped my throat. The only thing capable of stopping what was about to happen was back with Ness. My trusty mare was waiting in the forest. I wouldn't make it.

My tongue swelled, turned heavy and leaden. "Hey guy —" I swallowed thickly "—You got gold bullets in that gun?"

There was a beat of silence. "What other kind would I have?"

"Good." I blew out a breath. "That's good. I'm going to need you to shoot me."

"*What*?"

The walls crumbled. The dragon leaped for the surface.

"Fucking shoot me!"

I slammed to my knees as fire seared my organs. I convulsed and fell forward onto my hands. An agonized scream clawed up my throat. My fangs extended, slicing through my lips.

"What's happening?" the mortal shrieked.

"Shoot. Me." My back bowed as scales formed over my skin. The driver didn't move. Twisting back, I let him see my terrifying transformation. "Shoot me now, or you're going to die."

His eyes widened in horror. "W-What are you?"

"Pull the trigger!"

A savage pain tore through my calf. "Again!"

Another bullet buried in my left leg, but the dragon wasn't slowing.

"Keep shooting!"

Bang! Bang!

The driver peppered my legs with bullets. I screamed,

darkness curling at the edges of my vision. The gun clicked as he ran out of ammo.

"Use my gun," I shouted.

My spine snapped and reformed longer and stronger. I was seconds away from losing control.

"NOW."

He shot five more rounds into my legs, and finally, the dragon slowed. It teetered on its feet before it collapsed.

I slumped to the ground.

Ragged breaths tore from my lungs. The pain was paralyzing. I struggled to remain conscious.

It felt like hours passed before the bleeding stopped. Even after it had, I laid there for some time as the cold terror steadily leaked out.

Standing took more energy than I had. I used the edge of a broken window to hoist myself up. Hundreds of sharp needles stabbed into my calves, protesting the weight. My legs buckled, and I slipped back to the floor. This time I stayed there.

It took several minutes for the wave of pain to pass. When it did, my gaze bounced around, seeking the driver.

He was slumped in the corner with a small, jagged piece of metal sticking out of his side.

I dragged myself over to him. He tried to scuttle back but had to stop as blood pumped from his wound. "Wh-What do you want?"

"Give me the key to the train cars."

He whipped the leather string off his neck. "Here." He tossed it to me. "Ain't no point in protecting the gold anyway. The Enforcer's dead."

Icy shards injected into my heart.

"Where did you hear that?"

The driver whimpered at my sharp tone. His entire body

was shaking. I didn't blame him. I'd be terrified too after what he just witnessed.

"H-He escaped the gallows, but no one's seen him since. They say he died in the fire."

My brows slammed together. "He's not enforcing fae law?"

He shook his head. "Gold City's trying to keep it quiet, but word's getting around."

My pulse hammered in my ears. It couldn't be true. I made sure Ronan survived the fire. But what if someone had gotten to him after Marty's?

Thorny knots stabbed into my stomach.

No. He was almost fully healed when he left, and Boone would have gloated when I robbed him. Ronan was alive. He just wasn't enforcing fae law.

"Where are my weapons?"

The driver's eyes glazed with fear. He didn't answer, knowing what would happen if he did.

"Give them to me," I snapped.

With tremoring hands, he reached behind him, pulled out my weapons, and slid them over. I snatched up the gun and aimed it at his head. It had one bullet left, and I was close enough, I couldn't miss.

He knew this was coming, but his face still paled. "P-Please. I've got a son. He just turned three."

I tightened my grip on the gun. He'd seen me shift. He had to die, but no matter how much I urged my finger to pull the trigger, I couldn't.

Taking a forceful breath, I pinned him with a hard stare. "I know your face. You tell anyone what you saw, and I'll find you."

His throat rippled. "I ain't even sure what I saw."

"Good."

I dropped the gun and holstered it as he sagged with

relief. I did the same with my knife. "How long will it take the authorities to find you?"

"They'll be here by morning I reckon'. Fae have to have their gold by day after tomorrow."

I jerked my head in a nod.

Dismissing him, I turned on my elbows, and pulled myself out of the compartment, biting my cheek as my legs dragged over the edge. Fire radiated up my calves when they hit the ground.

There was no way I could stand, let alone open the compartments. Stealing the gold would have to wait.

I crawled across the gulley in the steadily dwindling light. When I reached the hillside, I attempted to claw my way up, but my arms were shaking too violently. I was only able to reach halfway before they couldn't hold me anymore.

I gave up and slid back down.

Then I passed out.

A rough tongue scraped my cheek. Peeling open an eye, I saw a horse's muzzle inches away. "Ness, what are you doing here?" I asked groggily.

She was supposed to wait for me in the forest.

I glanced around. I was in a clearing, surrounded by trees. Had I made it back to the forest and just didn't remember?

There was no way. I could barely crawl.

I sat up with a yawn and stretched. My brows compressed together when I didn't feel any pain.

I glanced at my legs and surprise rang through me. The bottom portion of my pants had been cut away. Bandages were wrapped around my calves. I flexed them. The bullets were gone.

On a hunch, I stood and peeked inside a saddlebag. Just as I suspected, it was filled with an array of dried meat and cheeses. Food had been magically appearing all month.

I peered between the trees. I couldn't see them, but I knew they were there. Someone had been stalking me since Mayhem.

I had only caught a glimpse of them once despite the numerous times I'd tried to confront them. They moved in shadows and whispers. I didn't know who they were, or what they wanted, but they were responsible for the food and bandages.

My eyes panned the landscape and settled on the train wreck. It was just past dawn. I had a couple of hours before the authorities arrived.

I searched for the key.

I'd had it on my person before I lost consciousness, but it was gone. Panic set in when I didn't see it anywhere. I ran my palms over the forest debris, hoping the key might be covered under some leaves. No luck.

Was it in a saddlebag?

I dug around but found nothing. "Ness, did you see where our spy put the key, girl?"

She threw her head toward the forest.

My gaze narrowed. They'd taken it.

I had attempted to rob fae gold numerous times but was only successful the twelve because despite my careful planning, some small piece went wrong.

It was the spy. The missing key was the most telling. They didn't want me to rob the fae and were one of the reasons I didn't believe the driver about Ronan. He was having me followed. Who else would have a vested interest in preventing me from breaking fae law?

Except, he wasn't acting as the Enforcer. Why would he care?

"Give me back the key, you bastard!"

Silence.

The compartment locks were impossible to pick with my talons, which left me with only one option, one I'd been avoiding. My body wasn't healing like it used to. Even now, several hours later and with the bullets removed, my legs ached.

I sighed heavily.

Half limping, half walking, I returned to the gulley and climbed down.

I slammed my fist repeatedly into one of the train's doors, tearing open my knuckles in the process. The lock broke open with a crack. Hundreds of pounds of gold were inside. My blows to the door shook the piles loose and caused an avalanche as soon as it opened.

I leaped back as thousands of gold nuggets spilled out.

The same thing happened when I forced open the other cars and found myself staring at a river of gold. This was the fae's entire month's supply.

Ronan couldn't ignore this.

I stuffed my pockets, boots, and arms with as much gold as I could carry, then I waited.

A half-hour passed.

Then another.

My shoulders sagged. He wasn't coming.

With the disappointment came a horrifying thought. What if the driver was right? What if Ronan was dead?

2

VERA

I tended to my split knuckles, changed into a new pair of pants, and reloaded my gun before heading a mile outside of Gold City.

The weather-beaten church was just as I remembered.

Years of brutal storms and wind had stripped the paint, revealing the wood paneling, and a hole had been punched through the roof. The boarded-up windows were new. The work had been done hastily, speaking to how quickly the Nighters had left.

Storm clouds coalesced overhead, and a shadow fell over the structure. Soothing scents of earth and clay filled the air. I sucked in a deep breath, and managed to smile despite the grim circumstances that brought me here.

I refused to believe Ronan was dead. There had to be an explanation for his disappearance, and I would find it here.

Dismounting Ness, I grabbed a lantern, hissing in pain as my hand curled around the handle. Those locks really did a number on my knuckles.

"Two stomps when it's here," I reminded her. On the ride over, I'd quickly thrown together a plan.

She threw her head down with a snort and I stared at her fondly.

I knew it wasn't normal we could understand one another, but we also had a bond unlike any other.

Ness had shown up at the Crone's cabin the day after I turned fifteen. By then, the torture was daily and slowly chipping away at my resilience. I'd stumbled outside, my shirt soaked in blood, despondent, to see a beautiful creature grazing inside the barrier.

She'd been emaciated and covered in scars. I instantly felt protective. It had taken an hour of coaxing and soothing words before she would allow me to get close. I'd spent the day feeding her and tending to her injuries.

In the evening, the Crone caught us.

I'd recognized the eager gleam in her eye. It was the look she wore whenever pain was imminent. I didn't think twice. I swung onto Ness's back and rode her as far away as possible.

I nursed her back to health as we made our way to Mayhem, not understanding at the time that she was saving me too.

I watched her affectionately, stroking her mane. "You're the best, you know that?"

Another head throw. I laughed and pulled away before making my way up the steps.

Thunder boomed overhead like an angry giant, rattling the church as I reached the entrance. The light outside dimmed seconds before rain fell in a light mist. I was grateful for the overhang as I opened the door and waited for the magic candle to appear.

Minutes dragged on. Where was that stupid thing? It had appeared in seconds last time I was here.

Squinting into the darkness, I searched the shadows. Lightning threw bright strips through the boarded windows, illuminating the dusty floor and decomposing pews. Like a magnet, my eyes were drawn to the pulpit, hiding the Nighters' den.

Were any of them still down there, or had they all fled to the Spirit Lands?

There was no sign of the candle.

I shouted for it over the din of the storm, but it didn't emerge. The Nighters must have taken it with them.

My gaze dropped to the floor. I needed to get safely across.

I tried to recall the path the candle had shown me, but the only thing I could remember was the area where my boot had sunken through. Even though the boards had been replaced, it was hard to forget almost falling to my death.

I held my lantern above the floor as I studied it, hoping to jog my memory. My eyes danced over the wood, but for the life of me, I couldn't discern the safe parts from the traps.

Slitted light flashed across the walls.

Wait . . . What was that?

I crouched. The lantern light didn't reach far, but just a few feet ahead, I could see footprints in the dust. They were clustered around a group of boards while the surrounding area remained undisturbed.

Thank you, Nighters.

Carefully, I picked my way across the floor, periodically stopping to find the next set of prints.

When I reached the safety of the platform, I stepped up, dropped the lantern, and flung my body down. The hard landing rattled my fangs but left my limbs at a believable angle. I raised a talon and sliced my forehead, adding yet another injury for my poor body to heal.

I shut my eyes as blood dripped down my face.

The rain came down harder. Thunder roared across the

sky. I strained my ears, listening for Ness's hooves. The signal came minutes later.

Stomp. Stomp.

My heart crashed against my ribs. I remained perfectly still as footfalls sounded near the entrance.

"What's she doing here?" a masculine voice mused. The spy was male and spoke in smooth, deep tones.

I knew he would follow me here. He was always one step behind me everywhere I went.

The moment he saw me, a curse sounded. One second, he was at the door, and the next he was kneeling over me.

None of the boards broke.

Son of Balor. How was I going to trap him now?

I needed leverage to make him give me answers about Ronan, and what better leverage than his freedom?

Rough palms whispered over my head and neck. "Where are you hurt?" he asked, but I knew he wasn't expecting a response.

I held still as he continued his inspection, mind racing to think of another plan. While he was busy feeling over my neck, I cracked an eye. A gold band was wrapped around a broad bicep with a sizable draoistone. He was high fae.

I jolted up and twisted his neck.

Shock flashed across his eyes.

I didn't have the strength to turn his head all the way. It caught at a sickening angle. *Oh Gods.* I quickly gave it another jerk and it snapped.

He went limp, landing on my legs. I cursed at the pain shooting over my tender calves. I shoved him off and massaged the muscles until the burning settled into a dull ache. Then I grabbed both his legs and started dragging him to the entrance, which wasn't easy. He was massive.

It was too dark to see much of him, but I caught

glimpses in the flashes of lightning: sharp cheekbones, dirty blond beard, and mischievous lips.

There was something vaguely familiar about him, but I couldn't place what.

I made it to the front, slightly out of breath from maneuvering his mass safely over the floor and pried up the boards. The spikes were concentrated in the center. I did my best to position him to land near the perimeter.

The pit was twenty feet deep with the walls sanded down. He wouldn't be able to climb out. My gaze shifted to his draoistone. Probably best to take it so he couldn't use magic to escape. I removed it and rolled him over the edge.

He hit the sandy bottom with a thud, one of the spikes slicing his abdomen.

I shrugged. He'd live.

I dabbed away the blood on my face and shook out my stinging knuckles. As I returned for my lantern, the pulpit caught my eye.

I slid the pit a look. It would take some time for the fae's healing to fix his broken neck. It couldn't hurt to do some exploring . . . See if the Nighters left anything useful behind.

I unsheathed my dagger—in case I ran into any of them —and entered the trap door.

My boots hit the ground with an echoing thud. The sound was deafening in the dead silence. Damp earth and mildew clung to the air. Darkness stretched in every direction, too thick for my lantern light to penetrate.

I took a step and splashed into a pool of water. Frowning, I angled my lantern down. Pockets of liquid reflected the light, spread out every couple of feet before the darkness swallowed them.

Strange. There hadn't been any flooding last time, but I could use it to my advantage. It would be difficult for someone to move around without making noise. Gripping the lantern in one hand, and my dagger in the other, I proceeded into the dark.

The Nighters' den was a twisting labyrinth of dirt tunnels. I couldn't tell if the passageways had been dug recently or were old remnants. They were surprisingly warm despite being twenty feet underground. I'd worn the thicker of my tunics and was starting to sweat from the humidity.

Every so often, the tunnels rounded out into archways covered in grated bars. Behind them, the space was laid with stone. Each one extended a few feet back and held a collection of bones.

These were cells and based on what I had seen during my first visit, they once held beasts. The labyrinth contained hundreds of prisons—possibly thousands—but I didn't venture far enough to find out. It was easy to get lost and they might not all be empty.

At least now, I knew how the Nighters had gotten into the Spirit Lands. They'd had a pooka in one of these cages. They never would have been able to find one on short notice otherwise.

Splashing sounded somewhere behind me.

I froze, the hair on the back of my neck prickling. I held my lantern out, but I couldn't see anything in the darkness beyond and hurried ahead.

The pools of water steadily increased in depth and frequency the further I trekked. Eventually, I came upon a thin corridor branching off the main one. It was flooded. From what I could tell, this section had been dug deeper than its parent, trapping the water.

I climbed three steps and followed another set down before I reached the bottom and sunk up to my ankles in cold water. It eddied around my legs before rippling out in the other direction.

I extended my lantern. A series of doors lined the hall. I splashed through the water, opening each one.

The first held a workshop. Nothing was left except tables and chairs dusted with metal filaments. This had to be where they'd been processing ore into iron dust.

A rush of water poured out when I opened the second door. Inside was the altar room—the place I'd been brought to on my first visit. The lantern light interrupted the span of darkness, rippling over the water's surface. It was deep, covering the bottom of the pews.

My boots flooded as I waded through the aisle, wondering where that rat bastard Ryder had been sitting when I'd come for the iron dust. I'd considered him a friend for seven years until he betrayed me, working with the Nighters to see me and Ronan hung.

I continued past the pulpit where I'd met the Nighters' leader, Bale. There was a small platform behind it with dark curtains, just tall enough to stand above the water. Stepping onto it, I parted the fabric and found an emblem carved into the wall—a white raven set against a black background. Below the bird was an inscription in a language I couldn't read.

To the right was an open door where the aibeya had come from. It sounded like there was a waterfall inside. I peered in.

Rain gushed from a hole cut into the ceiling. There was a door connected to it that had been tied open. The storm had just begun so it couldn't account for most of the flooding. The water had to have been accumulated from multiple storms.

Ancient chains were bolted on opposite walls, like something had been trapped inside.

My brows puckered. What was this room for? What were

the 'methods' Bale mentioned? More importantly, why were they collecting beasts?

I'd hoped to glean some insight into the mysterious Nighters, but so far, I was left with more questions than answers.

Disappointed, I exited into the hall, and froze as more splashing echoed from the left, much closer than before. Chills iced my spine. Whatever it was, it was large. I swiftly walked off in the opposite direction and turned down another corridor.

The moment I rounded the corner, a candle flew into my face.

I leaped back, placing a hand over my jackhammering heart. "It's not nice to sneak up on people." It careened toward me again, so close, it made me cross-eyed. I swatted it away, and it burned my hand.

I shook it, scowling. "No wonder the Nighters left you here. You're an asshole."

The candle zoomed off deeper into the hall, then stopped abruptly with its flame frozen. What was this thing's deal? I took a step, and it zipped a couple of yards back before freezing again.

I gathered it wanted me to follow.

My eyes narrowed in suspicion. It could be leading me into a trap.

I glanced in the direction the splashing had come from. I wasn't going that way, and if there was a chance the candle was taking me somewhere with answers, it was worth the risk.

Tightening the grip on my blade, I cautiously trailed the candle until it came to a stop outside an unmarked door. There were small rivulets flowing over the ground, but it was relatively dry.

I set my lantern down, took out my gun, and kicked

open the door. It banged against the other side and sent an echoing thud ringing through the tunnel.

The room was empty, save for a scroll.

It was just a rolled-up piece of paper, but I stared at it like it was a stick of dynamite. I scooted the lantern closer with a foot, scanning the shadows for booby traps. I didn't see anything, but I still wasn't convinced.

I took off a boot and launched it at the parchment. It sailed way past its mark and hit the far wall. I removed my other shoe and hurled it. It clipped the door frame and fell to the ground, ten feet shy of its target.

That goddam Eye was getting a dagger straight in the pupil.

I waited for another breath, then slunk into the room, one step at a time, approaching the scroll. When I wasn't blown to bits, I bent to pick it up, and my foot was torn out from under me.

My gun and dagger flew out of my hands as my face smacked into the floor. I barely had time to register the pain before I was being dragged out by my ankle. I managed to grab a hold of the door frame, but whatever had me tugged hard and broke my grip.

As soon as I was clear of the room, a stream of webbing pinned me to the ground. I struggled against it, trying to get out, but the delicate weaves were much stronger than they appeared and held me in place.

My face was free, but my arms were stuck at my sides. The material was sticky and dry. It burned my skin and set off a million itches.

I jerked my head around, searching for my attacker.

Pinpricks of purple glowed in a corner of the ceiling where a bodah waited.

It had a skeletal frame and hunched back. Most disconcerting were the disproportionately large, bony hands and fingers. They looked like leathery wings with the skin torn off. The beast had to hold them at an angle because of their size.

I frantically began scrabbling at the web with my talons. It was a slow process. The netting did not tear easily.

The bodah released a hair-raising snarl and lunged. Its massive form filled the tunnel as it descended on me. Sharp fangs sunk into my neck, sending searing pain coursing through my body.

My heart punched against my breastbone as I tore at the gossamer. I broke through the first layer, but the next one was denser. My talons worked furiously as the bodah twisted my head to the side and bit deeper.

I hissed at the fire shooting down my neck. I could feel its venom pumping through my veins.

I got through the second layer and managed to free my talons, but they were useless against the beast's impenetrable hide.

My right hand strained for the lantern as my left grappled with the beast, attempting to dislodge it. But the bodah was too strong, and its venom weakened me with each passing moment.

I stretched harder toward the light. My fingers glanced off the handle and knocked it over. I tried to lift my arm again, but it felt like a boulder, and remained useless on the ground. My vision faded in and out.

A soft scraping sounded somewhere, but my mind was too disoriented to pinpoint the source. Metal touched my hand and my fingers instinctually curled around it—the lantern.

Summoning my strength, I hurled it down on the bodah's back.

The glass shattered on impact. Flames erupted, its oily hair igniting in the blaze. With a deafening screech, it recoiled and shot off into the dark. Its agonized cries echoed off the walls before fading into silence.

I collapsed back, my heart thumping wildly in my ears, and wrenched out the fang the bodah left behind. Blood squirted from the wound, and I pressed a hand over it until my healing stemmed the flow.

I laid there and caught my breath. Aches pulsed over my body from the venom. Another minute and the bodah could have killed me.

After three quick breaths, I sat up and froze as the tunnel spun. There were two of everything. Nausea punched up my throat, and I leaned over, vomiting. When I finished, I felt surprisingly better.

I lurched to my feet, swaying, and managed to stumble into the room and collect my weapons, shoes, and the scroll.

On my way out, I had to rest against the door frame and saw the candle on the ground. Two small lines disturbed the dirt in front of it, leading to the lantern.

The candle had pushed it toward me.

I gave it a grateful, sluggish nod before fumbling with my shoes. Next, I tucked the scroll into the waistband of my pants, and holstered my gun but kept the dagger in hand.

The candle lifted off the ground and guided me back toward the entrance.

Until I was back on the surface, I was still in danger. Energy flooded my veins, helping to alleviate the effects of the venom. I stayed on alert, searching the shadows for the bodah, or any of its friends, but none appeared.

As we neared the trap door, there was a muted shout followed by banging.

The spy was awake.

3

VERA

I shot the candle furtive glances as I trailed it. Given it had saved me, I doubt it had been leading me into a trap. I believe the bodah had been left behind in one of the cells and had escaped. It'd probably been attracted to my lantern light.

We reached the door leading to the surface and the spy's shouting became clearer. "Trouble, you get your ass back here!"

Was he calling *me* Trouble?

Just for that, I took my time scaling the ladder. I didn't take orders from anyone, especially a fae.

I made it to the top rung and sheathed my blade. As soon as the trap door was open, the candle shot out, rustling my hair. "Thank you," I called, wondering where it was going in such a hurry. I hauled myself out and kicked the door shut.

Lightning flashed across the walls as I traversed the floorboards. The wind drove the rain sideways. It pinged off the side walls and windows like bullet casings hitting the floor.

I reached the pit and knelt over the lip. It was too deep

for much light to reach the bottom, but I could make out a silhouette and glowing gray eyes.

Said eyes narrowed a fraction. "That was a dirty trick." His deep voice echoed off the walls and carried up to me.

"Why are you following me?" I shouted.

His silhouette casually leaned against a spike. "Because you're trouble."

Trouble . . . Trouble . . .

The last word rang out twice before dying off.

My gaze thinned. I considered him long and hard.

The color of his eyes struck a chord of familiarity. Where Ronan's were dark graphite, his were a cloudy gray.

I ripped out my gun and fired blindly. The fae didn't move or make a sound. I couldn't tell if I had hit him until he dug something out near his shoulder.

White teeth flashed. "Careful, Trouble." His purr echoed powerfully. "Or I might think you're flirting."

Black threads swam in his gaze. It wasn't an instant transformation like Ronan's, but it was enough to tell he had a battle-mode, and if he had one, he had to be from House Taran.

My heart beat excitedly. "Ronan sent you."

The fae said nothing.

"Where is he?" I called, trying to mask the desperation in my voice. "He's not enforcing fae law."

The fae remained silent, but the slight widening of his eyes was answer enough.

My stomach sank.

He cocked his head. "What happened between the two of you anyway?" He projected his voice to be heard clearly. "One minute he's concerned with your weight and the next he's sending me to watch you."

How would he . . . ?

A bright burst of lightning illuminated his face. It lasted only a second, but it was enough to catch his smirk.

It clicked. "You were at the camp." I knew he looked familiar.

"Aw, you remember me." His gruff voice was at odds with his playful tone. "I'm Kian."

"I don't care. Where's Ronan?"

"Feisty." The murmur pinged softly off the walls, almost inaudible. His gaze slanted away a moment before returning. "I was supposed to provide him with weekly reports." I could hear the hesitancy, even in the echo. "But he hasn't answered any of my scries . . . Or anyone else's. Last I heard, he was looking for the Nighters."

It felt like an abca's stony hands grabbed my stomach. "By himself?"

"Yes."

Yes . . . Yes . . .

Those hands squeezed tighter with each echo. "They tried to kill him once. What if they succeeded?"

"Ronan's a big boy. He can handle himself."

Kian hadn't been at the gallows. Ronan was powerful, but he wasn't invincible, and the Nighters had plenty of iron dust, not to mention the godstone.

It was hard to breathe past the rising fear and panic. "Has he ever done this before?" My shrill voice was jarring. "Been out of contact?"

"Hey. Look at me." His tone was consoling, but firm. I met those luminescent eyes. "Take a deep breath. It's okay. He's okay."

"How do you know?" I snapped.

"Because I know Ronan."

"Has he ever been out of contact before?" I pressed.

"No . . . But I'm sure it's for a good reason."

Yeah, like he was dead. My heart pounded furiously in my ears. "I have to find him."

"Trouble," Kian's deep voice warned. "If Ronan doesn't want to be found, he won't be."

"So, you're just going to sit around, meanwhile he could be dead?" I gritted out.

"I am going to follow orders," he said patiently. "Because if he is alive, and he finds out I didn't, I'm dead."

I had taken a risk with Ronan's life once; I wasn't going to again. I palmed his draoistone, holding it out in a flash of lightning—it was growing fainter as the storm moved off—for him to see before I chucked it into the storm.

"Why you little minx," he growled. "What's the plan here?"

"I'm going to find Ronan."

His gaze sobered. "He wanted me to watch over you. I can't do that from here. Take me with you. We'll look for him together."

Corthshit. Did he think I was an idiot?

I flipped him off.

Then I covered the hole.

His muffled shouting dogged me as I jogged down the church steps. Outside, sunlight weakly broke through the cloud cover. The storm was slowly passing over and the rain was dwindling.

Ness shook out her mane as I approached, flinging bits of mud and water at me.

I laughed. "Good girl," I crooned, giving her neck a long stroke before swinging into the saddle. We headed back to the forest. The entire ride was through mud. By the time we arrived, we were covered in it, but at least the rain had stopped.

I brought us to the edge of the gulley. As I suspected, the mortals had already been by to collect their gold from the train wreck. They would have taken it to Gold City, to secure the metal and take inventory.

Robbing the train might not have gone the way I wanted, but it did give me an opportunity to sneak into the Faylands.

To meet the fae's deadline, the gold had to be delivered by tomorrow. In their rush to get it there on time, security would be lax. I could hitch a ride, and the mortals would bring me right to the tunnel leading inside the Faylands.

I was certain Ronan was there. Here, he was the feared Enforcer. That, in addition to his large stature, made it impossible for him to blend in. If he was in the Mortal Lands, he would have been spotted by now.

I turned Ness around and guided us deeper into the forest to our primitive campsite.

I'd tied together the tunics I'd stolen during my final visit to the Rogues and made a hammock. It hung between two trees and was pooled with water. A small campfire sat beside it with a dented pot suspended above. I'd swiped the latter off a traveling wagon.

Behind the camp was a small creek, bubbling as it flowed between rocks.

It wasn't much, but it'd been our home for the last month while I worked to get Ronan's attention.

I hopped off Ness, removed the saddlebags, and freed her to go nibble on the greenery.

My clothes were soaked through with mud, and it was starting to make my skin itch. I grabbed a cloth, approached the creek, and began stripping off my clothes. As I removed my pants, a paper fluttered to the ground.

I'd forgotten all about the scroll. I picked it up and gently unrolled it. Mud stained the edges. Thankfully it didn't obscure the image, but the ink was faded so heavily, I could barely tell it was a map.

I recognized the Mortal Lands, but the Faylands didn't look right.

Where the eastern edge should have ended in a jagged 'L', it continued, doubling in size. The rest of the topography looked correct, but nothing was marked. I was only able to distinguish the Faylands from the Mortal Lands because of the raised curvature of the mountains.

I turned it over. The back was blank. This thing was useless.

Why had the Nighters left it there, and why did the candle lead *me* to it?

Another unanswered question.

Sighing, I rolled it up, and tossed it in a saddlebag.

I returned to the creek and cleaned my clothes before hanging them to dry.

As I scrubbed the mud off my skin, the morning caught up to me. A band of pressure squeezed my skull, an aftereffect of the venom. It throbbed in time with my tender calves and split knuckles.

I left the creek feeling exhausted but forced myself to dress and keep moving. There wasn't time to rest yet. I had to prepare. The wagons would pass this way in the morning. By tomorrow evening, I'd be in the Faylands, searching for Ronan.

I had no idea what I would find on the other side of the mountain. He could be dead, severely injured, kidnapped— there was an infinite list of reasons for his silence, none of them good.

Fucking Boone and his wanted posters. I couldn't go near any of the cities with those plastered everywhere. If I had, I would have learned Ronan wasn't enforcing fae law weeks ago.

What was he thinking going after the Nighters alone?

The answer hit me, and my stomach pinched painfully tight.

He had to get the godstone back because his House was in danger.

Because of me.

I squeezed the bridge of my nose. *Fuck, you idiot. Why couldn't you have reacted like a normal person? Why was your first instinct to poison him?*

I gave myself a firm shake. I couldn't dwell on that now.

I opened my saddlebags and took inventory of my supplies. To be safe, I'd need at least a week's worth of food and water. Thanks to Kian, I was good on food, and water was a few steps away.

That left only one thing to worry about.

I pulled out the pouch and jerked it open. It was only a quarter of the way full. I needed to make more. I pocketed it and pressed through the brush in search of firewood.

Water dripped off the trees in soft plinks as gentle sunlight parted the canopy. The forest floor was muddy. All the dead leaves and fallen branches were too damp for kindling.

I took out my knife and cut away the outer skin of a tree trunk. The layer beneath was slightly wet but would still ignite. I sliced off two handfuls of strips and tucked them into my pocket, using my body heat to dry them as I hunted down branches.

There weren't many to choose from. Most of them were so soaked through, they wouldn't burn. I found what I could and carved off the wet layer before returning.

After arranging a bed of rocks to keep the fire off the damp ground, I laid the strips of bark on top, before arranging the branches last. I struck a talon over a piece of flint and ignited the kindling. It sizzled and spat steam before catching.

36

I opened the lid of the hanging pot and dumped in a handful of stolen gold nuggets, then I returned for more pieces of wood to keep the flames hot and stacked them beside the fire.

I peered up at the sky. It was late morning. It would take most of the day for the gold to melt. To pass the time, I unholstered my gun and practiced taking it apart and putting it together.

What used to take thirty seconds, took thirty minutes.

During my downtime this last month, I had trained relentlessly, desperate to regain what the Eye had stolen—the surrounding trees were littered with scars and pocked with bullet holes—but, regardless of how hard I worked, or how long I trained, it didn't matter.

There was a black void in my mind where all my fighting knowledge used to be, and it kept growing.

Daily exercises like this slowed the bleed but not much. The Eye's price was a slow poison, and I feared one day soon, I wouldn't even know what a gun or a dagger was, let alone how to handle either.

I grew frustrated when my mind blanked on how to remove the ammunition, and I tossed the weapon aside.

Crossing my legs, I sat back against a tree and watched the slowly melting gold, adding more logs when necessary.

At some point, I drifted off.

Smoke filled my lungs. It seared my throat and chest. I struggled to draw in another breath, choking on the acidic air. I yanked my tunic over my nose and mouth as I peered around. Mortals darted by, screaming. Some of them were on fire.

Children. I had to save the children.

Blindly, I ran into the dark plume of smoke. My eyes burned and watered, obscuring my vision, but I didn't stop. I couldn't. I had to save them.

Dashing through the streets, I frantically searched for their smaller forms. Flames licked up everything. The whole city was on fire. My gaze caught on a little girl standing on a stoop, crying for her mother as she clutched a doll. I skidded to a stop and kneeled before her.

"I'm going to get you out of here," I whispered.

Big, fat tears rolled down her soot-covered cheeks. She jerked away screaming, "I want Mama!"

"Shhhh. We'll find her."

The girl became unnaturally still. The doll slipped from her fingers and her eyes swung to me. They were milky and colorless. "Mama's dead," she said in an eerie, guttural voice. "And so am I."

More children joined her, surrounding me. Flesh melted off their faces until there was nothing left but bone. Their eye sockets were empty, their lips and noses gone.

Their skeletal mouths opened. "You killed us," they said in unison. "You killed us all."

I screamed.

I jerked awake and burst into tears. I dug my fists into my eyes as my chest shook with barely leashed sorrow and self-hatred.

The faces of the children I buried in the desert haunted me every time I shut my eyes.

I had burned them alive. Their last moments had been horrific, filled with pain and terror, and yet, I had almost let my dragon out again last night.

Rage blasted away the sorrow.

How could I have been so fucking careless? I lurched up and slammed my fist into the ground. I recoiled in pain, but it was my due. I had made a promise to those children, and I was damn well going to keep it.

Not just for their sake, but for every child's sake.

I didn't dress the hand, leaving it bared to the stinging air as punishment while I checked on the fire.

It was banked low, but the gold had melted into a thin

sheet. Flipping over my knife, I used the handle to break it into small pieces. After, I used a rock to ground it into a fine powder. The latter took hours.

By the time I finished, the sun was peeking below the trees. It was early evening by my estimate, but I didn't trust my timekeeping anymore. As the seasons changed, so did the sunset. It was coming a little earlier each day. I didn't want to risk it.

I pulled out the pouch and poured the powder inside. I raised the small blue velvet sack to my eyeline, and my mouth watered in bitter anticipation.

Do it fast.

Removing a pinch of the gold dust, I dropped it as far back in my throat as I could. The disgusting taste of vinegar, lemon, and metal made my eyes water. It burned down my throat and hit my stomach with an uncomfortable pang.

My stomach belched as bile surged up. I slapped a hand over my mouth to keep it from escaping. I worked my throat, forcing the disgusting concoction back down. My stomach gurgled once in protest before settling.

I dropped my hand and exhaled in relief.

Freeing my dragon at the gallows had devastating consequences beyond the death toll. The cage I had kept it in for the last twenty-two years shattered when I shifted. It was stronger and more powerful than ever.

The first night after I left Mayhem, I slept in chains and woke up in unbearable pain, shifting. I'd unloaded all my bullets into my thigh, and the shift had stopped. It happened again the next night, and I realized the chains were no longer enough.

I'd swallowed a handful of gold dust the next morning and was deathly ill for two days, but the dragon didn't stir. I continued tweaking the dose until I found the perfect amount to weaken the dragon while doing minimal damage to my body.

But even a pinch of gold dust had consequences. My healing window had doubled, and my energy and strength were cut in half, which only exacerbated my inability to fight. Still, the peace of mind was worth it.

Sure enough, the sun started to set thirty minutes later. I took a seat to watch my last sunset in the Mortal Lands for a while.

It illuminated the clouds from underneath, making them appear lavender. Lilacs and lilies—that's what the sky reminded me of. It was shocking that something so beautiful could exist in a world as ugly and broken as mine.

This world ain't right, but you already know that. You ever stop being afraid of yourself, you might just be the one to save it.

Ha!

If Marty could see me now, poisoning myself and begging to be shot just to survive another miserable day. I hung my head as tears pricked my eyes. Even with the Rogues, I had never felt so . . . Alone.

A fat tongue scraped my cheek. Oh, Ness. My wonderful Ness. I stood and threw my arms around her, hugging her tight. "You're right. I'm not alone," I whispered. "I don't know what I'd do without you." Ness was the only real friend I'd ever had.

No, that wasn't true.

The note burning a hole in my pocket said otherwise. I squeezed Ness once, before releasing her, and dug it out.

Darlin',

Don't be a stranger. It'd be nice to know you haven't gone and gotten yourself killed.

-Marty

He had slipped it into my things at some point during my stay. I hadn't responded or been back to see him since.

As much as I hated to admit it, Ryder's betrayal had rattled me. I wasn't keen on ever putting myself in that position again, and if Marty did turn on me, it would hurt so much worse. It was better not to give him a chance.

Releasing a hopeless sigh, I stared at the pile of gold I'd stolen. I'd taken two handfuls and left the rest with the train.

I didn't want it to go to waste.

I pricked my pointer finger with a talon, squeezing it until a bead of blood formed. I dipped a nail in the liquid then flipped over the note and hastily scrawled out a message.

Please give this to the children and take care of Ness.

Even though I couldn't trust him with my location, I knew Marty would do both for me. He'd give Ness a good life. I stuffed the note and gold into a saddlebag and strapped it to Ness. I squeezed her neck as tears welled in my eyes.

"I am so grateful you found me that day, girl. You saved me in so many ways. There isn't enough grass in The Lands to thank you." I pulled away, swiping at my cheeks and she went tromping off without a care.

Despair squeezed my chest.

She didn't know it yet, but tonight would be the last time we saw each other. After I found Ronan, I was going to the Crone.

4

VERA

Something sharp scraped over my back. I jerked awake with a hiss. My spine stung. Realizing where I was, I bit my tongue, but it was too late.

"Whoa! Whoa!"

The driver pulled the horses to a stop. Wood creaked as he climbed off the bench. Muscles tightening, I pulled myself higher off the ground.

I held my breath as he rounded the wagon. Boots appeared between the wheels. My heart beat a frenzied staccato. If he looked just a few inches lower, he would see me hanging underneath.

"Is someone there?"

The driver muttered under his breath before hauling himself inside.

I caught glimpses of him between the planks and air clenched in my lungs. The wood groaned as he twisted about the heavy barrels of gold, searching between them.

"Bradley? Why are you stopped?" Footfalls came toward me as Bradley jumped out.

"Thought I heard something. Must have been the wind."

There was a brief pause. "Well get a move on and don't stop again."

Bradley grumbled as he climbed back onto the bench, rocking the wagon. He clicked his tongue, and we set off.

I expelled a quiet lungful of relief and glared upside down at the rock that had almost gotten me caught. The damn thing had torn through my shirt and broken skin.

Relaxing my grip, I lowered to a less strenuous position, and the wagon swung me side to side as it continued over the rough terrain.

I'd heard the tell-tale rumbling of wagons at dawn. By the time they were passing through my patch of forest, I was waiting for them, strapped with my weapons and saddlebag. I had snuck onto the last wagon in line, the driver none the wiser.

After another tearful goodbye, I'd sent Ness off to Mayhem before bed. It was safer for her to travel in the dark.

I hadn't been able to sleep a wink, crying my eyes out over having to let her go, but the Faylands was too dangerous, and the Crone even more so.

Before Marty had told me the Nighters would try to go after Ronan again, returning to the Crone had been the plan, and nothing had changed.

The gold dust was a temporary measure until I found Ronan. It left too much room for error like what happened on the train. There was only one way to ensure my dragon couldn't hurt any more children. The Crone's torture would break my body but protect my soul.

Hours passed as the steady clomping of hooves lulled me into a sleepy stupor, but this time, I made sure to stay awake.

Peering through the wheels, I located where we were.

Sharp, fanged peaks pierced the cloud cover. Up close,

the size of the Fayette Mountains was incomprehensible. Gray stone threaded with veins of pink stretched endlessly in either direction.

There was an old wives' tale that a group of giants had been cursed by the Gods and turned to stone, and their bodies were brought to the edge of the Faylands to make the mountain. Observing the endless span of rock, I understood how the legend had started.

If I could see the mountain, that meant we'd be at our destination in under two hours.

Alarm bells rang through my mind. I was about to trespass into a strange, unknown land and hopefully find Ronan before some mercurial fae lord happened upon me. If they didn't kill me on sight for not having a fae brand, I could be forced to bear theirs.

I had no plan for finding Ronan beyond breaking into the fae's territory. His House would be the best place to start. If he wasn't there, Finn would know something. I'd need to figure out a way to make him talk and would be lying if I said I wasn't looking forward to it.

He wasn't the reason Ronan and I had broken up, but he sure as dark hadn't helped the situation.

Distant shouting interrupted my thoughts. "Checkpoint," was called down the line of wagons.

Creases cut into my forehead. Checkpoint? What checkpoint? They were coming up on their deadline to deliver the gold.

We still had a couple of miles before we would reach the mountain and evening was coming soon. There wasn't time to stop.

"What's going on?" Bradley asked, sounding equally confused.

"I don't know," someone called.

My gaze darted toward the forest on the left. I could roll

44

into it without being seen, but it was risky. If I got off the wagon now, I might not be able to get back on.

I couldn't afford to lose my only chance at finding the tunnel. Fae didn't leave their lands. The only time the entrance was used was for receiving gold and sending goods, which happened once a month.

I decided to risk it.

After several minutes, the other driver explained, "They're searching the wagons."

"For what?" Bradley asked.

"Guess we'll find out soon."

With agonizing slowness, the line of wagons crawled forward, periodically stopping. I couldn't get a good look at what was happening without risking being seen.

A clamor of crunching dirt reached my ears as the wagon moved closer to the commotion. No one was speaking, but I heard the groan of the other wagons as they were searched.

"You sure she's on one of these?" That voice sounded vaguely familiar, but I was too far away to be certain.

"Positive," a booming voice responded.

That one I'd recognize anywhere.

What in the dark was Boone doing here? Wait . . . Was he looking for me?

I knew if I tried to enter any of the cities, I'd be arrested, but Boone was here, hunting me. He had seen me shift into a dragon, the same dragon I'd threatened him with. He couldn't possibly be that stupid.

"Sweep the area. She might have gotten off. First one to find her will get a share of the reward," he announced.

My jaw clicked from how tight it clenched. He was ruining all my plans. I should have put a bullet through his skull when I had the chance.

Lowering slightly, I peered under the wagon as several

pairs of boots fanned out into the forest. More were standing around the wagons. If Boone was here, so were the Rogues. There had to be at least twenty of them.

I could run east toward the mountain, but that way was open fields. There was no place to hide, and I didn't like my chances of outrunning them. They were halflings. I was no match for their speed with the gold dust in my system.

Plus, my pride wouldn't let me run from these bastards.

My best chance was to not be found.

I pulled myself as flush against the underside of the wagon as I could. The position required more strength than I had, but I forced my muscles past their limits, hoping I could hold myself up long enough.

No part of me would be visible with my body hidden by the thin walls of the base. Someone would have to squat down and look up under it to see me. After a few minutes, my wagon moved forward, its turn to be searched.

Two sets of legs hopped into the back. Another approached the wheels. My muscles shook and sweat beaded my lip. My palms started to slip as a face appeared near an axle.

Hands, don't you dare give up on me now.

A spasm cinched my arms. They quivered violently. Fucking gold dust.

The head swiveled side to side, but not up.

Just a little longer.

The head disappeared. The footfalls receded too, and I exhaled silently.

Thank Gods—

One of my hands slipped.

I crashed to the ground.

Frozen, I stared wide-eyed at the bottom of the wagon as my heart pummeled my ribs. Maybe they didn't hear that. Maybe if I just—

"There she is!"

Guns cocking echoed around me, and I groaned. Why couldn't one thing go right? Just one?

I sighed and pulled off my saddlebag, dropping it before rolling onto my stomach and crawling out between the wheels. As I did, I caught sight of all the barrels aimed at my head. There was no way I could fight my way out, but the Rogues didn't know that. They also weren't aware that there wasn't a chance in the dark I would release my dragon again.

Time for threats and bluster.

Calmly, I rose and dusted myself off. The Rogues rushing toward me drew up short, startled at my sharp smile. Raising a talon, I drew it over the wagon's covering and tore through the fabric with each menacing step I took.

The ripping sound was jarring in the tense quiet. Some flinched. Others blanched.

I stopped ten feet away from the group, locking eyes with Boone. "Twenty against one." I clucked my tongue, smiling ruefully. "It's almost like you're afraid."

Boone's lips twisted into a sour pucker. Oh, he didn't like that.

He squared off against me. "We've come to take you in. You're outnumbered and outgunned."

"Then come and get me."

His hesitation betrayed his doubt. He didn't know if twenty of them would be enough. I pounced on it. "You've got balls bigger than a giant. I warned you what would happen if you came after me."

Eyes sparking with resolve, he tightened the grip on his gun, laughing humorlessly. "I'm not afraid of you."

"Then you're dumber than you look."

He scowled. "Go on then. Let it out."

I stared. He couldn't possibly know it was an empty threat, but the gleam in his gaze said otherwise.

"I thought she had put those scars on your wrists until I saw your room," he called.

Cold shards of panic burned through me. Even without the chains, it wouldn't have been hard to put together what caused the scarring on the bed posts. He knew I wasn't going to let the dragon out.

Fuck. I should have burned that room. I should have destroyed the whole damn compound.

Locking my jaw, I fought to keep the unease from my face.

"You really thought I'd let you get away with it?" Boone sneered. "We're still digging bodies out of the rubble."

I knew there would be consequences for Mayhem. I just thought I would be in the Faylands by now, beyond their reach.

"How'd you find me?" I was proud of how even my voice came out.

"I've been hunting you since Mayhem. Finally caught a break when you crashed that train. The driver put you in the area. We've been scouring the north for you."

Stupid, stupid, stupid.

"You can make this easy on yourself and come quietly."

I huffed out a bitter laugh.

Without the Rogues' protection, Mayhem would have hung me for burning that mortal. There was a better chance of shade in the Darklands than of me leaving with my life after what the dragon had done. If I went with Boone, it was to die.

"This only ends one way."

I tsked. "You know you don't have enough bullets."

A tier four beast would take a hundred to go down,

depending on the purity of the gold. I didn't know how many it would take to incapacitate me—less with the dose in my system—but I knew they'd need more than what they had.

If any of them had been willing to close the distance, I might have been worried. I doubted it would take more than a bullet to the head to end me, but they were all shit shots from this far.

"I only need one," Boone announced.

A Rogue appeared leading Ness. My heart dropped to my feet.

Duke put a gun to her head, looking conflicted.

Fire tore through my veins. "Don't you fucking touch her!" I ripped out my gun and leveled it at his head. "Let her go or I'll put a bullet between your eyes."

"Not before he puts one between hers," Boone warned. "Drop your gun."

Chest tight with panic, my gaze volleyed between Ness and Duke.

You could barely reload your weapon yesterday. You shoot even an inch to the right and she's dead.

I lowered my gun and tossed it aside.

It hit the dirt with a soft thunk. The noise rang loud and mocking in my ears. *You can't even protect Ness. Pathetic.*

The Rogues descended on me, kicking my gun away, and taking my knife before wrenching my arms behind my back. I was shoved to my knees. They held me down as Boone approached.

He bent over, putting his face inches from mine. Hatred warped his features. "We all lost someone in the fire," he whispered. "Friends, lovers. This is for them."

He backed up, nodding at the Rogues holding me. A fist gathered my hair and yanked violently, tearing out some of the strands. Air hissed between my teeth, but I molded my lips together, muting the sound. They weren't going to get the satisfaction.

A Rogue peeled away. I briefly recognized Vince's stupid face. "You had this coming," he whispered.

His fist crashed into my jaw. My head whipped sideways, blood flying from my mouth. Pain radiated out my cheek and down my neck.

I spat out a fang, smiling mockingly. "You call that a punch?"

His fist slammed into my gut. Breath wheezed through the gap in my teeth as another took his place. A boot connected with my ribs, and I choked down a pained gasp.

Boone signaled, and I was shoved to the ground. Eighteen pairs of fists and boots flew at me, hitting me repeatedly.

"This ain't right." I heard Duke's voice over the meaty thunk of knuckles hammering my flesh.

"One more word and you're next," Boone warned.

I couldn't fight back.

I couldn't scream.

I could barely breathe.

I curled my arms over my head, trying to shield it from the worst of the blows. My body jerked with each hit.

Pain was everywhere.

It sucked me into a horrible memory.

"Don't fight me darling and this will be over soon."

"Mama, please," I cried, tears streaming down my face. "It hurts. Please stop." My small hands tried to fight her off, but she used her weight to pin me and stab a knife in my back.

"Please!"

She didn't listen. She didn't care.

I could only lay there, helpless, as she stole what wasn't hers to take.

I hugged my knees to my chest, shaking, a spine shuddering sob building as the Rogues continued their assault.

I was grateful when the darkness came.

5

VERA

I woke in agony.

My body was a throbbing mass. I couldn't tell where the pain ended, and I began.

My jaw was too swollen to open. I had to breathe through an inflamed nose. Every gust of air burned. One eye was so bloated, it was sealed shut. The other had healed enough that I could slit it open, which meant I had been out for several hours.

It had been late afternoon when the Rogues captured me. It had to be the following morning at least.

I could make out distorted shapes and colors, but then double vision set in. I had four arms and legs covered in mottled bruises. I was surprised they weren't broken.

My eye fluttered shut with a pained groan.

I was in too much pain to move or fall back asleep. All I could do was lay there. Eventually, I fell unconscious, but sleep wasn't any better. I relived every brutal moment of the attack.

Even worse than the memory, was the poisonous shame.

I had worked so hard to learn how to protect myself after

the Crone. I had spent months training non-stop, and years maintaining my skills, and five minutes with the Eye had taken it all away. I was that same helpless little girl again.

The thought incited my fury as much as my disgust. I swore I would never be her again. Pre-Eye, I would have been able to take on all those bastards and make them pay.

And I thought I was going to protect Ronan?

How fucking stupid was I?

I woke up crying and hissed at salty tears touching raw skin. The sobs shook my battered chest and then I was crying from the pain. I couldn't even move my arm to wipe away the snot.

Black, bubbling tar seeped between my ribs. It was filled with searing self-loathing and misery. I was repugnant. I wanted to peel off my own skin.

I don't know how long I was out this time, but it was long enough that some of the swelling had gone down. My guess was a day.

Everything was still stiff and ached fiercely, especially my face. I think they might have cracked one of my cheekbones.

On a deep breath, I forced open my eyes, and hissed at the stinging pain.

I could feel abrasions all over my face where the skin was peeled off. I licked my teeth. They were coated in a disgusting fuzz. My tongue poked through the fresh gap where a fang used to be. I was surprised I hadn't lost more.

Overhead, wooden beams greeted me.

Where was I?

Gingerly twisting my head, I took in my surroundings as best I could.

I was in a cell, lying on a soft, feather-stuffed mattress. Across from me was an ornate desk and velvet chair. The floor was a cream tile run through with gold rivulets. Only one place would have a jail cell nicer than most homes.

What in the Gods was I doing in Gold City?

"Vera," someone whispered.

Clutching my ribs to keep them from being jostled, I slowly sat up. The movement inflamed my sore, sensitive muscles. I paused and let the blast of pain pass before moving again.

"Damn, you're in bad shape."

I carefully lifted my chin to see Duke in the cell across from me.

"What did you expect?" I snapped, and instantly regretted it. My jaw was still swollen and did not appreciate being used, but the white-hot fury glowing inside overrode self-preservation. "Twenty men against one woman. Fucking pathetic."

"Did they put you in here to watch me?" I growled at his silence.

They didn't need to bother. I was too damaged to cause any trouble.

Fingers speared through his white and silver hair. "No," he huffed. "I wasn't okay with what they did to you, and I let them know."

If he thought I'd show even an ounce of gratitude for his weak protest on my behalf, he was dead wrong. I tried to glare at him, but the skin around my eyes was too tender.

"You put a gun to an innocent animal's head."

"I was never going to hurt her, Vera. I swear it."

He could swear all he wanted. I didn't give a damn.

"Where is she?" I demanded.

"In the city stables. She's safe."

"Safe?" I scoffed. "She's not fucking safe."

Boone was using her to leverage good behavior out of

me, for now, but what would happen when they didn't need her anymore?

The stables were on the other side of the city. I'd never make it there in my condition. I needed to heal and get her to safety. Once she was out of their clutches, I'd return and make them all wish for death.

I did my best to leash the rage biting my insides. Duke was a shitty ally, but he was all I had.

"Why are we in Gold City?"

The crime was committed in Mayhem. Bringing me here didn't make any sense.

Duke rose from his bed and dragged a chair over to the bars. The legs glided smoothly over the expensive floor. He dropped into it, dangling his hands between his knees.

I shuffled closer to the candlelight, bringing my injuries into stark relief.

He sucked in a sharp breath. "Shit, Vera. I'm sorry. You and I have never seen eye to eye, and you need to stand trial for what you did, but that—" he flung a hand toward me "— no one deserves that."

"What *I* did?" I asked caustically. "What about what you did?" Just because I hadn't seen Duke at the gallows, didn't mean he wasn't there, cheering the Nighters on. "You knew me," I bit out. "I saved your ass more than once. I saved countless Rogue lives. I was innocent, but you were willing to let me hang."

Duke looked hesitant to say whatever was on his mind but did anyway. "You killed a mortal," he said quietly.

"It was an accident!"

I recoiled in pain. My body didn't appreciate the shouting.

Duke waited until I was able to meet his gaze again. "But that's the thing," he said softly. "When the rest of us have accidents, we don't wind up killing nobody."

Fine, but it wasn't his, or Boone's call to make. Besides, if Duke had been that upset over the mortal's death, why wait a month to have me hanged? It was just an excuse.

"Let's not corthshit each other. You wanted what the Nighters were offering and were willing to let me die to get it."

There was a brief pause before he admitted gruffly, "Yeah, I was."

I was taken aback by his bluntness but respected him for it.

"I started with the Rogues even younger than you. I've seen some shit. Shit, I'd want no child of mine to see." His voice grew rough. "That Bale fella can see stuff. He showed us a future where there were no beasts, or wondering where our next meal was coming from. A future where I might wanna raise a kid. You can think whatever you like of me, but yeah, I was willing to let you die for that."

I understood why Ryder had worked with the Nighters but hadn't been able to figure out why the rest of the Rogues had gone along.

There it was. I was speechless, and conflicted.

It didn't justify what happened, but in a way, it made things easier. If I was in Duke's position, I would have done the same.

All this talking was making me exhausted. I scooted back so I could rest against the wall. The bruising along my back screamed in protest. "Thanks for being honest. Now tell me why I'm in Gold City."

His lips set into a bloodless line. He took his sweet time answering. "Gold City would only agree to let us stop their wagons if we promised to bring you to them first for stealing their gold."

My brows touched. "How'd you know I would be on a wagon?"

He straightened in the chair. "That train was filled with gold, but you only stole a fraction. You weren't after it. You were looking for the Enforcer. Boone knew it would be your next move."

"But everyone thinks he's dead."

He shrugged. "Not you."

My stomach bunched into knots. "Did Marty tell him?"

He'd been the one to convince me to chase after Ronan, and I'd sent Ness to him.

A painful breath stuck in my lungs. After everything, I don't think I could bear it if Marty had betrayed me.

Duke shook his head. "Marty's in jail for trying to protect you."

A sharpness punctured my chest, a heavy mix of relief and guilt. I should have never doubted him. The Rogues must have caught Ness on her way to Mayhem.

"And you showed your hand when you barged into the compound without the Enforcer, threatening us if we went after him," he added.

I scrutinized him.

Duke was unexpectedly forthcoming. It was either guilt, or another trap.

I quickly dispelled the latter. He had been simple-natured and straightforward the whole time I'd known him. He didn't have a cunning bone in his body, and he'd been the only one to speak up during the attack.

Guilt was loosening his lips, but that didn't mean I would take everything he said as the truth.

"Why go through all the trouble of keeping the dragon attack quiet if this was the plan?" I asked. They could have had the entire Mortal Lands hunting me.

Another shrug. "We didn't want to cause a panic, but someone else beat us to it. In the days following the fire, anyone who spoke the word 'dragon' was found with their throat slit by morning."

It had to be Kian. I had trapped the one person who could help me. *Way to go, moron.*

Duke darted a look at the closed door before his gaze returned to me. "You know," he started in a whisper. "If you hadn't come to the compound and embarrassed Boone, he would have let this whole thing go. The Nighters want you alive."

Boone doing all this because I'd hurt his pride came as no surprise, but the second did. The Nighters had tried to kill me . . . But that was before Bale realized what I was, and it would explain the candle and the map. Maybe they wanted to add me to their collection.

"What happens now?" I asked.

When I found my way out of this, and I would, every man who put his hands on me would die—painfully. Ness would have to come with me to the Faylands after all. She wasn't any safer here than I was.

Duke rose, signaling our conversation was coming to an end. "I reckon Boone will wait for you to heal and then bring you before Gold City's council."

"Why wait? He wants me dead."

He lowered onto his bed, the wood groaning under his weight. "Mayhem signed your death warrant, but he still has to convince Gold City." He chose his next words carefully. "He . . . doesn't want you getting any sympathy on account of your condition."

I scoffed. "He doesn't want anyone knowing the Rogues beat the shit out of a woman."

His silence spoke volumes.

I turned away from him, laying back down to rest.

It was another two days before my body fully healed . . . almost. I still had abrasions on my face, but I no longer looked like a slab of meat on a butcher's block. The only bright side in all this was that I didn't have to worry about the dragon. It was as weak as I was. Good thing too because I'd lost the gold dust with my saddlebag.

The guards who were feeding me had to have been reporting to Boone because just an hour after I woke, relatively healed, the Rogues came for me.

It was Vince, and a twenty-year Rogue veteran, Butch. They watched me coldly through the bars. "Back up and sit on the bed," Butch ordered.

I crossed my arms, grateful to be feeling more like myself again. "Make me."

"Behave, or your horse is as good as dead," Butch warned.

My eyes spat fire, but I sat.

Vince wore a self-assured smirk.

The little shit was nowhere to be found when I'd broken into the Rogue's compound. I bet he had been hiding because he knew what I would have done to him if I had seen him. Intense satisfaction curled through me at the thought of him trembling in a closet somewhere.

Butch entered the cell and set down a basket of toiletries and fresh clothes while Vince, the coward, remained outside. "Clean yourself up. You have ten minutes."

This had nothing to do with decency. I was covered in dried blood. They wanted me to wash away the evidence of the beating.

I wanted to refuse on principle, but Ness's life wasn't worth my pride. Plus, I hadn't bathed in four days and stunk to high heaven. A bath sounded wonderful.

I grabbed the offerings and moved over to the small bureau with a wash basin behind the desk as the cell door shut with a clang. The granite bowl was filled with clean water. I dunked a cloth into it, scrubbed it with some soap, and began gently wiping my skin, hissing every time I hit a tender spot.

Next, I brushed my teeth.

The bowl wasn't big enough to wash my hair. I ran my talons through it, taming the waves as best I could before changing into clean clothes.

"Time's up, sweetheart," Butch announced just as I got the tunic over my head. "Time to face the music."

6

VERA

My gaze briefly met Duke's as Vince cuffed me. Though his smile was sympathetic, he didn't say a word.

Vince hauled me out and slammed my face into the bars. The broken cheekbone was still healing, and the impact sent up a flare of scalding pain. Butch tore him off before I could retaliate.

"Boone wants her in one piece," he growled, shoving Vince forward. "Go find the others."

Butch turned me toward him as Vince stalked out and roughly cleaned the cheek.

I bit back a hiss. The bastard had split open the skin.

When he finished, he spun me around and led me out by my hands.

I was brought into an expansive hall. Gold City's five council members sat atop a high dais, ten feet off the ground. Their gold-painted faces watched stoically as I was uncuffed and tossed inside a cage.

I recognized the councilor in the middle—Lucinda. She'd closed down Market Street for Ronan when we stopped in Gold City for supplies. "What happened to her?" she asked.

In addition to the fresh wound, there were old ones littering my face. They were faint, but visible. I stared at Boone, daring him to admit what he'd done.

"She refused to come in peacefully."

I rolled my eyes. "Corthshit. I surrendered my gun."

The councilor on Lucinda's right, the one with umber skin painted a deep shade of gold and light brown eyes, stared at me with heavy disdain. "Dear girl, the Rogues are highly respected members of the community. Why would they risk their reputations for *you*?"

He said 'you' like I was a steaming pile of shit.

I was under no illusion this would be a fair trial, but his question cemented just how prejudiced it would be. The Rogues, and especially Boone, had too much influence. I didn't dignify his question with a response, rubbing my nose with my middle finger.

His eyes narrowed.

Boone passed a stack of papers up to the council before coming to stand in the middle of the hall.

Lucinda shuffled through them. "I don't see her surname listed."

"She doesn't have one," Boone answered.

I craned my neck around, drowning out their conversation as she asked more mundane questions.

The Rogues were standing at the back with flinty expressions, wearing new vests. I'd made a bonfire with their old ones.

I caught their gazes and drew a talon across my throat.

They stood their ground, ignoring me, but I didn't miss the way some stiffened. My lips curled into a slow smile. *That's right boys. Guard your little dicks because I'm coming for each and every one.*

Vince met my gaze and breathed on his knuckles before rubbing them, like he was polishing his fist.

His dick would be first.

I was surprised to only see the Rogues. I would have thought Gold City would make a spectacle of me, but that would mean admitting they could be stolen from.

"She was raised in the Deadwood Forest by the Crone." Boone's voice pulled me from my thoughts.

I turned around in time to see shock ripple through the council except for Lucinda. I had been here plenty of times, but she was likely the only member who had seen my features up close and surmised I was different.

She reached the middle of the stack and paused, eyes skimming over what she found.

"Those are the eye-witness statements corroborating Vera was the one to start the fire," Boone explained.

Corroborating. I bet he had to look that word up.

Lucinda glanced at me. "Miss Vera, is that true?"

I didn't start the fire. My dragon did.

Locking my smug gaze with Boone's, I responded, "No."

"There are dozens of witnesses who say otherwise," the councilor on Lucinda's right spoke again in a haughty tone. A marble plaque sat in front of him, reading *Vaughn* in gold lettering.

Vaughn was a giant's sized asshole.

"Councilor," I started dryly. "What you have is a useless stack of paper. Anyone could have written those. Where are these dozens of witnesses?" I asked, head swiveling around. "I don't see any of them here."

Boone nodded to Vince, and he pulled open the double doors. Thirty or so mortals filed in, some of them children.

I glanced back to see Boone's gloating smile. "Those are statements from the ones who couldn't be here."

Shit.

Double shit.

Dolly was the first to testify. The brothel madam was quiet and subdued, wearing a long-sleeve dress falling to her ankles with her curly hair curtaining her face. Gone was the seductive woman, sashaying her hips. When she lifted her head, I saw why.

The right side of her face was severely burned, and if I had to guess based on the way she moved, those burns went all the way down. Dolly and I were the farthest thing from friends, but seeing her now, compared to before, it was like something in her had died, and that, that kicked me right in the stomach.

"My whole livelihood burned the night of the fire. Not just my brothel, but my body too. Men won't even—" her voice cracked. "I'm hideous."

"Miss Warton, who is responsible for your injuries?" Lucinda asked.

Dolly stabbed a finger at me. "Her." She sneered, glaring. "They should have hung you years ago."

"Thank you. That will be all."

The rest of the adults' testimony passed similarly. They spat vitriol at me while explaining to the council how I had destroyed their lives. Besides Dolly, I didn't know any of them, and I bet if they had seen me in Mayhem prior to the fire, I would have been met with the same disdain and disgust.

My talons and fangs had always made the mortals wary of me.

I let their sob stories roll off me, but then came the kids.

The first was Ana. She had dark brown skin that matched her curly hair, and big, sad eyes. Standing a little under waist height, she couldn't have been more than six or seven.

"Ana," Boone started in a gentle voice. "Can you tell

these nice people what you told me?" He gestured at the council.

Ana wrung her little hands in her threadbare dress. Her lip quivered and my heart twisted in my breast.

"Mama and Papa and I were eating dinner when—" sniffles interrupted her sentence "—when everything got really hot. Papa rushed me outside and then went back in for Mama, but they never came out."

An iron band tightened across my ribs.

"And who's taking care of you now, Ana?" Boone asked softly.

Her whole face bunched up as tears leaked down her cheeks. "No one," she whispered.

Tears strained at the edges of my eyes. *Oh Vera, what have you done?*

Judith came next. She had fiery red hair braided in pigtails and chocolate brown eyes. She was clutching a soot-covered teddy bear and was so soft-spoken, my ears had to tense to hear her.

"I was holding Mommy's hand. She started running and then there was a big ball of fire. It hurt her and she couldn't run anymore. I screamed for someone to help my mommy, but no one did."

"Can we show them your arm sweetheart?" Boone asked with an infinitely tender voice.

Judith jerked her head, and he helped her roll up her sleeve. Her forearm and hand were a raw, angry red. Blisters dotted the skin. That was the hand that had been holding her mother's.

She had watched her mother burn to death.

My stomach churned like it was filled with rancid meat. I threw up on the cage bars. I didn't care that everyone saw, or how guilty it made me look. I only cared about what poor Judith had suffered because of me.

When I cleaned off my mouth, and glanced back at the crowd, every disgusted, angry gaze was focused on me.

Ten more children testified after that.

Each story was worse than the last. There was no hate in their hearts, just confusion and pain. The dragon had taken everything from them but their lives. By the time the last one finished, I was numb and trembling.

The council filed out for their deliberation. It didn't take more than a few minutes for them to return.

"We agree with Mayhem's assessment. She is too dangerous to live," Lucinda announced. "Per the Rogues' request, she will be put before a firing squad."

She met my gaze. "You die at dawn."

With a prim tilt of her chin, Lucinda ordered me to be taken from the room.

I didn't fight. I didn't say a word.

I felt dizzy and weightless as I was dragged away. Time was warbled. Everything happened in slow movements. Mouths moved, but I couldn't hear a word over the loud ringing in my ears.

Suddenly, I was back in my cell on the bed, but I couldn't say how. I was just there.

I wrapped my arms around myself. I was so cold, colder than I could ever remember. It all felt surreal, like an impossible dream.

I raised my palms to my face. I expected blood. I expected there to be so much blood, but they were perfectly clean. How was that possible? How could my hands not have a single speck of blood after everything I'd done?

I didn't move an inch, staring at my hands, waiting for them to look as sullied as they felt. Hours passed in that fugue state. I drifted off at some point. When I woke, the gravity of what I'd done came crashing down, and I burst into tears.

I had killed children. That was terrible enough on its own, but they were at peace. Ana and Judith had to live with the horrible pain I had caused them every day for the rest of their lives.

Salty tears burned over still healing skin. I felt the weight of Duke's disturbed gaze as I cried hysterically.

His mouth opened and shut like a fish. He wanted to console me but struggled to grasp at the right words. He settled on, "Hey, it's okay. It'll be quick."

I sawed out a barbed laugh. "I hope not."

I hoped my death was slow.

I hoped it hurt.

The crinkles around his eyes deepened. He had no idea what to say.

"Why are you even talking to me?" I croaked miserably, swiping away tears. Duke and I had known each other for seven years, but we were acquaintances at best. He had steered clear of me like the rest of the Rogues. "Why did you try to stand up for me? You never cared before."

A long stretch of silence passed before he admitted, "Marty and I got to talking before he was locked up. He gave me an earful for how we treated you. How we were letting Boone stray us from what was right. I've known Marty for a long time. He's never talked about anyone like that."

My heart squeezed. *Oh, Marty, I don't deserve you.* "Why was he arrested?"

"He saw one of the wanted posters. He socked Boone good for it and threatened him if he touched you."

My lips trembled. I was so determined not to cry again, but knowing Marty was defending me after everything made the tears start fresh.

"You make sure he gets out," I choked, knowing I didn't have long left. "And Ness, please make sure they don't hurt her."

He bowed his head. "You have my word on both."

I swiped away more tears, nodding in thanks. I couldn't see if it was daylight or not, but I knew the Rogues would be coming for me soon, and I didn't want those bastards seeing me like this.

When I gathered my composure, Duke was staring at me strangely.

"What?"

"I've never known you to take anything lying down."

I shrugged sadly. "You were right. When other people lose control, someone might get hurt, but when I lose control, I burn half a city alive." Innocent children included.

That was the glaring truth.

I was too dangerous to live.

His expression turned grim.

The Rogues crashed into the jail, armed to the teeth. They were expecting me to fight, but I didn't. I didn't do anything as I was wrenched to my feet and my arms were shackled behind me.

Duke said goodbye with a lone nod as I was dragged out.

I'd looked death in the eye before, always with a steely determination to go out with a bang, but an odd sense of peace settled over me as I was towed through the gilded streets.

They brought me into the city square where a crowd was gathered. I was hauled up a small platform and tied to a wooden pole. Ropes crisscrossed my shoulders, torso, and legs. The Rogues lined up across from me, guns bared. Some mortals joined them, making it thirty in total.

My last act of defiance was staring down my executioners. I wasn't going to look away. I wasn't going to hide.

As hammers cocked, I waited for my life to flash before my eyes, but the only thing I saw was Ronan's steely gaze.

I'm sorry. I'm sorry for everything. Most of all, I'm sorry I didn't get to say goodbye.

Maybe he was dead too. Maybe there was no goodbye to say.

I thought I might feel a little fear, or apprehension at least, but the only thing I felt was relief. Relief that my dragon wouldn't be able to hurt any more children. Relief that I'd die before I became any more of a monster.

I shut my eyes, bracing for the first bullet.

Nothing happened for a long drag. Sharp whistling proceeded dead silence.

I opened my eyes to see every gaze fixed toward the sky.

A dark shape appeared between the clouds, barreling towards us with the speed of a bullet. I peered hard, trying to discern what it was. It took the shape of a figure seconds before it slammed into the city square.

The cobblestone cracked and sent fissures speeding in every direction. People leaped back as crevices opened under their feet. The figure unfurled into a giant. Chilling onyx eyes speared the crowd.

"Run."

They scattered, releasing a spray of screams.

I watched in stunned silence as Ronan came toward me and ascended the platform.

I knew this wasn't real. My mind was conjuring him in my final moments so I could say goodbye.

He cupped the back of my head in a gentle, loving embrace, but his eyes were full of hate. A gold blade flashed in his hand.

"What are you doing?" I mumbled deliriously.

He brought the tip of the dagger to my chest as his lips touched my ear. "Returning the favor."

He drove the blade into my heart.

7

VERA

I tumbled into blackness, landing in a dark lake. I sunk deep. There was no sound, heat, or cold. Just the water and me. I clawed for the surface, but anytime I thought I was close, I found more darkness.

It felt like years passed in that yawning midnight before a bright light pierced the water.

My eyes opened with a gasp.

Chest heaving, I sucked in great gulps of air, but it wasn't enough. Each wheezing breath felt like my heart was splitting in two.

Why couldn't I breathe?

Why was my chest on fire?

Panic cinched my lungs.

"Shhh. You're okay. Breathe." A strong hand brushed over my hair.

Breathe? How was I supposed to breathe with an axe buried in my chest?

"Inhale." They sucked in a breath, urging me to do the same. "Exhale." Air gusted out of their lips. "Inhale." Another deep breath. "Exhale."

The cadence of that rumble was hypnotic. I followed along, matching their pattern. Inhale. Pause. Exhale.

The pain subsided from a cleaving blade to a steady burn as the hand continued its tender movement. I arched into its warmth, desperate for comfort. It disappeared and I whimpered, begging for it to return.

It did at the same time cool metal pressed against my lips.

"Drink."

The hand in my hair cupped my head, lifting it. When the first taste of water touched my scorched throat, I moaned. I tried to suck it all down, but they held the cup away warning, "Slow."

My head did something resembling a nod.

The metal returned and I took small sips, groaning and licking my lips in between each one. The feel of the water hitting my empty stomach was bliss. Once I finished, the cup disappeared, and I was guided back down.

Furs were pulled over my shoulders. I snuggled into their warmth with a sigh. They held traces of my favorite scent.

"Rest more."

Their weight left the bed. I blindly reached for them. "Please don't go."

They took my hand as they lowered beside me and resumed that gentle stroke over my hair.

"Thank you," I whispered.

They squeezed my hand. Sleep was immediate.

When I woke again, I couldn't move my right hand, but my left one flew over my body in disbelief. I was alive.

A heavy mix of emotions followed—shock, anger, guilt, and a small degree of relief. The last one was confusing. I had been ready to die. I picked at it, trying to unearth its source.

Ronan.

If I was alive, I still had a chance to find him, protect him.

A soft snore jolted me out of my head.

Peeling open an eye, I found why my right hand couldn't move. It was intertwined with a much larger one. I dragged my gaze higher and froze.

Ronan was fast asleep in a chair too small for his giant frame. His thick, muscled legs were sprawled out and his head hung over the edge at an uncomfortable angle. The chair was pulled up beside the bed so he could hold my hand.

My heart beat sluggishly in my chest.

I blinked slowly, not believing my eyes. I saw him at the gallows, but I thought I was dreaming. He was here, the warmth of his palm against mine, undeniably real.

"Ronan," I whispered.

His head snapped up and liquid iron eyes flashed into mine.

The ball of dread and tension I'd been carrying since I learned he was missing exploded, releasing a shockwave of dizzying relief. Tears pricked my eyes. "You're alive."

I launched myself at him.

Ignoring the sharp pain in my chest, I threw my arms around him. His warmth and scent soaked into me; leather mixed with vanilla and amber wood. My favorite smell. I greedily sucked it in.

"I can't believe you're here," I whispered against his neck.

Fuck, I missed him. I missed him so much.

He was stiff for a beat, as if shocked by my reaction, before he wrapped his arms around me and clutched me just as fiercely.

We clung to one another for a long time.

Eventually, Ronan pulled back, but didn't let go.

The enormous relief I felt was reflected on his face. Words tumbled out of him in a rush. "You have no idea how good it is to see your beautiful gaze. You took so long to wake, I feared I used too much gold." He squeezed me tight, burying his face in the crook of my neck. "Fuck. I'm so glad you're okay."

We held each other for another stretch, our hearts beating in sync until he released me. I stepped back, dropping onto the bed.

His eyes swirled with guilt as they settled on my chest. "Is there any pain?"

Flashes of my last moments assaulted me—a gold dagger, excruciating agony, then blackness. My eyes widened. "Did I . . . die?"

"Your heart stopped briefly."

My brows inched up. "I'm immortal?"

He shook his head. "If I had stabbed you with a dagger made of pure gold, it would have killed you. The blade I used was made of a special gold alloy. Your body was able to heal from it."

A charged silence fell over us, filled with his unspoken act.

"And you stabbed me because . . .?"

"I'll explain everything shortly."

My eyes narrowed, but I let it go for now. I didn't want to break our temporary peace, or whatever was happening. I was just so damn relieved he was okay. Slowly, I examined the area where my chest protested each breath with an ache.

I was shirtless. Cream bandages were wrapped around my torso. Casting a brief look at him, I carefully peeled the cloth away. There was an angry red slit running between my breasts. The skin around it was black and blue.

It looked worse than it felt.

"I'm fine," I said answering his earlier question. "It's healing nicely."

"Let me know if that changes."

I nodded.

We stared at one another in silence, an awkward tension filling the air. Neither of us knew what to say. I'd been so focused on finding him, I'd never thought of what I would do once I did.

I cleared my throat, sticking to a safe subject. "How long was I out?"

"Three days."

That sounded right for a wound this severe. It also explained why the room was perfectly intact despite not having taken any gold dust.

There were no signs the dragon had attempted to escape. The injury had severely weakened it, and I'm sure Ronan's presence helped. The dishes piled against the wall told me he had been at my side the entire time.

He speared a hand through his hair. "It was three long fucking days."

My ribs grew tight at the waver in his voice. I slung my gaze back to his face, and really took him in.

Haggard was the first word that came to mind. His eyes were wild, ringed with dark circles, his normally sun-kissed skin was blotchy, and his blonde hair, now finger length, was in complete disarray.

He'd been desperate with worry, but I couldn't tell if it was guilt, or something more.

When I lifted my gaze back to his, I found him glaring at my cheek.

"Who touched you?" he asked in a low, dangerous voice.

I gingerly pressed a finger to the area. The skin was tender and likely bruised. It had still been healing when that rat bastard Vince had reinjured it.

"The Rogues."

He nodded like I confirmed what he'd already known.

More silence passed before he asked, "Are you hungry?"

The gold dust suppressed my appetite, but after eight days without it, and all the energy my body used to heal itself, I was ravenous.

"Starving."

For some reason that made him smile.

Oh.

When we first met, he had asked me the same thing, and instead of answering, I had bargained with him. That felt like a lifetime ago, but the fact that it was making him smile now had to mean something. A tiny tendril of hope crept into my heart.

I grinned back.

"One moment," he said. I didn't miss the quiet snick of the door locking on his way out, but it wasn't enough to quell my burgeoning hope. Given how things had ended, some distrust was expected.

He returned minutes later with a tray. A strawberry the size of my head sat on it beside a bowl. I had only seen the red fruit once before during a visit to Gold City, and it had been a quarter of the size.

Ronan chuckled at my comically wide eyes. The sound was much more reserved compared to our time in the Mortal Lands. He noticed at the same time, and we shared another uncomfortable moment.

"House Anu's powers make them excellent farmers," he explained, breaking the silence.

"What's that?" I pointed at the bowl of white liquid beside the fruit.

"Cream."

My brows dipped.

Even though the mortal's food supply came from the fae,

they were given the unwanted leftovers, which Gold City had first pick of. By the time Mayhem had its turn, it got the last of the odds and ends which included anemic meat and rotting vegetables. I'd never had cream before.

It was on the tip of my tongue to point out how messed up it was that the fae had food like this, meanwhile, children were starving on the other side of the mountain, but I bit back the complaint.

"It's like sugary milk," he said, saving me from having to ask.

He set the tray beside the bed, then squeezed into the chair next to it.

The strawberry was already split open. As I raised the knife and fork to cut off a piece, I saw a mark on my wrist.

I squeezed the utensils in a death grip.

"Ronan—" I sucked in a deep breath, trying so hard not to ruin this moment "—Did you brand me?"

"You can't survive in the Faylands without it."

I gripped the knife and fork so hard, the metal threatened to snap. "Why," I gritted out. I couldn't look at him. If I did, I might stab him.

"Magic saturates every particle of air," he explained patiently. "It feeds on organic material in order to create new life. The Faylands is in a constant cycle of death and rebirth. The only way to protect oneself is to be a conduit instead of a meal."

The brand was to protect me, and the halflings.

It had darker purposes like servitude, but that one surprised me. I loosened my grip with a rough breath.

I couldn't take my eyes off the snarling wolf burned into my wrist. The longer I stared, the harder I had to fight not to lash out. He had made me his property without my permission. I wouldn't have been able to give it at the time, and it was for my own good . . . *but still.*

I lifted my head. "You and I will be having a discussion about this." The way I said discussion made it sound like blades rather than words would be involved, which wasn't far off.

A hint of amusement shadowed his lips. "I expected nothing less."

Expelling a long breath, I pushed out my anger with the air. *We'll give him an earful later.* Holding my fork over the bowl, I glanced at Ronan, and he nodded encouragingly.

I dipped the piece of strawberry in the cream sparingly in case I didn't like it. A light, sugary flavor burst over my tongue, and I moaned. "This is delicious." I cut off a larger piece and dunked it.

When Ronan remained silent, I cast my gaze at him. He was watching me with an achingly sweet expression, pleased I was enjoying the food. As difficult as it was to keep my anger leashed about the brand, that look made it worth it.

Smiling, I kept my eyes connected with his, and the moment stretched into something intimate. The stiffness hanging over our interaction melted away as that magnetic force I had fought so hard in the beginning clicked into place.

My skin buzzed like live wire, desperately seeking his.

Our knees bumped together as we leaned forward to close the gap between us.

His gaze fell to my mouth.

Kiss me.

A clawing hunger glimmered in his eyes, but he didn't move closer. "Eat before the cream warms," he instructed.

He stood and stepped away.

Disappointment threaded through my chest, but I didn't let it show. This interaction was going better than I could have ever anticipated. I polished off the fruit in minutes.

I set the fork and knife aside as he approached with a tin of water. He held it to my lips, locking eyes with me. Some of it trickled out of the side of my mouth, and he swiped it up with his thumb, bringing it back to my lips.

My breathing hitched as his thumb parted my mouth. I sucked the water off, maintaining eye contact. His gaze hooded and a deep rumble shook his chest.

I stared expectantly, waiting for him to do more. He didn't, moving away, but he couldn't keep his eyes off me.

That tendril of hope blossomed, expanding through my whole chest.

In all my time chasing Ronan, I hadn't thought there was an inkling of a chance there would be a future for us, but I was starting to think otherwise.

Though attraction by itself didn't mean much, when combined with his rescue, his worry over my well-being, and sweet care, it meant he still had to feel something for me. And if there were feelings, there was hope.

Maybe, just maybe, I hadn't ruined things beyond repair.

The tin was set on the tray before he carried it to the door. "There are clothes in the wardrobe and a bathing chamber two doors over," he informed me. "Meet me downstairs when you're ready." His hand lingered on the doorknob. He cast a small smile over his shoulder. "I'm glad you're here."

More hope unfurled in my chest. I couldn't contain my grin. "Me too," I whispered, and he left.

Chest bubbling with a giddy sensation, I padded over to the wardrobe across from the bed.

Getting back with Ronan didn't absolve me of what I had done to those children, or fix the issue with my dragon, but it all felt infinitely more manageable with him by my side.

The bureau was stocked with an assortment of clothing

78

in my size and style. I picked out a cream-colored tunic, traded my dirty pants for clean leather ones, and snatched up my boots at the edge of the bed.

I found the bathing room he mentioned. It was a small space outfitted with a wide, wooden tub. The water was lukewarm, but I didn't care. I scrubbed my hair and body with the vanilla soap poised on its lip. I hadn't been able to wash my hair at the jail. It felt ten times lighter when all the dirt and grime was gone.

I grabbed a hanging linen as I stepped out and quickly dried and dressed, taming my wet hair into a braid.

I raced down the stairs, feeling buoyed and light, an uncontrollable smile stretching my lips. A fragile ball of hope filled my chest. I had been through so much this month. So much had gone wrong. But everything had been worth it for this moment right here.

Not only was Ronan alive and healthy, but there might be a chance for us after all.

I was dizzy with joy and excitement.

I followed the voices trailing out of one of the rooms. They led me into a warm, open kitchen.

Inside, a woman had her arms wrapped tightly around Ronan as he gazed down at her with a bright smile. Beautiful, chocolate curls, crystalline green eyes, and angelic wings. The latter was new, but there was no mistaking the rest of her.

It was the woman from the Eye's vision.

Ronan had found his mate.

8

VERA

I stumbled back, bumping into the wall. A coldness formed in my core and spread quickly. Ice pricked every nerve. I was shaking, my knees on the verge of buckling. I closed my eyes, praying it was a dream, or that the mortals had killed me after all.

When I opened them, nothing had changed.

Ronan had his arms around another woman, smiling like a lunatic, and she was smiling just as madly back.

He was a massive, dominant male, and she was a petite little beauty, barely reaching his chest. They fit together perfectly, looking deliriously happy in one another's arms.

My heart dropped to my feet. It felt like I'd been kicked by a giant.

A tiny noise of distress slipped past my lips. Every rotten emotion clawing into the soft tissue of my heart was relayed.

Their heads swung to me, and they leaped apart. Whatever Ronan saw on my face had his twisting with distress. *Oh, don't mind me. My world is just falling apart.* His mouth moved, but I couldn't hear anything over the loud buzzing in my ears. He started for me, and I knew, I just knew if he touched me, I'd shatter.

I darted left and bolted outside to panicked shouts of my name. Tears distorted my vision. I ran with no idea where I was going, and I didn't care as long as it was away from him.

Frantic footfalls thundered behind me. "Vera, stop," Ronan shouted. "It's not safe."

A scornful laugh churned in my throat. The only dangerous thing here was him.

I tried to run faster, but the wound in my chest sharpened every breath into a blade. The world around me spun, and I doubled over, vomiting. I threw up every last bit of strawberry and mourned the loss of the delicious treat.

His footfalls were gaining on me.

I was grateful for the lack of gold dust in my system. My speed and strength were at their peak. I launched back into a sprint, pushing past the pain.

"Stay away from me," I screamed, but his stampeding didn't slow. Why was he following me? Why couldn't he let me fall apart in peace?

His disappearance, his negligence of the fae laws—it all made sense. Ronan was never in any danger. *He was with her.*

A wretched sob built in my throat. Gods, I felt so stupid.

More tears came. I couldn't stop running. It was the only thing holding me together. If I stopped, I'd have to face reality. I'd have to recognize that the man I was hopelessly in love with had found his destiny.

The ground disappeared. Suddenly, I was falling. I'd run right off a cliff.

"VERA!" Ronan's roar blasted over the landscape.

Something clamped around my ankle mid-air and jerked me back. My spine slammed into rock. All the air burst from my lungs as I bounced off the cliffside, the momentum swinging me forward. I continued to swing back and forth, catching glimpses of blue as I went high, then gray as I swung low.

Whatever had my leg didn't let go. For a hopeful second, I thought it might be Ronan until I lifted my head.

A red vine spotted with white suckers had my ankle. As soon as my movement slowed, it tightened, crushing bone. Hundreds of vines slithered down the cliff face, racing toward me. The combined noise of their suckers moving over the rock made a hair-raising popping sound.

They snaked over my body until I was covered. Their suckers were slimy and disturbing. I managed to free a talon and stab it into the closest vine. It squealed and shrieked before retreating.

I tore into the others with my fangs. An acidic juice filled my mouth.

For every vine I destroyed, five more took its place. They wrapped around my torso and squeezed like a vise, crushing my ribs. I couldn't breathe. My vision blackened at the edges as I fought to stay conscious.

There was a roar above, followed by the sounds of a blade hacking. The vines' haunting squeals echoed around me, and then I was falling again.

I had a split-second to realize all the blue I had seen was water. I speared my arms in an arrow just before I hit it. The icy water swallowed me eagerly, pulling me down into its gullet.

There was no light penetrating the darkness and the frigid sea was stealing my air. My muscles cramped from the cold. I clawed for the surface like a rabid animal, but it was like swimming through tar. I kicked and kicked, getting nowhere.

The walls of my dark, wet prison closed in.

Terror gripped my throat.

This is how you die. Alone in the dark.

A figure shot toward me.

Hands hooked under my arms, and then I was rising out of my watery grave. We surfaced and I sputtered, gasping for air. My system was overwrought. I couldn't tell if it was from the cold, the fear, or the crushing despair.

Ronan took one look at me and cursed. "Hold on."

He wrapped my arms around his neck and paddled us to a small beach sitting below the cliffs. From there he scooped me into his arms, raced up a set of zig-zagging steps, and charged for the manor in the distance.

My teeth knocked together. My body felt like a block of ice.

He rushed us into a room where he set me on my feet and began frantically stripping off my wet clothes. I tried to help, but my arms were useless.

"I need furs," he shouted.

Ronan removed the last piece of clothing and blocked me from view as a figure bulldozed into the room, armed with blankets.

"She was attacked by fionain. Run to Lawrence for a poultice."

They left, and Ronan whipped around, swaddling me tightly in furs as he guided me over to a hearth.

"Sit."

I did, numb fingers gripping the furs as I stared into the flames.

Ronan removed a small pot hanging over the fire and disappeared. He returned, pressing a steaming mug into my hands.

Mechanically, I accepted it and took a sip. It had an earthy, nutty flavor with a hint of sweetness like bread and honey. He moved behind me and pulled me into his chest, giving me his heat. He gripped me tightly until the shaking in my limbs eased and I polished off the tea.

"What were you thinking?" he growled as he plucked the mug from my hands.

I didn't answer. I wasn't sure I was there. I knew my body was sitting in front of a fire, but I had drifted off somewhere else.

"Vera." He shook me gently. I didn't feel it, but I saw his arms moving.

The figure returned, handing Ronan a jar before departing. He gently pried the furs from my grip. I let them go without complaint and they pooled around my waist. I couldn't feel their warmth anyway. I couldn't feel anything.

Ronan's hand smoothed over my skin and a spike of pain broke through the numbness.

I hissed softly.

He paused. "I need to apply this before the numbing agent wears off," he murmured.

I nodded limply and he continued. As he smoothed the paste over my skin, I glanced down and saw I was covered in red, ring-shaped wounds. Each circle was created by hundreds of teeth marks.

"Were they drinking my blood?" I asked in an eerily calm voice.

"Yes. Their suckers secrete a numbing slime before they feed."

Huh. Was that why I didn't feel anything? No . . . I don't think that was it.

Belatedly, I realized he had brought me to the kitchen; to the place that had broken something inside me. My voice sounded strange and far away as I asked, "Why did you save me from the firing squad?"

I felt his confusion at my back. Then his anger. "You think I would have let you die?" he asked in a hard tone.

84

"Of course." He'd found his mate.

Ronan's mood became grim. His dark energy soured the air, but his touch remained gentle. The next several minutes were spent in a tense silence as he finished applying the ointment. He capped the jar and set it aside. "Why did you run?"

I stiffened. Was he really going to make me say it?

He prodded my arm, careful to avoid my wounds. I was too tired to fight him. On a heavy, dejected sigh, I admitted, "I know who she is, Ronan. The Eye showed me."

"Who?"

My hands clenched tightly at my sides. "Don't play stupid," I growled. Having this conversation was humiliating enough. At his silence, anger exploded through me. "Gods-damnit. I know she's your mate!"

Dead silence followed.

I peered over my shoulder. His mind was working a million miles a minute.

"Well?"

His gaze touched mine. "What did the Eye show you?"

I glanced away. This conversation was hollowing out my heart cavity, but I forced myself to explain, "You were cradling a baby and smiling like mad at that beautiful brunette."

Breath caught in my lungs as I waited, desperately waited for him to deny it, to tell me I was wrong.

"I'm sorry," he said quietly. "I didn't—"

My head whipped around. "What was that upstairs?" I interrupted, as my heart cracked open.

Ronan's gaze was gentle, if not a little guarded. "That was relief. I spent the last three days believing I had killed you. Do you have any idea what that was like?" he asked roughly.

I stared, eyes desperately roving over his face, searching for signs that weren't there. This—him—was all I had left. I wasn't ready to acknowledge I didn't have him either. "Why would you care?"

"I loved you. That doesn't just go away."

Loved. A spear lanced my chest.

The tide of misery swelling inside threatened to drown me. Anger was my lifeline. I clung to it. "You should have never gotten involved with me," I hissed. "You knew you had a mate out there this whole time."

His gaze remained soft. He was always so patient with me. I *hated* him for it.

"There have been no new mate pairings in five hundred years. I never considered it as a possibility. It just . . . happened."

I remember thinking that what we shared was too good to be true, that the Gods would remember I wasn't allowed to have anything good and take it away—and they had. Brutally. I should have known better. I didn't get a happy ending. I didn't deserve one.

It was too painful to meet his gaze. "Your mate is why you disappeared," I whispered. "Why you didn't come any of the times I broke fae law."

"That's part of the reason," he admitted gently.

"Why did you send Kian?"

"For your protection . . . And the fae's."

Of course. Bitterness lodged in my chest. I knew too many of their secrets. A long stretch of silence lapsed. There was nothing left to say. He had laid it all out.

"Do you—Do you want to be alone?"

I was too choked up to speak. I could only shake my head.

"Okay," he whispered. "I'll stay as long as you want."

I fought past the rock in my throat and somehow found the strength to meet his gaze again. "No," I croaked miserably. "I want to leave."

Ronan's face looked pained. He struggled with his next words. "You can't. King Desmond saw your wanted poster. He knows it was you in his dungeon. He's looking for you. I had to fake your death."

My insides withered. That's why he stabbed me.

"If he finds out what I've done before I can locate the godstone . . ." he trailed off.

If I left here, I would put both our lives at risk.

I released a sad sigh, knowing I would stay. I hadn't spent the last month chasing Ronan to protect him just to throw it all away. I averted my gaze as hot tears slipped down my cheeks. "I'll stay as long as you don't come near me again." My voice caught toward the end.

The prospect of cutting him out completely hurt almost as much as the alternative. I pushed off his hands, wrenched up the furs, and scooted closer to the flames. "You should go."

"Vera," Ronan said gently, attempting to turn me toward him.

I jerked away. "Leave. *Please.*"

I was seconds from falling apart and I couldn't bear to do it in front of him.

He hesitated before he did as I asked. "I'll be away for a few weeks searching for the Nighters. Kian will watch over you."

A cold spike of fear speared through the heartbreak. My gaze shot towards him. "Are you going alone?"

"Yes," he said, sounding confused by the question.

I was in no state to convince him what a terrible idea that was, and even if I was, the stubborn ass would never listen. I said nothing else, my gaze returning to the fire.

I heard him reach the door and couldn't stop myself from blurting out, "Do you love her?"

I braced for the answer. I didn't want to know, but I

needed to. When he didn't immediately respond, I swiped my tears and glanced over my shoulder.

His gray gaze swirled with an unreadable emotion, moving between mine, and in the softest of whispers he said, "With all my heart."

Then he was gone.

My heart didn't make a single sound when it shattered.

I sucked in a ragged breath, full of broken glass. I glanced down, expecting to see blood. Nothing. There was nothing.

I pulled the furs over me and blindly stumbled out of the kitchen, trying to find my way back to the room I'd woken in. The world was spinning. It felt like someone had shoved hot barbed wire between my ribs.

Somehow, I managed to find the room. I shut the door and slid to the ground, clutching my chest as my pulse hammered in my ears. Every breath burned. I threw off the furs like that might somehow alleviate the pain. It didn't. The cold prick of air only highlighted the fire raging inside.

I scored my talons into my skin.

The physical pain helped me focus. It gave purpose to the faceless monster clawing at my insides. Inhale. Exhale. Inhale. Exhale. I survived one breath at a time.

Eventually, the barbs stabbing into my lungs dissipated and the cry swelling at the back of my throat eased.

One breath in. One breath out.

The world slowed along with my pulse.

Rising, I collapsed on the bed, slipping under the covers, but no matter what I did, I couldn't get warm. It wasn't the fur's fault. The chill was bone deep.

I dug the heels of my palms into my eyes, pressing against another wave of tears.

I didn't think it was possible for things to be worse, but I should have known better.

Right before the Crone threw me in the well for the first time, I had stood up to her, adamant that she couldn't cause me any more pain.

She had laughed.

'Oh darling, as long as your heart beats, there will always be a greater pain awaiting you. It's the only guarantee there is.'

9

RONAN

I flexed my fingers. They ached from the number of times I'd broken them. A bone for each of her tears.

What transpired yesterday was unpleasant, but necessary.

Vera would thank me one day.

Kian appeared dragging a blubbering male by the scruff of his neck. His cheeks were fat with tears. I expected more from the men who protected Mayhem, but every last one had been pitiful. Half of them had pissed themselves.

"Is he the last?"

He jerked his head.

I threw open the pit door. Nineteen men stood huddled, trembling in the dark. The combined smell of their piss, shit, and sweat burned my nose. I kicked the last Rogue inside and locked the door.

Kian slanted a look toward it. "Should we get them a bucket?"

"No," I growled. "Let them soak in their own filth."

Twenty men against one woman. Spineless.

"What do you want to do with them?" he asked.

The things I had planned . . . Death would be a kindness.

"Skin off their brands. Leave the wrists."

Magic would eat at their bones and provide an excruciating experience until I could deal with them. I couldn't determine how the disgusting cowards had overpowered Vera, but no matter. They had put their hands on her, and they would pay.

"Give them food and water once a day," I ordered. "Mix in some mud from the shore."

It was infected with a nasty parasite. It would block their intestines and bloat their stomachs.

Kian shuddered. "Remind me to not get on your bad side."

I eyed him. "You already have."

Vera was an obstinate and willful creature. I understood he could not have prevented every attempt of hers to break fae law, but for one of my most elite warriors to be outwitted was unacceptable. Those pigs were able to put their hands on her, and she had been seconds away from death because of him.

Lucinda had scried me with the help of a witch and informed me of what the Rogues had done and Vera's impending execution. We'd made a deal. I would resume my Enforcer duties, and she would ensure everyone believed Gold City had executed Vera.

If Lucinda had not contacted me . . . My jaw clenched with fury. I had severed Kian's toes with a spelled blade. He wouldn't be able to walk properly for weeks.

He smartly lowered his gaze. "Any news on the godstone?"

After gathering intel on the Nighters, I learned they were hiding in the Spirit Lands. They managed to find a pooka to transport them, which was a feat that could not have been accomplished in between the godstone's discovery and the events in Mayhem.

The beasts were rare and even more difficult to capture. They had to have been planning this for years. It remained a mystery how they could have known the godstone would wash ashore after being lost for five centuries.

After pouring over House Cern's archives, I learned there was another way inside the Spirit Lands. The God of Death had created a door into his realm for his lover. Each record provided a different location, but they all agreed it was in The Wilds.

"I have several leads to track down," I informed him.

"And King Desmond?"

He had summoned me seven days ago.

The king sat at the head of his table, and he wasn't alone. Lady Belenus and her mate sat on his left. House Belenus had a sizable army, and though their powers were not as well adapted to war as mine, they outnumbered us two to one, and could fight on land as well as in the air.

Lord Brigid sat on his right. His House was composed entirely of healers. They could keep an army fighting at peak health for months.

Together, the two Houses made powerful allies . . . or enemies.

"Join us," King Desmond said, gesturing to the seat on Lord Brigid's right. It was presented as an invitation, but we both knew it was an order.

I remained standing.

King Desmond's eyes tightened at the provocation but didn't react. He snapped his fingers and a halfling presented me with a paper. It had Vera's face.

My blood ran cold, but I didn't allow my reaction to show as I glanced up from the paper. "Who is she?"

I thought I had known once. Not anymore.

"You tell me, Enforcer. I found her in my dungeon shortly after you left. Conspicuous, no?"

Rage hammered my veins. Vera had neglected to mention that.

I lowered the paper, leveling him with a dry look. "You summoned me because your House has a hole in its security?"

King Desmond stared through thinned lids, slamming a hand on the table, rattling the dishes and cutlery. "Where is my next course?"

A halfling rushed over, removing his dirty dishes with trembling hands as another carried over a fresh plate of venison and vegetables. The halfling with the dirty dishes wasn't watching where she was going in her haste and crashed into me.

The plates tumbled from her arms and shattered. She apologized profusely as she collected the shards. The king rose, eyes shooting fire.

I crouched. "Go." I took the shards from her, nicking myself in the process. She jerked her head and quickly scurried from the room. A few drops of blood stained the porcelain as I set the pieces down.

"Where is my godstone?" King Desmond demanded as I rose. He had returned to his seat.

Given the pressing situation, I ascertained truth was the best path. "The godstone is lost with the Nighters. They're going to use it to free the beasts on the next winter eclipse."

A scoff sounded. "How do we know you aren't simply keeping the godstone for yourself?" Lord Brigid asked. Copper eyes stared from a severe face. "The godstone in your hands makes us all uncomfortable."

My molars ground together. "I have paid for my crimes." I turned to the king. "As I am sure your spies already informed you, I do not have it."

"Yes, these so-called 'Nighters' stole it." He waved a dismissive hand. "I've never heard of such people."

"It is hard to hear of anything behind the safety of our border, your highness."

He stared coolly. "You think those mortals can overpower me?"

Dagda fae could steal powers. They couldn't wield them, and it wasn't permanent, but they could level the playing field for a time. The wall imprisoning the beasts was created from the combined powers of all the fae, but King Desmond was the conduit, feeding it our magic to maintain it.

"No, but the godstone can." It was forged by my ancestor, God Taranis.

"As long as I live, the wall will stand," he declared.

I shook my head. His arrogance would doom us all.

He signaled a squadron of guards over. "I warned you what would happen if you failed me, Enforcer."

There wasn't an ounce of concern for the threat to our people. He was only concerned with himself, but I had long been disillusioned by him. The only thing I felt was disgust for ever thinking we had chosen well for our king.

Briefly scanning the inbound men for threats, I dismissed them. They'd be dead on the floor before they could raise their weapons.

I flicked my gaze back to the king. "Do you remember what you told me when I came to you to change the way the fae laws were enforced?"

I had told Vera a half-truth when we met. I was the judge, jury, and executioner of lawbreakers, but I was beholden to every fae lord, lady, and the king.

Three hundred years ago, I felt the mortals were sufficiently cowed between the beasts and their infertile lands. There was no need to further demoralize them with automatic death sentences. Lawbreakers needed to be punished, but in a way that accounted for the circumstances surrounding their crime.

I stood in this room and made my case to King Desmond. He was quick to remind me how important it was for every House to play their part.

House Dagda maintained the walls.

House Cern recorded history.

House Belenus controlled the weather.

House Anu grew the food.

House Brigid healed.

And House Taran protected.

The magic in the Faylands created a vicious environment. We depended on one another for survival. It was a fragile ecosystem that worked as long as everyone contributed.

If I didn't continue my Enforcer duties, the other Houses would stop giving my House the things it couldn't provide itself. We would be denied food, healers, safe weather—everything my people's survival depended on.

King Desmond held up a hand, delaying his guards. "Go on."

"What would happen if I withdrew all my warriors from the outposts?"

There were four positioned throughout the Faylands to head off beast attacks from the sea. A water beast could survive days on land and amass a large fatality count if not stopped. My outpost soldiers were highly skilled and trained in water beast warfare. The same could not be said for the other Houses.

The king's answering smile was sharp. "Is it not fortuitous that Lady Belenus has agreed to supply as many soldiers as necessary, and Lord Brigid has pledged his best healers to oversee their health?"

There was the true purpose of this meeting: House Taran was expendable.

"That is fortuitous," I gritted out. "But who will act as Enforcer?"

He spread his hands. "You aren't enforcing fae law now."

I could ignore the pull of my Enforcer magic, but it was difficult, and painful. "The search for the weapon took precedence."

"And yet, you've nothing to show for it."

My jaw popped.

"I will give you one last chance, Enforcer," the king said. *"Deliver the godstone within two months' time, or all goods and services will be cut off from House Taran."*

An echoing silence proceeded the king's declaration. That was a death sentence.

"You'll have the godstone." I pivoted on my heel and gathered my Enforcer magic close, readying to leave.

"And Enforcer?"

Spine stiffening, I paused.

"If you fail, consider it justice for House Ogma."

"He's growing impatient," I told Kian. "We don't have long."

It was fortunate that I received the scry from Lucinda a day after I learned the king was looking for Vera. I had already been planning her retrieval. Kylah had flown me straight to Gold City.

"How much iron dust were you able to recover?" I asked. His main task was watching and protecting Vera, but his secondary assignment was collecting the iron dust dispersed in Mayhem.

"Ninety vials."

That meant only a handful remained with the mortals.

With the Nighters gone, the mortals would lose their bravery, but I'd had the mountain path blocked just in case.

"Excellent."

Vera appeared, marching toward us with a determined stride. Surprised flickered through me. I didn't expect to see her before I departed.

"She believes Kylah is my mate. Keep it that way," I ordered in a low voice.

"Kylah won't like it," he hissed.

Knowing how close he and Kylah were, I permitted the insolence. "I'm aware. You're dismissed."

He left just as she reached me.

Her face was puffy and red. I'd made her cry *again*.

I ignored the tightness in my chest. I'd done much worse for far less honorable reasons.

Pinning her shoulders back, she crossed her arms, and hit me with a stubborn glare. While she healed, I'd been denied the pleasure of that bewitching gaze—lavender with flecks of gold. I could stare into those eyes forever.

My hands itched to pull her close. I wanted to kiss her, love her, drop to my knees and worship her, but that's not who we were anymore.

She thrust up her chin, declaring, "I'm going with you to find the Nighters."

Her defiance was as infuriating as it was sexy. "No."

If looks could kill . . . *Don't smile.*

"I'm not just going to wait around," she snapped.

"Look at the mountains." I pointed south. "Do you see that shimmer?"

From this distance, the magical boundary was a faint ribbon of pink running along the peaks of the Fayette Mountains, but it could only be seen on this side.

She spun around, peering in that direction.

"It's the same kind of wall as in the Mortal Lands, only this one is designed to keep magic in. All the magic that once flowed freely over The Lands is now packed into a much smaller area. It wreaks havoc on everything from our plants and wildlife to our weather. Everything here wants to kill you, or have you already forgotten the fionain?"

She swiveled back, looking unimpressed. "I've been fighting the beasts since I was fifteen. I'm used to things wanting to kill me."

Another thing I would punish the Rogues for. What kind of men had young girls fighting on the front lines?

They didn't deserve to breathe the same air as her.

They didn't deserve to breathe at all.

I studied her, attempting to discern where this sudden interest had come from. The bruise on her cheek was glaring and sent rage ringing through my bones. I was going to tear those men apart.

"You told me to stay away from you," I reminded her gently. "And now you want to spend the coming weeks in my constant company?"

Her talons clicked together, but her voice rang out strong. "I made this mess. I'm going to help clean it up."

My brows rose. "You don't even know where I'm going."

"I don't care."

Discreetly, I scented her. A month ago, her emotions perfumed the air, constantly announcing her emotional state like a young fae before they learned the art of suppression, but now I could smell nothing. There was a wall around her, and I greatly disliked it.

"You're not coming," I said with finality. "It's too dangerous."

The northernmost tip of the Faylands was a cold hellscape. The weather could turn lethal in an instant, bringing with it an army of Magic-Born like the fionain, or a single misstep could cause a fatal fall into a crevasse, and those were the least pressing dangers.

In the Mortal Lands, I was feared. In the Faylands, I was hated. Any number of fae would kill Vera for simply being in my company.

"Yes, I am," Vera said softly. "Because if you leave without me, I swear to Gods, I'll hand myself over to the king."

My eyes narrowed. "You don't mean that."

She held her hands out to the sides. "I have *nothing* to lose."

"Only your life," I snapped.

"I don't care," she snapped back.

I tried to scent the air again and growled in frustration when I could smell nothing. I had no idea what was going through her mind.

"Take me with you, or give me to the king," she said point-blank.

She meant it. I could see it in her eyes.

Stubborn, infuriating woman.

I held her gaze, breathing roughly. "And you wonder why I said those things in Coldwater."

Her eyes flashed. "And you wonder why I poisoned you."

I snarled like a beast, glaring. The stubborn gleam in her eyes announced that nothing short of death would keep her from joining my search.

A solution came to me, and a slow smile curved my lips. I was going to do what I should have done in Coldwater. "Kian, there's been a change of plans," I called, knowing he hadn't gone far.

I barreled toward Vera and flung her over my shoulder.

A feral scream battered my ears as I headed for my manor. Skin ripped under the wild fury of her claws. Her fangs sunk into flesh. All her violence accomplished was making me hard. I adjusted myself as I ducked inside my home.

I carried her to the room I had prepared for her and set her down.

She punched me in the groin.

I grimaced, doubling over as she tried to dart for the door, but I got there first.

"You're not leaving."

Fire glittered in her eyes. "You try to lock me in this room, and I will bring this whole place down."

I scanned the floor for the chain I had installed while I was retrieving her. It was a thick chain with a cuff. She had previously slept with two, but I had it made from pure gold to strengthen its effectiveness so she would only need the one. It was intended to help her feel secure at night but would suit my purposes as well.

I spotted the chain, partially hidden by the bed. Using my powers, I thinned the metal cuff to make it large enough to fit around her neck.

Vera's wide eyes latched onto it as I picked it up and moved toward her.

"*Don't you dare*," she snapped, backing up.

I lunged and wrestled her to the ground. She fought admirably, but she was no match for my strength.

Her eyes burned with white-hot rage as I snapped the collar around her neck. I used my powers to meld the metal together and seal it.

"This is for your own good."

10

VERA

T he cold metal burned my skin. It wasn't tight, but the weight of its implication gripped my throat like a vise. There was only so much a person could take before they snapped. I had been beaten, stabbed, my heart shredded, and now this?

The rage inside was a bomb, steadily ticking down the minutes until I exploded.

"Oh, is this your idea of 'protection'?" I mocked. "You're demented. I didn't need your corthshit idea then and I certainly don't need it now."

Confusion cut creases around his eyes. He was taken aback by my outrage. Not about the collar, but about what transpired in the Mortal Lands. That was my fault. Back at Marty's, I had been so consumed with guilt, was so distraught over how close Ronan had come to dying, I never properly voiced how fucked up his actions were.

Instead of telling me the Faylands was too dangerous for me because of my dragon, he'd callously broken my heart with me and pushed me away.

Now that I knew he was safe, and any possibility of a

future between us was gone, I could see things clearly—see *him* clearly.

We wouldn't even be in this situation if it wasn't for him.

"You know what?" I whispered heatedly. "You're just as broken as I am, if not more. What kind of a man kidnaps a woman and forces her into a bargain because he's interested in her?"

I'd been delusional to think that was sweet.

Ronan's steadfast expression morphed into a child-like helplessness, like a kid being cornered by a bully. Acid washed through my stomach, but I ignored it. I refused to feel bad for speaking the truth.

My hands balled into fists the more I thought of everything he had done. "And then you left me without a word, ignored me for a month, and showed up out of nowhere to stab and brand me? *Who the fuck does that?*"

My chest heaved, hot with rage. That timer was getting dangerously close to zero.

Ronan remained silent through my tirade, and I plowed on.

"I don't care how long it's been since the last mate pairing. You knew you had one out there and you still pursued me, and then when you got what you wanted, when I fell in love with you, you ripped out my heart and said it was for my own good."

"You're wrong," he gritted out.

"Wrong? What do you mean wrong? *That all happened.*"

"No," he said quietly. "You never fell in love."

My eyes bulged.

I had spent my entire life ensuring the darkness inside was never freed, but I released it for him. I had *killed children*. And he had the audacity to claim I never loved him?

Rage beat my insides. Five . . . Four . . .

"I feel sorry for your mate. I couldn't think of a worse fate than being tied to you."

Ronan flinched. Actually flinched. Slowly, he shifted off his knees to sit back on his haunches. By the time he finished, any vestige of warmth was gone. Hate carved out his features.

There was the male from the gallows. A look like that couldn't be faked. I embraced his hatred, took pleasure in it. It breathed fresh life into my bones.

"If you're so good at protecting yourself," he started in a deceptively soft voice. "How did you get the bruise?"

A muscle ticked in my injured cheek. I could still feel the impact of every fist, and the shame—the deep, disgusting shame.

Three . . . Two . . .

The rage blasting through me was cataclysmic. I wanted to eviscerate him. I glared so hard, it was a wonder I didn't burn a hole through his face.

His lips lifted mockingly.

One.

"I wish I never saved you! I wish you were dead!"

His jaw clenched. He hooked my gaze with his and held it until it hurt.

"The feeling's mutual."

We glared as our bitter hatred thickened the air.

"Remove this collar right now, Ronan, or so help me Gods."

"No."

My mouth bled into a snarl. I dove for his leg. My fangs snapped together on air as he moved out of reach. He continued backing away until he was out of range altogether and strode over to the door.

"You're every bit the monster you warned me you were," I bit out.

He froze, back muscles bunching. He slammed the door behind him.

I glared at it with balls of fire in my eyes, wishing it would burst into flames.

He *wasn't* keeping me here.

I spent last night crying my eyes out. I cried for the orphans and the children I had killed. I cried for the love I had lost. In the morning came the *rage*.

I was pissed at Ronan for ever coming near me, and myself for letting him. I was pissed at the Crone for putting a monster inside me and the Rogues for never accepting me. I was pissed at the mortals for not killing me when they had the chance and Ronan for saving me.

I was pissed at everyone and everything.

But despite it all, I couldn't let Ronan go after the Nighters alone. They had almost killed him once, and he was going to waltz right back into their midst. As angry as I was, and as much as he didn't deserve my concern, I'd never forgive myself if something happened to him.

I knew the son of a bitch was too arrogant to even entertain the idea of bringing back up. I wasn't going to give him a choice.

The Nighters had left me that map. They wanted me. If it came down to it, I would trade my life for his. But first, I had to get free because the bastard had chained me up.

Redirecting my rage, I became focused on escaping.

I ran a hand over the metal circling my throat. It was as wide as a hand and thick. Feeling around, I located where it was secured to the chain, and tugged as hard as I could.

The angle made it difficult to get a good grip. I couldn't break it, and there was no lock to pick because he'd used his powers. Crawling, I followed the chain to where it ended at a metal plate. It was secured to the floor by thick bolts.

I leveraged my feet against the frame and pulled until

my arms grew numb. None of it made a difference. Those bolts were in there good. I dropped the chain with a huff, shaking out my cramping arms.

The vine bites on them had healed. My chest wound throbbed angrily from the exertion, but it was already substantially better than yesterday.

I needed something heavy if I was going to get out of this collar. I peered around the room.

There was a bed, a wardrobe, a rocking chair, a table, and a fireplace. I already knew the wardrobe didn't have anything other than clothes. My eyes caught on the numerous candles littering the room. Their silver bases looked hefty.

I strode over to the closest one, blew it out, and plucked off the wax, then weighed it in my hand. It was a solid piece of silver. I nodded. *I could bludgeon someone with this.*

I returned to the chain's base and began hammering away at a section of links, but the candlestick was no match for the metal. All I succeeded in doing was denting the silver.

The top of it had a spike for holding candles in place. I tested the pad of my finger against it and drew back with a hiss. It was sharp. It could do some damage.

I hid it under the bed for later just as my jailor entered.

Bending my neck back, I dragged my gaze up Kian's towering form. I hadn't been able to see much of him at the church, but now I could see all six-foot-five of him. Dark breeches hugged muscular legs. A tunic with sleeves rolled up fit snuggly over his broad chest. The collar was notched tightly up to his neck where the edge of a tattoo peeked out.

His ears were pierced with small rings and his dirty blonde hair was pulled into a bun. A short, well-groomed beard partially concealed marble cheekbones and framed his lush lips. His eyes danced with mirth as they landed on me.

"Hey Trouble," he rumbled. "Bet you didn't think you'd be seeing me again."

"How did you get out of the pit?" I asked, my voice pitched with shock.

He carried a tray over to one of the nightstands. The muscles on his forearm rippled as he set it down.

The tray had two head-sized strawberries with cream and a bowl of nuts. I licked my lips, salivating at the sight. If I accepted this food, I accepted my imprisonment, but I'd also thrown up the only thing I'd eaten in days. I settled on waiting until he left.

Kian faced me, crossing his arms. The movement pulled his tunic taut across his chest and revealed bar-shaped impressions. My eyes widened. His nipples were pierced.

"Secret door," he grunted, drawing my attention back to his face.

My brows slanted down. Why would the Nighters put a way out of their trap?

"After I escaped, I crossed paths with Ronan on his way home with you," he continued. "He beat me bloody."

There was an expectant pause where a good person would have apologized.

Realizing that wasn't going to happen, he kept going. "Then he told me what happened. You and that horse were joined at the hip. I assumed she'd been captured with you and tracked her down. If you're good, I'll take you to see her when Ronan's back."

I struggled to follow what he was saying until my mind seized on one phrase: *That horse.*

My heart slammed into bone with the force of a giant's fist. Ness! *Five days, Vera. Five days and you hadn't thought of her once.* To be fair, I'd been unconscious for four of those, but guilt still twisted up my insides.

Duke promised to look after her, but I had no guarantee he would.

"You know where she is?" I blurted. "Is she okay?"

"She's fine. She's at House Taran."

My lungs deflated on an exhale.

I studied Kian. Ness was safe because of him. I'd locked him in a pit, which he'd been punished severely for, and afterward, he'd tracked down my horse.

My lips bunched up at the swelling gratitude. "Thank . . . you." I sounded like I was eating mud. Then, I processed the rest of his statement—that he would take me to see her when Ronan returned—and that gratitude shriveled up.

"You're not going to free me," I said flatly.

"Afraid I can't do that."

He was a Taranis fae and would have the same powers as Ronan. He could free me if he wanted. I bared my teeth. "Get me out of this collar right now, or you're going to regret it."

He fought a smile. "Is that so?"

My hand slipped under the bed and wrapped around the candlestick.

I swung hard, aiming for a completely different area than my goal, and what do you know, I hit right where I wanted—his boot. The point sank clean through and stopped with a reverberating thud as it met the floor.

What the . . .?

My head snapped up.

Kian wore a mild expression as he reached down and jerked the pointed end from his boot. "Nice try, but Ronan cut off all my toes."

"Why?"

He cocked a brow. "Why do you think?"

"Because you failed to follow orders."

"I think you mean because you played damsel in distress, tricked me, shot me, and locked me in a pit."

I shrugged. "Semantics."

He let out a low laugh. "I don't know why, but I like you."

"Can't say the same."

He chuckled and sent me a wink. "You will."

"Doubtful."

Gesturing at the collar, he explained, "Only Ronan can remove that."

"You're from the same House. Don't you have the same powers?"

He shook his head. "It used to be that way when the first fae were created. They were all born with the powers of the God that created them, but those powers have been diluted over several millennia. Nowadays, fae magic amplifies and enhances what's already there. Most fae at the same House will have similar abilities because of the skills and knowledge that have passed down through generations."

I made a small sound of surprise before frowning. I'd wasted my only weapon. Well, if he wasn't going to free me, or take me to see Ness, then there was nothing else to discuss. I gave him my back.

"Oh, don't pout. Ronan will be home before you know it and you can go back to trapping people in pits."

I briefly debated telling him I wanted to be freed so I could watch over Ronan, but Kian had made his opinion on that clear. I heard him depart briefly before he returned and dumped my saddlebag beside me.

"That was with your horse," he announced.

I peered up at him. "You sure she's safe at House Taran?"

"There's a treachna in the moat, and if someone manages to get past it, there are a hundred of the Lands' best fighters inside."

The tier four beast was capable of capsizing boats. I had no idea how they managed to keep one at House Taran, but it was genius. They were incredibly territorial. If any lower tier beasts tried to attack on a full moon, the treachna would send them running.

I gave him a small nod, and he left.

I sorted through the saddlebag to ensure the Rogues hadn't stolen anything. My note to Marty was missing. The map was inside—I'd left it with Ness thinking it was useless. Surprisingly, all the gold was there too. I wonder why they hadn't taken any. Maybe they feared reprisal after seeing the Enforcer was alive.

My hand stumbled onto a waxy surface. Confusion flitted through me as I withdrew the candle from the church. It was carved with the same strange lettering as I'd seen below the emblem.

"How did you get in here?" I whispered.

It didn't give an answer.

My eyes caught on the tray as I shoved it back inside. I hurried over and inhaled the strawberries, cream, and nuts. I was overly full when I finished, but the feeling of food in my stomach was bliss.

Curious where I was, I moved over to a pair of curtains and pushed them aside to find a shuttered window. I had just enough chain to open it. Soft sunlight and the sound of crashing waves filtered in. An expanse of water, swirling with every blue imaginable, greeted me.

My gaze lifted to the sky, and I sucked in an awed breath. It was threaded with ribbons of turquoise and lavender. They reached across its expanse, intertwining in some places, and separating in others.

As gorgeous as the view was, it was limited. I couldn't see what was to the West.

Was this entire place surrounded by water? If so, that

would pose another problem if I managed to get out of this collar. Chewing my lip, I glanced at the chain. That was a big if.

I paced the room for hours, trying to think of a way.

Even with the sunlight streaming in through the window, the room was dimly lit. To compensate, or maybe it was Ronan's knowledge of my fear of the dark, lit candles were planted all over.

An idea sparked. My smile was evil.

I locked the shutters, then moved around tipping over every candle. Once I finished, I grabbed my saddlebag and took a seat in the middle of the bed and waited for the room to set ablaze.

It took some time for the curtains to ignite. The flames licked up the fabric and spread across the furniture as heat washed over my face. Popping and shattering glass sounded.

The rumble of the fire grew louder as it doubled in size, roaring in my ears. It wasn't long before the fire reached the bed and smoke consumed the room. I choked on the thick plumes, eyes watering.

Kian burst inside. He took in the scene with wide eyes and disappeared a second before returning with an axe. With one powerful swing, he cleaved the chain in half.

He grabbed me and we vanished, moving in a flash. One minute we were surrounded by fire, and the next we were outside. I bent over coughing, expelling the smoke from my lungs. "How did you do that?" I rasped as I straightened.

"Running is my specialty."

A thick cloud of smoke billowed off the building.

Kian glanced down at me. "Ronan's not going to be happy."

My shoulders rose and fell in a careless shrug. If Ronan didn't want his house burned down, he shouldn't have locked me inside.

He laughed, shaking his head. "You're Trouble with a capital 'T'."

"What now?"

"I scry Ronan."

A beam disintegrated in the middle and crashed to the ground, taking part of the roof with it. Set against the late afternoon sky, the red and orange flames made a pretty picture.

"You going in there to get a mirror?" I asked.

Kian cursed.

"Take me to him," I suggested. "Let him decide what to do with me."

He scrubbed a hand down his face, muttering, "I'm a dead man." He spread his arms and beckoned me over. "I'm going to run us to the mainland."

I stepped into his arms, and in the time it took to blink, we were standing on a cliff's edge, opposite from where we just were.

My gaze pinged to the island where we'd come from. It was in the shape of a horseshoe with the open side to the west and the closed facing east. The burning manor looked like a small bonfire.

"Is that House Taran?" I pointed at the large stone castle on the island's southeast edge.

"No. That is." Kian jerked his head to the right.

Just a couple miles away, a dark stone castle dominated the cliffs. It had rising black spire towers on each of the four corners, and a huge moat, the size of a lake. The moat had to be where they were keeping the treachna.

I glanced back with a probing gaze. "If that's House Taran, whose castle is that?" I gestured to the island.

And why did Ronan have a house there?

"Finn's."

"*Finn has a castle*?" I peered in the distance. It was too far to see any of the castle's details. I turned back to Kian. "If Finn has a castle, what's he doing working for Ronan?"

He slid me an unreadable look. "That's a question for Finn."

Well, since I wasn't planning on speaking to that asshole again, I guess I would never know.

There were three miles of water between the island and the mainland. It would have taken thirty minutes to travel by boat without Kian. That explained how he was able to evade me so easily in the Mortal Lands.

I eyed the draoistone on his bicep. Guess he'd been able to find it.

"Give me your bag."

I hid it behind my back. "Why?"

"Because it will feel ten times heavier once I start running."

"Fine." Begrudgingly, I gave it. "Careful, it's heavy," I warned even though he would have already known.

He held it one-handed, testing its weight. "What have you got in here? Rocks?"

"The dicks of all my enemies," I deadpanned.

I wished that were true. Vince's would make a great necklace.

He broke into uproarious laughter. "Come on, Trouble. Depending on Ronan's mood, you might be adding mine."

11

VERA

K ian darted a look at the blazing manor. "Finn needs to know about the fire. One second."

He flashed away.

I shrugged, my gaze sweeping around.

Green was too mediocre a word to describe the dazzling, endless grasslands and hills stretching West. Amethyst, ruby, blue topaz—flowers and plants in every shade of gemstone speckled the vista.

Along the cliff line, stalks of knee-high, golden grass, like a sea of glittering yellow sapphires, swayed hypnotically in the breeze. Beyond them, the sea was spread out. It started pale blue in the shallows and bled into a blue-green as the water deepened before turning indigo with the plunging depths.

Everywhere I looked, there was a new color. It was nothing like the anemic, barren landscape of the Mortal Lands. The vibrancy and lushness overloaded my senses. It was all so alive. So magical. No wonder the fae never left.

An outcrop of trees caught my eye. They had a mass of leaves and vines dangling from their limbs like hair. The trees were stark white, and with the way the tendrils hanging off their branches refracted the light, they appeared frozen. Soft blue beams pulsated along the crystalline structures.

Outlining the trees were shimmering, iridescent auras. I'd never seen anything like it. Mesmerized, I drifted closer, needing to know what it was.

A heavy, sulfuric scent hit my nostrils, and I wrinkled my nose.

"You might be pretty, but you stink worse than Mayhem's meat market," I whispered, pressing my palm against it. It was cold and sticky, wet almost. I pushed my hand all the way inside and my eyes gaped as my talons transformed into ordinary fingers.

"What are you," I asked in quiet awe.

The longer I kept my hand inside, the colder the colorful gas became. Painful pricks bit into my palm and traveled up my arm just before it scalded me. I ripped my hand away so quickly, I fell.

Cradling the offended limb, I scrambled back into the grass, and something hooked into my bicep. I tried to tug myself free, but each pull embedded whatever it was deeper. Hissing in pain, I glanced down to see a handful of thorns writhing under my skin, burrowing further.

"Ah, fuck!"

I leaped to my feet, swatting at my arm, trying to stop their movement, but they continued squirming under my skin like worms. In a panic, I used my talons to break the skin and dig them out.

I flung them free of my arm, and when they hit the ground, they started wiggling toward me. I smashed them under my boot, and they stopped.

When I lifted my shoe, a viscous slime dripped from the bottom. I shook it off with a grimace.

Gods. What were those things?

I braved a peek at the area where the tiny attackers had come from. Hidden within the blades of grass, were brown, fingernail-sized burrs with sharp barbs curved like fish-hooks, designed to snag flesh. They also had tiny mouths filled with razor-like teeth for eating through skin.

Note to self: Stay away from the trees and grass.

I straightened and ran a more discerning eye over the landscape.

The turquoise and lavender threads in the sky were outlined in a faint, poisonous-looking smog. The stalks of grass, which had appeared soft and gentle from a distance, were full of those monstrous burrs. The rolling hills had deadly, sharp drop-offs and were covered with those red vines.

As a bird flew overhead, one shot into the air, but before it could reach it, a ten-foot-tall, aquamarine plant with teeth clamped its large mouth around it and slurped the vine down like a noodle.

Its dying squeal was loud enough to be heard from here.

I shuddered.

And I thought dealing with the beasts was bad.

Kian returned a few moments later, raising a brow at where my arms hugged my chest in an attempt not to touch anything.

"Got your first taste of the Faylands, huh?" His lips twitched. "You'll get used to everything wanting to kill you."

I shrugged off the comment, swiping a piece of hair out of my face.

Kian presented his hand again, and I laid my palm over it.

"Hold on."

We sped forward, moving so fast, my lips peeled away from my fangs. The arm-length of chain still attached to the collar flew behind me. A kaleidoscope of colors zipped past.

I grew nauseous staring. Kian was the only thing I could focus on without getting dizzy.

His head swiveled around, searching for Ronan. I knew the moment he found him because he warned, "Brace yourself."

We stopped, and the only thing keeping my body from catapulting forward was Kian's grip, but his hand didn't stop the momentum of my head. It flung forward while the rest of me remained still.

I cursed at the whiplash, sending Kian a glare.

A guilty smile formed. "Sorry. I should have told you to watch your head."

I clutched it, glancing around. "Where are we?" The landscape was steeper here, washed in dry tones of blue, green, and gray.

"The Hill Lands ten miles south of The Wilds."

"What the fuck is she doing here?"

Kian and I froze at Ronan's furious voice.

The sound of it was a spark, reigniting my fury.

Hot rage spiraled through my limbs and chest. My head snapped his way, but the scathing retort on my tongue withered as soon as I laid eyes on him.

A white failin hide sat on his broad shoulders with the wolf's muzzle covering his head. He was shirtless, leather straps crisscrossing his chest to secure a bag to his back and clad in only a white loin cloth.

The scant amount of clothing left little to the imagination. Every ridge and valley of his powerful body was on display.

His ink was different, or more detailed to be accurate. Graphite flames outlined in black licked over every inch of bronzed skin. I imagined it's what fire looked like in the Darklands—grim, violent, and all-consuming.

My gaze connected with his and the murderous intent in his eyes melted into something darkly lustful.

The look caught me off guard. I'd seen him look at me like he wanted me before, but never like he wanted to *devour* me. Heat licked through my core, tightening my insides.

Stop it, you idiot. One, he's got a mate. Two, we want to strangle him, not fuck him.

"She burned down your manor," Kian tattled, dispelling the crackling tension.

Ronan reared back. "What?"

I skewered Kian with a fiery gaze before dismissing him and locking gazes with Ronan. I pushed aside my body's reaction and mustered the sweetest smile I could. "It was for your own good."

Black instantly overtook gray. Ronan's lips peeled back in a snarl like a pissed off failin. That dark gaze narrowed on Kian. "Get out of my sight."

A shudder tripped down my spine and the command wasn't even directed at me.

Kian slowly backed away.

I shot him a dirty look, hissing, "Coward."

"Sorry, Trouble," he said in his deep rasp. "I like you, but I like living more."

"*You're immortal.*"

"I won't be if I stay."

Fine.

I'd deal with Ronan on my own. He didn't scare me, and neither did his battle-mode. He had *no right* to lock me up, and besides, that was just a guest house. He had an entire castle.

I steeled my spine and thrust up my chin. "I'm not apologizing."

"Oh no." His whisper was a silk-wrapped blade. "We are way past apologies."

He lunged, tackling me, and in a flash, he had me bent over his knee. In the time it took my mind to catch up to what just happened, he had my hands trapped behind me with the chain. The position forced me to bow my back or be choked by the collar.

"Ronan." I could only kick my feet and rock helplessly on his lap. It pissed me off something fierce. "Let me go," I screamed.

His fingertips trailed down my spine, searing my skin through the fabric. I bit the inside of my lip to hold off a shudder.

"I've wanted to do this since the day we met," he said in a velvet purr.

His palm cracked down on my ass.

I froze, eyes flaring wide as fire radiated down the back of my thighs.

Did he ... just ... *spank me*?

I could feel the heat of his hand hovering over my bottom like a scalding pan, poised to do it again.

A veil of red crashed over my vision. "Don't. You. Dare."

Another crack.

I pitched forward, shock reverberating through me. I'd never been spanked before, and a part of me couldn't believe it was happening, it was so absurd.

I screamed a string of obscenities at him, thrashing violently in his lap, but the movement pulled tightly on the collar, and I had to stop before I choked. "I swear to Gods, Ronan, do that again, and I will—"

A strong hand smoothed over the inflamed cheek. He kneaded the injured flesh and the pain morphed into something else. To my horror, hot tingles broke out in my stomach.

Heat spread across my face.

No.

I was not turned on by this.

I refused to believe I enjoyed being held down and spanked like a child. But as he continued massaging my burning cheek, I couldn't contain the moan building in my throat.

An iron bar pressed into my stomach. "You look so sexy like this," he said, his voice dripping with desire. "All chained up. I could do anything to you."

I clamped my thighs together as an image of him jerking down my pants and slipping his fingers between my folds flashed across my mind, unbidden. He inhaled deeply and groaned.

My cheeks flamed. He could smell my arousal.

Get it together, I mentally chastised. Somehow, I managed to pull back a thread of sanity, and warned, "Spank me again and it'll be the last thing you ever do."

He released a throaty laugh as his lips came to my ear. "I can smell how wet you are."

His hand came down in rapid fire, dividing his attention between each cheek. Heat stirred low in my belly, arousal mingling with the pain. I was mortified, aroused, and infuriated all at the same time.

He has a mate! What are you doing?

Better yet, what was he doing?

"You have a mate," I snapped.

I rocked forward with enough momentum that my mouth touched his thigh. I sank my fangs in deep, locking my jaw, and a coppery taste flooded my mouth. That iron bar grew impossibly harder—the sick bastard—but he released me.

I flopped off his lap, landing on my side, and jerked at the chains until I freed my arms. Sitting up, I panted at the cool relief against my bottom, and spat out his blood.

We stared at each other, our quick breaths filling the

silence. The black steadily disappeared from his gaze as it cooled, but the hunger remained.

Ronan appraised me for a length of time until the lust settled into vexation. "You burned down my home," he accused quietly.

I scoffed. "That wasn't your home. You have a castle."

A pulse feathered over his jaw. He said nothing.

"If you're done being an asshole, I'll show you how to find the Nighters."

I rose and dusted myself off. My bottom smarted as my hands brushed over it and I hid a wince. He tracked every movement with an agitated stare. I glared back. I might want him alive, but that didn't mean I'd tolerate his corthshit.

I stormed over to where Kian waited. There was a steadily blooming smirk on his face. I tore my bag from his hands. "Not a fucking word."

I dug around in the saddlebag and removed the candle, the map, and a piece of flint.

Ronan reached us just as I was unrolling the scroll. He didn't spare me a glance as he took in the paper over my shoulder. It was like the last five minutes never happened.

I wish *we* never happened. I wish I could get back the two months I wasted on this asshole.

"Why are we staring at a blank piece of paper?" said asshole asked.

"It's not blank," I snapped. "It's a map of The Lands."

Kian peered over my other shoulder. "I don't see anything."

I held the map up to my face, staring at the outline of the Lands. "You guys don't see this?"

"No," they said at the same time.

Any doubt the Nighters had left this for me vanished. It was spelled for my eyes only.

"Describe the map to us," Ronan said.

I threw him a poisonous look for giving me an order, but secretly, I was glad he did. I was grateful for every infuriating thing he was doing. Each act added kindling to the rage inside me and kept it burning bright and hot.

Anger was the only way I was going to get through this with my heart intact.

"It's of The Lands, but there is a huge land mass connected to the Faylands where there should be sea."

At their silence, I twisted around in time to see them share a look.

"What?"

"The landmass you see was broken off during the War of the Gods many millennia ago. Whoever made that map had to be among the Sons and Daughters. They were the Gods' first creations," Ronan explained, meeting my gaze. "Where did you get this?"

I could have given a half-truth, but I desperately wanted to piss him off. "The Nighters left it for me."

Black lightning flashed through his eyes. He snatched the map out of my hands. "They left you a way to find them and you thought it was a good idea to use it?" he growled.

"Yes," I snarled, snatching the map back. I hid it behind me as I retreated several steps. "They want me alive." Duke would have no reason to lie about that.

He stalked toward me until our boots met and glowered down his nose at me. I had to crane my neck back to see his face. I'd forgotten how large he was, but this close, there was no ignoring the bristling, six-foot-six wall of muscle and tattoos looming over me.

I was only six inches shorter than him, but his intensity always made the height difference feel much greater.

"Alive and well are two very different things."

That deep, sensuous voice made my lower stomach crackle with heat, and I hated it.

I locked my spine, leaning up on my tip toes so I could stare coldly right into his eyes. "You lost any right to an opinion."

I lowered back as his jaw worked in a tight circle.

"What's your plan?" he asked hotly. "Walk into their ranks and somehow avoid capture, something you couldn't do with the Rogues?"

Rage whipped through my core. I was so close to shoving him out of my space, but I couldn't trust what my hands would do if I touched him. It was a toss-up between ripping out his heart, or running over his abs.

"What's yours?" I snapped. "Walk aimlessly hoping you'll stumble into them?"

He glowered.

"That's what I thought."

If it was so easy to find them, he would have done it already.

The items behind my back were wrenched from my grip. I whipped around as the dirty traitor, Kian, tossed them to Ronan. I charged him, but he easily held them out of reach.

"You're going to House Taran." He tipped his chin at Kian.

The fuck I was.

His henchman grabbed my elbow, and I slammed it into his stomach, surging forward to leap for the items, but Ronan kept them above his head. I drew back with a frustrated growl. "How do you expect to find the Nighters with a map you can't use?"

You don't know how to use it either . . .

So? *He doesn't need to know that.*

It wasn't hard to put together my plan for the flint and candle. I silently prayed it didn't work as Ronan lit it. The candle sprang to life, vibrating in his hand until he released it, and it shot into the air.

"Try and follow it," I sassed, crossing my talons behind my back.

Ronan approached and the candle did nothing. *Ha!*

Kian tried next, and it still didn't move.

I took two steps, and the candle zoomed off, then stopped, waiting for me to continue. When I did, it flew off again, and paused.

My gaze was smug as it met Ronan's. "The candle is spelled to lead me right to the Nighters. I don't know what your plan is, but I can guarantee it's not going to be easier or faster than this."

Ronan pinned me with a cold stare. "If I'm such a monster, why do you want to help?"

Because even worse than the idea of having to spend time in your constant company knowing I can never have you is the thought of living in this world without you.

"The sooner we find the godstone, the sooner I can go home and never have to see your face again."

12

VERA

Something flashed across Ronan's face too quick to catch. Hurt? No, why in the world would he be hurt by that?

"I can't wait," he growled.

Definitely wasn't hurt I saw.

"Me either," I snapped.

Kian glanced between us, wearing a huge grin. "Oh, this is going to be fun."

Ronan marched over to him and slammed his fist so hard into Kian's face, it caved in. Eyes, nose, teeth—it all sunk into a bloody, grotesque crater. I could see straight into his throat, which was making an awful keening sound.

Was he crying?

"He's fine," Ronan grunted at my look of horror.

"I don't recall asking you a question."

You can't wait to be rid of me? Well, fuck you, I couldn't wait even more. The second he was safe from the Nighters, I was getting as far away from him as possible.

He slanted me a look, then dismissed me brusquely.

I lapped up our hostility like cream.

As if to punctuate his point, Kian's muscle and tissue

rebuilt before our eyes. In a matter of seconds, his face was whole, and I realized the sound he was making was laughter —a deep braying noise that shook his body.

"That's for allowing her to burn down my home," Ronan said in a clipped tone.

"It's your fault," I was more than happy to point out. "You left the candles."

His icy gaze sliced to me. "I don't believe I was speaking to you."

My nose was so itchy, I had to use both middle fingers to scratch it.

He ignored the gesture, focusing on Kian. "You will return home."

Kian glanced between us looking disappointed he didn't get to stay and enjoy the show.

He bowed curtly. "Yes, My Lord."

As he passed me, he whispered, "Good luck." Then he shot off into the distance. I could see a tiny speck on the horizon that disappeared as soon as I caught sight of it.

Ronan faced me with a severe expression. "You will do everything I say, when I say it. Without question."

Please. It was like he didn't know me at all. But I knew if I didn't agree, he'd scry Kian back here to drag me to House Taran, candle or not.

"Sure."

"Swear it."

My eyes thinned in annoyance. "I swear," I bit out.

Ronan wasn't satisfied, but he left it at that. "We need to get going," he said, striding over to a black war mount waiting up ahead. His arm muscles flexed as he pulled himself into the saddle.

When I made no move to follow, he glanced back growling, "Get on."

"I'm not sharing a horse with you."

His gaze narrowed dangerously. "What did I just say?"

Silence.

"You want another spanking?" he asked coolly.

I glared even as prickles of excitement heated my belly. "You wouldn't."

He launched off the horse, charged over and grabbed hold of the chain, and forced me to arch into him, or choke. I was sorely tempted to choke.

His lips brushed my ear as my breasts pressed into his chest. "I would," he said in a gluttonous whisper. "I greatly enjoyed spanking your ass and you did too." He pulled away, face transforming into an intimidating mask. "It's the only discipline you respond to. I'll turn your ass red if that's what it takes to get you to listen. Are we clear?"

Gods, I wished I could just let him go on his own.

"What would your mate think of you putting your hands on another woman?" I asked sharply.

"We are free to do as we wish until we bond as is fae custom."

That meant Ronan could be with other women. My stomach soured. Had he been with someone else since me?

I shoved the thought away. Hard.

I wasn't going there. I was here to make sure the asshole survived his encounter with the Nighters. Nothing more, nothing less.

He dropped the chain, and I quickly reeled it in.

"Remove the collar and I'll ride with you." There was no way in the dark night I was going to let him continue using it to manhandle me.

He stared for a moment before flicking his hand. The weight around my throat vanished, and the metal hit the ground with a clank. I lifted my hand to my throat, rubbing feeling into it.

I sighed in relief, then begrudgingly followed him to the

horse and climbed into the saddle. He hauled himself up behind me, his groin plastering against my ass. He was still hard.

I stiffened, inching forward.

He reached around me for the reins, flooding my nostrils with his delicious scent.

"You smell terrible."

A half-truth. It was terrible how good he smelled.

He stiffened, just minutely, and amusement curled through me. I shouldn't have enjoyed insulting him as much as I did.

Ronan's nose touched the hollow of my neck, and I froze. He inhaled deeply, releasing an obscene groan that had my stomach clenching.

"You smell like a rotten egg covered in shit."

I tamped down the urge to smell myself, raised a middle finger, and scooted up as far as the saddle would allow. The distance would be worth the discomfort.

Ronan clicked his teeth, and we set off at a steady pace. Neither of us said a word. Our animosity crackled in the air like static electricity, buzzing over my skin.

Less than a day after reuniting and we were already at each other's throats. It felt just like it had in the beginning, only worse because we knew each other well enough to get under each other's skin.

I did my best to put him out of my mind and enjoy the scenery.

Sweeping miles of undulating, lush hills were bordered by mountains and rushing rivers. We followed a well-trodden grass path. It curved smoothly around the hills, bisecting impassable sections of river and steep grades.

Around every bend was a new surprise. Sometimes it was ancient woods, others it was a white sand beach, or a small fae village.

Periodically, I glanced down at my wrist to maintain my well of rage. The wolf burned into my skin did the trick every time.

"If we get separated for any reason, that will allow me to locate you," Ronan said, mistaking my glances for interest.

I whipped around, brows touching my hairline. "You can track me with this? How?"

"Halflings are our most vulnerable population. Every brand is imbued with a locator spell. A drop of my blood over a map and a few words in Déithe, and I can see your exact location."

Déithe—the divine tongue. All the Crone's spell books were written in the language of the Gods.

Ronan's explanation was meant to make me feel safe, but it only further embittered me toward the brand. "The halflings aren't vulnerable," I spat. "They're enslaved."

The scar cutting through his lips whitened imperceptibly. He took pride in the fact that his halflings were paid, but were they educated? Literate? Taught valuable skills that could earn them a living outside his House?

"A comfortable prison is still a prison," I informed him.

"What you consider prison, many of them see as a good life."

I rolled my eyes. Arguing with him was pointless. I spun around and didn't make a peep for the next several hours.

The light started retreating higher on the hilltops. I tensed, waiting for the dragon to make a move, but it didn't stir. My earlier assumption had been right. Ronan's presence calmed it.

The last tendrils of sunlight disappeared, and twilight settled over the Hill Lands. This close to a new moon, there was no moonlight, but the sky was clear and the bands of turquoise and lavender glowed brightly.

Glowing eyes started to appear on the hilltops. Dozens of yellow pinpricks dogged us.

"Ronan," I whispered uneasily.

"They're creasugas. They're harmless."

I peered at him, brows lifting.

"Rock creatures," he clarified. "They are similar to abcas, but much friendlier."

Some of the braver ones rolled down the hills to greet us. They were the size of my head with moss and vines for hair, and gentle yellow eyes. They chittered at us as we passed.

"What do they eat?"

"Each other."

"Lovely."

I kept an eye on them until we stopped for the night.

"We'll set up camp and head into The Wilds in the morning," Ronan said, as he swung out of the saddle. He'd chosen the base below a small hill.

I squinted at him as he undid one of his saddlebags. A strip of turquoise light fell over his eyes, painting them a sea green.

His face was impassive. The aggravation from earlier had tempered during the ride.

Oh, no. We can't have that. I needed him angry. I needed him mean. It was the only way my heart was going to survive the coming days, or weeks—however long we were stuck together.

"Kill any innocents lately?"

His head shot up, and the light spilled over his face. The glittering turquoise played over his sharp cheekbones, giving him an otherworldly beauty. He looked like a cruel, fallen God. "Poison anyone this week?"

I hopped off the horse, and stepped up to him, tipping

my chin back. In the blue light, his eyes were intensely bright and hard to meet. "You deserved it."

The light disappeared, and his features fell into shadows, but not before pain briefly tightened them. His gaze flicked to my cheek. The bruise was almost gone, but there was a faint outline left. "So did you."

I reared back and scored his cheek. His eyes flashed black as three deep gashes opened in his skin. They sealed just as quickly as I'd made them.

"Don't you ever say that again."

"If you want to be cruel, then so will I."

I raised my hand to hit him again.

He snatched my wrist and jerked me to him. I caught myself on his chest and sucked in a sharp breath at the hardness digging into my stomach.

"You feel that?" he whispered darkly. "Slap me again and I'm going to fuck you into oblivion."

My nostrils flared as I tried to jerk free. "I wouldn't touch you if you were the last man in The Lands."

He angled close until I could feel his breath on my lips. "I'm not a man. You'd do well to remember that."

He released me and I tore away as a loud trilling filled the air.

Ronan shot me an irate look before withdrawing his scrying mirror. He opened the connection with a wave, and a menacing expression stole over his face.

"Who are you?" he growled.

"Where's Vera?" the caller asked frantically. "She's there with you, ain't she?"

My whole face brightened at the sound of Marty's voice. I rushed over and plucked the mirror from Ronan's hands.

"Who the fuck is that?" he asked, stalking me.

"*My lover*," I snarked, backing up.

He charged after me.

"One second!" I told Marty, then bolted.

When I didn't hear Ronan following, I glanced behind me. He stood with his arms crossed, wearing an expression that promised retribution.

That was future Vera's problem.

I returned my attention to the mirror.

Marty's face filled the reflection. His silver hair was longer than I'd ever seen it, strands falling near his brow line, with the rest slicked back away from his face. A white beard peppered with black framed his mouth.

He smiled crookedly, his warm brown eyes crinkling at the corners. "Hey, Darlin'."

I grinned back, immense relief sweeping through me. "It's good to see you, old man."

His head tipped back with laughter. "Baby girl, it's good to see you too. I heard the Rogues got to you and-and—"

"I'm okay," I assured him, heart pinching at the waver in his voice. "Are you okay?" I asked. "Duke told me you'd been arrested."

"They released me on account of Boone's disappearance. No one was left to press charges." He squinted. "You know anything about that?"

"No . . ." I wish I did. I wish I had a chance to give those bastards what they deserved.

"Well, that's a damn shame."

"It is."

I couldn't contain my smile. It was so good to see his face. I missed him. Then something occurred to me. "Wait, how are you using a scrying mirror?"

All he had to do was imagine Ronan's face to make the connection, but to operate the mirror, he needed magic. Unless Marty had managed to keep that a secret all these years, there was no way he was doing this on his own.

"We'll get to that. How are you doing, Darlin'?"

"Fine," I said, glazing right over that question. "How did you know I would be with Ronan?" In my peripheral, I saw the fucker slyly moving closer to eavesdrop and retreated a few steps.

"I saw him leaving my place that day looking like a kicked dog. You two made up yet?"

The image of Ronan holding his mate flashed through my mind, and the grief I was trying so hard to bury pierced the shroud of anger, clawing its way up my throat.

Do you love her?

With all my heart.

I glanced to the side, blinking furiously. I refused to cry. The moment I started, I wouldn't be able to stop. "No," I said a little harsher than I meant to, but it couldn't be helped. "We haven't."

And we never will.

Thankfully, Marty wasn't put off by my tone. "You'll get there," he said confidently. "Just takes time."

I reached deep, and dragged up a smile, not wanting him to worry, though it was brittle. "I'm sure."

Based on his frown, I wasn't very convincing, but he let it go.

"One second," he said. "I want you to meet someone."

His face was replaced by the saloon's ceiling.

I was grateful for the reprieve. My composure was hanging by a thread. I released several long, drawn-out breaths as I wrangled my emotions back under control and slapped on an overly bright expression as Marty returned.

A dark-haired woman with a hawk-like nose and bright green eyes was with him.

"Esma, this is Vera. Vera meet Esma."

"Good to see you again," she said with a warm smile.

"You too."

Marty glanced between us. "You know each other?"

132

"I went to her for a spell." Specifically, one that would remove the Crone's curse, but Marty didn't know that part of my history, and I didn't want to get into the details.

"Did you ever find anyone who could help?" she asked gently.

"No, sadly not."

Her lips pursed. "That's a pity, dear."

It was.

We were quiet for a moment before her face brightened. "Well, it's so good to see you again. Marty has been talking my ear off about you," she said, another grin forming.

I silently chastised myself for making this about me and forced a polite smile. "How did you two meet?"

If I recalled correctly, Esma lived in Greene.

A coy smile stole over her face. "I was visiting my brother in jail."

Laughter burst out of me. "You met her while you were in jail? Marty, you dog."

He flashed a toothy grin off to the side.

My heart warmed. It was nice to see him so happy. He deserved that.

But his budding love was a thorn in a raw wound. Every smile, every tender look they shared was a sore reminder of what I'd lost. I was stiff the rest of the conversation, but forced myself to continue, asking Esma more questions about herself.

Her answers were a blur. I couldn't recall a single one if my life depended on it. I was grateful when we ran out of things to talk about.

"I need to go," I said, proud of how even my voice came out. "But thanks for the scry. Keep in touch, okay?"

Marty sensed something was off, but nodded, knowing I wouldn't appreciate his prying.

"Bye, Darlin'. You be safe."

"You guys too."

Their faces disappeared and my shoulders slumped. The mirror dangled from my fingertips as I struggled to rein in my emotions.

The extra time didn't help much. I kept my head down as I returned the scrying mirror to Ronan.

"Why do you look like you're about to cry?" My head snapped up at his vicious voice. His teeth gnashed together. "What did he say to you?"

I shoved the mirror into his chest. "Like you fucking care."

His anger deflated into a heavy sigh. He ran a hand down his face, suddenly looking exhausted. "I don't enjoy fighting with you, not like this. Must we be enemies?"

If I didn't hate him, I would have to face the fact that I loved him, and waiting on the other side of that love was devastation. In the short time I'd allowed myself to feel it, it had almost broken me.

My anger was the only thing carrying me from one minute to the next.

Without it, I had *nothing*.

I didn't have much when Ronan and I met, but it had been enough for me at the time. Then he swept into my life and taught me to want more, and somehow, I had ended up with less than what I'd started with.

No vest, no Rogues, no home, no family, no friends, no love; only a child-murdering-monster inside me and a child-abusing-monster for a mother. That's all I had left to my name.

I met his gaze with a stare that was as empty as I felt.

"We're not enemies, Ronan. We're nothing."

13

RONAN

She grabbed her saddlebag, and picked a spot as far away as she could.

The tether inside my chest writhed angrily, demanding I make things right.

Every fiber of my being strained toward her, yearning to touch her and kiss away her pain, but that's not what Vera needed. She craved my cruelty. With each cruel act and word, I saw relief tangled with her anger.

Allowing this friction to continue would become agonizing, but if it helped her heal, I would gladly bear it.

I would be her villain.

It would be easy for her to believe. She already saw me as one.

My fists clenched and unclenched at my sides. I took shallow breaths through my nostrils, fighting my instincts.

Once I regained control, I walked off a distance to scry Kian, but ensured Vera was in my line of sight, both for my safety and hers. She'd already tried to poison me once when she was upset. There was nothing stopping her from trying again.

The sooner we find the godstone, the sooner I can go home and never have to see your face again.

Though her motivation for coming on this journey came as no surprise, it still smarted.

She was a complication I didn't need, but I had no choice.

With fifty-three, soon to be fifty-two, days left to meet the king's deadline, and hundreds of miles of treacherous tundra to cover, I couldn't chance it, not when she had a map and candle that would lead her straight to the Nighters.

Kian's smirking face appeared in the reflection. "That didn't take long. Want me to come get—"

"I need you to run to the Mortal Lands and track down a man named Marty."

"And when I find him?"

"Kill him."

No one made my Little Thief cry.

He canted his head. "Is this about her?"

"Just do it," I growled.

"Look, whatever's going on between you two, is none of my business, but you should know, she looked ready to burn the world down when she thought you were missing."

Vera cared for me. I knew that. She had unleashed her dragon to save my life at the gallows. But she could never love me the way I loved her, not when she thought the worst of me.

"Why would she think I was missing?"

"Uh." He rubbed the back of his neck. "I might have mentioned something."

I raised a brow.

"You weren't answering any of my scries," he said quickly. "What was I supposed to think?"

I growled, furious he had made her worry.

"Why did you go dark?" he braved.

"It's none of your concern. Take care of the halfling."

I ended the connection and cast my gaze to Vera. She had settled on the hard ground with only her thin clothes as a barrier.

Marching over, I dropped my bedroll and failin hide beside her. She appraised the items with an impassive stare before dismissing them. I picked them up and dumped them on top of her.

She slapped them off, gaze snapping up to me. "Fuck off."

There it was again. A flicker of relief was hidden beneath the irritation.

"You have five seconds before I spank your ass so hard, you can't sit right for a week."

Her nostrils flared wide.

I secretly hoped she disobeyed. I would give anything to touch her again.

"Five."

She didn't move and I quirked a brow as my heart revved excitedly in my chest. "Four."

"Three."

"Two."

I started rubbing my hands together to get them warmed up, tamping down an eager grin.

"Godsdamnit," she snarled. "Fine." She snatched up the bedroll and started unrolling it.

"Good girl," I crooned, despite the disappointment coursing through me.

She shot me a death glare as she jerked the hide over her and plopped her head on her saddle bag. I settled on the ground across from her and her eyes slitted. "What do you think you're doing?"

"I assumed you wanted me close since you haven't brought out any chains."

"I don't need them anymore," she growled, turning on her side. "So go sleep somewhere else."

My brows pinched together. She didn't need them anymore?

She had been so terrified to sleep without them in the Mortal Lands, she had agreed to sleep chained to me when she would have rather 'let a dullah rip out her spine' than be anywhere near me.

"Why not?"

She scoffed. "Yeah, like I'd ever tell you anything about my dragon again."

She didn't trust me. That was just as well. I didn't trust her either.

Rising, I moved away, and cleared an area of rocks. I removed my dagger and placed it on the ground. I felt naked without a sword but hadn't the time nor clear mind to make a replacement.

I laid down facing the dark sky. The turquoise and lavender bands glowed magnificently, dancing across its expanse.

They had formed during the Dark Wars as a result of magic pollution. We had sent so much magic out into the air, it couldn't be recycled properly. It rose into the clouds where it's stayed for the last five hundred years, never letting us forget that painful time.

Never letting me forget.

I waited until Vera drifted off before scrying the only friend I had left in the world, knowing he would be awake at this hour. Finn slept as little as I did.

Finn's face appeared in the mirror, alert and focused. Zeroing in on my cheek, his cerulean eyes sparked with amusement. "I see things are going well."

He had been my first scry shortly after I left Mayhem. He'd been brought up to speed on everything and received periodic updates while I searched the archives. Without even having to discuss it, Finn knew I wanted to be left in peace, and kept our communications a secret.

I touched the area that had caught his attention.

It was where Vera had slashed my cheek. The wound had healed quickly, but not before it bled.

She had seen the monster peeking out, seen the tension vibrating through me. Anyone else would have been terrified, or at least had the sense to back down, but what had that beautiful fool done?

She'd raised her hand to hit me again.

Blood flooded my cock, remembering the fierceness in her eyes.

My fingers came back covered in dried flecks of blood. I smeared them between my fingertips, gaze darting back to the mirror. "I'm sure you've seen my manor."

"Kian informed me of the incident. I dispatched men to put out the fire, but I'm afraid we were too late," he said with a note of apology. "It's all gone."

My jaw burned. I'd likely lost everything in the fire.

"Please dig out what you can from the rubble."

"Of course. Should I have your old rooms prepared as well?"

"Yes, thank you."

He nodded. A brief pause followed. "Does this . . . change anything?"

"No. The House will operate as it always has. I'll have a new manor built when I return."

Finn was more than a steward. He ran my House and all its affairs. I only made an appearance when someone or something required a more . . . *heavy* hand. It was an arrangement that worked well for both of us, and I knew Finn greatly enjoyed the position. I would never take it from him.

He released a tight breath. "Thank you." He peered into the darkness framing my reflection. "Where are you?"

"Near The Wilds. I'll be out of contact soon."

It was storm season. The storms drew a disproportionate amount of magic from the air, making its use unreliable.

"Stay safe."

"Always my friend."

I ended the scry, seeking Vera in the darkness.

Her body twitched, her face contorting into a grimace. A muffled cry parted her lips.

I *knew* her dragon still plagued her sleep. She had been too prideful to admit it.

Careful not to wake her, I settled behind her and wrapped my arms around her. The moment our skin touched, sweet relief crashed into me like a missing limb had been returned. I shuddered in bliss.

Her spasms stopped and her breathing evened out. I held her through the night, delighting in the feel of her in my arms, in her hair tickling my skin. I couldn't bring myself to sleep and miss out on what might be my last opportunity to hold her.

When the sun crested over the hills, it took all my strength to release her. I quietly rose and braced to take up my villain role once more.

"Vera," I barked.

Her eyes popped open with a glare.

"Get ready. We need to make a stop." She was ill-dressed for The Wilds, and I had only packed enough supplies for myself. She sat up, her hair adorably mused from sleep. "And do something with that rat's nest on your head."

She blinked, still groggy, then launched a rock at my head. Her aim was so poor, I had to lean far to the right to catch it. I attributed it to her sleepy state.

"Were you *trying* to hit me?"

"Shut up."

I danced out of the way as she threw another just as poorly and left her to get ready while I tended to Loach.

When I finished, she was nowhere to be found.

"Vera?"

"What?" Her irritated shout came from behind a boulder.

My gaze narrowed, instantly suspicious. "What are you doing?"

"None of your business."

There was a large clang of rock hitting rock . . . Or iron ore being ground into a digestible powder.

I had snuck a peek inside her saddlebag while she slept. I didn't find anything other than some stolen gold, the map, candle, and a shirt, but I hadn't checked her person.

I marched over, hoping to catch her in the act.

"You really think you can poison me—"

My words died in my throat as I glimpsed the silken swell of her breasts. My mouth watered. The rosy peaks were just begging to be sucked.

"What the fuck," Vera shrieked, an arm flying to her chest. "Get out of here, you perv."

I widened my stance, crossing my arms, but averted my gaze. "I thought—"

"What?" Fabric slid down her torso. "That I had some iron dust shoved up my ass?"

I met her gaze again. She was dressed in a form fitting tunic and pants. Vera had a slender build. She lacked the bulk of many of my female warriors, but she still managed to be strong and lithe.

My eyes narrowed a fraction. "I wouldn't put it past you."

She shook her head in disbelief.

"What was that racket you were making then?"

She stabbed a talon at a vampiric centipede, known as a

bogfala, crushed under a rock. Its millions of fanged legs still twitched.

"My mistake."

She glared before stalking past me with a huff.

I whistled for Loach, and he came trotting over. I swung into the saddle and waited as Vera finished getting ready. She fastened her saddlebag to Loach's flank, then lifted her gaze to me.

"Put this on." I offered my failin hide. "And before you argue, there will be curious eyes where we're going. King Desmond has spies everywhere." If Lucinda had done her job, the king would think Vera was dead, but if he received any news to the contrary, his search would continue.

I could glamour her, but we would only be making a quick stop, and it required a vast amount of magic to create a new one properly.

She accepted it with flattened lips and swung into the front of the saddle.

Knowing my face would not be a welcome sight, I threw on a glamour I often used when traveling, lightening my eyes, darkening my hair, and smoothing my facial features. The villagers would see an ordinary Taranis soldier, but I would appear the same to Vera.

We crested the peak of the hill we'd camped below, before following the slope down to the base of another, much larger one, and riding up it. Deiridh Village was on the other side.

The rising sun cast a warm glow over the thatched roofs set into the hillside. Every home was painted in soft pastels, faded by magic to reveal the clay walls beneath. Within a few years, the magic in the air would consume the structures, as it did with all organics. Stone and metal were the only safe materials, which made them too expensive for many.

The villagers lived above the market which was nestled at the hill's base. Rock walls and sloping paths connected the two.

We dismounted a safe distance away. As I weighed down Loach's reigns, I caught sight of ten warriors exiting the village; dressed in white furs with large, fighter builds, they were unmistakable.

Saor.

I pushed Vera behind me.

My gaze flitted across each of their faces. One had been there for my mother's death—Kian's brother, Lark.

Flashes of his fist wrapped in her hair, dragging her, pummeled my mind. Fury pumped through me as darkness coated my vision. My battle-mode pressed against my skin, demanding vengeance.

The image shifted to Lark, nothing but a bloody torso with his limbs torn off.

Blood roared through my veins.

Kill him.

Kill him.

Do it now.

"Ronan," Vera hissed. "What's going on?"

I blinked and blocked her as she tried to move around me. "Stay behind me." I returned my attention to the men just in time to catch a glimpse of the paper several of them carried.

It was Vera's wanted poster.

My heart stopped.

They hadn't seen us yet, but they would soon. I could have them dead on the ground with a snap of my fingers, but a trail of bodies would arouse suspicion, and there were hundreds more to take their place.

My gaze cut right and left. There was a large boulder

that would block us from the village's view, but the Saor would see us once they passed.

I dragged Vera behind it and pushed her up against the stone. "Kiss me."

She shoved at my shoulders. "Are you out of your mind? No."

I let her see the urgency in my gaze. "*Kiss me.*"

She drew up to her tippy toes, bringing her face as close to mine as possible. "I'd rather let a beast eat me alive."

"You are maddening," I snarled.

An icy smile crawled over her lips. "I learned from the best."

"Witch."

"Asshole."

I slammed my lips down on hers.

Her mouth was stiff at first, barely grazing mine, but it quickly transformed as I claimed her lips. Drinking deeply, I pulled soft moans from her throat. She arched into me, talons scrabbling at my chest, unsure if she wanted to push me away or pull me close.

As I devoured her lips with broad sweeping strokes of my tongue, my world narrowed to the feel of her mouth moving against mine; to the thundering of her pulse; to the exquisite scent of her arousal. It was sweet and flavorful like my favorite puffed dessert with a dash of cinnamon.

A tiny mewl of pleasure escaped her before she scraped her fangs over my tongue and drew blood. I growled, rolling my swollen cock against her.

She hissed, back arching as I sucked greedily on her tongue like it was her sex.

My hand shot out, wrapping around her throat. I collared her and molded every inch of my body against hers, pinning her against the rock. Then I kissed her so deeply she forgot whose air she was breathing. She responded beautifully, moaning, chasing her tongue with mine.

I dragged my free hand down to her hips and fisted the fabric of her pants, desperately wanting to tear it off.

I was seconds away from doing just that, spinning her, and sheathing my aching cock inside her when outside sounds filtered in.

By some heroic feat, I managed to wrench myself away, and glance back. The Saor were gone. They had overlooked two lovers as they made their way out of the village.

I glanced down at Vera, breathing heavily.

Black swallowed all but a small ring of lavender in her eyes. The color was mesmerizing. So was the pink flush tinting her cheeks. It made me painfully hard. She looked so bewitching, so innocent.

I had treated the subject of sex delicately in the Mortal Lands, afraid if she knew the true extent of my dark appetites, I'd frighten her away, but I had no such qualms now.

I wanted to drag her down into my sinful darkness and touch her places no others had. I wanted to sear my touch so deep into her skin, there would be no getting it out. Anytime another man touched her, her only thought would be of me.

But I feared once I started, there'd be no end.

I traced her swollen lips.

"I want to ruin you," I whispered.

Every ounce of softness bled from her. She shoved me away and swiped her hand across her lips, disgust pinching her face. "That was awful."

Her face was filled with revulsion, but her eyes were desperate. 'Make me hate you,' they begged.

I could never say no to those eyes.

I slapped a hand over her head and leaned close. "Whatever you need to tell yourself, sweetheart, but we both know you were all but begging to be fucked."

14

VERA

He managed a smile that was even more condescending than his words.

Oh, this fucker had forgotten who he was dealing with. The Eye might have stolen my fighting abilities, but it hadn't taken my backbone.

Even with his hand gone, the heat of it lingered like a brand. I itched to sink my talons into him for daring to touch me—kiss me—like that, but that would be letting him off too easy. He needed to be taught a lesson.

Batting my lashes the same way I'd seen Dolly do, I stepped toward him, and dragged a finger down his chest. His cocky smile fell, intense desire flaring in his eyes. He wanted me just as badly as I wanted him. It frightened me how pleased I was by that.

I threaded a hand through his hair and pulled his head to mine. I softly brushed my lips against his, and he responded with vigor, banding an arm around my back.

Ronan might not be a man, but he was just as simple-minded as one.

I led the kiss, licking at the seam of his lips. They eagerly parted on a groan, Ronan's hands clenching in my tunic. I slipped my tongue inside. It flicked and tangled against his as I made all the expected moans and trills—not that I had to pretend much, he kissed as well as he killed.

I let it go on for a minute, to disarm him, before I opened my eyes, glaring. His were closed, face taut with lust.

Sweetheart this you son of a bitch.

I scraped my fangs over his tongue.

Just the way he liked.

Then I clamped down with all my strength.

Warm liquid squirted in my mouth as Ronan's tongue severed in half.

Bastard didn't even flinch.

He tore away with a grunt and spat out a pool of blood.

I expected him to be angry, but when he lifted his head, his eyes were bright with hunger. The edge of his mouth hooked up. "What did I tell you about biting?"

His words were slightly slurred by his injury.

If you bite me, I'll want to do a lot more than look at your leg.

"Try it, and your dick is next," I barked. "I don't care if you can do as you please, stay the fuck away from me."

I wouldn't touch Ronan with a ten-foot pole for a multitude of reasons. He was a monster who had crushed my heart, stabbed me, branded me, and then broke my heart again. There were a lot of complicated, sticky emotions where he was involved. Oh, and then there was that pesky little issue of HIS MATE.

His eyes hooded. "I was trying to protect you." There was no slur to his words now. His tongue had healed. "They were Saor. They are defectors from my House, turned mercenaries for hire. They had your wanted poster."

I'd only caught a brief glimpse of some men before Ronan was shoving me behind him.

He'd kissed me so they wouldn't see me . . .

"Next time, let them catch me."

"I believe the word you're looking for is *thank you*."

I shrugged, leaning back against the rock. The same rock he just had me pinned up against. I could still feel his fist gripping my pants, his monster erection grinding into me. I'd forgotten how large he was.

Heat coiled low in my belly, but I ignored it.

Ronan looked skyward, pinching the bridge of his nose as he muttered, "You could test the patience of a fucking saint."

I pretended he wasn't there, drumming my fingers against the rock.

Hired killers had a picture of me.

Where there should have been fear or concern, there was only indifference. I was going to die one day soon— whether it was at the hands of the Saor, the Nighters, or the Crone, it didn't matter, but I had to see this prick to safety first.

"Who could have hired the Saor? Doesn't the king think I'm dead?"

When Ronan didn't answer, my gaze slid to him. He was scrubbing his jaw, staring like he could as easily crush me as kiss me. "Yes," he said tersely. "I would have heard from him otherwise."

My tapping stuttered to a stop as cold dread pinched my stomach. "Do you think someone knows what I am?"

While death didn't frighten me, another person after the dragon's powers did.

The fear in my voice had him frowning. "No, if word had gotten out, the entire Faylands would be hunting you. I believe this has to do with me. I know a secret about Lord Cern he doesn't want shared. I threatened him with it to gain access to his archives. The Saor are retaliation."

My brows rose in a slow arc. "But how does he know about me, and why not go after your mate?"

The more I said the word out loud, the less it cut.

You're a dirty liar.

"Liam can access minds," Ronan explained. "He's incredibly powerful and likely entered mine without me realizing it. Kylah is the rightful heir to House Belenus. To go after her would be a provocation."

His mate was an heir to a fae House. Fucking of course. She couldn't just be drop dead gorgeous, she had to be powerful too.

I blew out a raspberry because the alternative was crying.

"So, he chose the nobody instead," I said bitterly.

"I don't think he'll have you harmed," he assured me. "I believe it was meant as a warning, but we can't be sure. The Wilds is the Saor's territory. They'll be looking for you there too. We'll need to take precautions."

"Like?"

"I'll have to glamour you to look more like a halfling."

That sounded easy enough. "Okay."

"That's not all . . ." he said like a tier four beast was suddenly standing in front of him. I preened at his wariness. It'd been too long since I'd frightened anyone. "We'll need a cover story."

It was my turn to be wary. I crossed my arms, peering up at him. He really needed to put on a shirt. No one wanted to see all those bulging, tatted muscles.

Alright, I was a dirty liar.

"Why?"

"A Taranis soldier and a halfling all the way out here will draw attention."

Damnit. If the Saor were looking for me, they'd be looking for him too. We'd both have to wear glamour.

"Fine. What's our cover story?"

He peered around the boulder, and I did the same,

watching some fae tie off their horses outside the village. They were wearing a dark, supple material I'd never seen before with satchels slung over their shoulders.

"Who are they?" I whispered.

"Gem hunters."

I threw him a questioning look as we retreated behind the boulder.

"The storm systems mixed with magic in The Wilds produce The Lands' largest gems. Mining them is incredibly dangerous work, but the rewards are immense." Ronan's gaze connected with mine. "We're newlyweds. We're headed into The Wilds to collect enough gems to fund our new life."

I burst into laughter. It sputtered out when I realized he was serious.

"We can't lie," I hissed. "No one's going to believe we're newlyweds."

"We would have convinced anyone watching that kiss." His lips twitched. "The one where you didn't bite off my tongue."

"We have the chemistry for it." I ignored the spike of pain that came with that admission. "But people will expect us to be in *love*." I hissed the last part like it was a dirty word.

"I do love you. It's not the way you might love me, but it's sufficient for our needs."

I pinched my eyes shut as a wave of nausea crashed over me. Gods, this was all so fucked.

I took a deep, stabilizing breath, and forced open my eyes.

"There has to be another way. What if I'm your servant?"

He shook his head. Halflings don't leave the safety of their House unless it's to run away to the Mortal Lands and a common soldier wouldn't have a personal servant."

"Ronan—"

"No." He straightened to his full height, staring me

151

down. "I'm not putting you at risk. It's either marriage or you're going to House Taran," he declared with finality.

His gaze was dead sober. He meant it.

My jaw clenched.

Either let him face the Nighters alone, and possibly die, or be his wife for the time being. They were both shitty options, but only one I could live with.

I snarled under my breath. "I guess we're getting married."

He flicked a finger, beckoning me over.

I glared before I took a hesitant step closer. "How does glamour work exactly?"

I was familiar with it because of the Crone. She'd worn one for as long as I could remember. It was like a layer of camouflage over your face, but I didn't know anything beyond that.

"I can change your appearance to a certain degree. I can't disguise your height, frame, or give you a new face, but I can manipulate your features, distort them like smudging ink on paper. Your appearance will be different to everyone else but me. However, if anyone peers closely enough, they can see through it so don't give them a reason to."

As in, I had to make everyone think I was a halfling. I'd spent my whole life believing I was one so it shouldn't be too hard. Except, halflings here were vastly different than in the Mortal Lands.

I lifted my gaze to his and wished I hadn't. Those swirling mercury eyes sucked me in and wouldn't let go. This close, I could see flecks of green buried in the gray. Huh. I'd never noticed that before.

Ugh. The last thing we need is to find him more attractive.

Infuriatingly, the events of the last couple days had done nothing to temper my attraction. If anything, it had grown since the Mortal Lands.

My body was a goddamn idiot. I, thankfully, wasn't.

"How would a Taranis halfling act?" I asked.

"They aren't fighters, but they aren't meek."

I nodded.

He raised his hand and waved it over my face. My skin prickled and grew hot a moment before the sensation vanished. Ronan stepped away and returned, offering his scrying mirror.

I flipped around as I held it up.

My hair was shorter and still silver but with less shine. My eyes had changed to a muted brown and the rest of my features had been flattened. It all blended into a seamlessly plain face. It would be impossible to distinguish me from other halflings.

I opened my mouth and my eyes widened. My teeth were square and blunt. I peeked at my talons. Gone were the razor-sharp claws. They were as normal looking as my teeth.

I'd always wanted to look like everyone else but now that I did, I felt . . . ordinary. I dropped the mirror with a strange sense of disappointment.

Ronan's gaze was watchful as I returned it, but he said nothing.

"Why didn't you just glamour me and leave me in the Mortal Lands?" I asked.

"There isn't enough magic there for me to maintain it."

A gold nugget floated out of my saddlebag and landed in his palm. He began molding the metal between his hands.

My eyes narrowed. "How did you know that was in there?"

"I went through your things."

Why was I not surprised?

Oh yeah, because he'd snuck up on me while I was changing to accuse me and my boobs of colluding against him. I shook my head at the absurdity of this plan. I didn't trust him, he didn't trust me, but somehow, we were going to convince everyone we were happily in love.

Ronan finished whatever he was making. He put a gold ring on his thumb.

"Why the thumb?" I asked. Mortals wore their rings on their fourth to last finger.

"It's closest to the heart."

He gestured for my left hand, and I presented my thumb. He slid on a ring ending in a small dagger. The blade portion had the same shape as the pointed end of a quill and stopped halfway above the knuckle. When I bent my finger, the ring could act as a small weapon.

"There," he said softly.

I lifted my gaze to his. "That's it, we're married?"

He dipped his head. "There's usually more ceremony, but that is how it is done these days."

His fingers lingered on mine longer than necessary. They were warm and calloused. "You're my wife now," he continued. "For however short a time that might be. I won't take that duty lightly."

I wasn't surprised Ronan was going to treat this like a real marriage, because not only would it help our case, but the man didn't do anything in half measures. He went all in, or not at all.

"Does that duty include fidelity?" As soon as the words were out of my mouth, I wanted to suck them back in. My whole face pinched tight. "Please don't answer th—"

"I haven't been with another woman since you."

Confusion smacked my face.

"You look surprised," he said softly. "Of course you are."

"What does that mean?"

"It means, you think I'm so cold and heartless, I'd be able to move on so quickly."

"She's not just anyone, Ronan. She's your mate."

His steel eyes stared intensely. "You weren't just anyone either, Vera."

I didn't want to have this conversation. My plan was to avoid any emotions besides anger when it came to Ronan.

A strange expression crossed his face. "I need to go."

"What? Where?"

"To enforce fae law," he said crossing over to his horse.

"I thought you weren't doing that anymore."

He swung into the saddle and tossed me a pouch. "Get yourself some clothes for The Wilds and whatever else you want. I'll be back as soon as I can."

"You're just going to leave me here?"

A smile ghosted his lips. "You're the most capable woman I know, Wife."

And with that, he clicked his teeth and raced back up the hill we'd come down before disappearing from sight.

I stood motionless for several moments, vacillating between flattery, annoyance, and a lot of confusion. Thirty minutes ago, I was throwing rocks at his head, and now we were married—temporarily—and he'd admitted he hadn't been with anyone else since me.

I had no idea what to make of the latter.

Don't make anything of it. We're avoiding.

The abrupt turn of events was giving me a serious case of whiplash.

As I glanced down at the pouch, the brand caught my eye. I was glamoured, and if I got into any real trouble, Ronan could find me with it.

Time to shop.

An archway marked the village entrance. The light amber wood was heavily worn with 'Deiridh' burned into the center. Beyond it was an open area framed by the sloping walls of the hill.

Low, squat tables were clustered around the edges. They

were steadily filling with fae filing down from the houses above, carrying barrels on their heads, likely full of whatever goods they were selling. By the time I reached the entrance, every table was full, and the area was bustling with gem hunters.

Every House was represented inside. The assortment of smells, colors, and new dialects was dizzying. I was hit with an extreme sense of alienation, like I very much didn't belong, but I'd never belonged anywhere so, in a way, I was right at home.

My eyes locked on a winged fae at the first table.

White, downy feathers covered the appendages. He was on the shorter side, but what he lacked in height, he made up for in muscle. He was a Belenus fae. I didn't know much about them beyond they could fly and manipulate the weather.

Black body suits were laid out over his table—the same ones I'd seen the gem hunters wearing. Thick padding covered the chest and stomach area.

"Get your lightning-proof gear here!" he called.

As I passed, he shot me a glare.

I frowned and kept walking.

I continued through the market, and realized he wasn't the only one shooting me dirty looks. Scornful eyes watched me from disapproving faces. I glanced down. My talons had a faint shimmer over them still so what was with all the looks?

A few tables over, a female fae was dressed in the ceremonial burnished robes of House Cern with a stack of books neatly set out. Gold-brown eyes met mine. "Would you like a copy of the most comprehensive list of gemstones and how to identify each one?"

Seeing she was the most approachable so far, I stopped

beside her table. "No, thank you. Do you know where I could find clothes for The Wilds?"

"There's a pair of Anu siblings that'll have what you need." The Cern fae gestured to a table on the other side of the market.

I thanked her and wheeled in that direction.

More dirty looks and snide whispers tracked my steps, coming from both the vendors and gem hunters. The only thing I could think of was garnering this kind of reaction was the fact that I was an outsider.

I reached the table. Manning it was a male with verdant eyes and short, tawny hair. His shirt and pants were made of a moss-like material. Spiders dangled from his lobes like earrings.

He was an Anu fae. Their powers revolved around nature.

Crates full of enormous fruits and vegetables were stacked on top of one another. Various furs and animal fabric hung above them.

"What are those?" I pointed at the jars lining the table. Each was filled with swirling black smoke and a bright fire. I could feel heat emanating from the glass.

"Eternal flame," the fae responded. "An endless fire for your light and heating needs." He recited the pitch dryly like he'd rather be doing anything other than dealing with me, but his whole demeanor changed when I set the pouch of silver on his table.

"I'll take one."

I scanned the other items adorning the table and my gaze landed on a strange flower encased in a dome of glass. It had glittering, silver gossamer petals. The effect reminded me of moonlight hitting sand at just the right angle, making the particles shine like precious jewels. The stem was black and covered in small thorns.

My eyes were riveted to it. I felt this intense pull, drawing me in, and shuffled closer.

"It's a moon rose," the fae said, noticing my attention. He carefully lifted it off the table. "It blooms in darkness and can only be found in one spot in the Enchanted Forest where the thicket of trees is so dense, no light can penetrate."

Up close, the petals looked woven from bodah silk. The way their color danced and sparkled in the sunlight was enchanting.

"I'll take it."

He nodded and set it down.

As he packaged up my purchases, I caught the layer of bark covering his hands. The skin was scaled, dark, and dry. His fingers had trouble bending properly and every movement looked painful.

I recalled Ronan mentioning that every fae paid a price for their powers. I wondered if this was his.

A woman—I assumed to be his sister based on their similar features—appeared. At first glance, I thought she had long braids in her hair, but they moved and shifted. They were vines.

I tucked the fire and moon rose into my saddlebag and found her appraising me beneath dark lashes. The vines on her head seemed equally as interested, stretching toward me like snakes. "What's a Taranis halfling doing all the way out here? Looking for the Saor?"

I frowned. Why would one of Ronan's halflings seek out the Saor?

"Cressida," the male chastised. "Don't be nosy."

"What? No one would blame her is all."

"It's fine," I said, grateful for Ronan's thoroughness, otherwise, I couldn't have spoken my next words. "My husband and I just got married. We're out here gem hunting to fund our new life."

I made sure to flash my ring finger as I buckled my saddlebag. The gold winked in the light, mocking me. I had the urge to tear the thing off.

"Ah, the soldier, right?" she asked. "Saw you two together outside the village."

I nodded.

"Is there anything else we can help you with?" the brother asked, bumping his sister out of the way.

"I need some clothes made."

"Cressida is the village's best seamstress. She'll get you whatever you need."

I quickly rattled off my measurements and order.

"Come back in thirty minutes, and I'll have them ready for you," she instructed.

I moved back into the market, and a table caught my eye. It stood out from the rest because it was selling a medley of fae goods without a common theme connecting them like the others, as if they had been collected from various areas and were being resold at a higher price. The glint of steel had me beelining for it.

I needed a real weapon.

I felt naked without one and I couldn't use my talons with the glamour over them. It would draw unwanted attention if my blunt nails were suddenly capable of tearing through flesh.

Plus, I hadn't practiced with my gun since the night before the Rogues captured me. Who knows how far my knowledge had degraded since then. Practice might just go better now that I didn't have to take gold dust for the time being. The dragon was quiet with Ronan nearby.

Strangely, I hadn't had any nightmares either.

A fae stood behind the table, conversing with a group of

hunters. They were placing bets on where they thought the first storm of the season would make landfall.

I picked up the small dagger, turning it over in my palm. It had a solid weight to it. Pressing the pad of my finger to the tip, I gently touched it, testing its sharpness. Just light pressure drew blood.

I took out the pouch and dropped it on the table like I had with the Anu fae. "How much for the blade?"

The seller's ears twitched in my direction, confirming he'd heard, but he continued his conversation like he hadn't.

"Excuse me," I said more forcefully. "How much for the blade?"

The largest of the hunters, a hulking Dagda fae, twisted toward me with a sneer. "Didn't your Lord teach you any manners? Don't interrupt."

That's what all the disdainful looks were for. . . Because I was a halfling.

My temper flared.

I stabbed the knife into the table.

The group's conversation cut off. Six faces swung toward me, their mouths' angry slashes.

"This halfling doesn't know her place."

"Someone ought to teach her."

The men exchanged looks. Means smirks settled over their faces.

It registered too late that I'd made a grave mistake.

These weren't mortals. These men were predators, packing some serious power based on their draoistones. Each one was bristling with muscle and towered over me.

They crowded me, trapping me between them. I couldn't see beyond the press of their bodies.

Unease dripped like cold sweat down my spine. I backed up, bumping into one of them, and lurched forward.

"Aw, look at the little rabbit run."

A quick glance told me the knife was just out of reach. I'd have to somehow make it past the two largest of the men to get to it. All I had were my talons, but I don't think they would be much use against their armor-scaled suits.

Hiding my nerves, I thrust up my chin and met the vendor's gaze. He seemed like the most reasonable of the bunch. "I just want to buy the knife."

A jeering smile. "How did a halfling get all those silvers?"

"My husband gave them to me." Gods, I hated how pathetic I sounded.

The largest of the group scoffed. "I don't see any husband."

"He'll be back soon." Inwardly, I flinched. The words sounded weak and foolish, even to my ears.

"Better finish before he gets here then."

Knuckles and necks cracked. As my gaze flitted over each of their faces, they transformed into the Rogues. Phantom fists and legs hit my flesh, and my muscles quivered with each invisible blow.

Please, no. Not again.

I shielded my head with my arms, curling forward, preparing for the assault. *Let it be over quick*, I silently begged.

"Look. She's shaking," one said with a smile in their voice, sounding so much like Boone.

Dark, sticky shame swamped me as a burn flared behind my eyes. I hated how fucking helpless I was.

The large hunter leaned forward. I could feel his breath on my neck. "Let this be a lesson to you, Halfling, you are nothing. Less than noth—"

When he didn't finish, I glanced up.

My eyes traced over the knife at his throat, tightening in confusion until they hit Ronan.

He stood behind the hunter, wearing a terrifying expression. "Go on," he whispered darkly. "Finish insulting my wife, so I know how many bones to break."

The fae canted his eyes over his shoulder, took one look at Ronan, and terror lit his face. The behemoth crumbled. "I'm-m s-s-sorry, sir. I didn't realize. My mis-stake." The knife dug deeper, precious seconds from doing serious damage.

"Don't apologize to me. Apologize to her."

Terrified eyes met mine. He looked like he was about to pee himself. "I'm—" he had to pause to swallow "—I'm sorry."

Ronan leaned down, putting his face right near the fae's. "Try again."

"I am deeply sorry for the way I spoke to you."

Ronan released him and the hunter shriveled to the ground.

Hard eyes met each of the hunters. "You know who I am?"

Their heads dipped, throats bobbing.

"If any of you so much as breathes a word I was here, I'll track you down, burn your homes, slaughter your children, wives . . . Anyone you've ever loved. Anyone you've even thought about loving."

The scent of urine drifted up. The vendor was shaking like a leaf.

"We won't tell a soul," one swore, and the others nodded, affirming it.

Ronan surveyed the group, a vicious edge to his face. "Good. Don't let me see your faces again."

The men scattered.

I grabbed the knife, battling tears.

"You okay?" Ronan asked.

"Fine," I croaked, hiding my face. "I'm going to get my clothes."

I rushed off to the Anu table before Ronan could question me.

I collected my order, and we departed the village in silence. As soon as we were safely out of earshot, Ronan grabbed my arm and turned me toward him.

"What's wrong? Did those men—"

I wrenched my wrist away, eyes flashing. "You shouldn't have fucking left me!"

Surprise flitted across his face. His brows slowly rose. "I had to. I made a deal with Lucinda to enforce fae law in exchange for covering up your death."

"I didn't even have a weapon," I said in a low, heated voice.

"Since when do you need one? I've seen you fight."

My jaw clenched tight. I was trying so goddamn hard not to cry.

He peered hard, and I saw the moment he connected the dots. His voice became so soft and sincere, I wanted to claw his eyes out. "I am deeply sorry for mocking you before. Please tell me what happened with the Rogues."

"No."

"Please."

"I said no," I snapped.

"Vera . . ."

"No!"

"Why won't you tell me?" he demanded, losing his patience.

I met his gaze with an acidic stare. "Because the last time I told you something personal, you loaded it into a gun and used it to shoot me right through the goddamn heart."

He frowned. Without warning, he plucked the blade from my fingers.

"You'll get this back when you're ready to talk."

15

VERA

I glared at the knife strapped to Ronan's thigh. I could see it every time his hide billowed out as we walked through the snow.

A blizzard had delayed our arrival in The Wilds for two days.

We had reached the entrance, just as the snowstorm hit, and were forced to wait it out in a hunting lodge at the border. Fortunately, we had been given our own room.

For two days, Ronan had taunted me with the knife, leaving it seemingly forgotten in different places in the room, only to threaten me with a spanking whenever I'd gotten close. At night, the bastard had used his powers to turn the blade into a useless pile of nails.

Not only had he teased me with the weapon but he'd also teased me with his body.

For forty-eight excruciatingly long hours, I was trapped with Ronan's tantalizing scent, forced to gaze at his near nakedness, with all those layers of muscle and tattoos. He knew what he was doing, walking around in just a loin cloth.

He'd smirked every time he caught me looking. He was

mocking me, challenging my claim that I wouldn't touch him if he was the last man in The Lands.

Thank Gods we'd woken to a clear morning today and were able to leave. The horse had been left at the lodge because it was too dangerous to keep him with us.

Now it was a couple hours later, and we were following the candle in The Wilds.

No one had blinked an eye at the floating stick of wax. I guess it was hardly a novelty in a land of magic.

Like the rest of the Faylands, the Wilds was stunning.

Crystalline covered trees and shrubbery spread out in every direction. Dazzling white filaments dusted everything, sparkling in the sun. The air was biting, like a blade digging into soft skin, but the way it moved around the landscape created a lyrical humming.

In the distance, crescent-shaped mountains arced toward the sky and ended in fanged peaks. Craggy formations punched through the snow like bone.

It was beauty and violence, deadly yet inviting.

I marched through the snow, wearing a white fur top with laces starting under my breasts and running up to my collarbone. My pants were a similar material, cinched at the ankle, and sat low on my hips, leaving a slither of flesh visible. Fur boots and a cloak tied it all together.

Sunlight glinted off the fresh snow, making it shine like fine crystal, but it did little to dispel the cold.

Every breath came out as a plume, and no matter how tightly I tied my thick cloak, the arctic air managed to find a way in, leaving stinging bites in its wake.

Ronan seemed to be faring better despite wearing less clothing. He'd traded his loin cloth for a pair of brown leather pants that molded to his toned ass and legs and donned his failin hide. The wolf head over his gave him a savage edge.

Unfortunately, he was still shirtless, his tattooed abs flexing with every step.

Our boots crunched rhythmically over the snow as we held hands. I hadn't even fought him when he insisted on the intimate touch.

The last two days had given me time to adjust to the idea of our ruse. If I stared hard enough, I could see his glamour, see the face of a soldier who looked like Ronan, but different enough I could pretend he was someone else.

I wasn't holding hands with Ronan. I was holding hands with a handsome soldier named Rolan. Rolan hadn't broken my heart or found his mate. We were madly in love.

That's what I let myself imagine every time we had to touch, and so far, the delusion was working.

A large pack of gem hunters kept pace with us. They had gotten stuck at the hunting lodge and were headed in the same direction, toward the mountains.

Another rush of cold air billowed Ronan's hide, revealing the stolen dagger strapped to his thigh.

My eyes narrowed on it.

I'd tried to get it back right after he'd stolen it, but the threat of a spanking had quickly ended the attempt.

I had learned my lesson after the kiss. Letting him touch me like that was too dangerous. I might know it was wrong for us to be intimate while he had a mate, but my body didn't share my scruples, and knowing he hadn't been with anyone else since me only heightened the temptation.

Which was strange. Ronan had told me he loved her so why hadn't they been intimate yet?

You weren't just anyone either Vera.

I slapped his words away. Avoid, avoid, avoid.

My attention dragged back to the knife.

I wasn't going to tell him what happened with the Rogues because one, it wasn't any of his goddamn business, and two, I trusted him as far as I could throw a giant, which was not at all.

But I was going to get that damn knife back.

Every day that passed without practice, more knowledge was sucked into the Eye's void, and we could be at our destination any day.

I needed to be as prepared as possible. Even if all went well, and there was no need to trade myself to the Nighters, I wanted to be able to defend myself when I inevitably returned to the Crone.

Although I needed her torture to help keep my dragon weak, I couldn't stomach letting her without putting up a fight.

Ronan's flank brushed against me, sending gooseflesh pebbling up my side. I glared at him from under my hood. He did it again and smirked when my eyes narrowed further.

"Stop it," I hissed. "It's bad enough we have to hold hands."

The Rolan fantasy didn't work when Ronan was antagonizing me.

"Behave, Wife," he whispered out the side of his mouth. "We're being watched."

I glanced around. A couple of the hunters' eyes were on us.

I'd overheard people talking as we left the hunting lodge. That gossip Cressida had told everyone what I told her. I supposed that was to our benefit though. The Saor wouldn't think anything of some newlyweds.

He brushed his thumb over my knuckles and sent hot tingles racing up my arm.

"Touch me one more time," I warned quietly. "And I'll saw off your dick with a dull, rusty blade."

He stopped us and angled close. A teasing gleam

168

sparked in his eyes as he ducked near my hood and brought his face inches from mine. Hot breath skated over my lips, contrasting starkly with the biting cold, and made my pulse leap against my throat.

"You'd have to touch it first."

I pressed my hands against his chest, ignoring the hard ridges under my fingers, and readied to shove him out of my space when I remembered we had an audience.

I dragged them down his chest instead, eyes tracing over his scars, like I was admiring them. "Are you proud of all the lives you've taken, Husband?" I whispered sweetly.

The teasing spark hardened into steel. He removed my hands.

I waited to feel satisfaction for getting under his skin, but it didn't come. I glanced down at the brand, hoping it would do the trick. The snarling wolf stirred annoyance, but I couldn't muster the same anger as before.

Well, that was a problem.

He took my hand again and we continued into the snow. His movements were stiff, announcing his agitation, but I didn't address it. I didn't care if he was upset.

The niggling guilt in my stomach said otherwise.

We marched through the snow for hours, taking brief breaks for food and water.

His body heat soaked into my flank, and his annoyingly delicious scent tickled my nostrils every few minutes. I was in a constant state of arousal and aggravation. How could my attraction possibly have grown?

It didn't make sense. Unless . . .

We'd only been together once, and we'd made love. Maybe this maddening attraction stemmed from the fact that we'd never fucked. Yes, that was it. Maybe I just needed to fuck him once, and I'd be rid of this infuriating attraction.

"You're plotting." Ronan's voice interrupted my thoughts.

I glanced at him. His expression was stoic. The irritation wasn't gone—some still lingered around his eyes—but it was severely reduced.

"Am not."

He lifted his brows. "I can practically hear it, Wife."

"Stop calling me that," I said under my breath.

"No."

I huffed. "I liked it better when you were upset."

He slanted me a look that bordered on annoyance but said nothing else.

Endless crunching filled my ears as we walked. The snow looked like it went on forever.

Toward dusk, I noticed thick clouds shadowing the horizon, several miles up ahead. They darkened the landscape far more than it should have been for the hour.

A bolt of lightning arced across the sky. Thunder followed, so loud, it sounded right overhead.

Whoops and cheers exploded from the surrounding hunters. My brows furrowed, taking in their excited faces. "What's going on?"

"It's the first storm of the season," Ronan explained. "It's early, which is a good omen."

The hunters, previously quiet and subdued, turned animated, chatting and laughing with one another. At least someone from every House was present in the group, except for Ronan's—well, besides us.

As we drew closer, I could make out dark dots, like splotches of ink, in the storm, multiplying every second. Their shadows were ghastly contortions, some standing ten feet tall with limbs protruding at every angle. Others looked like mere ants. Their snarls and shrieks floated on the wind.

"What are those?" I whispered.

"Magic-born. The magic the storm is pulling in creates them."

I recalled the giant plant sucking down the vine like a noodle and shuddered.

Humanoid forms crept among the magic-born, digging through the snow. My brows sunk low over my eyes. "Why in the world would those fae willingly go out with all those creatures?"

"They're gem hunting," Ronan said. He pointed as lightning shot down from the sky. "When a bolt is hot enough, and the magic strong enough, it creates the perfect conditions when it meets the layer of sediment beneath the snow. You've got to get the gem while it's still hot, or the snow might cool it before it has a chance to fully form. The trick is to be quick."

A giant silhouette sprouted from the ground, rising until it was thirty feet tall. I couldn't be sure from this far away, but its upper body appeared to be a skeleton while its lower half ended in a fishtail. Distant screams erupted as its long, bony arms swiped out at hunters, and its tail crushed them.

I winced, glad we weren't a part of that.

We walked for another thirty minutes and stopped before the sun fully set. It was a waxing crescent so there wouldn't be any moonlight to use to set up camp once the sun was gone. It was cloudy as well, which meant the light from the turquoise and lavender bands wouldn't be reliable.

Some of the gem hunters continued on, but most settled in for the night. Thankfully, it was miles of unobstructed terrain, and everyone could spread out.

Ronan laid three furs out in the snow and draped two more on top. "It's a nice night. We'll sleep under the stars."

I bit my lip, staring at how close we'd be sleeping to one another.

"I'll be a perfect gentleman," he assured me.

"You better."

I pulled out the eternal flame and stuck it in the snow, at

the edge of the furs. For its size, it put out a surprising amount of heat.

We ate dinner—some jerky and cheese—as the last rays of sun retreated.

Brief spurts of ribbon and starlight shined down as the clouds moved beneath them, but for the most part, it was exceptionally dark. I tensed, accustomed to the dragon stirring as soon as night fell, but for the fourth night in a row, it did nothing.

Releasing a quiet, relieved breath, I sat back, resting my weight on my hands as I stretched out my legs. Physically, I felt better than I had all month. Without any gold dust, all my wounds had healed, and my strength and energy were at peak levels.

I knew it wouldn't last. As soon as Ronan and I parted ways, I'd have to go back to taking it, but I would enjoy the reprieve while it lasted. A brief, sharp pain rose at the thought of what would happen at the end of this, but I quickly squashed it.

I glanced over at Ronan and found him watching me with an intensity that made me want to squirm.

"You're staring."

"You make it hard not to."

"No one's listening," I hissed. "You don't have to pretend, Husband."

"I'm not."

"Why would I believe you?"

He watched me for a moment before laying down, crossing his arms under his head, and shrugging.

"Goodnight," he said, shutting his eyes.

"Night."

As I moved to lay down, my eyes caught on the dagger. It was strapped to his upper thigh. Either he'd forgotten to hide it, or he thought I'd given up stealing it back. I laid down as calmly as I could despite the excited drum of my heart. I used the top fur as a blanket and my saddlebag as a pillow.

Ronan's warm flank pressed into me as he shifted closer. I made a sharp sound of displeasure but left it alone.

The closest camp was a hundred feet away, but someone might wander during the night, and it would be odd to see newlyweds sleeping apart.

I watched the clouds slowly meander across the sky, listening as the thunder and growls in the distance faded as the storm came to an end. Periodically, I darted glances at Ronan to check if he was awake.

The moment his face went slack with sleep, I made my move.

Slowly, silently, I wormed out from beneath the fur, careful not to disturb him.

His body dwarfed me as I sat beside it. He was shirtless with the fur thrown off. Thickly coiled muscles, honed from centuries of battle and war greeted me. Dark flames encircled the tattoo near his collarbone before spreading out over the delicious expanse of tanned flesh.

Sometimes I forgot how large and dangerous he was.

The dagger glinted in the firelight, beckoning me.

I snuck a glance at his face to confirm he was still sleeping, then I pushed to my knees, stretched over him, and wrapped my hand around the handle. I gave it a gentle tug, expecting it to come loose, but it didn't.

I pulled harder. Still nothing. I couldn't get a strong enough grip from this angle.

Sitting back, I chewed thoughtfully on my lip. How badly did I need this dagger?

Badly. If you don't practice soon, there's not going to be anything left by the time you return.

If I returned.

My lack of fighting abilities wouldn't matter if I was dead, but I didn't have it in me to give up. I had already lost so much. I couldn't lose this too.

On a deep breath, I braced myself, stretched a leg over his broad waist, and lightly sat over him. I could feel his girth beneath the leather and sticky heat flushed through me.

It felt distinctly wrong to get turned on by someone as they slept, but my body didn't care that he was sleeping, or that he had a mate. It simply *wanted*, and no amount of self-recrimination or shame could stop the madness.

Flexing my stomach to maintain my balance while touching as little of him as possible, I gripped the knife. The handle was ice cold, but I attributed it to the temperature.

I slowly pulled it out. It cleared the sheath, and I smiled in triumph.

Until the thing dissolved in my hand.

No, not dissolved—melted.

It was made of ice.

White teeth flashed in the dark. "Looking for this?"

A blade pressed against my throat, and I froze. The pressure was light but firm. One slip and I would bleed out.

Ronan rolled me beneath him and trapped my arms overhead.

A dark thrill coursed through me as my pulse hammered against the blade. Being held immobile by the press of his body, combined with the threat of the knife was intoxicating.

I felt a little drunk but managed to push past the cloud of lust to accuse, "You tricked me."

The bastard had made a decoy.

The jarred flame threw shadows across his face, but it was impossible to miss the depraved curve of his lips. He pressed me deeper into the furs, his hardness digging into my thigh.

"You don't sound too upset," he whispered, dragging the knife down the column of my throat. I held deathly still as my heart pounded away in my chest. His nose came to the soft curve of my neck and inhaled deeply. "You love this, don't you?"

The blade continued between my breasts, and I shivered against the metal as it grazed the bare skin between the shirt's laces. It was as cold and unfeeling as the snow beneath the furs, yet somehow set my skin ablaze.

He skillfully kept just enough pressure, so I felt the sharpness without it breaking the skin.

"Answer me." The knife paused over my sternum and dug a little deeper, causing a prickling of pain.

I shook my head, but my body betrayed me, arching into the blade as he dragged the flat end over a breast.

His dark chuckle was dripping in sin.

The knife sliced through my top. It split open, and cold air hit my breasts. Ronan's eyes glazed with need as they fixed on the pointed peaks.

I groaned as he dragged the blade over each nipple. The feel of the sharp metal against the sensitive tips had me gasping. I fought hard not to arch into it.

"Please." It was a moan and a plea wrapped in one.

"Tell me to stop," he murmured. "Tell me you don't want this."

"I can't," I panted.

I needed this, needed to be rid of this infuriating attraction.

But I also couldn't bring myself to fuck a mated man.

I peered hard, seeing his glamour. I couldn't fuck Ronan, but there was nothing wrong with fucking Rolan.

Rolan's face twisted savagely. He lapped at a hard peak

before teasing it with the blade. The contrast between the warmth of his tongue and the coldness of the knife sent a delicious shudder down my spine.

He kissed down my stomach while using his power to keep the blade's attention on my breasts. When his mouth reached my waistband, he wrenched down my pants, and stared hungrily at my center.

His head lowered and my body coiled tight in anticipation. I could feel the heat of his breath through my underwear.

I licked my lips, somehow managing to get out between strained breaths, "What happened . . . to being . . . a gentleman?"

His gaze met mine as a finger dragged down my cloth covered slit, tracing the damp outline before pushing it to the side.

"I lied."

His tongue speared my folds.

My body arched off the furs with a strangled cry. The blade flowed deftly with my movement without breaking contact, continuing its slow tortuous circles around my nipples as Rolan feasted on me.

He pushed a finger inside and turned his mouth on my clit, sucking hard on the swollen nub as his digit worked in slow, deep strokes. My body wound tighter and tighter, clenching around his finger as my back bowed.

"Rolan," I cried out, on the edge of exploding.

His finger and tongue vanished.

I bolted up to find Rolan crouched off to the side, fury lighting up his eyes.

"What are you doing?" I growled.

The knife moved to my throat. "Lay down."

I did.

He kneeled over me with a dark smile, dragging the tip

176

of the blade between my breasts. I shuddered. "Were you imagining someone else eating your sweet pussy, Wife?"

I said nothing.

The blade traced my stomach, pebbling my feverish skin.

My heart beat furiously, but I forced myself to remain still as the blade circled each hip before slipping down to my center. Rolan melted his blade and sent the material to the ends of the knife poised at my entrance, covering the sharp edges.

It brushed my clit and my whole body jerked. The flat end of the blade continued lightly strumming my clit, and my insides sang.

Without warning, it sank into me.

I choked on air. It felt cold and wrong, but strangely erotic. The blade slowly worked in and out of me, as Rolan stared with desperate, hungry eyes.

The blade paused and I whimpered.

"Look at me."

My eyes snapped to his. He'd dropped his glamour. Rolan was gone. I bit back a frustrated cry.

The knife eased in and out of me with excruciating slowness. "Who's fucking you?"

I lifted my hips, demanding he go faster.

The knife stopped.

I growled in aggravation.

"Who's fucking you?"

"You are," I snapped. The son of a bitch couldn't let me have this, could he? He just wanted to take and take until I had nothing left.

"And who am I?"

"Ronan," I hissed.

"Ronan who?"

"Ronan Taran," I said defeatedly.

"That's right. You want to fuck me. No one else. Do you understand?"

"No," I whispered. "I don't." I didn't understand why my body craved him, despite everything. It left me feeling empty and ashamed.

"Then allow me to show you."

The knife started moving again, pistoning in and out at a furious pace. Each time it returned, it hit deep, right where I needed.

He took himself out, wrapped his hand around his swollen, tattooed cock, and began pleasuring himself. A slick of wetness coated the knife. Dear Gods. That sight alone was enough to get me off.

He watched me take the knife with a feral expression, slowly stroking up and down his shaft.

The knife sunk deep, and I gasped, gripping the furs.

His teeth gnashed together as he pumped furiously into his fist. The thrusts of the blade grew faster and deeper, coiling me tighter . . . higher. Black spots dotted my vision.

"Oh, fuck."

"Say my name," he snarled.

I shook my head. He'd taken my fantasy away, but I could still pretend he was someone else. I could pretend he wasn't the man I was madly in love with, fated for another.

The blade slowed.

"Say it."

"Ronan," I moaned, anger and desperation riding my tone.

The blade resumed with quick strokes, and I shattered around it.

No calming high or relief came with my release. There was only shame and heartache.

Ronan groaned gutturally and then he was spilling his

seed into the snow. He tucked himself away and threw back on his glamour, but the damage was already done.

He tried to pull me against him, and I shoved him away.

"Don't touch me," I hissed.

Ronan stared, brows furrowing. "What's wrong? Did I hurt you?"

More than you'll ever know.

Avoid, avoid, avoid.

I tried to shove my emotions down deep, but they rioted in my chest, demanding recognition.

The back of my throat swelled. "That can't happen again," I choked out.

"Why?"

"*Why*?" I repeated, a tide of anger rising—at me, at him, at the situation.

"Because none of this is real. None of it matters. At the end of this, you'll be going home to her."

16

RONAN

A towering column of violet-blue flames bit into the night sky. The unusual color meant the magic in the air was exceptionally potent tonight. I could feel its wild energy crackling over my skin.

The fire shined brilliantly in the darkness with the bands of turquoise and lavender intertwining overhead. Silhouettes danced around the bonfire, their drunken revelry carrying up with the smoke.

Eternal flames speckled the horizon.

Dozens of hunters had stopped to partake in celebrating the first storm of the season. There wasn't room to spread far with the concentration of rocks and trees. We had neighbors within ten feet on either side.

I laid out all the materials for our tent—I'd picked up some more before we left the village to ensure there was room for Vera—and put it together for warmth and privacy.

After setting down two layers of furs, I spaced posts around them before driving them into the ground. The thick layer of ice made it a slow process.

I slanted Vera a look as I worked. Her hood was down, her hair lying in a soft braid. A fur sat beneath her as she leaned back on her hands, watching the celebration in the distance. She'd been quiet as we followed the candle all day.

We hadn't spoken since our coupling the night before. She'd regretted it, which was a shame because it was all I could think about.

The image of her taking the knife, her face twisted in ecstasy, was seared into my mind, and made me painfully hard every time I thought about it. I'd pleasured myself to the memory of it three more times after she'd gone to sleep.

When I made the decoy, I had promised myself I wasn't going to touch her, knowing it would only exacerbate the intense need to feel her skin on mine.

I was a fool to think it would make a difference. If anything, it had intensified the need. The tether in my chest buzzed desperately, begging and pleading to pull her against us.

It didn't understand that Vera had been imagining someone else while we were together, someone who wasn't a monster.

What I couldn't figure out was why Vera was so distraught over Kylah, given how she saw me.

Her reaction went far beyond anything I expected. Perhaps it was a matter of pride. Vera had more than anyone I knew, and for her to be set aside for another, must burn.

I felt Vera's eyes on me when I finished the first post.

"Why are halflings so despised?"

I flashed her a glance. Shadows danced over her troubled expression.

I disliked that I had to leave her alone, and she had an unpleasant experience in the village. If I had failed to uphold our agreement, Lucinda would have ensured everyone knew that I was responsible for Vera's 'death', and the king would have questions I couldn't answer.

"Are we speaking again?" I asked lightly.

She shrugged.

The rapping of my blade handle against the post filled the silence as I debated how best to respond. "It depends on who you ask."

"Rolan . . ."

I paused, quirking a brow. That's the name she had cried out last night.

She leaned back on her arms. "We need new names."

So, she'd been staring at my glamour, pretending she was fucking a soldier. Jealous fury tore through me, but I didn't let it show.

A visual sweep of the campgrounds confirmed no one was listening, but I kept my voice low as I resumed hammering. "Vera is fine. No one knows you here."

I supposed Rolan was fine as well. It was close enough to my name that we flirted with the line of lying without stepping over it.

I finished setting the remaining posts under her watchful stare, knowing she was waiting for an answer, and that none I could give would appease her.

Once the frame was set, I draped two overlapping furs on top. The fifth and remaining fur would serve as a blanket. The resulting structure was four feet high, about eight feet long, and two people wide.

"Well?"

"I liked it better when you were upset," I teased.

She glared.

I sighed, as I sat back, resting an arm on my knee.

Vera cared about halflings for the same reason she did children. She felt deeply about those she perceived as powerless, but there was much she didn't know or understand about fae and halfling history.

"The answer is long and complicated."

"And you don't trust me with it," she was quick to add.

I didn't want to broach that unpleasant topic. I twirled the stolen blade between my fingers before stopping and offering it to her.

Her brows raised. "But I didn't tell you about the Rogues."

A playful smile tugged at my lips. "You more than earned it."

She scowled, swiping it out of my hand, and I laughed lightly.

"Would you like to see the bonfire?"

We had some time to kill before bed.

She turned toward it, staring for a moment before facing me. "Why not? We've got nothing better to do."

I stood, offered my hand, and we made our way there together, cutting through the throng of tents.

We chose a spot on the outskirts, outside the dancing zone, but we could still feel the heat of the fire. The flames were giant, reaching fifteen feet. This close, I could pick out the individual flares of blue and violet.

I sat down and Vera sat stiffly on my right.

A pair of nearby hunters raised their hands in greeting. I returned the gesture.

"Act like you like me, Wife," I hissed out the side of my mouth, nudging Vera.

Reluctantly, she scooted closer, and I tucked her against me.

As I held her, watching the drunken foolery of the dancing hunters, a peaceful, contented hum buzzed in my chest, telling me all was right in the world.

My thumb smoothed over her ring and satisfaction thrummed through me. Vera would be furious to learn we didn't have to be married.

I saw an opportunity and I took it.

I'd lied by omission. Halflings as a whole never left the

safety of their Houses, but on a very rare occasion, some of mine did, to join the Saor.

Someone tripped over themselves as they danced around the fire and Vera laughed loudly. The sound bordered on hysteria. She clapped a hand over her mouth as nearby hunters shot us looks. "Sorry, that was weird."

I pulled her tighter against me, and we sat in silence, listening to the muffled conversations and drunken laughter filling the night.

As time wore on, I noticed Vera's pupils growing abnormally large. A giddy smile kept popping up on her face. She would squash it, only for it to return a minute later.

"Are you alright?"

She burst into laughter, then pinched her lips together, eyes wide. "I feel strange."

I gently removed her hood and felt her forehead. "You're not running a fever." I scanned her face. Her pupils were blown, and her cheeks were flushed. "Did you take something?"

This close, I could see flecks of silver glitter dusting her nose and cheeks. The glitter was unmistakable. I jerked back. "Did you touch a moon rose?"

"I bought one at the market."

She must have brought it out at the campsite.

"Its pollen contains a potent hallucinogen. Were you not warned?"

Her lips slanted into an adorably lopsided grin. "No."

A thread of sense broke through the haze and panicked eyes met mine. "I don't like this," she whispered. "I've never even had a drink."

The drug was slowly stealing her sense of control and Vera thrived on control. It made her feel safe and protected.

"Do you ... want me to ... pet your hair?"

"Pet my hair?" she parroted.

I rubbed the back of my neck. "Yes, you—you liked when I did that before."

She burst into giggles, but I could see she was shaking.

I moved behind her and pulled her into my chest. She tremored in my arms, and I stroked her hair. "Shhh. You're okay. I won't let anything happen to you."

Some of the flower dust fell from her cheeks onto my arms, igniting a fire under my skin, but I ignored it.

She met my gaze over her shoulder with a small smile. "I know."

My brows lifted lightly. "I thought you didn't trust me."

"I don't . . . with most things, but with my life? Absolutely."

Strangely, I felt the same. Vera might be willing to poison me and harm me herself, but she'd guard me fiercely against anyone who tried to do the same. It was a dysfunctional dynamic, but it was ours.

And that, that was something.

A smile softened my lips.

I held her tightly as her mind was steadily overtaken by the drug.

She twirled her fingers in front of her face, watching raptly at whatever she was witnessing. "Can you see this?" she whispered, glancing back.

"No."

Releasing a trill of laughter, she twisted around and climbed into my lap. Her arms wove around my neck, putting us face to face.

More dust sloughed off onto my chest, searing my skin.

There was only a small ring of violet left in her eyes. The rest was engulfed in black. I was fascinated by the color, by seeing her like this.

Vera was a loaded gun, always wound so tight, ready to

185

go off at the slightest provocation, but right now she was serene.

Something cold landed on my chest.

I glanced up to see a light snow starting, the snowflakes glistening in the firelight as they floated to the ground.

Vera tilted her head back and sucked in a deep breath of arctic air. Though her cheeks were ruddy, the tip of her nose bright red from the biting cold, a relaxed smile graced her lips.

A stray snowflake settled on her nose. She released a delighted laugh as it melted.

I froze.

"Do that again," I said roughly.

She peered at me sideways, frowning. "Do what?"

"Laugh."

She bit her lip, a mischievous look sneaking across her face. "I will for another knife."

"Done."

"No, I want ten thousand silvers."

"They're yours."

She paused, meeting my eyes. "Really?"

I nodded.

She tapped her lips. "No, no, I want a castle."

She was so adorable like this. I leaned forward with a roughish grin. "I'll build you one by hand."

Her head tipped back with bubbly laughter.

She shifted, putting all her weight on me as she threaded her fingers through my hair. I groaned low in my throat. This position—with her legs wrapped around my waist—left our most intimate parts touching. I don't think she noticed, but I was hyperaware.

She accidentally brushed over my member as she moved, and my breath expelled in a slow hiss.

Freezing, her eyes darted to mine, and a seductive smile

broke out. She rolled her hips once, twice. "You want to fuck me, don't you?" she whispered in a husky voice, like a mermer luring its victim into the sea.

I'd let her. I'd let her devour me if only to keep her eyes on me.

I laughed darkly, loving this side of her. I wouldn't touch her, not while she couldn't properly consent, but I would play along.

"I didn't know what a little seductress my wife was." I leaned forward, pressing my lips to the shell of her ear. "The things I want to do to you would frighten you."

"Like what?" she asked breathlessly.

I pinched a finger down her spine, one notch at a time. "I'd lick your tight little asshole." I nipped her ear. "Then I'd shove my cock inside."

She shuddered. "I've never been touched there. I want you to be the first."

"Fuck." I dropped my hands to the snow, squeezing it to keep from doing just that.

She climbed off my lap and started tugging me, glancing in the direction of the tent. She meant tonight. I cursed again and gently broke her grip. She wasn't in her right mind.

She pouted for all of five seconds before shrugging me off. "I feel like dancing."

Not in her right mind at all.

She popped to her feet and started swaying her hips in tune to inaudible music as she shook out her hair, letting it fall in soft waves. The dance was hypnotic. She moved with carnal abandon, the firelight lending it a sultry edge.

Vera wasn't just beautiful, she was a goddess.

Abruptly, she stopped and started dancing around the fire with the drunks. She twirled, yipping and laughing, her hair fanning out behind her. Her eyes were bright, her smile carefree. I'd never seen her so relaxed.

She deserved a night of fun, and I was going to ensure she had it.

"I'm hot," she complained as she circled back to me.

She started stripping off her clothes. The glamour would act as a camouflage, disguising her real body, but I didn't like the idea that these men would think they were seeing her naked.

I stopped her in the middle of her removing her shirt. "That's enough."

"*Please*," she begged. "I'm burning up."

I was a goddamn sucker when she used that word. That, combined with the distress in her voice had me relenting. "Fine, but the boots stay on."

I didn't want her running barefoot through the snow. She nodded and I released her.

She feverishly removed the rest of her clothes until she was naked. It was sweet fucking torture. She took off towards the campgrounds and I trailed closely behind.

Her streaking drew the attention of every male. I stared down each one, inciting the fear of the Gods into them, and they smartly averted their eyes.

Vera caught me glaring and burst into a fit of giggles. I found myself smiling despite the scalding pain slowly spreading over my skin.

She did two loops before circling back to our camp.

My scrying mirror was pulsing with urgency when we arrived. I picked it up and waved a hand over it. Kian's bloody face appeared.

"Stay right there," I warned her. "I'll only be a minute."

She nodded and started twirling around the eternal flame.

I stepped out of earshot. "What is it?"

"This halfling's crazy," Kian shouted as he ducked under an axe swing. A sharp thud followed as the blade sunk into wood.

"Keep your voice down," I warned. Vera would not be pleased to learn I had ordered Marty's death. I peeked over the mirror's frame to check on her and saw she was still spinning in circles, howling at the moon.

I fought a grin. It abruptly fell when I caught one of the neighbors watching her. He'd been at the bonfire with us a moment ago, and had already been warned.

I pulled out a dagger, flipping it over in my hand.

My attention flicked back to the mirror. Kian's face was replaced by the inside of a saloon. Images flickered by, blurred by his frantic movements.

A glimpse of an axe appeared in the mirror's upper right corner as it arced down, aimed at Kian's head.

The halfling was not as easy prey as he appeared, and there were more pressing concerns at the moment. "Abandon the mission," I told him. "I'll deal with it when I return."

I ended the connection and stalked over to the neighboring campsite. The fool was too busy watching my wife to see me coming. I kicked him to the ground and held him there as I stabbed his eye.

The blade sunk through. I stopped it just shy of hitting bone.

I wrenched the knife out, taking his eye with it. He screamed, writhing on the ground, cradling his face. I clapped a hand over his mouth. "Keep screaming and I'll take the other."

He went deathly still. I tapped his cheek and wiped the blade on his shirt before returning to camp.

For a second, I didn't see Vera anywhere and my heart dropped until I glimpsed a boot sticking out of the tent. Vera was fast asleep inside, snoring loudly. My lips twitched into a soft smile.

Careful not to disturb her, I unlaced each of her boots before gently removing them. Then I draped the unused fur over the flame to warm it up before bringing both inside. After gingerly laying the blanket over her, I crawled in behind her, and pulled her into my chest. She stirred briefly, twisting toward me.

"Shh. Go to sleep, my little wife."

A sad smile bloomed. "I wish I was really your wife," she whispered.

I froze.

A million questions raced to my tongue. I asked the one that had been protruding into my thoughts more every day. "Why didn't you tell me what the Eye showed you?" I asked softly.

She stretched her arms, yawning. "Because I . . ." her sleepy voice trailed off.

"Because what?" I gently shook her.

Her soft snores filled the night.

17

VERA

Sunlight filtered through my eyelids. I groaned, throwing an arm over my face.

My head was pounding, and my throat was stuffed with cobwebs. I had to peel my tongue off the roof of my mouth to swallow, but it didn't help much.

Blindly, I patted around for the water skin, and fur brushed over my nipples. My eyes flew open. What the . . .?

I sat up and a wave of dizziness crashed over me. I clutched my aching head as everything spun. What in the dark happened last night?

As soon as the spinning eased, I peeked under the fur. Why in the Gods was I naked?

Had Ronan and I . . .?

I tensed, gaze cutting to him. The other night was bad enough. I don't know what I'd do if I let it happen again.

He was sound asleep with his back to me—fully clothed. If only one of us was naked, it was unlikely we had been intimate. My shoulders sagged in relief.

But why was *I* naked?

I glanced around for my clothes and found them neatly folded at the edge of the tent.

The flap was parted thinly, allowing sunlight and cold air to spill in, but the tent was surprisingly warm from the jar set in the corner.

Huh. Ronan must have put it there.

I couldn't remember coming in here or taking off my clothes. In fact, I couldn't recall much of anything from last night.

My eyes landed on Ronan's saddlebag, and I reached forward, hunting through it. I found the waterskin and took a deep pull. The rush of cool liquid against my dry throat was bliss.

I replaced it and grabbed my clothes. There wasn't room to stand. I had to wiggle into them while sitting. Once I finished, my eyes drifted to Ronan.

He was fast asleep with the furs tucked up over his collarbone. Even in sleep, he maintained an intimidating air from his broad, sculpted shoulders to the twin graphite flames stretching over his thick neck. Every inch of him was intense.

I was surprised he was still asleep. Ronan always rose before me. I shook his shoulder. "It's well past sunrise. We should get going."

It took him a moment to stir. He tensed, bolting upright, then released a sharp breath when he saw it was me. "What time is it?"

I shrugged. "Late morning?"

He scrubbed a hand down his face. His cheeks had lost some color.

"Are you okay? You look a little pale."

"I'm fine," he grunted, throwing off the furs. He was wearing a dark tunic that matched his pants.

Surprise spread over my face. He'd been shirtless this whole trip.

"Are you sure?"

He cut me an annoyed look. "No one's watching, Wife. You don't have to pretend."

Guilt pinched my stomach. I hadn't been the most pleasant person on this trip, and while there was a good reason for that, I didn't have it in me to be angry anymore.

It wasn't like Ronan had found his mate to hurt me. If I was a better person, I would be happy for him. I couldn't be, but I didn't have to be an asshole either.

"Is that truce still on the table?"

His gaze narrowed in suspicion. "Why?"

"I'd like to accept."

Surprise flashed through his eyes, but it didn't wash away the distrust.

I offered my hand—a peace treaty and apology wrapped in one.

He watched it for a moment, like he was expecting it to bite him, before his long, calloused fingers wrapped around mine.

Warmth infused my belly the second our hands met. I lifted my gaze to his and saw an unreadable emotion churning in his eyes. His thumb gently brushed over my knuckle, and I felt myself leaning toward him, toward his lips.

I caught myself and jerked away, pulling my hand from his.

I turned away and started packing. I felt his stare burning into my back for a moment before he joined me.

Once the inside was all packed, we exited and broke down the tent.

Ronan put away the last of our things, and I freed the candle and lit it before releasing it into the air.

Our fellow campmates had already departed. As we passed the neighboring site, my gaze snagged a blood stain in the snow. "Was there a fight last night?"

"Something like that," Ronan murmured.

"What else happened?" I asked as we continued through the empty camp.

"You got high off the moon rose dust."

I froze as vague memories returned. I remembered Ronan telling me it could cause hallucinations, something the Anu fae had neglected to mention. If we stopped at the village on the way back, I'd make sure to give him a piece of my mind.

I also recalled pulling out the flower as Ronan set up the tent, wanting to know if it smelled as lovely as it looked.

Beyond that, I couldn't remember anything.

"And . . ." A tiny smile played on his lips. "You streaked through camp."

"I did not."

He grinned. "You did."

I wished I could remember. I resumed walking, and Ronan fell into step with me. "Anything else?"

My question held an expectant weight, making it clear I was asking if anything happened between us. Just because we didn't have sex, didn't mean I hadn't tried something else embarrassing.

"Nothing you need to worry about," he assured me, and I relaxed.

Once we made it past the outcrops of trees framing the camp, the space opened into a vast area of white. There was snow for miles in every direction with a path of footprints cutting through it.

We marched through the powdery dust for hours, guided by the candle. Toward late morning, I noticed Ronan wasn't keeping pace with me anymore.

I glanced back to see him clutching his stomach and he immediately dropped his hand. A sickly sheen coated his face.

"Rolan . . ."

"I'm fine."

He wasn't wearing his failin hide. I could see a small patch of blood blooming near his shoulder. I charged over and jerked his saddlebag aside. His entire shoulder was soaked through. "What the fuck," I said shrilly.

I tried to peel the fabric away to find the source, but he wouldn't let me, brushing my hand aside. "I said I'm fine."

My eyes snapped to his. "You're not fine."

"Leave it," he said softly, annoyance clear in his voice.

Frustration burned through me. "Stop being stubborn and let me help you."

"Tell me what happened with the Rogues."

My eyes ran over his face. His expression was obstinate and unyielding.

"Good gods," I muttered, blowing out a sharp breath. "You're not going to let that go, are you?"

"No more than you'll let this go."

I stared for a moment, grinding my teeth. I didn't want to tell him, but I also couldn't stand he was in pain. What was the harm if we'd be at our destination soon and would be parting ways? He couldn't use the information against me if we weren't together.

"Fine. I tell you, and you let me look at you."

"Deal."

I closed my eyes, inhaling deeply through my nostrils. *Just say it fast.*

"IlostmyfightingknowledgetotheEyeandcouldn'tdefend-myself."

"Come again?"

I drove out a harsh sigh. "I lost my fighting ability to the Eye and couldn't defend myself."

Ronan didn't respond for a long moment, and I peeked open an eye.

His face was stricken. "You—" his throat had to work several times before he could get his next words out "—You couldn't defend yourself . . .?"

I shook my head.

His face took on a sickly sheen. He got down on his knees, hands clasped together, and looked up at me with pleading eyes. "Please forgive me. If I'd known . . ."

He never would have mocked me. I grabbed him and tugged him up. "It's fine." It's not like he'd taken my knowledge.

He sent me a sharp glance as he got to his feet. "It's the farthest thing from fine."

"What do you want me to say?" I asked, shrugging.

"That you'll let me help you get your knowledge back."

He looked so sincere, I didn't have it in me to tell him that I'd already tried; that it was hopeless.

"Fine, now let me look at you."

He remained still as I stepped over to him, and carefully peeled away his shirt. His shoulder was covered in blisters leaking a dark viscous liquid that was leaving painful lesions in his skin. The smell alone made me want to vomit.

I inspected the rest of his chest. His skin was red and swollen, peppered with black blisters. It looked like he'd been burned and poisoned at the same time.

"What happened?" I asked, meeting his gaze.

"I . . . I am allergic to moon rose dust."

"Why didn't you say something?"

"You were frightened."

I frowned. Another memory flashed across my mind—of Ronan holding me and stroking my hair. He'd known what the dust would to do him and had put my comfort before his own.

A warm thread of tenderness snaked through my chest

196

despite my best effort to tamp it down. I couldn't afford to feel that way toward him.

"I need to get a better look."

He opened his mouth to argue, but smartly closed it at the glare I shot him. He'd looked after me. I was damn well going to look after him.

I hunted down a large rock that blocked most of the wind chill and laid out a fur in front of it. "Sit."

He did, propping against the rock.

I checked his forehead. He wasn't running a fever, and his face looked healthy compared to the rest of his body.

There was a toxic plant that grew in some areas of the Cold River called blisterweed. It was named after the nasty welts it left if you accidentally brushed against it. Ronan's blisters looked a lot like those welts. Cold had made mine feel better. I bet it would help him too.

First, I needed to wash and dress the boils. Some were leaking puss and looked like they might be infected.

"Take off your shirt."

He obeyed without argument.

I tore strips off a clean tunic with my teeth. I dabbed what remained of the shirt with water and began gently cleaning the worst of the boils.

"You don't have to do this," Ronan whispered.

My gaze drifted up to his as I worked. His voice held no agitation, but it was evident in his flexed jaw and the tight lines drawn around his eyes. I dismissed it as male ego, of not wanting to be seen as weak, but the longer I studied his face, I realized it wasn't agitation I was seeing, it was discomfort.

He was uncomfortable with being cared for, and if he was uncomfortable with it, it was likely because he had little experience being cared for.

I felt a twinge of pain in my chest.

"You can't always be the strong one."

He frowned, watching me with a quizzical expression like I was some strange creature he'd never encountered before.

"Last night," he started in a low voice. "Before you fell asleep, you were going to tell me why you didn't share what the Eye had shown you."

I said nothing for a stretch, focusing on cleaning his chest.

Once I finished, I used the dry end of the cloth to carefully soak up any excess moisture, and the strips to dress the wounds. I laid them in horizontal lines across his torso and pressed them as flush to the boils as possible.

"Lean forward."

He did, and I tied the ends off at his back.

Ronan watched me intently the whole time, waiting for an answer.

I sighed as he sat back. "It doesn't matter."

"Tell me."

"No."

His lids thinned, but I refused to cave. "Get some rest. You're in no condition to walk."

His eyes narrowed further. "This conversation isn't over."

It was as far as I was concerned, but I didn't want to argue with him while he was sick.

I tucked the candle away before fishing out the eternal flame and some food for us to nibble on. By the time I finished, Ronan had passed out.

The stubborn ass would have walked until he collapsed if it was up to him.

Grumbling under my breath, I tucked the jar under the fur to keep him warm and took a seat beside him. I chewed on some dried meat and bread as I peered up at the sky.

It was clear, with the ribbons of turquoise and lavender dancing through it.

Thick clouds suddenly formed overhead, eclipsing the sun. My brows slanted together as I shoved the last of the food in my mouth.

The sudden drop in light was eerie. Everything was cast in shades of gray. The wind picked up, growing into a howling cacophony. Static electricity saturated the air. It was so strong, it prickled the hair at the back of my neck.

I gently shook Ronan's shoulders. "Wake up. I think something's wrong."

He didn't stir.

I shook him harder, raising my voice. "Ronan, wake up!"

Still nothing.

Red lightning streaked across the sky to the south. Set against the dark clouds, it was beautiful and terrifying.

I counted to thirty, but no percussive boom followed. Where was the thunder? It was impossible to locate how far, or how close, the lightning was without it.

It grew impossibly darker. I pulled out the eternal flame from beneath the furs. It provided a small halo of light, but it didn't extend far.

Another red flash of lightning lit up the sky, much closer.

The first drops of rain fell. The water was so cold it burned like acid on impact. The pain only lasted for a split second before the liquid warmed against my skin, but the horribly cold rain kept coming, sizzling and stinging exposed flesh.

I kneeled at Ronan's side and hurriedly covered every inch of him with furs while intermittently tapping his cheeks to wake him up. He was out cold.

I stood and threw my hood over my head and fastened the laces to keep the fabric tightly against me.

More bolts of lightning cut across the sky, one right after the other.

A bolt flashed down and hit several yards away, exploding a frozen bush. Shards of ice flew everywhere. One impaled the ground near my boot.

Fuck. Fuck. Fuck. What do I do?

My gaze dashed around, searching for cover. There was nothing for miles. We were totally exposed to the storm rolling in from the south, but further north, I could make out clear skies. If we could just make it there, we'd be fine.

Biting my lip, I stared down at Ronan's unconscious form.

How was I going to get *him* there?

A solution hit me, and I sprang into action.

I used the tent poles and strips of my last tunic to haphazardly erect a sled. I rolled Ronan's mass onto it, elevating his head with our saddlebags, and covered as much of him as I could with two of the furs.

I shredded the third, knotted some of the pieces together to form a makeshift rope, and secured Ronan to the poles. With the leftovers, I made a second rope, tying one end to the sled and carrying the other over my shoulder.

I set off as another lightning bolt lit up the sky blood red, moving over the snow as quickly as I could, but Ronan's weight made it difficult to gain any speed.

Behind me, another thunderbolt hit, and then another.

Hundreds of lightning strikes hit the ground in rapid succession, spraying chunks of snow everywhere. I flinched at each one. The cumulative force of all the strikes created an ear-splitting sound ten times as loud as any banshee wail.

A flaming spear of black ice sailed overhead and hit the snow with a wet thunk. Another whizzed right past my ear, so close, I could feel its heat. My head swerved around to see a fiery trail behind me.

What the fuck is happening?

This looked nothing like the first storm.

A cluster of fire spears landed in my path at the same time I hit a deep patch of snow, and I tripped, skidding face first into the white dust. Dirt and slush filled my mouth. I spat them out and rushed to my feet, grabbing the rope.

More spears sunk into the ground ahead, forcing me to weave around.

Flames were everywhere, bathing the darkness in a fiery glow.

Smoke rose in thin, wiry columns between the curtain of frozen rain. Lightning split open the sky like a knife tearing through flesh, leaving a bloody streak before disappearing.

The air was thick with static and made it hard to breathe. At the halfway point, I was panting.

As I drew closer to the clear skies, they seemed to stretch farther out of reach. Had I misjudged the distance?

I peered behind me and saw the rock where we'd come from, then looked back to the area where the storm hadn't reached. The distance had increased. The storm was growing, swallowing up the safety I'd been depending on.

Fuck. I needed to outpace the storm.

I took off at a slow run, gritting my teeth as I dragged Ronan behind me. I pushed more strength into my legs, trying to go as fast as possible, but no matter how much speed I gained, the clear skies seemed farther and farther off.

A blinding bolt of electricity struck the ground between us, and I went flying into the air and smacked into the snow.

It felt like a gun had gone off in my ears. Excruciating pain spread through my head and jaw. Loud ringing echoed inside my skull, drowning out all other noise. I clutched my ears, curling into a fetal position, and screamed as blood seeped between my fingers.

"Vera," Ronan groaned weakly, reaching for me, but didn't have the strength to move.

Slowly I unfurled, grimacing in pain with every jarring pace forward, but managed to make my way over to him just as his eyes fluttered shut. I checked on him, breathing in relief when I saw he was unharmed. The sled was another story. It was scattered in charred pieces.

The storm was growing stronger in the distance and Ronan was already weakened. Who knew how much damage the storm's magic would do to him if we were caught in the middle of it. I had to get him out of here.

I stumbled to my feet and lost my balance a moment before I was able to steady myself. My head and ears were ringing. I couldn't see straight, but I forced myself to keep moving.

I tied the saddlebags to Ronan.

I grabbed his arms and began pulling him through the snow. It took several starts—I kept losing my balance and slipping into the snow—but eventually I fell into a rhythm and continued for miles as the storm steadily crawled toward us; fire and ice rained down from the skies like some sort of divine curse.

My muscles were cramping from the cold and my feet and hands were numb. I dragged Ronan for as long as I could until my muscles gave out. I collapsed to the ground. The small distance I'd managed to gain on the storm was lost.

Acid rain, fire spears, and deadly lightning converged on us.

I used the last of my energy to cover my body with his and prayed for the best.

18

RONAN

My first sensation was cold. Not the biting chill I had come to expect from the Wilds, but a bitter, bone-numbing freeze.

I tried to move, but my limbs felt impossibly heavy. I couldn't tell if it was from the temperature, or the lingering effects of the moon rose.

Slowly, painstakingly, I blinked away the layer of ice encrusting my eyelids. Darkness greeted me, broken up by faint glimmers of sunlight filtering through a canopy of snow and the dim light of the eternal flame. I could feel the latter wedged between me and the wall of snow on my left.

There was snow on my right as well, and at my feet and head. I was buried in it.

A weight shifted on my chest and my favorite scent tickled my nostrils.

"Vera," I croaked, my voice barely a whisper.

A soft groan answered. The weight moved again, more deliberately, and a cascade of silver hair tumbled into my field of vision.

Vera's face emerged from the snow. Her eyes fluttered

open, confusion clouding them before she realized where she was. Her gaze landed on me, and she exhaled sharply. "You're alive."

I mustered a weak smile. "I am."

I willed my arm to move. It responded sluggishly, but I was able to lift it and brush the snow off her face. Her cheeks felt like ice.

"You're freezing," I said in a hushed tone. "How long have we been here?"

She lifted a shoulder. "Hours."

"Hold on."

Gathering my strength, I banded one arm around her back and used the other to break through the snow above. Stinging air and sunlight rushed in.

The exertion left me breathless. The moon rose dust hadn't left my system yet. I collapsed back, clutching Vera.

My heavy breathing filled the silence. It was interrupted by voices floating through the freshly made holes.

"Have you . . . Any information that leads . . ."

I strained my ears but wasn't able to catch more before the voices died off and the sound of crunching snow filled my ears.

Several sets of boots passed overhead and stopped just on the boundary of where we lay.

From this angle, I gleaned they were large men, dressed in white furs. One of them raised a piece of paper. "Have you seen this woman? We're offering fifty-thousand silvers for any information that leads to her whereabouts."

My blood chilled. The Saor were here, and they were offering a hefty reward for Vera now.

Her wide eyes latched onto mine.

I pressed a finger to my lips.

Whoever they were speaking to must have shaken their

head because no response came before the Saor said, "If that changes, scry us."

The boots disappeared, and the footfalls gradually receded.

I waited another minute before I pushed through one of the holes I'd made, taking Vera with me. Cool sunlight and frigid air hit me the moment we cleared the snow.

I glanced back to see the Saor's forms off in the distance. "We have to move quickly," I whispered urgently, helping Vera to her feet. "They could come back any moment."

She nodded.

We raced to collect our belongings before throwing on our hoods.

I extended my hand. Vera clasped it easily, like we'd been holding hands our whole lives. There was none of the familiar frowning, or grumbling I'd grown accustomed to.

I glanced between our hands and her face, brows arched in surprise.

Her shoulder rose and fell in an unconcerned shrug. "We're married, aren't we?"

I hid a smile as we set off.

We crossed through what looked like a war zone.

Smoke drifted from black patches of snow. Ghastly ice sculptures erupted from the ground where lightning had struck a layer of sand. Huge snow drifts had exploded and laid in scattered pieces.

Hunters were scavenging for gems amidst the wreckage, which explained why the Saor were here.

"Was there a storm?" I asked.

"Yeah. A pretty bad one. It didn't look anything like the first storm we'd seen."

I stopped us. "What do you mean?"

"There were no magic-born. It was lightning, really cold rain, and fire spears."

I scrubbed my jaw. "That sounds like the storms House Belenus can conjure." But I didn't have a clue what they'd be doing out here. My brows furrowed as I took in the scene around us. We had to be miles from where I'd fallen unconscious. "How did we get here?"

Vera glanced up at me, then quickly looked away. "I dragged you," she said quietly.

House Belenus storms couldn't be outrun . . . And I found her on top of me. Had she . . .

No, she wouldn't . . .

"Did you shield me with your body?"

She rolled her shoulders, looking uncomfortable. "It's not a big deal. Okay? You were out cold."

I gave her a long, intense look. Why would she protect a monster?

As my eyes ran over her face, searching for an answer, she turned away.

"Why didn't you tell me what the Eye showed you?" I asked softly. I'd tried and failed to come up with an explanation.

An exasperated sound exploded from her lips—part sigh, part growl—before her head snapped back to me. "Drop it. We need to get out of here."

My eyes narrowed. I let it go for now, only because I'd said the same thing.

We resumed our brisk pace through the snow.

"Let's take out the candle," I suggested once we'd gotten a safe distance away. I shrugged her saddlebag off my shoulder and offered it to her.

"How are you feeling?" she asked as she accepted.

I flexed my arms and chest. The boils were gone, but I felt weaker than I would have liked.

"I'm on the mend, thanks to you."

She sent me an unreadable look before opening the bag

and digging through it. She frowned and upturned the bag. The contents landed in the snow with a dull crunch, and she squatted, shifting through them. Her search grew frenzied. Items were tossed over her shoulder in a bid to get them out of the way.

Panicked eyes met mine. "It's gone."

I kneeled and helped her search. It was just as she said. The candle was missing.

"Is it possible it was lost during the storm?" I asked.

"No, I made sure it was in here before I stopped." She growled in frustration, searching some more. "Everything else is here. Could the Saor have taken it?"

"I don't see why they would have taken it, but not you. Besides, we were hidden under the snow."

And we had looked thoroughly for everything before we departed.

She kicked the saddlebag away in agitation.

"What about the map?"

She bit her lip, and my eyes were drawn to it. A delicate fang pressed into her supple bottom lip. "I might have neglected to mention that it's useless."

I shot her a sharp glance, but I didn't have it in me to be upset that she had fibbed her way into my search, not when it meant we got more time together.

"Take it out. Let's have a look."

She retrieved it and laid it flatly over the snow. Her eyes traced over the page, studying it as her tongue adorably peeked out between her fangs. It was something that happened often when she concentrated.

The scroll appeared blank to me. I had no idea what she was seeing.

"It's useless." She shoved it aside with a huff.

I took it and straightened it in front of her. "You said the Nighters left this for you," I said patiently, ignoring the surge of anger at that information. When we found the door, I'd be the only one going through it. "There had to be a reason. Try again."

She stared for another minute before sitting back with a sigh. "I'm telling you, there's nothing there."

I peered at the eternal flame discarded in the snow, before glancing at the map. "I have an idea."

I grabbed the jar and lifted the map, holding the flame beneath. "During the War of the Gods, encoded messages were often sent with invisible ink that could only be revealed through heat."

She leaned forward, staring intently. "I see something! Move it a little to the right." Her gaze bobbed between the map and a section of mountain in the distance. She stabbed a finger. "There."

I couldn't tell where she was pointing, but if she was sure, that was enough for me.

I handed her the jar and map. "I'll follow you."

She started in that direction while I stayed behind to quickly pack up her belongings.

She held the jar below the map, guiding us through the snow. An hour in, as we neared the mountains, a blistering gale force slammed into us.

The strong gust swelled, creating an ominous howling as it swept over the icy wasteland. Snow started to fall in a thick sheet, covering our tracks. With every hard-earned step forward, our boots sank deep into the fine powder.

A whiteout was starting.

I had only experienced the extreme weather once before during the Dark Wars. The world had turned completely white, erasing all shadows and definitions my men and I could use to navigate. We hadn't been able to see the pack of beasts hunting us.

"What's happening?" Vera shouted.

"A whiteout!"

There was only three feet of distance between us, and we could hardly hear each other over the roar of the wind. The map flapped violently in her hand.

"Should we wait it out?"

"We have no shelter." I struggled to be heard. "It's safer to keep moving."

The sheet of snow thickened, reducing visibility to only a couple feet ahead. We trudged forward, pushing against the brutal wind for hours. Glimpses of looming rock walls appeared between the blanket of snow, surrounding us.

We'd reached the mountains.

They acted as a buffer against the extreme conditions, lessening the snow and increasing visibility.

We came upon the frozen lake sitting at their base. It extended for half a mile and sounded like a taut rope was bouncing up and down beneath the ice.

"Is it safe to cross?" Vera shouted.

"It should be. The ice is thick this time of year. Step where I step."

The wind howled across the frozen expanse, whipping up flurries of snow that stung our faces as we carefully navigated the treacherous stretch of ice. It creaked and groaned beneath our boots, a present reminder it was shifting and could break apart at any moment.

Each step was a calculated risk, my eyes scanning the ground for any signs of weakness. I kept pace with Vera, ensuring I was never more than a foot ahead in case the ice gave way.

The vast, icy landscape stretched out around us, a world of white and gray, cold and unforgiving.

As we reached the halfway point, I glanced at Vera. Her hood covered head was tilted down, focused on her measured steps across the ice.

We would be at the door soon. I had to know why she never disclosed the Eye's vision, and I was running out of time.

"Vera," I called out, my voice barely audible over the howling wind.

The hood slipped down as her head raised, revealing her wind-nipped nose and cheeks. "Yes?"

"Why didn't you tell me what the Eye showed you?"

Her lips flattened, annoyance sparking in her gaze. "This isn't the time."

"If not now, when?"

Her lips pinched together.

"I need to know," I said, frustration and desperation leaking into my tone. I couldn't live with the uncertainty. I had to know, regardless of the answer.

A guarded expression came over her face. Her head sliced right and left. "We need to focus on getting across safely."

My jaw tightened as my frustration boiled over.

In a moment of reckless resolve, I stepped off the safe path, my weight pressing onto a patch of ice that immediately began to crack beneath me.

"Ronan!" Vera shouted, eyes wide as she watched the web of fractures spreading out from my feet. "You're not fully healed yet! You could drown!"

The ice groaned ominously beneath me, but I remained determined. "Tell me, Vera."

Her eyes filled with panic and anger. "Stop being an idiot and get back here!"

"Not until you answer me."

She glowered, eyes spitting fire. "No, it doesn't matter."

The ice splintered further, and her gaze turned fearful. "Ronan, please," she said taking a cautious step toward me. "You're going to fall through."

"Why didn't you tell me what the Eye showed you?" I gritted out.

A large crack sounded. I felt the ice separating beneath me.

I didn't move.

"Because I wanted it to be me!"

I leaped off just as the ice caved. The broken chunks splashed into the icy water beneath.

My heart beat a feral rhythm against my chest as a cautious hope formed inside. I locked eyes with Vera. "Truly?"

Her teeth ground together. "Yes, and fuck you for making me say it."

"Why?"

Her breathing came in quick, angry breaths. "Because for the last goddamn time, none of this matters!"

She stalked off.

I remained where I was, watching her retreating form through the shroud of snow.

"What if it did?" I shouted over the wind. "What if it mattered very much?"

Vera crashed to a halt, her backbone snapping straight. She didn't turn around. "It can't. You have a mate."

"But what if it did?" I repeated.

She shot a careful, guarded glance over her shoulder. "I don't know."

"Yes, you do."

She scrutinized me for a long moment before resuming her stride.

I quickly caught up to her as we reached the end of the ice, between the start of the two crescent shaped mountains. She held the jar beneath the map and searched for where to go next.

"Vera . . ."

She ignored me.

Her brows pinched together before excitedly springing apart. "We're here."

She shot off before I could demand an answer.

I reluctantly followed as she raced for a rock face in the distance.

She climbed five feet in the air before urgently patting her hands over the stone. An opening revealed itself.

"Wait," I said sharply, stopping her from entering. "I'll go first."

I climbed up and crawled through the opening. Suddenly, the world tilted, and I fell.

I landed in sand. The air was warm. I glanced up and could see the blizzard raging above me through the shifting mass of magic I had fallen through. I was in a deep pocket that had been cut out of the mountain.

Vera's head peeked through the opening. "Do you see the door?"

"It's too dark to tell."

"I'll get the jar."

She disappeared and returned a moment later, climbing inside. I held out my arms, caught her, and set her on her feet. I wouldn't steal her triumph of finding the door, but as soon as we laid eyes on it, she was returning outside.

The jar's flame couldn't penetrate the darkness more than a few feet ahead, but we could see a small mountain of rocks separating us from the rest of the cavern.

We climbed to the top and stared into the vacuum below. It was deep, perhaps thirty feet.

"Ronan . . ." Distress clung to Vera's voice. "Look."

My gaze followed her finger.

Red glass and skulls lay shattered over the ground. I'd seen the pieces before, in a drawing in the archives, only they were intact, and melded together to form a large, arching entrance into the Spirit Lands.

The door was destroyed.

"Could it have been like this the whole time?" Vera whispered.

I peered at wisps of magic streaming off the door debris. If it had been destroyed long ago, the magic would have dissipated by now.

"No," I hissed, jaw clenching. "This is recent."

Anger rose inside me, sharp and acidic. My only chance to save my House was gone. My fingers clenched around a rock. I hurled it into the vacuum with a roar. It smashed into a piece of red glass and magic exploded through the space, knocking Vera and I back from our perch.

The walls started to tremble. Rocks and debris rained down from the ceiling.

"The pocket is collapsing. We have to go."

Wrapping an arm around her waist, I helped Vera over the rocks, shielding her body with mine. The rockfall created a great plume of dust that made it difficult to breathe.

I lifted Vera to the opening before pulling myself out. We clamored to the base of the mountain as the hole sucked down more stone. When all the shaking finally stopped, there was a large crater in the rock face.

We collapsed, clutching one another as we caught our breath, reeling over what had just happened.

"Ronan, who could have done that?" Vera whispered.

"I don't know."

I didn't know anything in that moment—how I was going to protect my people, how we were going to stop the Nighters', or how Vera felt about me. All I had were questions.

My scrying mirror pulsed urgently in my bag, vibrating

against where it was fixed to my chest. I withdrew it and waved a hand over the glass.

I was met with King Desmond's face.

Every muscle coiled tight. Discreetly, I squeezed Vera's arm, warning her to remain still and silent. The king couldn't see her from this angle, but it would only take a slight movement for that to change.

It took a monumental effort to keep the strain from my face as I met King Desmond's gaze.

"Do you have my godstone?" His voice was clipped.

Vera stiffened.

"I'm working on it," I growled.

"I thought you might say that." His smile was sharp enough to cut glass. "Do you remember our conversation in my dungeon?"

He'd informed me he was searching for a way to weaponize the beasts, to use their powers to kill his enemies. Many before him had died attempting to do so.

"Yes."

"I wanted you to be the first to know, I've accomplished my goal. You won't have to worry about your House starving to death if you fail me again. I'll have my beasts put your people out of their misery."

His face vanished.

The mirror slipped from my fingers and landed with a dull crunch in the snow. My heart hammered away, roaring in my ears.

My gaze found Vera's. Her dragon was the only thing that could save us now.

"Vera..."

The color drained from her face. She leaped to her feet and slowly backed away, furiously shaking her head. "I can't."

I matched her steps. "Vera, please," I implored. "You saw

his dungeon. It goes on for a mile. He has hundreds of beasts he's going to send after my people when he learns the godstone is lost. You can control them. You can stop him."

She stopped her retreat, gaze planting on mine. Her eyes were pinched and bleak.

"I'm sorry." A current of breath carried her words. "I'm so sorry, but I can't."

My steps faltered. "I don't understand . . . You released your dragon for me at the gallows. How is this any different?"

Her gaze dropped to the snow. Her silence grew and swelled like a throbbing wound. "I'm sorry," she repeated hoarsely.

"I don't want your apology. I want your help."

She stared at the ground for what felt like an eternity before her eyes finally found mine. Silent tears slipped down her cheeks.

Truth dawned, and with it a legion of pain. It was hard to breathe past the fist violently gripping my heart.

"You didn't free your dragon to save me. You did it for yourself."

Vera flinched as if she'd been struck but said nothing.

Agony punched through my chest.

I couldn't fathom why she wanted to be the woman in the Eye's vision, but I was certain it wasn't out of love.

It felt like the world had been dropped on top of me. It took everything in me to remain standing.

"Did you ever care for me?" I asked venomously. "Was any of it real?"

Pain twisted her features. She opened her mouth, but I raised a hand.

"Don't answer that." Some truths were better left in the dark.

I let black leak into my gaze. Ice settled into my bones,

freezing the pain. I breathed in relief at the blissful numbness. I couldn't feel a thing.

Heavy lines cut into the sides of her mouth at my transformation.

The faintest trace of anger rose. I let more black bleed into my gaze, smiling sharply. "Give me your ring. We're done here."

19

VERA

An aching lump formed in my throat as I pulled off the ring. Ronan took it, melted the metal into a useless pile, and discarded it.

He didn't look at me once.

He picked up his scrying mirror from where it'd fallen. I knew what was happening even before I heard Kian's voice. The conversation was brief. Only a handful of words were exchanged before the scry ended.

My heart pounded wildly in my chest.

It would take Kian ten minutes to arrive. I had ten minutes to make a decision.

Two parts raged inside me.

One wanted to spill my guts and tell Ronan everything; to desperately erase the heart-shattering look I'd seen just before he shifted. It was the look of a man who had been surviving on hope from day to day and just had it viciously taken.

The other didn't want to say a thing.

I'd told Ronan that nothing we were doing here mattered, and that hadn't changed, no matter how much I wished otherwise.

The lines may have blurred as we played out our fake marriage. I might have even let myself forget it was a ruse at times, but him asking me to use my dragon had brought me back to reality.

And reality was, Ronan and I could never work.

Best case scenario, if he had never found his mate, and we were free to be together, we had no trust. Even now, when I was breaking his heart by letting him think I hadn't freed my dragon to save him, I couldn't bring myself to tell him the truth.

Worst case—I'd often thought of the moment in the kitchen when I'd seen him with his mate. His eyes had been alight, and the hard angles of his face soft. He'd appeared wholly at peace in her arms.

That look was joy. Pure, radiant joy.

I made Ronan laugh, pissed him off, frustrated him, teased him, loved him, but not once had I made him happy, not like that.

The awful truth was, I never could.

His mate could give him the one thing I couldn't, and somehow that realization hurt more than anything else. Maybe because it reaffirmed something I had known all along. The same thing Ronan had said in Coldwater.

You're broken, Vera.

I hadn't thought twice about pouring the iron dust into his food. He had broken up with me, and my response had been to poison him. I'd regretted it moments later, but my instinct, that internal guiding force when my brain was incapable of decision, thought the best course of action to a hurtful conversation was to poison the man I was in love with.

Broken was too light a word for what I was.

Worst of all . . . If I was put in a similar situation, I'd do it again.

As long as I didn't trust Ronan, I'd keep hurting him, and that was the last thing I wanted. The great irony was I'd come on this journey to protect him from the Nighters, but *I* was the one he needed protection from.

I felt his black stare burning into the side of my face and pitched my gaze to meet it. There wasn't an ounce of emotion in his eyes' inky depths, but the lines around them were drawn tight.

Kian would be here any moment. It was time to decide.

I said nothing.

Kian arrived a minute later, and I caught an anguished flicker in Ronan's eyes before he tore them away.

"Vera will be serving as a halfling at House Taran," he said tonelessly.

If he was expecting a reaction, I didn't give one. With his manor burned down, and the danger with the king, House Taran was the only option. I was glamoured to look like a halfling. It would be suspicious for me to be anything else.

Kian took in our faces and announced bluntly, "Who died?"

"Leave it," Ronan said quietly. "Bring her to Finn. He'll get her settled like the others."

He set off into the snow without another word.

"Where are you going?" Kian called.

Ronan's head swung over his shoulder. "The godstone is lost. I have to find a way to protect our people." His condemning gaze briefly met mine before he stalked off.

Heavy guilt and shame spiraled through me. My entire purpose here was to protect Ronan and I couldn't, not the way he needed me to. The only thing I could do now was serve at House Taran and pray he found another way to protect his people.

Kian glanced at me, a question in his eyes.

"It's . . . complicated."

He made a sound somewhere between a snort and a laugh. "It always is with you two." His gaze dragged over me and his lips quirked.

"What?"

"Did you do something different with your hair?"

He knew I was glamoured. Ronan had mentioned it during their scry. I couldn't fathom where it came from, but a strangled laugh bubbled up my throat. "You're an idiot."

Dimples popped out with his grin. He opened his arms. "Come on, Trouble. You know the drill."

I shot Ronan's retreating form a parting glance.

With a long sigh, I handed Kian my saddlebag and stepped into his hold. We took off, and minutes later, we arrived at House Taran, and he returned it.

The castle was far more intimidating up close.

Walls made of a dark gray volcanic stone loomed like giants. Black steel spires rose from each of the four corners. A huge barbican guarded the entrance, and the entire structure was surrounded by a murky lake. The castle sat on a small, raised block of land, enveloped by a mile of water in every direction.

Cutting vertically through the moat was a narrow bridgeway connecting the castle to the land. It ended a quarter short of the barbican where a drawbridge took its place.

Kian had brought us to the bridgeway. The drawbridge was down, but the entrance gate under the barbican was shut.

Soft thwacks reverberated above. I craned my neck toward the battlements, shielding my eyes against the cool sun. Ten stony-faced archers had arrows aimed at us.

"Stand down," Kian told them.

"We don't take orders from the Lord's dog," one sneered.

A tense quiet descended, intermittently broken up by the lapping of the moat and waves crashing in the distance.

Rattling chains cut through the tension.

The gate started to rise. A figure appeared in the entryway, silhouetted against the sun. "Stand down."

After a moment of glaring, the soldiers' bows reluctantly dropped.

The figure stepped out of the shadow of the barbican, revealing a familiar, unwelcome face.

The mess of emotions I was battling over the way I'd left things with Ronan was shoved aside, replaced by bitter hatred for the fae in front of me. Icy cerulean eyes, silky black hair, and an arrogantly upturned nose—Finn was just as annoyingly good-looking as I remembered.

"Well, are you just going to stand there all day looking stupid, halfling, or are you going to come inside?"

The archers snickered.

Either Finn was this much of an asshole to everyone, which was likely, or Ronan had informed him of my arrival. Probably both.

A muscle pulsed in my jaw as I fought not to insult him with all the eyes on us. I was still at risk of discovery. The Saor were offering a pretty silver for my whereabouts, and if the king got wind I was alive, the consequences would be even worse. I couldn't give anyone watching a reason to stare too closely.

I settled for mouthing, 'I hoped you were dead.'

'Likewise.'

The drawbridge separated us. I stepped over the threshold, boldly meeting his gaze until I remembered there was a treachna in the moat. My eyes darted around for the beast. The moat's surface was calm, but that only meant it was lurking in wait.

What if Finn was luring me into a trap?

"The treachna's been fed," Kian murmured behind me. "You're safe."

I flashed him a small smile.

Finn tapped a foot. "I don't have all day."

I sent him a quick, scathing look. I was having a crap day and the last thing I needed was his corthshit.

Contempt overrode everything else. Locking gazes with him, I took the smallest steps possible. It took me a minute to go a foot.

Kian chuckled under his breath. "*Tra—bowl.*"

I sold my slow pace as fear, wide eyes dropping to the moat just enough to not arouse any suspicion that I was doing this solely to piss Finn off, but he knew, and that's what mattered.

As I continued my steady shuffle, Finn's face grew redder by the second.

"I think he might explode," Kian whispered.

I gagged on a laugh, glancing behind me. "Should I take pity on him?"

"Absolutely not."

This time I didn't hold back my laughter. I moved swifter, but not much. It was another ten minutes before I stepped off the drawbridge. Finn's eyes were bulging, his nostrils flared like a beast.

As soon as I was under the cover of the barbican, he snatched a hold of my arm and started dragging me while ordering for the bridge to be raised. Kian easily caught up, and with a hard twist, broke Finn's grip and nearly his wrist.

"No touching, Finney Boy." His light tone was at odds with his hard eyes.

Kian and Finn were the only ones I knew at House Taran, and while I didn't know Kian well, he felt like my only ally. I sent him a grateful smile and he winked.

Finn pinned him with a blistering stare. "I am Steward of this castle. You take orders from me."

He reached for me again and was met with a blade.

Kian clucked his tongue. "I work for Ronan and only Ronan, and he wants her looked after."

If impending murder was a fashionable look, Finn wore it well. "Then you can show this snake around," he snapped, turned on his heel, and stalked off.

Kian watched him disappear before turning to me. "You sure know how to get his panties in a twist."

"He's awful."

"He can be," he murmured. "But he's got a good reason to be."

I couldn't care less about Finn's reason. He'd been an asshole to me since the moment we met, and I would never forgive him for his cruelty in Coldwater. It burned even more that he'd been right.

"Well, guess it's just you and me, Trouble." Kian flashed a dimpled grin. "Shall we?" He gestured to the archway.

I jerked my head, and together, we crossed under it.

There was another fortified area separating the barbican from the castle. It formed a square, running along the periphery of the main structure, putting two layers of walls between the innermost part of House Taran and the outside.

In between the two walls were several nondescript buildings. Based on the group of soldiers lingering outside, I'd say they were barracks.

Kian took a sharp left and led me around the back to a row of stalls. "Thought you'd want to check on her."

A wide smile split my face.

I burst into a run, glancing inside each stall as I passed. "Ness, where are you girl?"

Loud neighing sounded and I rushed toward it.

She looked tiny inside the stall built for a horse twice

her size. I threw my arms around her and nuzzled her neck. "Gods, I missed you girl."

I squeezed her tight for a long moment before releasing her and checking her over. There were no new scars or markings. I exhaled in relief. Either Kian had gotten to her before the Rogues could do any damage, or Duke had kept his word.

Her coat was shiny and thoroughly brushed, and her stall was clean and dry, piled with hay. "They're taking good care of you here, huh?"

She pushed her head into my hand, demanding more pets. I laughed and obliged. I stayed with her for several minutes, catching her up on what happened while we were separated before returning to Kian.

"Thank you," I said sincerely.

He grinned. "You're very welcome."

We circled back to the front and walked under an archway that led into a sprawling courtyard.

Halflings were bustling about between buildings. At least a dozen soldiers were sparring, going at each other with swords. Others were slicing into wooden practice posts lining one of the walls.

"Why is no one looking at us?" I whispered. I expected at least a few curious stares, but no one was paying us any attention.

Kian leaned close. "They see new halflings come in every month or so. Ronan spares mortals, glamours them, and sends them to Finn to take credit for saving them from the Saor. You're nothing special."

"Oh." My brows pinched. "Wait, why does Finn take the credit?"

Kian shrugged. "You'd have to ask Ronan."

We weren't exactly on speaking terms.

It's better this way.

It certainly didn't *feel* better.

Ronan had mentioned the Saor were defectors from his House. I hadn't thought to ask more at the time, but now my curiosity was peaked.

It *was* nice not to be gawked at for once.

Bordering the courtyard was a high wall connected by four towers, one on each corner like outside, but these were made of stone. There were a handful of structures flush against the walls, leaving an open space.

At its center was a gargantuan tree, like the one that had burned me. My heart started to pound the closer we got. It felt like I'd taken a shot of energy.

"What kind of tree is that?" I asked.

"It's a draoi tree."

I peered up at it. The highest branches stood well above the castle walls. "Like the stone?"

He nodded. "They come from these trees." He unsheathed a dagger and dug into the trunk to reveal part of its blue, crystalline center.

"Huh. Interesting." That sulfuric scent hit me, and I wrinkled my nose, backing up. "Why do they smell like that?"

"That's magic."

Frowning, my gaze cast to the pink shimmer coalescing around the tree, to the cold gas that had turned my talons into normal fingers. "That's *magic?* How is that even possible?"

Kian sheathed his knife, and the small cut he'd made in the trunk closed. "Draoi trees are as ancient as the Gods. They feed off magic. When a Taranis fae dies, we bury them here. The tree sucks the magic from the bones and recycles it."

"These trees *eat* people?" I leaped back another step.

He shot me an amused glance. "When a fae dies, their

soul leaves their body, but not their magic. Every Taranis fae that has passed has been buried beneath its roots."

"That's . . . disturbing."

A shrug. "Maybe, but this is the epicenter of House Taran's strength. The cumulative magic of all our ancestors is being endlessly recycled by this tree. Our magic is strongest behind these walls."

I could feel that power now, pumping through my blood. It was invigorating.

We stepped away and I migrated over to one of the fires scattered around the courtyard. The air sweeping in from the sea was icy, but the fires helped to dissipate some of the chill.

Kian followed and proceeded to give me the world's worst tour.

He flung his hand at the largest structure in the courtyard. "That's where we all get drunk." He pointed at a tower. "That's where Finn strangles animals for fun." His hand moved toward another tower. "That's where Ronan broods. And finally." He faced the last tower. "That's where the lovely Kylah sleeps," he finished, looking proud of himself.

Kylah . . . Ronan's mate. My insides tightened.

If I thought I'd be here long, I would have asked for a proper tour, but as it stood, I didn't need one.

"Annnnd," he slung an arm over my shoulder, facing me toward a long, squat building. "That's where the halflings make babies."

"I take it that's where I'm staying?"

"Yep, let's find you a room."

We entered the building to a long stretch of doors. Kian started kicking them in one by one.

The first three were unoccupied but didn't have whatever he was looking for. Someone screamed in the fourth. A shoe was thrown out of the fifth.

"You could knock you know," I said, holding in a laugh as he rubbed his temple.

He smirked. "Where's the fun in that?"

I was learning Kian was an agent of chaos. He loved starting it, or stoking it, didn't matter.

He continued kicking in doors, and in the eleventh one, found what he was looking for. "This one's empty," he called.

I'd stayed a little behind to avoid flying objects.

I strode down the hall and stepped inside. It was twice the size of my room at the Rogue compound, and simply furnished. There was a bed pushed under a window, a nightstand to the left of it with a candle set on top. Sitting in front of the bed was a chest and a cata-cornered chair.

It was warm and had a cozy feel to it, but it was missing one thing. "There's no fireplace," I noted.

I would need to start taking gold dust again, and my supply had been lost during the Rogue attack. I had plenty of gold, but no way to melt it.

"Only the towers have them," Kian informed me.

Well, that was a problem. "Can we go sit in front of one? I just spent the last week freezing my ass off." I knew it was a weird request, but there was no half-truth I could make up for needing to melt a bunch of gold nuggets to keep my bloodthirsty dragon quiet.

"It's better if you stay in this room. You pissed Finn off earlier, and he's not the forgiving type. Give him some time to cool down."

Pffttt. I wasn't going to tiptoe around Finn's mood swings. Guess I was sneaking out tonight.

I shrugged like it wasn't a problem and took a seat on the bed. "So, what's this about me being rescued from the Saor?"

"One second." Kian closed the door and propped a

227

shoulder against the wall, crossing his arms. The fabric pulled taut across his chest, displaying his nipple piercings.

He caught me staring and wagged his brows. "You like? I've got more." He poked out his tongue. A small ball pierced the flesh. He started undoing his pant laces next.

I delayed him with a hand. "No one wants to see that."

He made a sound of disbelief. "The ladies love my pierced co—"

"Kian."

He released a slow, deep laugh. "Fine. The Saor. Finn came up with the idea. Halflings can't change House allegiances like fae. Ronan couldn't bring any home without raising some eyebrows."

"You were in The Wilds," he continued. "You know the environment. If anyone asks about your time with the Saor, just describe your time there."

"Sounds easy enough."

He inclined his head. "Well, unfortunately, this is where I leave you. I've got some errands to run."

"You mean biding to do."

He laughed. "That too. I'll be by to bring you some dinner. Stay out of trouble until then."

I gave him a smart-ass salute that had him chuckling as he left the room.

True to his word, Kian brought me dinner in the evening. It was a simple plate of meat and vegetables, but after a week of dried food, the warm meal was sublime.

He departed, and I had to wait until the golden light filtering through the window dimmed before I snuck out. The gold dust would take a couple of hours to make. I was cutting it close, but I didn't have another option.

I watched through my window as the courtyard steadily emptied of halflings and soldiers.

Once I heard the last door shut in my building, I crept out of my room and down the hallway to outside.

As I slipped between the buildings, I wished Kian had given me a better tour. I assumed 'This is where everyone gets drunk' building meant there was a kitchen inside, and a kitchen would have a fireplace.

After glancing around the corner to check it was clear, I peeled away and rushed forward. I was about halfway there when someone stepped into my path.

Icy blue eyes sparking with contempt glowed in the firelight.

Finn. Godsdamnit.

The retreating sunlight hit the top of the courtyard walls, and the dragon's eyes flashed open. Panic wrapped around my throat.

"I can't explain it right now, but something bad is going to happen if I don't get into the kitchen," I said urgently, playing to his conscience.

I should have known better than to think he had one.

"In that case." Finn's lips curled into a vengeful smirk. "You will return to your room immediately and not come out until sunrise."

I was about to tell him right where he could stick that command when a soothing wave of magic crashed over me like honey dripping down a sore throat. On its own accord, my body did an about-face and started marching.

Eyes wide, I tried to stop, but my legs weren't responding. I glanced over my shoulder as my feet continued without my permission and was met with Finn's gloating smile.

I knew, I just knew, this motherfucker had used his powers on me.

I viciously fought myself the whole way back to staff

quarters, but no matter what I did, I couldn't overcome his magic.

As soon as I crossed the threshold of my room, my control returned, and I tried to lunge out the door . . . Only to fall flat on my face. My boots were cemented to the floor.

Gritting my teeth, I put all my energy into lifting my legs, but they were stuck.

Hissing, spitting mad, I pushed myself off the floor. The moment I stepped away from the door, my feet unglued themselves, only to root right back when I moved toward it.

I was trapped.

The last tendrils of light filtering in disappeared, and the dragon leaped for the surface.

20

RONAN

Snow and ice raged around me, but I was numb. I was numb to everything, but the raw pain clawing at my chest.

Not even my battle-mode could alleviate it.

I'd made peace with the knowledge that Vera could never love me the way I loved her but had taken solace in the fact that she cared for me in her own way. If she didn't, she wouldn't have freed her dragon to save me at the gallows.

It was the one thing I had clung to, the one thing that had gotten me through the long nights; the one thing that made me certain our time in the Mortal Lands hadn't been a lie.

And when Vera revealed she hadn't shared the Eye's vision because she wanted it to be her, I'd let my guard down. I'd let myself hope that Vera might actually love me, but none of it had been real.

She hadn't freed her dragon for me. If I had been the only one hanging, Vera would have let me perish. Saving me was a matter of convenience. *My life* was a matter of convenience. The realization cut more viciously than any blade.

I felt like a fucking fool.

I was a fool.

I hunched against the brutal wind, failin hide gripped tightly in my fists, and shoved away the image of her face crumpling when I demanded the ring back. She wasn't going to play with my emotions anymore.

My boots struggled in the tall snow drifts. The roar of the wind buffeted my ears, drowning out all noise. A blanket of snow chased away all shadow and definition, cloaking everything in white. I pressed blindly forward, guided by memory.

I'd traveled north, following the valley between the crescent mountains. The stone had protected me from the worst of the storm but left me to its mercy when the looming walls had given way to an endless canvas of white.

At midday, I reached the Crevasse Plains. The earth was broken up by hundreds of fissures splitting the ground.

I stopped at the edge. In the current conditions, only half of the cracks were visible, but I knew they extended for miles in every direction.

Each crack represented a deadly drop. Crevasses could be anywhere from ten to hundreds of feet deep. On a clear day, one could navigate the plains with extreme care, and perhaps survive, but not during a whiteout.

There was no safe way to cross, and the magic in the air was too thin to use my powers. However, the longer I waited, the more cracks would be covered by the snow.

I had no choice but to plunge forward, one cautious step at a time.

Some of the crevasses were hairline fractures while others were gorges. I was stepping, then leaping. It felt like walking a tightrope over a bottomless canyon.

One boot slipped off the edge of a crevasse, and I almost

went tumbling into the dark, but righted myself in time, and continued on.

It took hours to reach the end. Ice had formed around my brows and hair. My skin was numb, and my fingertips were turning an unsettling purple.

On the other side, a pillar of smoke rose from a copse of snow-laden trees. Between the trunks and snow drifts, glimpses of a log hut were visible. The solitary structure was the only refuge amidst miles of stark wilderness.

As I trudged closer, more details came into view. Frozen animal trappings hung from the slanted roof among the icicles. Furniture parts poked out from beneath snow piles lining the front yard. A lone piece of wood with an axe buried in the head sat on a chopping block.

I reached the trees and breathed in relief as they blocked the worst of the storm.

A wall of snow partially covered the door. The parts that could be seen were iced over. I banged on the wood and sent piles of snow sloughing off the roof. I waited, listening for any movement inside.

It was dead quiet.

I hiked over to a window and brushed aside the snow to peer through the frosted glass. A low fire crackled in a small stone hearth. It was the only sign of life inside. The owner wasn't home, but the fire told me he would be back soon.

I returned to the step and kicked the piles of snow loose before opening the door. The hinges were frozen. It groaned, then opened sharply.

I kicked it shut behind me as warm air blasted my frozen skin. I was so cold that the heat stung, but my body quickly adjusted, and the pain shifted into relief. Rubbing my frost-bitten hands together, I made for the fire.

I crouched in front of it, stretching out my palms. The tips of my fingers were black. The nerve endings were dead.

I couldn't feel a thing despite how close they were to the flames.

As warmth flowed into my bones, the ice coating my face and hair melted. The color steadily returned to my fingers as my healing kicked in, and I was able to unfurl them.

Peering over my shoulder, I surveyed the space. My old friend had lived here for five centuries, but I'd never been invited to visit.

Dark pelts lined the floor. Rustic, handmade furniture painted black was scattered over the space. Skulls and antlers decorated the walls. An artic rabbit hung next to the fire along with a smattering of herbs.

I retreated to the window to watch for my host's return. Half an hour later, a dark form appeared between the trees, an animal carcass slung over their shoulder.

I backed away and took up position in the center of the room.

The door opened, letting in a blast of icy air. A sharp pang hit my chest as I laid eyes on the man I once considered a brother.

Standing at my height, Hunt wore his signature all-black look from the dark cap to the fur vest and pants. He'd put on more muscle and his jet-black hair had grown to his shoulders since I'd last seen him. The beard was new. It was as wild and unruly as his cold copper eyes.

A red lig root dangled between his lips. The end glowed cherry red in the faint light from the fire. Lig root was similar to the mortals' tobacco but provided a calming high.

He ducked inside, shaking off the snow, and shuffled the wild fox off his shoulder.

"Hunt."

His full name was Huntley, but there was only one person allowed to call him that, and she had passed long before her time.

His head snapped up. The moment his eyes landed on me, they ignited with hate. He stalked over until he was in my space.

He took a deep drag of his lig root, blowing the smoke in my face. "You've got some big fucking balls coming here."

"I just want to talk."

He rubbed a tattooed thumb over his lips, appraising me. "Talk, huh?"

"Yes."

He turned away. His hand curled around a chair solid enough to support the weight of a giant. "Yeah, let's talk."

He lifted the chair and hurled it at me.

I only had a moment to react and threw my arms up in defense. The chair crashed into me and knocked me to the ground. Hunt lunged on top of me and rained his fists down.

His knuckles crashed repeatedly into my face before I managed to get my arms up. I angled one over my face to absorb the hits and slammed the other into his ribs, shattering bone. He froze for a second, and I used the time to free a leg and smash it into his gut.

He went flying back and smacked into the wall.

He was on his feet in seconds. So was I.

We collided.

We rained blows down on one another, rolling and grappling over the ground. We crashed into furniture and walls, shattering everything in our path.

I realized too late he'd maneuvered us near the fireplace.

He got behind me, wrestled me into a headlock, and shoved my head into the flames.

I grunted sharply as scalding heat consumed my hair and skin. Stone bit into my palms as I attempted to push back, but Hunt used his body weight to keep me pinned.

My hand slapped out and wrapped around a fire poker. I reached behind me and stabbed him with it.

He reared back with a grunt, his weight disappearing.

I twisted to see the metal sticking out either side of his skull. He wrenched it out in one sharp pull, sending up a spray of blood, and flung it aside. He staggered sideways and collapsed in a chair.

I caught my breath, waiting for the scalding pain over my head and face to vanish before heaving to my feet.

The hut was a mess. A lone antler on the wall remained unscathed. The rest of the decor lay in pieces on the ground. Holes and cracks littered the walls. Some of the furniture had survived, but not much. I grabbed a chair and dragged it over to Hunt, sitting across from him.

"I'll pay for the damages."

He fished out a new lig root, lighting it with a nearby candle. He took a few puffs, glaring. "I don't want your fucking money. Get out."

"Hunt . . ."

Shadows coalesced around him. Black wisps danced between his fingertips. I'd been on the receiving end of his death magic once. I wasn't keen on experiencing it again.

"I need your help."

A low mocking laugh rumbled up from his throat. "You've gotta be *desperate*." He cocked his head to the side. "Give me one good reason."

"House Taran is in danger."

He eyed me, rolling the lig root around his lips. The shadows dissipated. "What have you done this time?"

His question struck me like a blow, but I was quick to cover it. "King Desmond wants the godstone."

He quietly puffed on the root before leaning back, tossing his arm over the chair. "So, give it to him."

"I can't. It's hidden in the Spirit Lands. King Desmond will bring war to House Taran when I fail to deliver it in time."

Smoke streamed out of his nostrils before he popped the lig root out of his mouth. "And what the fuck am I supposed to do about that?"

"House Belenus and House Brigid will join him." Hunt was estranged from his father, Lord Brigid, but he was his only son. If anyone could persuade him, he could. "I need you to speak to your father, dissuade him from siding with House Dagda."

Lord Brigid was well respected by the other Houses. If he changed allegiances, House Belenus would follow.

His eyes sharpened. "And why would I do that? Sounds like you're getting exactly what you deserve."

I released a grunted breath, spearing my hands through my hair. "House Taran was your home once. Hers too."

My eyes fell to the name tattooed across his knuckles, to the only person Hunt had ever loved. Moira was born and raised at House Taran.

He cracked his neck and extinguished the lig root on the chair arm. "That's fucking low, even for you."

"You said it yourself, I'm desperate."

He growled, shoved out of the chair, and stalked around the hut. The space filled with banging and dull thuds as he rifled through the debris. He wrenched a sack out from beneath a broken table and began packing.

He faced me once he finished. "Let's go before I change my mind."

My brows pinched. "Go where?"

I didn't expect he would leave with me.

"House Taran before you fuck up anymore."

I rose, hiding my surprise, and threw a sharp glance at his unruly beard.

"What?"

"You might want to shave that animal on your face first."

21

VERA

A knock startled me awake. Opening bleary, bloodshot eyes, I glared at the door, before yanking a pillow over my head.

I'd *just* gotten to sleep.

There were shooting pains all over my body. It felt like I'd been run over by a train.

The dragon and I had spent the night playing a terrifying game of tug of war. It would gain control, and we would partially shift, before I managed to wrangle my body back in time. This went on and on. I'd clung to my control by a thread the whole time.

I was spent. I barely had the energy to get out of bed, let alone answer the door. Whatever it was could wait.

The knock came again, more urgent. "New girl, you need to wake up. The Head of House is on his way."

I stayed silent, pretending to be asleep.

"He'll make us do extra chores if anyone is late," she hissed.

Having Finn as an enemy was bad enough. The bastard's powers involved compulsion of some sort, which meant he could make me do whatever he wanted, whenever he wanted. It was a terrifying prospect.

I didn't need anyone else gunning for me.

Groaning, I threw off the covers. "One second."

The stone floor felt like ice under my feet. There really should be fireplaces in these rooms. I'd lodge a complaint with the man in charge as soon as he was speaking to me again, which would likely be never.

He would if you told him what was happening, like with your fighting skills.

This is different.

My dragon was the source of my greatest vulnerability and shame. I'd already been vulnerable with Ronan about it once, and he'd used it to strike a vicious blow, one I still hadn't recovered from.

I wouldn't survive a second.

Blowing hot air into my hands, I padded over to the door and froze midway seeing the collection of feathers clinging to my clothes. Peering back, I saw the mattress was shredded. *Fucking dragon.* I had to get my hands on some gold dust today.

"New girl," the stranger whispered. "You need to hurry."

"Almost ready."

I rushed to the bed and stuffed all the feathers under the furs, out of sight, before throwing on a clean pair of clothes and opening the door.

The female was there. She had smooth brown eyes and a freckled nose and cheeks and wore a white bonnet and blouse paired with red skirts. A few loose ringlets of silver hair peeked out beneath the hairpiece.

Her lips were pinched in irritation until she took in my face. "Rough night?"

"You could say that."

She dropped her voice, whispering, "It's a lot to take in at first, but you get used to it."

I peered at her more closely and caught the faint shimmer of glamour over her face. She was one of the mortals Ronan had spared.

She stuck out her hand. "Gisa."

Some of the mortals here might recognize me by my talons and eyes, but none of them would know my name.

I clasped her hand, a tired smile quirking my lips. "Vera."

There was a commotion at the end of the hall and Gisa's back shot straight. "Milton's here. Quick, stand there." She pointed to my door before moving in front of her own.

Everyone was lined up in the hall. There were close to a hundred halflings in total. At least a quarter of them were glamoured mortals. My eyes stopped on a woman and young boy and widened.

It was the mother and son I'd tried to save outside the train.

Ronan *had* spared them.

"What's going on?" I whispered.

"Morning inspections."

A short, bowl-shaped halfling appeared. He wore a soft red vest over a silver dress shirt and dark breeches. His thinning hair was slicked into a short ponytail, and his thick boots were polished to a shine.

He halted in front of the first set of doors and the staff in front of them, running an appraising eye over their uniforms.

This had to be Milton. He was the reason I had to get out of bed at the butt crack of dawn.

He turned up his long, pointed nose at the first female. "I shouldn't be able to see any of your hair beneath that bonnet. Tuck it in," he ordered in a nasally voice.

Gisa rushed to push her loose hair out of sight.

He moved to the man next to her. "I should be able to see my face in those shoes," he said snidely.

Continuing down the hall, Milton found fault with everyone. Men's shirts weren't tucked into his standard; women's skirts had too many wrinkles. He even commented that someone's shoes weren't tied properly. Apparently, there was a wrong way to tie shoes.

With a long, disappointed sigh, Milton addressed the group. "When you leave these quarters, you are not only representing House Taran, you are representing me. My family has served this House for seven generations and built a reputation for excellence. I will not have you tarnishing our good name with your—" his eyes, eyes much too small for his broad face, ran over the wrinkled shirt of the closest halfling "—Unkempt appearances."

This is what I'd been woken up for?

I'd never wanted to punch someone in the mouth so badly.

He waved his hands, shooing everyone away like chickens. "Back to your rooms. You have five minutes to make yourselves presentable."

What was he going to do if they didn't? Beat them over the head with his impeccable manners?

He'd have to be able to reach their heads first.

Someone gasped.

Fuck. I'd said it out loud.

Milton's head whipped around. His pale, puffy cheeks were tinged red. "*Excuse me*?"

He strode over, his shoes clipping the ground. Nervous glances darted my way and I cursed under my breath. I was supposed to blend in, not draw attention.

Folding his hands behind his back, he tipped up his chin and tried to affect a menacing air as he glowered up at me, but I couldn't take him seriously when he was half my size.

"I am the Head of House. They listen because I hold each of their fates in my hand. One word from me and they will be outside these gates, begging for work."

I remained quiet as his flat stare skipped over my rumpled clothes, looking entirely unimpressed. "What's your name?"

"Vera," I muttered.

"Vera, you are new here so I will forgive your indiscretion. The lot of you Saor cannot help your boorish upbringing." He dragged his disdain filled gaze over me once more before turning away.

"The rest of you are dismissed," he called. "Make yourselves presentable and report to your stations, and if I hear any complaints about the quality of your work, your wages will suffer."

Everyone jumped at his command, adjusting their uniforms before they scurried away.

He snapped his fingers at me like a dog. "Come along."

My left eye twitched.

You're doing this for Ronan.

I couldn't use my dragon, but at the very least, I could stay out of trouble.

I blew out a breath and trudged after Milton.

"I expect the highest work ethic from the halflings under my command. I've no patience for slouches or idlers. You earn the same as everyone else so you will do the same amount of work. Are we clear?" Milton asked over his shoulder.

"Yes," I gritted out.

He stopped and rounded on me. "Yes, what?"

I stared.

Milton sighed as if the weight of the entire Lands sat on his shoulders. "The Steward ought to pay me double for putting up with you people. No head for manners or respect." He gestured toward himself. "Sir. You will address me as Sir."

He wasn't serious . . .

Threading his hands behind his back, he rose up and down on his toes, waiting.

He was.

The murderous eye tick started again. My fangs ground together. *Deep breath. We can do this.*

"Yes . . . Sir." The last word tasted like corth acid on my tongue.

He gave an approving nod, then continued down the hall, and led me to a linen closet stocked with uniforms and handed me three pairs. "That is your work uniform. I expect you to be waiting outside your door at five am sharp every morning looking presentable. Understand?"

"Yes—Sir."

Gods, that would take some getting used to. Hopefully, I wouldn't be here long enough for that to happen.

"You have five minutes to meet me outside." He spun and marched back the way we came. I scowled at his back until he passed by my door, then ran to my room.

I had just finished yanking on the long red skirts when I heard, "Stop your dallying!" near my window.

Oh, the things I would do to that little man once this was over . . .

"Two minutes!"

Growling, I yanked on the apron and hastily tied it around my waist. I wrenched the stockings up my legs, nearly ripping them in the process, then shoved my feet into some flat, leather shoes.

I ran from the room as I stuffed my hair under the

bonnet. The skirts twisted around my ankles, and I fell face first onto the floor.

I allowed myself a breath to collect my dignity—what little remained—then shoved up with a grunt. Fisting the front of the skirts, I raced the rest of the way down the hall.

Breathless, I flew out the door to hear Milton counting down the seconds. "Five. Four. Three—"

"I'm here," I said on a huff of breath, then checked my face to make sure no hairs had gotten loose during my sprint.

Milton ran an inquiring eye over me. "That'll do for now. Time for a tour." He moved under the canopy of the draoi tree as I trailed him.

"The inner castle is comprised of four towers as you can see. The high fae occupy the top floor of two of the towers, and then of course Lord Taran has his own tower as well. Their personal staff lives on the floors below them."

"You aren't allowed inside any of the towers unless you have express permission from the high fae living there or have received a station assignment from me. You do not speak to them unless spoken to and you will curtsy any time your paths cross." He eyed me with that disdainful expression I was starting to think was permanent. "You do know how to curtsy, don't you?"

At my blank stare, Milton blew out his cheeks. "Of course, you don't. Watch closely." With graceful poise, he swept out his arms, pinching his imaginary skirt. He extended his right foot behind his left, then slowly dipped until he was almost touching the ground.

My lips twitched, a laugh threatening to spill out. "You'd make a very pretty lady . . . Sir."

"Etiquette is no laughing matter, young lady," he chided as he straightened. "Now, let me see your curtsy."

Mimicking Milton's movements, I grabbed the edges of my skirts and slowly dipped.

"Straighten your back. Head down."

I obeyed as best I could, teetering on my feet the deeper I went.

"Lower," he ordered. "Your right knee should almost touch the ground."

My thighs shook with the strain of holding my weight. I lost my balance and toppled sideways, catching myself just shy of falling into the mud.

"Rude and graceless," Milton mumbled as I stood, shaking off my muddy hand. "You need more practice, but you'll have to do that on your own time. You're needed in the northeast tower."

He turned and headed that way. I slowly followed.

An earthy, clay scent hit me as we entered. The ground level was a filthy mess. It looked like someone had taken a bucket of mud and tried to paint the walls and floor.

Brown spatter decorated the wall portraits and antique decor. The stone floor was so smeared with mud streaks, I couldn't say what the original color was.

Milton ignored my raised brows, shouting, "Gisa!"

A familiar face came bounding down the stairs with a duster in hand. "Yes, Sir?"

"Vera will be assisting you today. I trust you will show her the way we do things at House Taran."

"Of course, Sir."

Somehow, Milton managed to walk over the mud caked ground without getting a single speck on his shoes. He retrieved a bucket and some cleaning rags and dropped them at my feet. "I don't care how long it takes. I want this floor to sparkle."

Blood flooded my mouth from how hard I bit my tongue. "Yes. Sir," I said tightly.

"And be on your best behavior." Milton's gaze dragged over me. "Even if the standard for your 'best' is buried six feet under. Do try," he said before leaving.

I made a rude gesture at his back. He was like a mini-Finn.

"You don't want to get on his bad side," Gisa said, stepping off the stairs. "He'll give you the worst assignments."

My gaze dragged over the space. The mud was still damp, which meant it'd be even harder to clean. It would take hours, possibly days.

I picked the bucket up with a sigh. "Too late."

She chuckled. "Just keep your head down, do good work, and you'll be fine. There's a water trough by the kitchen."

"Thanks."

She nodded before disappearing upstairs.

I quickly filled the bucket and set to work.

The surface of the stone was broken up by small divots. Each one had to be scrubbed individually to clean out all the mud, and the sharp, uneven surface scraped my knees raw as I crawled over it.

I had barely made a dent by the time we broke for breakfast a couple of hours later.

We were served mushy oats in the building whose real name was the Great Hall. When we returned to the tower, Gisa offered to let me help her dust for a little while to give my knees a rest.

I was dusting around some furniture on the top floor when Gisa burst breathlessly into the room. "Lord Taran is here."

My brows furrowed as she crossed to the window overlooking the barbican. "Doesn't he live here?" I asked, joining her.

She glanced briefly at me before turning her attention to

the glass. "I've been here ten years and I've only seen him here a handful of times."

Frowning, I followed her line of sight, and watched two riders enter. One was a dark-haired fae I'd never seen before, and the other was Ronan. Only the top of his head was visible, but an ache still blossomed in my chest.

He crossed out of sight, and we raced to the balcony on the other side of the room. A dozen other halflings were gathered on the balconies of the neighboring towers.

"Who's that with Lord Taran?" I whispered as the pair reappeared.

The dark-haired companion was Ronan's height and clad head to toe in black leather. He had this tragic air about him like he desperately needed a hug, but he'd rip the head off anyone who tried.

"I don't know. I've never seen him before."

They dismounted in the outer bailey, and all the soldiers stopped. After a stunned second, they were crowding the dark-haired fae, smiling, clapping him on the back.

Not a single one spared a glance at Ronan.

The strange behavior continued in the courtyard. Halflings bowed and curtsied warily as he was met with hard stares from his soldiers. Even stranger was Ronan's reaction. He was acting like everything was perfectly normal. The only sign anything was wrong was the faint tightness around his eyes.

I recalled Ronan telling me that even his own people feared him, but why would they? He was the Enforcer. He protected them.

"Why are they looking at him like that?"

Gisa glanced at me out of the corner of her eye. "I don't know. It's been that way since I arrived." Her hand flew to her mouth. "He's missing his sword," she said, aghast.

"So?"

Shocked eyes met mine. "A Taranis fae *never* surrenders their sword. It's the height of humiliation and disgrace. They would rather die."

Ronan hadn't surrendered his, it had been taken by the Nighters. I had a feeling that was even worse.

A figure strolled out below us. My eyes narrowed on Finn's back as he approached Ronan. He'd come from this tower, which meant it was his residence.

That bastard was going to pay for using his powers on me.

Maybe I'd take a shit on his bed.

He greeted Ronan with what would be considered a mild expression on anyone else, but for someone with the emotional capacity of a frozen shit, Finn's face was downright warm.

"Welcome home, Brother."

They clapped one another on the back and the tension around Ronan's eyes dissolved.

That made me hate Finn just the teeniest, tiniest bit less.

Finn turned sharply to the soldiers. "Why are you still standing?" he snapped. "Bow before your lord."

A wave of, "Yes, Steward," was mumbled among the men and women. They fell to their knees, pressing their fists over their hearts.

Finn whispered something to Ronan as they rose. Ronan glanced up, his gaze unerringly finding mine. His expression was blank—no anger or hurt. Nothing.

"He's caught us." Gisa gasped and ducked under the railing, even though she could still be seen between the bars. Her hand slapped at the air, trying to tug me down with her.

I let her pull me down but didn't break eye contact with Ronan.

He was the one to break it as a beautiful brunette came bounding out. Ronan's face lit up. He grinned, catching her, and lifted her into his arms; Kylah—his gorgeous mate.

His eyes met mine for the briefest of seconds, and then he kissed her.

Reality delivered a cold, brutal slap across the face.

Gisa made a comment, but I couldn't hear her over the hammering blows of my pulse. My stomach bunched into a thousand knots, pushing bile into my throat. I rose, stumbling back as I fought tears.

I'd known all along that this would happen, that he'd come home to her, but it didn't make it any easier.

Gisa glanced up at me. Her mouth moved; her face pinched with concern. I should have offered a reassuring smile, or word, but I couldn't do either. All I could do was run.

I turned and dashed away.

I flew down the stairs and raced for the exit.

Sense returned as I reached for the doorknob. What was I doing? I couldn't just run off. I was a halfling, and I had to act like it.

I sank to the ground, shoulders shaking with the tidal wave of tears I was holding back.

"Vera, are you okay?" Gisa called down the stairs.

I fought past the clog in my throat, forcing myself to rise. "Yeah. Just . . . Just wanted to get a head start on the floor."

There was a beat of silence. "Are you sure?"

"Yep!" I said with fake brightness.

I threw myself into scrubbing, doing it loudly to cover the sound of my anguished sobs.

Her footsteps receded, but I didn't stop cleaning.

I scoured the floor as if my life depended on it.

The uneven surface cut my knees, but I didn't mind the pain. It gave me something else to focus on.

The image of Ronan kissing his mate popped into my

mind and I choked down a sob. Just as I predicted, nothing that happened in The Wilds had mattered. The fact that I'd been right didn't give me any solace.

I ground the brush vigorously over the stone, channeling all my heartache and grief into each scrub. I spent hours cleaning. Nothing existed outside of the quiet, steady rasp of the bristles grinding over the stone.

I slowly made my way over the floor, not thinking, not feeling, just focusing on the movement of the brush under my hand.

"Wow, you're almost finished."

I startled at Gisa's voice and glanced up. She was surveying my work with an impressed stare.

I sank back on my haunches and took in the floor. It didn't shine, but it was as polished as stone could be.

I didn't realize how much I had cleaned.

"Yeah, I guess I am." I kept my head bowed so she wouldn't see my red rimmed eyes and tossed the brush into the bucket. Chunks of dirt floated in the dirty brown liquid. It reeked.

I rose and stretched out my aching back. "What time is it?"

"Dinnertime. I'm headed that way if you want to join?"

"I'll catch up. I want to finish first." The spatter on the wall décor still needed to be cleaned, and I needed time for the evidence of my crying to fade.

She nodded and headed for the door.

Finn entered as she was leaving. Gisa dipped into a flawless curtsy, and Finn smiled softly in return. He leaned in and whispered something that had her blushing as she left.

My eyes rounded.

Finn being pleasant? The sun had risen in the Darklands. It was the only explanation.

His gaze immediately found mine and turned frosty. "Halflings curtsy before their superiors."

"Which is why I haven't," I said, stepping up to a painting to keep my face hidden.

No one was with him, so I felt no obligation to play along. I ignored him, and gently dabbed away the flecks of mud over the delicate paint.

"Did you enjoy your task? I dirtied the floor, just for you."

I said nothing, focusing on the painting.

I heard his footfalls come toward me. He stopped beside me, and I felt his eyes running over my profile. There was no hiding my tear-stained face. It took everything in me not to grimace.

A barbed smile twisted his lips. "Ronan and Kylah make a lovely couple, don't they?"

His question was like nails on raw skin. I flinched, tears brimming in my eyes. "Don't," I whispered hoarsely, trying my hardest not to cry.

He laughed, and I flinched again. "Don't what?" He leaned close, teeth flashing. "Don't remind you of how insignificant you are? Or how little you meant to him?"

My eyes cut to him. "Fuck you."

"Go on," he whispered. "Tell me I'm wrong."

I opened my mouth, but the words wouldn't come.

He pulled away, laughing loudly, each note cold and mocking. "That's right. You can't because it would be a lie."

He strode off. As he passed the bucket, he kicked it over and sent the muddy water rushing over the freshly cleaned floor.

"You missed a spot."

22

RONAN

I'd made my new sword and Lord Cern's blood would be the first to christen it.

His House was carved from stone high in the Fayette Mountains. It was an impenetrable fortress if one hadn't spent enough time inside to learn its weaknesses. Biting the blade, I scaled the mountain face leading up to his balcony and vaulted over the edge, landing in a silent crouch.

Frosted glass doors were the only defense against invaders, or so Liam would have one think.

His House was comprised of scholars. It had no army, no warriors to speak of, and if forced onto a battlefield, it would decidedly lose. But it never had to fight on one because House Cern waged war in the mind—capable of stealing memories, implanting false ones, or erasing a person's experiences altogether.

Additionally, their study of history gave them a keen understanding of fae's nature and made them unrivaled strategists. His House was always ten steps ahead of everyone else.

And Liam . . . He was twenty.

His brilliant mind was pivotal to winning the Dark Wars.

After studying the beasts for a brief period, he was able to anticipate their behavior, and in turn, their every move.

I peered through the glass and spotted him sprawled on a bed, thumbing through a book.

He prided himself on his appearance. Every inch of him was meticulously put together, from his short, neatly styled auburn hair and burnished orange frock coat set over a cream tunic, to the gold chain inset with a draoistone centered perfectly over his sternum.

Beside him on a table was a cluster of familiar objects. Some were remnants of his time with his mate, but most were new acquisitions. A lock of hair, a precious necklace from her mother—it had caused quite a crisis when it went missing—and lastly, something I wasn't proud of, a pair of her undergarments.

They were the only things the bastard would accept in trade for memory draughts.

"Peeping doesn't suit you." Liam's voice carried through the glass, muffled, but audible. He wet his thumb, flipping to the next page. "You're about as stealthy as a newborn calf."

There was no gaining the upper hand on Liam. He would have been expecting my visit from the moment he hired the Saor.

I kicked open the doors and stormed inside.

"Two visits in the span of a month," he whispered in a mock, scandalized tone. "What will people say?"

I sent my sword flying at his throat and stopped it a second before it would have cut clean through. I'd dipped it in a special poison. I dug the sword in, just enough to break skin, and black veins erupted around the site.

A flash of surprise lit Liam's features, spurring confusion.

He should have seen this coming.

Despite his surprise, he was unperturbed, only briefly

taking attention away from his book. "Come to kill me?" he asked with a heavy air of indifference, lazily raising his hand. "Good luck."

A crushing band of force seized my skull.

I pressed the blade deeper into his throat. It was centimeters away from severing an artery.

Black continued to leach into Liam's veins, too quick for his immortality to catch. The poison wouldn't kill him, but he would be in an excruciating amount of pain until I provided the antidote.

It was known as torthaí in the divine tongue, but fae called it the death fruit. One bite would stop a low fae's heart.

His fingers touched over the infected area and returned covered in black. "Poison?" He set the book aside and irritated, golden eyes met mine. "I'd call you clever, but only a fool would attack his only ally."

The tension around my head increased, and I grit my teeth. My skull was on the verge of shattering. It wouldn't be the first time he'd done it. "I know what you did," I growled. "Did you really think I wouldn't know it was you?"

The pressure abruptly vanished and I called back the sword. It had served its purpose. The poison would reach his heart soon.

Liam stared intently, eyes glinting with curiosity. "And what, pray, is it you think I've done?"

"You hired the Saor."

His eyes narrowed a fraction, annoyance washing away any thread of interest. "You really think I'd waste perfectly good silvers on you?" Two notes of a deep laugh. "I could kill you for free and entertain myself at the same time. People would call me a hero."

On the latter, I agreed. The other Houses would throw a festival in his honor.

I scrutinized his face, pouring over the last five minutes, assessing every detail of our interaction. I would never take a fae's word at face value. We made skirting the truth look like an art form, but the eyes, the eyes could never lie nearly as well, and his had shown genuine surprise when I attacked.

Liam was not a man that was ever surprised.

"I threatened to expose your secret," I reminded him, not that he needed it. Liam's mind was a steel trap. He remembered everything. He could recite every book he'd ever read, every conversation he'd ever had, and if you angered him—Gods save you. He never forgot.

After gathering intel on the Nighters' whereabouts, I had come straight to House Cern and demanded to see the archives Liam and his ancestors had painstakingly built over hundreds of centuries, and whose secrets they guarded fiercely. It was the seat of House Cern's power.

Liam had been understandably reluctant to grant me access until I reminded him of the confession he'd given to assuage me from war when I arrived, seeking vengeance for his mate so many years ago.

Lord Cern's mouth twitched into a smirk, a fragment of the old him showing. The laughter lines framing his saffron eyes were remnants of another time, another him. They had been set aside like one of his well-loved tomes, left to gather dust.

"We both know you were never going to expose me. You'd never harm *her* in such a manner, and neither would I."

Such a manner being the key phrase. Liam had already caused irreparable damage.

My brows slowly rose. "If you didn't believe me, why did you let me into the archives?"

He looked at me like he was questioning my intelligence.

"If you were desperate enough to threaten me, something had to be deeply wrong at House Taran."

We had an unspoken agreement. I looked after his mate for him—not that I needed any incentive—and Lord Cern looked after House Taran. He had warned me of impending attacks days before they would occur and saved my House countless times.

He had given me access for her sake.

All of his actions and responses lined up, but Liam was cunning. It would take more to convince me.

"Who else would hire the Saor?"

Genuine, amused laughter sputtered from his lips. "I don't know . . . *Everyone*?"

"No one is that stupid," I growled.

His amusement cooled into an unsettling mask. "History will show there is often little intelligence involved in hatred."

Liam rose and approached a mirror.

"They didn't come after me directly though," I murmured, watching him examine his wound, trying to discern the kind of poison used. The black veins had spread to his cheeks. The poison would reach his heart any second now.

If someone had sent the Saor after me, the list of possible suspects would be endless, but they hadn't. They had gone after Vera, and few knew about her.

A tight fist squeezed my heart at the thought of her. I hadn't seen her since I arrived yesterday.

Liam made a thoughtful noise at the back of his throat, twisting toward me. "They went after someone no one should know about," he guessed. "And if no one should know about them, you've got a leaky ship, which shouldn't come as a surprise. You're about as likable as the firean plague."

I glowered. The sickness had swept through the Faylands during the War of the Gods, started by the Goddess Brigidis to decimate Houses pledged to her enemy. It was named for the red flush and boils it left on the skin as the victim slowly burned from the inside out.

An unsettling idea occurred. I was furious with myself for not thinking of it before.

Anyone paying attention could have seen me rowing Vera's body to the island. I had done it under the cover of night, but if someone was determined, they could have glimpsed enough details in the moonlight.

Liam stepped away from the mirror. The slight twitch in his hand was the only indication the poison had reached his heart, but his cool demeanor didn't slip despite how much pain I knew he was in.

"I assume you have the antidote."

That brought us to the second reason I had come. I showed him the vial. "I'm willing to make a trade. I'll give you this in exchange for a draught to restore lost knowledge."

His smile was razor-sharp. "I don't think so, Lord Taran. I'll consider the antidote reparation for attacking me in my own home. If you want the draught, you will pay full price."

A tremor shook his hand. He curled it into a fist.

"You're not in a position to barter."

He pressed a hand to his heart, his face twisted in mock pain. "It hurts you think so little of me." His hand dropped as his expression hardened. "I can have my own antidote made within a day."

"You will be in a great deal of pain until then."

"Care to wager which of us can hold out longer? I promise it won't be you."

I stared for a long moment, debating. I knew Liam well enough to know he wouldn't yield, and under any other circumstances, neither would I, but I couldn't leave without a cure. Reluctantly, I handed over the vial.

He drank it, finishing with a sigh. The black veins slowly retreated, and the color returned to his face.

"We'll conduct our business in my office."

He led me into the adjacent room. It was cluttered with various scrolls and skulls and smelled of old books. He rounded the large desk at its center as I took the seat across from him.

Leaning back in his chair, he steepled his fingers. "How did she lose this knowledge?"

"I never said it was a she."

He sent me a sharp, insulted glance.

"The All-Seeing Eye."

He drummed his fingers together. "Oh, that's nasty magic." Reaching into a drawer, he withdrew an empty vile. His hand circled the air and wisps of gold materialized. He directed them into the container and sealed it. "What the Eye took cannot be returned, but we can stop the bleed, and the knowledge can be relearned quicker than before."

I reached for it, but he held it away. "I require payment upfront."

"What's your price," I gritted out.

"If you want an important piece returned, I require an equally important piece from you."

I knew what he wanted. Cern fae glutted themselves on the memories of others. The darker, the better. The chair scraped over the ground from the force of my movement.

"No." I slapped my hands on his desk. "I'll give you anything else."

He dismissed me with a hand. "Then be on your way."

My jaw worked in tight circles as I leveled him with a burning glare, but he was unphased. He had me by the balls and he knew it. I shoved away. "Deal. Get on with it."

Pinpricks of magic encircled my head, digging in like a band of needles. Liam's face was the last thing I saw before the office fell away.

The wash bowl turned dark pink as I viciously scrubbed away the blood. My whole body was stained with it—my hands, my face, my soul.

Blood. Blood. Blood.

It was everywhere.

I scrubbed harder, flaying my skin raw with the pumice stone, but no matter how many times I scrubbed, the blood remained. It stained the pads of my fingers and beneath my nails.

Voices echoed through my skull.

"Please, don't do this."

"You don't have to do this."

"Spare her. She's just a girl."

"My family is innocent."

I could see each one of their faces, their horrified faces, right before I struck them down.

Scrub. Scrub. Scrub.

I lifted my head, staring into the mirror. Blood matted my hair and splattered my face. I dragged the pumice stone over my cheeks, peeling away the skin, but somehow the blood remained.

Strips of skin splashed into the basin.

Scrub. Scrub. Scrub.

The door ripped open.

Mother stood on the other side, nuzzling a blood-spattered babe. Her eyes were as cold as her words. "I want you gone."

The memory vanished, and I stood back in the office, battered by the emotions it stirred. They rioted inside. I remained perfectly still, breathing shallowly as I struggled not to let any slip through. Liam could have the memory, but he wouldn't get those too.

Once I regained enough control, I met his gaze with a placid expression. "Satisfied?"

"Quite." He passed me the draught.

I stormed through the halls of House Cern and made my way back to the castle. I found Vera scrubbing the floor of Finn's tower.

She glanced in my direction, then quickly averted her gaze.

"Everything okay?"

It took her a moment to answer. "Just great." She sounded off.

Guilt tightened my stomach. I'd gone too far kissing Kylah. If Vera had stayed a moment longer, she would have seen Kylah slap me across the face.

I set the draught down.

She set her brush aside and picked it up. "What's this?" She wouldn't look at me.

"That will restore what the Eye took. You'll need to use it immediately or risk losing it again. Kian will train you starting tomorrow."

"Thank you," she whispered, then cleared her throat, still staring at the wall. "What are—What are you going to do about the king?"

"It doesn't concern you."

She said nothing, and I strode off.

"Why does it matter why I released my dragon?" Her voice carried down the hall. I turned to see she was still looking away. "You got everything you wanted."

"No," I said quietly. "I didn't get anything I wanted."

23

VERA

How someone could move in the blink of an eye and still be late was beyond me. Kian had instructed me to meet him in the level below Ronan's tower at sunset. Thirty minutes later, and there was no sign of him.

Heaving a sigh, I shucked off my cloak—at the very least, it was nice to be back in my pants and tunic again—and draped it over the lone chair furnishing the space.

Aches and pains throbbed all over my body, especially in my knees.

I'd finished recleaning the floor yesterday, only to find a bigger mess waiting for me this morning. Finn had made it his personal mission to torment me.

I sat heavily in the chair and buried the heels of my hands in my eyes. I was tired. Bone tired. The kind of tired that made it feel like I was dragging anchors around with every step.

Part of it was gold dust—I'd finally been able to sneak out and make some in the kitchen—but the other part was . . . Hopelessness.

The Gods had taken everything but Ness, and she didn't need me anymore. She was well taken care of here.

I'd lost the drive to relearn my fighting skills. Ronan had a whole castle of experienced warriors. He didn't need me, and I was going to let the Crone do whatever she wanted to me. What was the point in fighting her?

It just prolonged the inevitable.

I was only here because Ronan had gone through the trouble of getting the draught for me and felt like I owed it to him.

I was just biding my time until he found a way to deal with the king, and I could return to the Crone.

I dragged my hands down my face, then lifted my head. Still no Kian. Sighing, I surveyed the space.

It was a large open room with pillars supporting the ceiling and built from stone. The temperature was cool, just on the edge of cold. Torches washed it in a dim glow.

My eyes ran over the armory spanning one of the walls. Axes, swords, maces, and several weapons I didn't recognize were mounted at varying levels. With nothing else to do, I got up and wandered over to one of the unfamiliar weapons.

It was a long, metal tube with two handles jutting out from the bottom on opposite ends. I felt along one of the handles and my fingers caught on a trigger. I lightly pressed it and a stream of flames burst out.

The fire glanced off a suit of black armor and shot into the air before dissipating. A scorch mark was left over the red wolf's head on the chest plate.

"Woah."

Another weapon was a harmless looking stick. I wrapped my hand around it and two long, sharp spears burst out of the ends. One nearly pierced my thigh.

I jerked back and left the foreign weapons alone and approached one of the swords.

The ebony handle was intricately designed. I wrapped my hand around it and lifted the blade to my eyeline, running a finger over the gleaming metal. The pad of my index finger glided over it like ice.

The steel was flawlessly made—smooth and balanced in a way that only an expert blacksmith could achieve. I couldn't find a sword like this in the Mortal Lands.

The quality also meant it was heavy. Holding it for only a few moments left me dizzy and winded, but the gold dust was to blame more than the weight.

My dragon was stronger than ever after a break from gold dust. To subdue it, I had to take four times my previous dose. It left me with a constant headache, and made it feel like I was dragging a boulder around.

That much gold couldn't be healthy, but the side effects were worth the peaceful nights.

Before I realized what was happening, the sword slipped through my fingers.

A rush of wind rustled my hair as a blur shot by and caught it before it would have cut through my foot.

Kian materialized. Black leather covered his powerful thighs. A tunic fit tightly over his broad shoulders with the strings cinched at his throat. His dirty blond hair was pulled back into a loose bun at his nape. Some of the tendrils had escaped and hung near his pierced ears, giving him a roguish appearance.

He hefted the sword over his shoulder, his bicep bulging as he smirked. "Trouble . . . What have I told you about pointy objects?"

"That I should use them on you?"

He chuckled, returning the sword to its bracket.

"You're late." I crossed my arms and leveled him with a flat stare.

"You can blame the boss for that."

The mention of Ronan twisted my insides. His parting words had been eating at me. How could he possibly not have gotten everything he wanted? He'd gotten *her*.

I shoved the thought aside.

I felt around in my pocket for the vial and withdrew it. "Should I take this now?"

His head moved swiftly left and right. "Save it and follow me."

He led me to the spiraling staircase I'd taken to get to this level, and we took it all the way to the top where it ended at an aged wooden door, embellished with metal trees and looping circles.

Kian flipped over his blade and used the handle to crack the lock.

He pushed open the door, and the sounds of night flooded in. It was alive with chirping insects, whistling in tandem with waves lapping in the distance. A hair-raising screech cut through the soft ambience and the insect noise died off before gradually returning.

I breathed in sharply at the sky. The ribbons of turquoise and lavender were vivid against the starry night.

The door led onto the southern battlements. Torches flickered in the gaps, casting long shadows over the faces of the assembled archers.

"Wait here," Kian instructed and stepped out.

I stayed hidden in the shadow of the doorway.

The archers slanted looks Kian's way as he traversed the narrow walkway.

He clapped the first one on the shoulder. "Congrats. You're all getting the night off." The group exchanged glances before shrugging and filing off through the opposite door.

With the way cleared, Kian moved into the middle, and impatiently gestured for me to join. I threw my arms out for balance and carefully trapezed across the thin ledge.

"It's beautiful, isn't it?" he asked when I reached him, gazing east.

The sea was spread out across the inky horizon. Moonlight glittered over the cresting waves as they lapped softly against the cliffs. The bands of turquoise and lavender were reflected in the pale light over the water, giving it an ethereal glow.

"It is," I agreed. "But what are we doing here?"

He slung an arm over my shoulder and drew me into his flank. "That's an excellent question." He turned us west. "See that?"

I followed the line of his finger to the moat thirty feet below. In the daylight, the water was a pale yellow, but at night, it took on a green hue. The lake was choppy and cloudy, and seemed to swallow, rather than reflect the moonlight.

There was no drawbridge or walkway like at the entrance. It was one unbroken expanse of water.

"The moat?" I asked incredulously. "What's that got to do with anything?"

"Patience, Violent One," he said stoically. "Vial please."

I placed it in his palm, and his hand snapped closed around it.

Then he shoved me off the wall.

I slapped down on the water, face first. Fire blasted across my abdomen.

"Oh, shit," he called down. "Sorry, that sounded like it hurt."

I shoved a mop of wet hair out of my eyes, glaring up at him as I treaded water. Against the backdrop of the moonlight, he was a faceless shadow, but he could see my murderous expression.

"What the fuck, Kian?" I screeched.

"Your strength and endurance are shit. We need to build them up."

"And this is what you came up with?"

He nodded sagely. "Death is an excellent motivator."

"Kian," I growled, slapping the water. I was not in the mood for his corthshit.

"I wouldn't do that if I were you."

"Do what?" I snapped.

"Make all that noise."

I heard the tell-tale splash of something massive moving just before a series of monster waves rocked me.

The treachna.

Panicking, whipping around in a circle, I searched for somewhere I could get out before Kian's asinine antics got me eaten. All the exit points except the castle—whose stone was too flat, and slime-covered to climb—were half a mile away.

"*Kian,*" I hissed. "This isn't funny."

Ridges punctured the water's surface, heading straight for me.

"I'd start swimming if I were you!"

Motherfucker. I threw up a middle finger and caught Kian's laughter before I plunged under. My tunic ballooned around me as I swam hard.

The water had cooled with the night and was steadily growing colder. The chilly temperature cramped my muscles. That, in combination with the gold dose, made every stroke a fight.

I dared a glance over my shoulder as I swam. It was impossible to see much in the murky water, but I could just make out a faint column of bubbles rising fifty yards off. There was no sign of the creature who'd made them.

I surfaced to see if I could pick out the ridges, but they were gone too.

The moat was eerily quiet. The tiny hairs at the back of my neck shot to attention. The treachna had to know where I was. It could have easily attacked by now.

It was playing with its food.

I aimed my eyes up at Kian, seeking an indication of where it'd gone. The asshat waved.

A burst of pressure beneath the water pushed me back. I focused on the sensation. That had to be the treachna moving, and if I could feel it, it was too damn close.

I dove back into swimming, alternating between underwater and surfacing when I couldn't hold my breath any longer. I moved in a zig-zag pattern to confuse the beast.

Its mass made it a slow swimmer, but it was relentless in its pursuit and didn't seem to tire. Forty-five minutes in and I was exhausted, starting to lose feeling in my arms.

"Kian," I called tiredly. "I don't know how much longer I can do this."

His shoulders rose and fell in a shrug. "Finn told Ronan training you was a waste of time. Looks like he was right."

Scorn, fury, and an unhealthy degree of pride burned through me.

No way in the dark was I going to let that asshole be right. Not again. I grit my teeth, ignoring the ache and lethargy blooming in my muscles, and threw myself into swimming.

My arms cut through the water as I kicked hard. The treachna took it as a challenge and it turned from hunting to chasing. Vibrations pulsed through the water every few seconds.

We swam across the length of the moat. When I neared the castle, I turned and pushed off, moving through the water diagonally to avoid the approaching beast.

We did this continuously over the next hour. I managed to outpace it by a narrow margin.

Despite my determination not to quit, the exercise was pushing my muscles past their limits, and they started to cramp. The pain increased until they seized up and I went under.

I tried to flail my arms and swim for the surface, but my limbs wouldn't cooperate. The pulses grew stronger, pushing my body back with each one as a dark mass encroached.

My lungs started to burn.

The treachna prowled closer and closer. My heart pounded feverishly in my ears. Tentacles stretched toward me in the darkness, writhing like snakes.

Why are we fighting?

I froze.

Why *was* I fighting?

So, I could return to the Crone to be tortured? Why not let it end now?

I stopped moving, and shut my eyes, letting myself hang suspended in the water. I could feel the vibrations pulsing every second. The tentacles would reach me any moment.

I was wrenched to the surface.

Air flooded my lungs. I sucked in gasping breaths.

A million, tiny splashes reached my ears, and I belatedly realized Kian had me in his arms and was running on the surface of the moat. He raced me to land and gently set me down.

I collapsed on my knees and emptied my stomach.

Kian was silent when I finished. I was half expecting him to tease or mock me for my terrible fitness.

I wiped my mouth, twisted around, and found him watching me with a serious expression.

My heart lurched. Had he seen me stop fighting? Did he know what I had intended?

The moment extended uncomfortably long. Until he cracked a smile.

"What?"

"I can see your nipples."

I glanced down. Sure enough, the tips were peeking through my wet tunic.

Laughter exploded from me. My body shook with the force of it. Gods, it felt good to laugh.

I smacked him as I got to my feet, saying lightheartedly, "Asshole."

He grinned.

My legs felt like noodles. I had to clutch Kian's shoulder to stay upright.

"You did great," he said brightly. "You should be ready to hold a sword after a week."

I sent him a sharp glance. "I'm not getting in the moat again."

"That's fine," he agreed easily. "I need to run you back into your room so no one sees you." His arm spread.

I watched him through thinned lids as I stepped into his hold. "What else do you have planned?"

His eyes sparked with mischief. "You'll have to wait and see."

I groaned.

"Oh, cheer up. It'll be fun."

Kian's definition of fun and mine were quite different.

The next evening, he made me run up and down hills while vines chased me. The following night, he bated the sea, and I spent the whole time trying not to be eaten by water beasts. The fourth, he dropped me in the middle of The Wilds and made me outrun a storm and magic-born.

I'd never admit it to him, but his insane methods were working. Between my halfling chores, and nights with Kian,

I had already built up a small amount of muscle, and despite the high gold dose, my energy was returning.

I would also never admit it to him, but there were worse people to spend time with.

On the fifth day, Kian instructed me to meet him in the underground level.

I'd been assigned to muck out the stables during the week, but the new assignment hadn't deterred Finn. Just this morning, he shoved me into a pile of manure while my back was turned. The clever bastard had done it in front of witnesses so I couldn't retaliate.

He would get his.

Kian was waiting for me when I arrived.

He wrinkled his nose. "What's that smell?"

I'd taken three baths, but the scent of horse shit still clung to me. "You don't want to know."

He shrugged, dangling the vial. "You ready?"

I nodded and he handed it over.

An orange-gold smoke swirled inside the glass. It didn't appear powerful enough to overcome the ancient magic of the All-Seeing-Eye, but Ronan believed it was.

He'd made himself scarce since giving it to me. I'd only seen him once, passing between his tower and Finn's. Not a single soldier had acknowledged him, like the day he arrived. Ronan was their Lord. I couldn't figure out why they would act that way toward him.

I'd tried asking Kian, but he gave a non-answer.

I popped off the lid, and the smoke spiraled out, flowing into my nostrils.

It tingled my airway as it spiraled up into my brain where it lit a fire. I grabbed my head, hissing in pain. My vision blurred. It felt like a banshee was screaming in my skull. I teetered on my feet, tipping sideways.

Kian caught me and eased me to the ground. "Trouble,

are you okay? What's happening?"

I was in too much pain to answer. I could feel the new magic fighting the old, sinking claws into one another, and my mind was the battlefield. It was paralyzing. I could only grit my teeth and wait for it to stop.

After several minutes, the pain started to ease, and I relaxed, blowing out a long breath. A hand appeared in my eyeline, and Kian helped me to my feet. He hovered nearby, ready to catch me if I fell.

"How are you doing?" he asked.

I licked my lips. "I'm okay," I rasped.

I didn't feel any different, but I also hadn't after the Eye so hopefully that was a good sign.

Kian scrutinized me. "You sure?"

I nodded.

"Alright. Time for your first lesson then." He moved deeper into the room. "I want you to hit me."

After his corthshit with the moat? "Gladly."

I rolled my shoulders before shaking them out, and bounced on my heels, loosening up my muscles. We squared off in the center of the room.

I circled him, but he didn't move. His feet stayed in place while his upper body swiveled to keep me in sight.

Abruptly, I swung hard at his face, hoping to catch him by surprise, but he easily danced out of the way. The same thing happened when I tried an uppercut, a left hook, and a kick. Each time, he easily ducked or slipped in the opposite direction.

It was like trying to fight air.

"Quit using your powers," I hissed.

"I'm not," he said with a laugh, skating left, avoiding the knuckles coming for his head. "You're just slow."

I tried again and again, exhausting myself in the process. It was pathetic how far my skills had degraded since the

Eye. By the end of the night, all I'd accomplished was embarrassing myself.

"You'll get there," Kian said as we stopped for the evening.

"Probably won't be alive long enough to," I muttered, too quiet for him to hear.

Finn visited the stables the next morning, released all the horses, and blamed me for it. Milton made me forgo lunch and dinner.

I showed up for training that evening in a foul mood.

Kian didn't even have a chance to greet me before I started attacking, taking out all my frustration and anger on him.

Again, he moved seamlessly, impossible to hit.

"There are snails faster than you," he teased.

It was going to take more than simple punches and kicks to land a hit. Complex combinations teased at the edges of my mind but were too hazy to latch onto.

My hands clenched at my sides. Bitter frustration reared up. I used to be able to do those combinations with my eyes closed, and now I couldn't remember them for the life of me.

"I can't remember how to fight. I need you to teach me, not mock me," I snapped.

Kian stopped abruptly. "Hey," he said gently. "I'm sorry. I'm going about this the wrong way. Let's start over."

My distrustful gaze met his and he chuckled softly.

"Come here."

He pulled me in for a short hug. I let him, but I wasn't happy about it.

He released me, eyes running over me. "Are you okay? You look more tired than usual."

I'd always been this tired. I just didn't have the energy to hide it anymore.

My lips formed into a thin smile. "I'm fine."

His gaze tightened in concern. We both knew it was corthshit, but thankfully he didn't call me on it.

Instead, he walked me through a series of fighting combinations, patiently correcting my posture and stance no matter how many times I got it wrong. He treated me with gentleness, but he didn't make me feel like I was fragile, and I was grateful for it.

At the end of our session, I was no closer to regaining my fighting knowledge, but I did feel better about my teacher.

The following day during my halfling duties, I snuck frequent breaks to practice the moves Kian had shown me.

When I met with him again, we focused on my technique. I kept making the same mistakes, but Kian didn't tease me, or get frustrated once. He was infinitely patient with every error.

On the ninth night since we started training, and after stealing more time away from my halfling duties to practice, I was feeling the teeniest bit confident.

Kian gestured for me to come at him. I did, throwing a series of combination moves.

Jab—Cross—Left Hook—Low Kick. Inside Kick—Cross—Left Hook—Right Body Kick. Nothing landed, but the more I moved, the smoother and more measured each hit became.

I still couldn't hit him though.

A realization crashed into me, and I stopped.

"Holy shit. I'm remembering."

Kian kicked my legs out from under me. Air fled my lungs as I landed hard on my back.

"That's great, but you've still got a long way to go."

Pushing off with my hands, I sprung to my feet, staying low, and swept out a leg, attempting to knock him down, but he skirted out of reach. It should have been impossible for a man his size to move as quickly as he did.

"Fight me, will you?" I gritted out. "Enough with the dancing."

His expression sobered. "You aren't ready for that, Trouble."

I launched into another series of attacks. He dipped, dodged, weaved, and even backflipped his way out of each one. Eventually, I had to stop to catch my breath, meanwhile, he looked like he'd been standing still the whole time.

"I think that's enough for tonight."

"No," I gritted out. "We're not leaving here until I hit you."

I staggered to my feet and flew at him again, though slower than at the start. Again, he blocked or evaded every single one of my attacks.

A wave of fatigue hit me, and I had to stop.

I slid against the wall and laid my head against my arms as tears burned at the edges of my eyes. Footfalls stopped beside me.

"This is pointless. I'm never going to get my fighting skills back."

Kian crouched, resting a hand on my knee. "You're doing great. Really."

I smacked his hand away and stood. "It's not good enough." I brushed past him.

The next day, I could barely get out of bed. All the gold dust was catching up with me. I was taking more than ever before and not even all the exercise could offset the effects. I worked sluggishly in the stables all morning, then left to grab lunch in the great hall.

Chatting and the clank of utensils filled my ears as I entered. Almost every seat was full.

"Vera!" someone barked, and I stiffened.

I slowly turned to see Finn wearing a smug grin as he stood on the small platform at the edge of the hall. He crooked a finger at me, and I knew I wasn't going like whatever was about to happen.

"Now, halfling," he snapped when I wasn't quick enough.

All eyes moved to me. He was doing this in front of all these witnesses to force my hand. A halfling couldn't disobey the lord's steward.

Godsdamnit.

Snarling, I grit my teeth and crossed over to him.

I curtsied, which only made his grin widen, then straightened and waited to see what corthshit he was about to pull.

Finn stepped to the edge of the dais. It was level with my waist.

"Kiss my boot."

My brows crinkled. I couldn't have heard correctly. I peered up at his face. "What?"

"Did I stutter?" His gaze shifted to the audience behind us. "Did your steward stutter?" he called out to them.

"No, Sir," the hall shouted in unison.

I felt the weight of their gazes on my back. Watching. Judging. There would be scrutiny if I disobeyed. I couldn't afford that, and Finn knew it.

My talons flexed at my sides as I snarled under my breath. Through a slitted gaze, I glared up at him, quietly seething. *You'll pay for this*, I mouthed.

Compulsion powers or not.

Though every fiber of my being rebelled against it, I lowered my head to his boot.

A black whip of smoke materialized between my lips and the leather. Eyes wide, I pulled back as it wrapped around Finn's ankle and yanked.

He tripped and landed on his back. Everyone sucked in a sharp breath and averted their eyes as Finn lurched to his feet, spitting mad.

I followed his glare and found the dark-haired stranger leaning against a wall. The black shadows retreated, disappearing into his fingertips.

Without a word, he shoved off the wall and left.

Finn turned his glare on me. I quickly followed the stranger before Finn could make me finish the job.

The stranger was outside with a boot kicked up against the wall. I got a look at him for the first time.

He had shoulder-length raven hair. His skin was on the paler side, but still maintained a healthy glow.

An arrogant nose led to full lips. A fresh shave revealed a strong jawline and lean cheeks. There was a tattoo wrapped around his throat. It was a grim skull with yellow flowers sprouting through the eye sockets.

A black tunic with a deep cut provided a glimpse of a sculpted chest. Matching leather pants clung to muscular thighs. The fae had some sort of red root dangling between his lips, the end burning.

He took a drag, cracked his neck back—stretching the skull—and blew out a plume of smoke.

"Thank you for saving me back there."

He shoved off the wall and slinked forward, moving in a fluid way that only a predator could, and didn't stop until our boots met. He loomed in my space, peering into my eyes. His were an intense, electric pink orange.

"I didn't do it for you."

His voice was deeper than Ronan's but lacked its richness. It was a raw masculine rasp.

He said nothing else, staring. His eyes were powerful, invasive. I had an insane desire to wither under that stare. Which I'm sure was his intention.

I jutted up my chin, and met his gaze head on, letting him know whatever intimidation corthshit he was trying to pull wouldn't work.

His lips curved around the root. "Kitty's got claws."

"You're Ronan's friend."

The smirk vanished. "Ronan doesn't have any fucking friends."

He took another pull of the root and blew the accompanying smoke in my face. I scowled, swatting it away.

"And if you know what's good for you, you'll stay away."

"How do you—"

"You reek of him."

I narrowed my eyes. "Are you threatening me?"

His smile was all teeth. "Just some friendly advice."

And with that, he strode off, leaving me staring after him.

My stomach rumbled, reminding me I hadn't eaten lunch. Knowing Finn was still in the Great Hall, I opted to return to my room and munch on some leftover meat and cheese.

A note was waiting for me on the bed.

No lesson tonight. We're going out for some fun.

-Kian

24

VERA

I swung into Ness's saddle, then bent over to pet her flank. "Ready to stretch those legs, girl?"

The only upside of stable duty was that I got to spend time with Ness, but sadly, between chores and training, I hadn't had a chance to take her riding.

"I really hate to be the one to tell you this . . . but . . . she can't understand you. She's a horse."

I fixed a heatless glare on Kian. He sat atop his own mount, staring at me like I was adorably, irrevocably insane.

"Hush you."

I continued stroking Ness, whispering in a baby voice. "He doesn't know what he's talking about, does he?" Ness brayed, shaking out her mane and head at the same time. I raised my head, sending Kian a 'would you look at that' look.

He released a low chuckle, his Adam's apple dipping in his throat.

A flood of comforting warmth flushed through me. He had a nice laugh. It was deep and contagious. I scowled. When had I started noticing his laugh?

Since you spent the last week with him, and he was nothing but patient, kind, and had the annoying ability to make you smile when it was the last thing you wanted to do.

Fine, but it didn't mean I had to like it.

He directed his horse north, and lightly dug in his heels before setting off.

I followed suit, riding on his right. "Where are we going?"

"A nearby village."

It was a cloudy night. The ribbon and moonlight struggled to break through the cloud cover, leaving it too dark to see much on the way until we crested a hill.

Below, a quaint village was washed in a brilliant blue glow from strings of draoistones. The village was small, but it had a warm feel. There were a handful of structures made of stone with thatched roofs.

We pulled up in front of a tavern standing on short stilts. They were uneven, slanting the building slightly to the right. It had a tiled, sloping roof. A sign hung over the door with 'Crooked Keep' painted in white.

I hopped off Ness and tied her to a post before vaulting up the steps leading inside.

Kian was right behind me. "Keep your hood on," he instructed. I jerked my head and pulled it down as far as it would go before he pushed open the door.

Drunken laughter and music spilled out. The tavern was packed. Every table was full.

Candlelight cast the inside in a warm glow from the circular light fixtures hanging from rafters to the sticks of wax adorning each table. A band played on a small stage at the back, plucking at fiddles, whistling into flutes, and thumping a low drum.

The cozy, upbeat music was at odds with the rowdy crowd, shouting demands at the barmaids as they weaved between tables.

279

Kian scanned the sea of patrons. His face lit up when he found whatever he was looking for.

I followed his line of sight and saw the dark-haired stranger at one of the tables.

His face was shadowed by a hood, head bent low over his drink. The only reason I recognized him was from the grim tattoo spread over his throat.

Kian grabbed my hand and beelined for him.

"He doesn't look like he wants company," I hissed.

He met my gaze, his eyes alight with mischief. "All the more fun."

I groaned. Chaos. He was absolute chaos.

We meandered through the smattering of tables as the first song ended and a folksy flute beat took its place. A pair of drunken fae stumbled from their chairs and linked arms, skipping and swinging in a circle until they crashed into a neighboring table. Shouting ensued. A fight quickly broke out.

Kian ducked and danced under swinging fists, shoving the assailants out of the way to clear a path for me until we reached the stranger.

"Hunt," Kian said in greeting.

Hunt's head snapped up; copper eyes tapered in annoyance. "You followed me."

His voice came out rawer when he was angry, sounding like the rattle of an ungreased gatling gun.

"I did," Kian answered unapologetically.

Out for some fun my ass. I slanted him a sharp look he didn't see.

"Why?" Hunt asked gruffly.

Smiling, Kian circled to one of the chairs, and sat uninvited. "Because you're such delightful company."

"Ronan," Hunt growled under his breath.

Kian neither confirmed nor denied, gesturing for me to take the seat on his left.

I did . . . reluctantly.

"This wasn't my idea," I told Hunt. I didn't know him, but our brief interaction was enough for me to know I didn't want to get on his bad side. Kian, however, didn't seem to give two shits about that.

He carelessly plucked a piece of meat off Hunt's plate and tossed it into his mouth.

Hunt growled like a territorial beast, slamming his fist on the table, but it wasn't enough to deter Kian from reaching for his plate a second time. Hunt intercepted the hand and twisted. A sharp crack sounded.

Kian laughed loudly, withdrawing his mangled wrist. By the time it reached his body, the bone had already snapped back into place. "I love it when you play hard to get." He blew Hunt a kiss.

Hunt lunged for him, and Kian danced out of the way, his chair scraping over the ground.

"I need another fucking drink," Hunt grumbled and cut a path for the bar.

Kian returned to his chair and leaned toward me while keeping Hunt in his line of sight. "He doesn't know it, but we're best friends."

I snorted. "He's going to kill you."

He rocked back with a quiet laugh. "He already has. Plenty of times. Abuse is how bullies show their love."

"You're an idiot." I could only shake my head. "An annoyingly loveable one." My eyes rounded. "I didn't mean that."

A short laugh of triumph burst from him. He stood, addressing the tavern. "Did you hear that? She thinks I'm loveable."

Some heads turned our way, but thankfully, most weren't paying attention.

I tugged at his shirt. "Sit down."

He did, beaming at me, his dimples popping out in full force. "No takebacks. We're friends."

I planted a cheek on my hand, studying him.

Kian was attractive with his well-filled out frame, handsome face, and contagious smile. He was also incredibly easy to be around. I laughed and smiled more in his presence than anyone else, but sadly, he didn't stir any of the same feelings as Ronan.

Hunt returned to our table, and sat heavily in his chair, a mug of poitin in each hand.

He tipped his chin at Kian while glancing at me. "You friends with this jackass?"

"Not willingly."

"Good enough."

He slid the second mug to me.

Kian grinned at the obvious smite, mouthing, 'What did I tell you? Best. Friends.'

He stiffened as a vibrating pulse filled the air and pulled out a scrying mirror. I saw a flash of Ronan's agitated face before Kian excused himself.

Hunt kicked up his boots and withdrew another of those red roots from beneath his cloak, before he placed it between his lips and leaned forward to light it with the candle. My gaze caught on his knuckles. They were tattooed. Each had a letter, spelling out M-O-I-R-A.

He puffed on the root, appraising me with a cool stare as a fiddle and tambourine played in the background.

"What's with the talons?"

I froze, my heart throwing itself against my ribs.

"Relax," he drawled lazily, releasing a puff of smoke. "Your secret's safe with me."

"What's with the name?" I pointed at his knuckles, smiling sharply. "Your secret's safe with me."

A shadow flitted across his face. He sucked in a long drag and blew a stream of smoke toward the ceiling. "Point taken."

The music changed to a slow melody, filled with flute and harp sounds as I slowly sipped from my mug. I cupped it, staring into the murky liquid. "Why did you help with Finn?" I asked.

He took three quick puffs of the root before removing it and holding it between his index and middle finger. "I don't like bullies." He popped the root back into his mouth and softly puffed on it. "What'd you do to piss him off?"

I chuckled humorlessly, twisting the mug between my hands. "Exist."

His gaze left mine, surveying the room.

"How do you and Ronan know each other? Are you here to help with the king?"

They hadn't seemed friendly with one another when they arrived at House Taran together, but Ronan had said he was going to find another way to stop King Desmond, and then he'd returned with Hunt.

I could only guess that's why he was here.

His eyes sliced back to me, brows raised. "What's with all the questions?"

I shrugged. "Just making conversation."

"I'd prefer if you didn't."

Kian appeared. He ran a hand down his face, looking flustered. "Ronan's not happy I took you off castle grounds."

"Too bad." I sat back, taking a small drink of the poitín. "He might be your boss, but he's not mine."

Kian sighed loudly, dropping into his chair. "Thirty minutes and then I need to get you home."

The door banged open before I could argue, and a group

of winged fae entered. They swaggered through the tables to the back corner, opposite us, and kicked out the three fae sitting there.

Hunt's hand curled into a fist. His eyes cut to Kian. "What the fuck is this?"

Kian raised his hands. "I've got nothing to do with it."

Hunt puffed furiously on his lig root before flicking it to the ground and rising.

Kian shot up and gripped his shoulder. "Don't do anything stupid," he said in a low voice.

Hunt shrugged off Kian's hold. Glaring at the Belenus fae, Hunt pounded the rest of his drink, and slammed it on the table before turning to leave.

"Look at the Fallen Prince run."

Hunt stiffened, and slowly pivoted to face the speaker.

It was one of the Belenus fae. He was leaning with his hands on the table, staring at Hunt with vicious hate. He was five-ten with glossy midnight wings, dark hair, and jade eyes, and wore a dark body suit that molded to his lithe frame.

"We don't want any trouble, Bellamy," Kian said, subtly pressing closer to me.

"Speak for yourself." Hunt threw off his cloak and the music cut off with a screech. Every eye was trained on Hunt and Bellamy.

Kian cursed, glancing down at me. "You need to get out of here," he said, his voice uncharacteristically sober.

"What are you going to do?"

"Have Hunt's back."

My gaze darted to the table. It would be ten against two. "Who's going to have your back?"

"Trouble, I appreciate the concern, but—"

"Who's the girl?"

We both turned to Bellamy as his eyes scraped over me.

Hunt and Kian's massive frames stepped in front of me, shielding me from view.

"No one," Hunt grunted.

"I don't know. She looks like she could be some fun."

"You don't want to do this," Kian said in a deathly cold voice. From his profile, I could see his eyes were black. The fun-loving Kian was gone.

"Or do I?"

"Leave it," Hunt growled.

"What are you going to do if I don't?" I couldn't see him, but I imagined Bellamy cocking his head, sporting a taunting smirk. "Watch her bleed out?" Cold laughter followed.

Hunt turned rigid as stone. He didn't say a word as a black whip of smoke materialized at his fingertips. He lashed out, giving me a view of Bellamy and the cord coiled around his throat.

Bellamy tugged at it with wide eyes. "What the fuck is this?"

Hunt's smile could have given The Wilds a run for its money. "Learned some new tricks."

Bellamy's head started to grow. It turned bulbous and continued expanding as his friends rushed to help him, but they couldn't stop it. His head ballooned to gargantuan proportions before exploding, and spraying brain matter everywhere.

The Belenus fae all flared their wings, vibrating with tension. Hunt and Kian wore matching bloodthirsty grins. The impending violence thickened the air and sucked all the oxygen out of the tavern.

The other patrons started to scatter.

Kian turned to me. "You stay right there," he warned.

He and Hunt exchanged a look, and together, they rushed forward, slamming into the Belenus fae.

Fists and blood flew. A Belenus fae lifted into the air briefly to slam back down as he threw his fist toward Kian's face. Kian dodged the punch, snatched a hold of the fae's arm, and flashed behind him, kicking the limb clean out of its socket.

Hunt kicked up one of the chairs and swung it into the stomach of a Belenus fae while throwing his blade into the eye of another.

They both moved with a lethal grace I'd never seen before. Well, besides Ronan.

Not one to sit out a fight, I waded into the battle. This was the perfect test to see if I'd gotten any of my fighting skills back. Just because I couldn't hit Kian, didn't mean I couldn't hit one of these guys.

A Belenus fae flew over my head and knocked me to the ground from behind. Dirty little cheater.

I rebounded quickly, whipping around, and swiped out my fist. I managed to catch his arm and he growled, throwing out a leg. My reaction time was too slow. It crashed into my stomach and knocked me back. All the air whooshed from my lungs as I collided with a table.

Definitely not at my fighting peak, but at least I wasn't completely missing anymore.

"Duck," I heard Kian call. Instinctively, I did.

A chair came flying and crashed into my attacker. As he fell to the floor, I leaped back to my feet and scowled at Kian over my shoulder. "I had him!"

"Sure, you did, Trouble." He winked and turned away.

There were only a handful of the Belenus fae left standing and Kian and Hunt weren't even breaking a sweat. Amidst all the chaos, no one noticed Bellamy stagger to his feet, his head completely repaired.

He was high fae.

His draoistone flared.

Thunder rumbled overhead. A bright light lit up the windows.

His gaze was locked on Hunt.

Panic crawled up my throat. I didn't know how Hunt was supposed to help fight King Desmond, but I knew Ronan needed him—a lot more than he needed me.

I didn't think.

I ran, throwing my body in front of him as a blinding flash of light burst through the roof.

The light slammed into me, and a shock of electricity burst through me.

I fell to my knees screaming. Debilitating pain cracked over my ear. It felt like my eardrums had ruptured. There was a deafening ringing in my ears. I couldn't hear, or see, but I could smell burnt flesh.

Hands grabbed my elbows and lifted me off the ground.

Kian roared something, but I had no idea what he was saying. He froze at the sight of the blood dripping out of my ears, his face paling.

He scooped me into his arms and took off running with Hunt right behind us.

Everything went black.

25

RONAN

"You will answer your Lord's questions honestly." Finn's draoistone flared brightly over the dark dungeon walls.

Milton sat in a chair between us, twitching, as Finn's compulsion washed over him. Once Finn used his powers, he'd be voiceless for a time. He nodded at me to start.

I spun a chair around, and sat, facing Milton, arms crossed over the top. He squirmed under my intense stare.

"My Lord, what is this about?"

"I'll ask the questions."

He swallowed thickly, nodding.

"Are you now, or have you ever been, a spy for King Desmond?"

"N-No, my Lord," he sputtered. "I would never."

"Has King Desmond, or anyone from his House ever approached you for information?"

His thick brows touched together. "No, My Lord. And even if they had—"

I held up a hand, and he quieted.

"Are you now, or have you ever, fed information about House Taran to an outsider?"

He paled. His hands shook as he threaded them together.

I leaned forward, spearing him with my gaze. "Answer."

"I-I told a woman at a tavern about my position once, but I swear it was only to impress her!"

I sat back, exchanging a look with Finn. He gave a lone nod of agreement. Milton wasn't our traitor.

I rose. "You're dismissed," I told Milton. "Don't breathe a word about this to anyone."

He scrambled to his feet, bowed hastily, and beat a fast retreat for the stairs.

"How many is that?" I asked.

"Twen—" Finn's hoarse voice cracked. "Twenty."

We'd begun interrogations shortly after my visit with Liam. A traitor inside these walls had leaked information about Vera to the Saor. We had no leads. The whole House had to be questioned.

"Have the outposts been contacted?"

"Yes." His voice came out as a low rasp. He pressed a hand to his throat. "Yes. The generals are sending their best fighters."

The castle soldiers hadn't had the same exposure to water beasts as the outposts. I'd requested the best men to come here and train them. King Desmond had more than water beasts at his disposal, but neutralizing air and land beasts would be similar.

I checked my scrying mirror. I still hadn't heard from Kian. He was supposed to scry when he and Vera were on their way back.

Finn glanced between me and the mirror, putting together who this was about. "What are your plans for her?" His voice was gravelly, but stronger. Compelling honesty didn't require a large degree of magic, and therefore the price was minimal.

"Release her once she can defend herself and the traitor has been caught."

My chest ached at the thought of letting her go, but I couldn't keep her here forever.

I glanced at the mirror, urging Kian to scry. When nothing came through, I envisioned Kian's face, and initiated the scry myself. The mirror pulsed in my hands, but there was no answer.

I tried once more. Nothing.

A tendril of unease snaked through me.

"I have to go. Let's pick this up tomorrow."

He bowed his head, and I strode off.

As I reached the castle gate, the thunder of hooves sounded in the distance. The urgent pace froze my stomach. "Lower the bridge," I bellowed.

The massive plank groaned against its chains until it hit the ground, sending up a spray of dirt.

The galloping intensified. A rider appeared on the horizon with a figure slung over their horse, but it was too far to see who.

"Bring me my horse," I roared.

A guard ran out with Loach.

I threw myself into the saddle and whipped the reins, taking off at a sprint. The rider was headed toward the healer's cottage perched on the edge of the cliff. I caught up as they leaped off their horse.

It was Kian. He raced inside with Vera in his arms.

My blood turned to ice.

I launched off Loach and charged in behind them. "What the fuck happened?"

Lawrence was lounging in the back with a book. He rose swiftly and cleared the table. "Set her here."

Kian's panicked eyes darted to me, but his words were for Lawrence. "She was hit by a lightning strike."

My gut tightened as rage roared through my veins.

Kian gently laid her down. Her pale face stood out starkly against the wood. She wasn't moving.

My stomach plummeted. "Tell me she's breathing."

Lawrence pressed an ear to her mouth. "Yes, but not for long."

I stepped back as he rounded the table and cut away her shirt. When he neared her chest, I shot Kian a look. He nodded gruffly and stepped outside.

I pushed as much magic into Vera's glamour as possible. Lawrence had been loaned to House Taran after the Dark Wars. His loyalty was to House Brigid and its Lord.

The last of Vera's tunic fell away, and I dragged in a violent breath. A network of jagged marks bisected charred, blistered skin.

My pleading eyes fell to Lawrence. "Help her," I rasped.

He nodded somberly.

With practiced precision, his hands roved over her injuries, his palms emitting a blue light.

Most Brigid fae had healing specialties. Some were skilled at identifying rare illnesses, others could sense disease at the earliest onset. The more powerful were capable of limb and organ regeneration, and Lord Brigid could bring back the dead.

Lawrence was considered a generalist. He did not possess a specialty in one area but was proficient in a variety and could see injuries invisible to the eye.

His head twisted over his shoulder. "I've identified the damage."

"Heal it."

The golden band encircling his wrist filled the dimly lit cottage with a bright glow. Vera twitched, grimacing in pain. My hands clenched at my sides.

"You're hurting her," I snapped.

Lawrence's brows rose but he didn't take his focus away. "If you cannot control yourself, Lord Taran, you may leave."

"I can control myself," I bit out.

I wasn't a godsdamn animal.

I started pacing furiously, cracking my knuckles. I did a decent job ignoring Vera's shudders of pain . . . Until her back bowed off the table, her face contorting in agony.

I lunged for Lawrence, grabbing fistfuls of his shirt, and lifted him off the ground.

He stared pointedly at my hands before dragging his eyes to my face.

"I'll wait outside."

I set him down.

Pressing through the door, I found Kian pacing.

He jerked to a stop. "How is she?"

"Unconscious." I cut him a glare, folding my arms. "Start talking."

"Bellamy showed up with some friends," he said grimly.

A hot curse flew off my tongue. Bellamy had been in love with Hunt's mate, Moira, since they were children. He'd never gotten over her death, and blamed Hunt for it.

"He conjured up a lightning strike for Hunt and Vera jumped in front of it."

"*She what*?" Rage singed every nerve. "*Why*?"

He scrubbed his jaw, gaze darting to the cabin. Mine followed. Only the bright glow of Lawrence's draoistone was visible through the window. "I don't know," he said, turning back. "She hasn't been the same since she arrived."

The light cut off and the door opened. Lawrence appeared, drying his hands. "I was able to stabilize her, but she will require lots of rest."

"Thank fuck," Kian said at the same time I drove out a harsh, relieved sigh.

Lawrence disappeared, the door clicking shut behind

him. My eyes ran over the horse grazing among the grass. Kian must have used too much of his powers to run Vera here.

"Where is Hunt?" I demanded.

"Hunting Bellamy and his friends."

I pinched the bridge of my nose. This was the last thing I needed. "Inform Kylah."

She was from House Belenus. Hopefully, she could smooth over tensions before we had a war on our hands.

He hesitated, sliding a look at the window.

"You heard Lawrence. She needs rest. You can visit when she's awake."

Nodding tightly, he hopped back on the horse and took off toward the castle.

I returned to the cabin. Vera was fast asleep on the table. Gooseflesh pebbled her skin where it was exposed by the split fabric. I grabbed a blanket and gently draped it over her.

My gaze clung to her chest, steadily rising and falling with each breath.

Lawrence righted the items he'd knocked to the floor. He cleared his throat, setting a dried herb on the counter. "I was able to heal the damage from the lightning strike, but . . . there's more."

My eyes cut to his face as he turned toward me. His expression was grave.

"More?"

He inclined his head. "She has severe organ damage. Far beyond the scope of my capabilities."

My pulse buffeted my ears. "What do you mean?"

"She . . . shows signs of prolonged poisoning."

"I don't understand."

"Her body is reacting to a toxicity. It could be in her environment, or in her food, or . . ."

"Or what?" I growled.

"The damage is extensive. The symptoms would have been severe and impossible to go unnoticed."

His accusation hung in the air, ignorant and unfounded.

"Vera wouldn't poison herself," I snarled. She was the fiercest, most vivacious spirit I'd ever known. "You don't know of what you speak. If you value your tongue, I advise you not to do so again."

Lawrence's mouth spread into a grim line. "Whatever it is, it must stop. Her body cannot sustain it for much longer. If it continues, the consequences will be dire." He met my gaze as he delivered the final warning.

Eager to get her away from him, I gently pressed my hands underneath her and lifted her into my arms, adjusting the blanket to keep her covered.

"I'll oversee her recovery."

Lawrence frowned but said nothing as I carried her out.

Hunt was outside, leaning against the cabin, puffing on a lig root. I sighed in aggravation. My mind was reeling, a band of pressure forming. He was the last person I wanted to deal with.

He tipped his chin at Vera. "How's she doing?"

"Fine, no thanks to you," I clipped out.

He lazily shrugged a shoulder. "I didn't ask her to do that."

"You could have healed her at least."

His eyes narrowed. "You know I don't do that shit anymore."

"I don't know anything. We haven't spoken for the last five hundred years."

Another shrug.

"Did you find them?"

"A couple. The rest made it home."

"Good. I don't need you causing any more problems for House Taran."

He laughed caustically. "That's rich coming from you." His eyes ran over Vera as he took a deep pull from his lig root and blew out a stream of smoke. "You ruin everything you touch." He flicked the root into the grass and smashed it under his boot. "If you've got even an ounce of light left in your black soul, you'll stay away from her."

He shoved off the wall and stalked past me.

"If it was Moira, could you?" I called.

He froze like he'd been struck. Twisting, he gave me his profile. Barely leashed grief tightened his face. "Keep her name out of your fucking mouth." He stormed off and was quickly swallowed by the night.

Hunt had no reason to worry. Vera had ensured I would stay away.

I whistled for Loach to follow and quietly carried her to the castle.

I entered my room and gently laid her in my bed. She stirred slightly as I pulled the covers over her but sleep quickly took her again. My gaze roved her features softened in sleep. She was so beautiful, it made my chest ache.

I took a chair, running over the conversation with Lawrence. I couldn't wrap my mind around his allegation. She wouldn't poison herself. *She wouldn't.*

But as I considered our interactions over the last month, things weren't adding up. She suddenly didn't need chains. Then there was the Rogues' attack. Even without her fighting abilities, her dragon would have been able to take those men down with a single breath.

Doubt started to creep in. I left to search her room.

Wide eyes trailed me as I marched through staff quarters. Halflings pressed against the walls in a bid to escape my notice.

"Vera's room. Now," I barked.

Shaking fingers directed me to a door.

I entered and immediately smelled her scent.

There were few nooks and crannies for secrets, something I'd done intentionally to remove the temptation for betrayal. I had long lost the love of my people, but found fear was an equally powerful motivator for loyalty.

The chest at the edge of the bed was the only cover. I rifled through it, tossing clothes over my shoulder until I found what I was looking for.

A lone pouch sat at the bottom.

I'd had my suspicions, but when I saw the metal flecks inside, I wasn't prepared.

As I poured the dust into my palm, the burnished yellow flecks glinting in the candlelight, there was no denying what Vera had done.

I clenched the pouch as a liquid fire roared through my veins. The rage consuming me was paralyzing. My vision blurred and every line of my body tightened to the point of pain.

Vera was poisoning herself with gold dust.

She was slowly killing herself.

I returned to my room and paced by her bedside, trying to calm down.

I cracked my neck to alleviate the tension. Every muscle was stretched taut, on the verge of snapping. I wanted to tear something apart, rip it to shreds, to relieve some of the pressure in my skull.

The source of my anger lay peacefully swaddled in furs. She hadn't moved, sleeping deeply as she remained blissfully unaware of me raging a few feet away.

My initial reaction was to reason her actions weren't intentional. She wouldn't purposely harm herself. But the more I reflected on her behavior over the last few weeks, the more I understood.

Setting fire to a room while she was still in it, threatening to offer herself to the king if I didn't allow her to come on a dangerous journey, and now this . . . diving in front of a lightning bolt intended for someone else. She had a death wish.

My teeth ground together, fists flexing at my sides.

I wanted to shake her awake and demand answers. Demand to know why she would want to hurt herself. But she needed sleep . . . because the damned fool was poisoning herself. No, I didn't want to shake her awake, I wanted to strangle her. Choke some goddamn sense into that dense skull of hers.

I squeezed the pouch with enough force to break bone.

Oh, how I wished I had Vera's power at that moment, desperate to incinerate the source of her agony into ashes.

Now, that was an idea . . .

I marched to the fireplace. Noticing the fire was low I added another log. The flames shot higher, and a wave of heat hit me.

"Ronan," Vera called groggily from bed.

Gripping the pouch, I shot a quick glance over my shoulder.

She was sitting up, hair rumpled, a hand holding the furs to her chest. Despite the fatigue lining her features, her sun-kissed skin had a healthier glow and the shadows under her eyes were barely visible.

The ruined shirt had slipped off, catching in the crook of her elbows. Under different circumstances, the tantalizing view of her bare shoulders would have ignited my desire, but I was far too angry for that.

She offered a small smile before rubbing her eyes. I didn't return it.

Her eyes snagged on the pouch, and she froze. "Ronan . . . What are you doing with that?"

I tossed it into the fire.

"No!" She launched off the bed and dove for the fireplace, but I caught her and hauled her back to the mattress, forcing her to sit.

Her indignant glare shot up to me. "What's your problem?" she snapped. "I needed that."

I crowded her between my arms. She pushed and shoved at my chest demanding space, but I didn't give an inch. All the rage simmering in my veins bled into my expression, contorting it into something murderous—something monstrous. I was close enough, I could see it reflected in her gaze.

My battle mode was dangerously close to exploding out of me. She recognized the monster peeking at her and glared. I couldn't tell if it was bravery or stupidity.

I brought my face inches from hers. Our breaths mingled.

"How. Fucking. Dare. You."

If I thought this mulish woman would give even an inch, I was gravely mistaken. Her gaze narrowed to slits. "How dare I?" She threw her hand at the fireplace, where the pouch slowly wilted as it was consumed. "That didn't belong to you."

"And what was it? Hmm?" I dragged a finger down her throat, both a caress and a threat.

Her breathing stuttered, but her stare was bold. Defiant. "You know what it was."

My hand wrapped around her throat. I kept the pressure light, not enough to restrict air, just enough to remind her who was in control. "Say it."

"Gold dust."

Those two words penetrated my chest like she stabbed a

hot poker clean through it. My control hung by a thread, but somehow, I managed to calmly ask, "And why were you taking it?"

She tried to pull away, but my hand around her throat kept her in place. I squeezed it once, urging her to answer. Scowling, she tipped her head all the way back to meet my gaze.

"It's none of your fucking business."

I released her, tearing myself away as rage flooded my veins with renewed vigor. I had to stand on the other side of the room. I couldn't even look at her. If I did, I would lose control.

"You're killing yourself," I snarled. "Of course, it's my business."

She glanced away for a moment and when she looked at me again, I saw everything. I saw the desolation, the hopelessness, the *absolute misery*. "No, Ronan," she whispered. "It's not."

My anger was instantly drowned out by concern.

In three quick strides, I was kneeling at her feet. "What's going on?" I asked, gripping her knees. "Talk to me."

Her lips set into a bloodless line.

The dancing firelight cast shadows over her face, darkening it, but that wasn't the source of the tightness constricting my ribcage. No, it was the haunted expression she wore—the hollowness in her eyes.

She stared at me for a long moment, jaw clenched, fighting to hold back whatever was distressing her.

She released a mournful sigh, and the fight fled.

Tears welled in her gaze. They fell freely, slipping down her cheeks. "Do you know why I went with you to find the Nighters?"

"So we could find the godstone and you could return home."

She shook her head. "Because the Nighters want me. I don't know why, but they do. I knew that if they tried to kill you again, I could trade myself to save you."

A rush of anger and confusion spiraled through me. I ignored both.

"Why, Vera?" My voice cracked with emotion. "*Why are you so eager to throw your life away?*"

"Better I die than another innocent child," she whispered hoarsely. "I can—I can still see their faces—" she choked on the words "—I can still see their tiny, charred bodies every time I close my eyes. Hear them screaming for their mothers." Her gaze flitted to me, no longer vacant. It was bitter, mournful, glistening with tears. "I murdered innocent children when I released my dragon in Mayhem. As much as I hate myself for what I did to you, I hate myself even more for that."

Her admission gutted me.

"I can't control the dragon anymore," she said defeatedly. "It's too strong."

That's why she was taking the gold dust. To subdue it.

Rage filled me. I was livid at myself for being so fucking blind and selfish. Not once had I thought of the consequences Vera endured for releasing her dragon.

"When I was standing before the firing squad, knowing I was about to die, do you know what I felt?" she said in a forlorn whisper. "I was grateful." Her gaze lifted to mine. "I was so grateful and relieved that they were going to do what I couldn't. They were going to keep my dragon from hurting any more children."

Her words slammed into my chest with the force of a battering ram. Shock, horror, guilt, rage—so many emotions hit me at once it was hard to seize onto one.

"You wanted to die."

She shook her head. "I wanted my dragon to die and if that meant I had to die too, so be it."

"You should have told me," I said softly. "My presence calms your dragon."

"You hate me," she croaked.

I squeezed her knees. "Oh, Little Thief I could never."

She lifted her watery gaze to mine.

I wanted to hold her. I wanted to wipe those tears away and tell her everything would be okay, but comfort wasn't going to save her.

"You'll be sleeping in here from now on," I said, rising.

Her lips pinched. I knew she wanted to argue, but she also knew it was a losing battle.

"I appreciate the offer, but it's not going to fix anything. I *need* to take the gold dust."

"Lawrence examined you," I said slowly. "If you continue taking it, you will die."

Her head tipped back, strong and defiant. "Then I die."

My jaw clenched so hard I thought it might snap. "You will sleep. We will discuss this again when you're feeling better."

I strode to the door and quietly shut it behind me.

"I can't be saved." Vera's voice floated through the wood. "I've made peace with it. So should you."

26

RONAN

"Milton," I bellowed as I stormed into the courtyard. Halflings scattered as my soldiers threw me sharp, wary glances. They knew better than to disobey but had no compunctions about making their disdain clear. Normally, their behavior would weigh on me, but right then all I cared about was Vera.

The Head of House appeared and swept into a bow. "How may I be of service, My Lord?"

"I want anything gold not bolted down to be collected and locked in the dungeon. Personal items included."

Milton was too professional to show if he found my request odd.

"I will handle it at once."

"And Vera is to be given the week off. She isn't feeling well."

A tiny glimmer of curiosity sparked in his eyes, but he was quick to cover it. "Of course, My Lord."

He barked orders to the halflings milling around, and the courtyard burst into a flurry of activity.

I strode inside the Great Hall to oversee the gold collection as the space housed more than the rest of the castle combined. From the frames depicting my ancestors, to the weapon's display, it all had to be removed and hidden.

Kylah entered holding a bowl. She paused mid-step, gaze flitting around at the halflings dismantling the room before it landed on me. "What's all this?"

I sighed. "It's a long story."

"I have time." She smiled. "An eternity's worth in fact." She gestured at the long mess table before sitting.

Reluctantly, I joined her, lowering onto the opposite bench.

She brought a spoonful of onion and garlic custard to her lips, and I grimaced. "I don't know how you eat that."

Her eyes glazed over. She peered down at the bulbous yellow slime jiggling on her spoon, looking a little lost. "I've always just eaten it." She spooned it into her mouth, humming. "I wouldn't call it good. The taste is just . . ." Her brows pinched. "It's familiar. Comforting."

Her shoulders lifted daintily and the strange look vanished. She twirled the utensil at me. "Tell me what's going on."

I tapped a finger against the wood. "Were you able to smooth things over with House Belenus?"

She raised a brow at the subject change, but still answered, "Helena made me beg in front of our entire House, but yes, there will be no retaliation."

Her sister was rotten to the core. "Thank you," I said sincerely. I gave her a long look. "If you ever want to take your House back, I will stand behind you."

"Short of death, Helena will never give it up."

I stared pointedly.

She waved me off. "No. She can keep my crown. I've made my peace with it. If you truly want to thank me, you can tell me what is going on."

My gaze gripped hers and held it for a long moment.

Kylah had refused to speak to me for centuries, and then one day while I'd been visiting to put an unruly general in his place, she walked up and given me a hug. Our friendship wasn't what it used to be when we were younger, but it was miles better than what it was.

"What changed your mind?" I asked quietly, adding, "About me."

"Kian. He is one of your most fervent defenders, you know. He doesn't tolerate anyone speaking ill of you."

My brows raised. I was shocked she hadn't said Finn. Whenever someone was bold enough to voice their true thoughts about me, he was always the first to my defense.

Kian and I had a working relationship, but I didn't consider us close.

Kylah's spoon landed in her bowl with a soft clink as she scooped out another helping. When she finished, she pointed it at me. "You've avoided long enough. Speak."

I groaned, dropping my head into my hands, and peeked at her through my fingers. She stared stubbornly back, quirking a brow.

I lifted my head, drumming my fingers against the table as I gave her a petulant stare. "Perhaps I should have never accepted your oath of loyalty."

Fae didn't wear brands like halflings. Many stayed in the Houses they were born into, but some changed allegiances for one reason or another, mainly to be with their mate. To be accepted into the new House, they had to swear an oath of loyalty to its lord or lady.

Kylah's mother and mine had been close. We had spent most of our summers together growing up. When her younger sister usurped the throne, and banished her, I welcomed Kylah into my House.

Trills of laughter erupted from her. She reached across

the table and lightly smacked my arm. "You need me, and you know it."

It was true. Not only did Kylah serve as House Taran's eyes in the sky, providing air reconnaissance that had saved us from an incoming enemy more than once, she was my diplomat, solving inter-House conflicts when fear and violence would not bring peace.

Her gaze sobered, glinting with a strange light. "I've missed this. You haven't been yourself in quite a long time."

I wasn't here to discuss me.

"Vera's been poisoning herself with gold dust," I said bluntly. Kylah, Finn, and Kian were the only ones who knew about her dragon.

The spoon clattered to the bowl. All amusement wiped clean from her features. "Why would she do such a thing?"

Vera was a private person. It was one thing to expose her inner beast. It was another to share intimate details about her life, but Kylah and Vera were not so different. If anyone knew how to help Vera, it was her.

"This must be kept in confidence."

"Of course."

I told her everything—from how Vera and I first met, to the Crone, to the iron poisoning and now the gold poisoning. She listened attentively throughout.

"I don't know what to do," I finished. "I don't know how to help her." My fists tightened under the table. "She's willing to die."

I was a lord, a leader. I was used to knowing what to do, but in this instance, I didn't have a clue. I'd never felt so lost before.

"I assume you have seen the scars on her back?"

"How did you—?"

"When I stayed with her briefly. They were barely visible beneath the bandages, but I have an eye for that sort of thing." She tried to play off the last part with a light tone, but she couldn't hide the tightness in her eyes.

Kylah had watched Vera for an hour at my manor while I attended to House business with Finn.

"They're old. Probably from when she was a child," she guessed.

I had left the Crone's abuse out of my tale. That wasn't mine to share.

I neither confirmed nor denied, waiting to see where Kylah was going with this.

She folded her hands under her chin, leaning forward to confirm she had my full attention. "We all carry weights with us from our childhood. Some more than others, and most aren't aware we are carrying anything at all." Kylah forced a thin smile. "Children are supposed to be cherished and protected. The ones who aren't grow up with two choices. They can either pass on their pain, or fight."

Kylah settled back on the bench. "Vera is choosing to fight."

"She is *choosing* to poison herself," I hissed.

"Because she would rather die than become like whoever left those scars on her back," she said simply.

The solution, the answer to Vera's problems, slammed into my gut. My fingers rapped against the wood. I hated the idea with every fiber of my being, but I could see no other way. "I need a favor."

Kylah dabbed her lips with a cloth, before giving me a small smile. "How can I help?"

An hour later, Kylah was setting us down. Her gaze flickered around the ring of massive stones.

"Where are we?" she asked.

"A worship site."

Vines strangled the stones. They scraped against the

hard surface with the wind, creating an ominous rustling in the quiet.

"It looks abandoned," she observed.

"It is."

Kylah pulled her gaze to me. "Why are we here?"

I didn't answer, pressing between the stones into the meadow beyond. I heard Kylah's light, sure steps behind me and gestured to the field of wildflowers.

She hummed under her breath as she leaned down to examine a purple flower. She plucked it, then straightened, a teasing smile curving her lips.

"They're pretty, Ronan, but this seems a bit far to travel for flowers."

"We aren't here for them." I dug out my mother's brooch and placed it gently among the grass. Thankfully, I always carried it with me, so it had escaped the fire.

Kylah stared at the brooch, brows tightening, before her gaze touched mine. "Why are you . . .?"

"This is an offering site for the Crone."

Understanding lit her gaze. She ran a speculative eye over the meadow. "I will accompany you then."

"No." My tone was gentle, but commanding. "I need you to watch over Vera while I'm away. She has wings. Perhaps you can give her a flying lesson."

Kylah could draw out Vera's wings with magic. There was no need to get her dragon involved, and the distraction would be good for her.

"I'd be delighted."

I smiled softly. "Thank you."

She nodded, stretching out her wings.

"And Kylah?"

"Hm?"

"Vera still thinks we're mates. Keep it that way."

Kylah shot me a venomous glance. She was still upset

over the kiss—understandably so. "I will keep your secret for now, but you need to tell her. Soon," she said sharply.

"I will."

She left, and I took in the meadow.

It hadn't changed since my visit with Vera.

I stared at the log we'd shared, trying to riddle out why she hadn't freed her dragon for me, but she'd been willing to sacrifice herself to the Nighters to protect me.

I couldn't make sense of it.

The vortex of wind appeared, and I stepped inside. Violent wind whipped around me, tugging at my clothes and hair as I was lifted off the ground and transported to the Crone. It dissipated and I stood inside a familiar cabin.

She'd transported me right inside her lair.

I had been here once before I visited with Vera, half a millennia ago. The space had been decaying, primordial ooze bleeding through the cracks with no windows or warmth. The smell of rot and death had hung in the air.

It'd been transformed into a bright, airy space full of life. Sunlight poured through the wall-length windows, vines and flowers blossomed over the walls, and colorful, nature themed décor dotted the floor.

It'd been made into a home.

"Hello, Enforcer."

I turned to face my host.

Startling familiar eyes, the same color as Vera's, stared coolly at me, but they lacked her spark, her passion. The Crone's delicate hands were folded neatly in front of a lilac dress. Her outfit was feminine, meant to distract from her black soul.

Her eyes ran over the assortment of weapons I carried—I'd come prepared to use violence to get answers—and a hint of a smile grew.

My knuckles coiled and bleached as black flickered

across my vision. I wanted to tear off her head and paint the walls in her blood for what she had done to Vera. Eyes burning with hate, I thrust them at her. "I should kill you."

I would one day. One day soon.

The edge of her mouth curved up, amusement glittering in her eyes. She gestured toward the sitting area.

If she wasn't the only one who could help Vera, I would have slit her throat and been done with it.

I lowered into the chair opposite the witch. It groaned under my weight. Between us, a tea set perched on a low, wide tree stump. She sipped gingerly from one of the cups and didn't offer me any, knowing I wouldn't accept.

"What is wrong with my daughter?" she asked without preamble.

My brows inched up my forehead. "How could you possibly know why I am here?"

"Why else would you come, if not for her?"

"To kill you."

I was sorely tempted. So tempted, my hands shook. She was close enough, I could reach over and wrap my hands around her throat and crush it.

The shadow of a smile formed as she set her cup down and waited for a real answer.

I blew out a harsh breath, glaring at my fists clenched in my lap.

"You are the last person I ever wanted to come to," I gritted out. "I want to kill you. What you did to her—" I exhaled roughly "—I want to rip out your black fucking heart. This visit doesn't change that."

"I wouldn't expect it to, Enforcer."

My head snapped up. "Why did you pretend you didn't know me when I was here with Vera?"

A stiff smile breezed over her lips. "I had my reasons. Now tell me what is wrong with my daughter."

My jaw hardened. Knowing the Crone was the only one who might be able to save Vera did not make it any easier to share intimate knowledge about her with her abuser. Vera would hate me for it, but her life was at stake.

"She is poisoning herself with gold dust."

She took a dainty sip from her teacup. "Vera has always been dramatic, even as a child."

"Dramatic?" I lifted off the chair, ready to damn it all and kill her anyway. "Nothing about Vera's actions is dramatic," I snarled. "*She's terrified of becoming you.*"

My eyes flared wide.

I hadn't realized it until now, until I was sitting in front of the wretched woman who had raised her. Vera's drastic measures to keep her dragon subdued, even at the cost of her own life, was rooted in a paralyzing fear of turning into the Crone, of harming innocent children, like she'd done to Vera her whole childhood.

Kylah was right.

"Coming here was a mistake." I shoved to my feet. "I take back what I said about ripping out your heart. There is nothing to take."

I strode for the exit.

"Sit. Down."

A blinding light filled the cabin. I shielded my eyes, twisting toward it. The halo was coming from the Crone, or what had once been the Crone, because I was gazing at an entirely different creature.

Her skin was wrinkled and leathered like all the water had been sucked from her bones. Tufts of silver hair sprouted from a bald skull. The strands floated above her head like she was underwater. Serrated teeth filled her mouth; wicked looking claws gripped the chair arms.

Her eyes had elongated along with her pupils, creating two milky, white orbs that didn't blink as they stared at me.

They held the dawn of time in their depths and were as terrifying as they were ancient.

She wasn't like any being I had ever encountered before. She was ethereal, otherworldly, and wholly dangerous. Power pulsed through the air, sucking the oxygen from the room. It squeezed my lungs in an escapable vise.

"Kneel."

My body obeyed without permission. I slammed to my knees.

The vise around my lungs tightened. Darkness spotted my vision.

I was on the cusp of blacking out when the pressure vanished. I sucked in air, coughing, grabbing at my throat. When I glanced over, the Crone was the pink-lipped, rosy cheeked witch again.

"You and I are not even in the same league, Enforcer." She leaned back casually. "You have threatened and insulted me in my home. The only reason I am allowing you to draw breath is out of respect for what you mean to my daughter, but even that has its limits." She took another sip of her tea, then smiled coolly over the rim. "Have a care. For her sake."

I could only blink in shock for a stretch before I sat.

The cup returned to the table. "Vera is poisoning herself. For how long?"

"Since she freed her dragon to save her neck from the gallows."

Her smile was coy. "You've been misled, Enforcer."

My brows stitched together. "What do you mean?"

"Vera would never have freed the dragon for herself."

Her statement hung in the air, pointed and jarring.

"But she—"

"*Never.*"

I had no idea what to make of that. It's possible she could be lying, but what purpose would that serve?

I steered the conversation back to the issue at hand. "Vera has been poisoning herself for months."

This conversation reignited my fear and frustration. I rubbed my throbbing temple. I wanted to protect Vera, but I had no idea how. I was at the mercy of this fickle, callous woman. At her silence, my head jerked up. "Well?" I snapped.

She quirked a brow at my tone.

Drawing the Crone's ire didn't frighten me. Losing Vera did. "If you wish to kill me for worrying over your self-destructive daughter, you go right ahead."

She rose and crossed the room, returning with my mother's brooch. I held her gaze with a hard, determined stare. "I'm not leaving without answers."

"I cannot accept this."

I stared at the red lacquered nails clutching the brooch, before lifting my gaze to her face. "Why?"

"Two reasons. The first—my daughter and I bargained for it."

My mouth tightened. "What are you talking about?"

"She didn't tell you?" Her gaze flattened. "The self-sacrificing little fool. Did she learn nothing?" She heaved a sigh. "My daughter traded that comb in exchange for another visit with me."

Cold dread blasted through me. It wrapped around my heart with icy, burning tendrils.

"No . . . She wouldn't . . ."

I saw the damage after Vera's first visit, how much pain she was in. The Crone had shredded her back. She would never agree to go through that again.

"Oh yes. She offered herself for the same reason she freed her dragon. *For you.*"

"How could you . . ."

"I know everything, Enforcer."

312

I pushed it away. "Take it back. Keep the brooch."

"The bargain has already been struck." She dropped it in my lap.

I stared at the brooch in abject horror. *Vera, what did you do?*

My chest constricted painfully. Vera had traded time with the woman she abhorred, just so I could have this piece of my mother back. Not only that, but she'd also freed her dragon for me as well.

Why?

The answer hit me with the force of a battering ram. I nearly fell out of the chair.

Love.

Vera had done it out of a great, intense love—the same kind I felt toward her. With the revelation came horror.

Good Gods, what have I done?

"And the second reason." The Crone pulled me from my thoughts. "That's not your most prized possession anymore."

My gaze jerked to hers. "How do I help Vera?" I rushed out.

"She needs to trust her dragon."

"That's impossible," I growled. "She'd rather poison herself to death than ever give it control again."

"Then help her remember."

"Remember what?"

"Her dragon isn't the monster she thinks it is."

I didn't miss a beat. "You are though."

She shrugged her shoulders as if my statement was of little consequence. "I have never pretended otherwise, Enforcer. I am and always will be the villain in my daughter's eyes. The fates made it so."

I was on my feet, in the Crone's space, in half a second. Damn the consequences. This was about Vera.

I loomed over her, growling, "The fates didn't make you do all those horrible things to her."

"You are correct," she said indifferently, like Vera's pain meant nothing.

And yet she had offered me advice to help her without receiving anything in return. I didn't understand this witch, this thing—whatever she was.

Tearing myself away from her before I got myself killed, I walked over to the door but paused fingers lingering on the handle.

I glanced sharply over my shoulder. "I don't care what you are, or how powerful, I will find a way to kill you for what you did to her."

A small smile curved her lips. "I believe you will try. Why do you think I chose you?"

"Chose? But—"

She waved, her smile broadening. "Goodbye now."

A vortex of wind swept me out of the cabin.

27

VERA

There was a light knock. I groaned and lifted my head. There was a slither of light snaking through the curtains. Someone had been in to draw them closed. Kian had opened them when he stopped by this morning.

I had a feeling it was Ronan. I hadn't seen or heard anyone else coming in or out of his rooms.

I hadn't seen him since our argument the day before.

I've never seen him so angry, but he had no right to be upset. I was doing what I had to, and I wasn't going to apologize. Besides, we weren't anything to each other. He didn't get a say in my choices.

I think he had slept in one of the adjacent rooms because his scent was strong enough through the night to keep my dragon calm. It hadn't woken me once.

I glanced at the curtains. Based on the amount of light, it had to be early afternoon at least. I sat up, clutching my chest. It still throbbed from where I'd been struck.

Another soft knock.

"Come in," I called, expecting it to be Kian. He'd promised he'd pop in later after spending half the morning fussing over me, fluffing my pillows, and asking if I needed anything every five seconds.

No matter how many times I told him it wasn't his fault, he wasn't convinced.

"Good morning," a lyrical voice softly announced.

I blinked at the woman standing at the edge of the bed.

She wore a royal blue dress with a matching mantle. Gold chains, hanging from a lightning bolt adjournment, clasped each shoulder. Fine white gloves, woven from bodah silk, covered her hands. The upper part of her hair was woven into an elegant, braided crown, with soft brown curls sitting below it, and her wings were tucked neatly at her sides.

It took a moment for my groggy brain to register it was Ronan's mate.

I jackknifed into a sitting position, and tensed, waiting to be yelled at for being in his bed. Her spring green gaze glowed with a confusing warmth as she gingerly perched on the edge.

"Nothing happened, I swear. I was just injured and—"

"It's quite all right," she interrupted in a smooth, practiced way that made me forget I was speaking to begin with. At the same time, she lightly squeezed my hand.

The unsolicited touch of a stranger would normally raise my hackles, but she projected a calm, gentle auora that had the opposite effect. I had this bizarre desire to be her friend.

Fucking Kian. If it wasn't for him, I wouldn't even be thinking about having friends. The bastard was worming his way under my skin.

"It's a pleasure to finally meet you, Vera. I'm Kylah. Would you like to get some fresh air?"

Shock tied my tongue. Apprehension swiftly followed.

Was this friendly act a ruse? Did she plan on luring me

from the safety of this room to kill me? Bonded or not, Ronan might have told her what happened in The Wilds, and she could be here for revenge.

She took one look at my face, and her grip tightened reassuringly. "Ronan asked me to look after you while he takes care of a few things."

The tension in my muscles loosened. That made more sense than her being here to kill me.

Ronan was her mate, hand-picked by the Gods. No matter what happened between us, he'd come back to her. I was no threat.

I appraised her for a beat longer before agreeing, "Some fresh air would be nice."

Anything was better than being stuck in this room, even spending time with the woman fated for the man I loved.

She released me, and rose with a swift, fluid grace like she was made of silk. "I'll wait for you outside."

I quickly changed and met her in the hall. Now that we were standing, I could see how petite she was. Her head barely reached my chest.

"So." She began gliding down the hall, her mantle trailing behind her, while delicately clasping her hands at her waist. "I hear you have wings."

Suppressing a growl, I fell in step beside her. "Ronan told you."

"He did."

She flitted to a stop, her wings extending.

They were gorgeous and angelic with the width of two arm spans. They couldn't stretch out fully and had to curve around the walls.

The feathers looked so soft. I wanted to reach out and—

"You're welcome to touch them. I'm sure you're curious."

"No. That's okay." Despite her affable nature, that

seemed too intimate for someone I had just met, especially given who she was.

She didn't push. Her wings folded into her sides, and we resumed walking. Well, *I* walked. She gracefully skated forward.

It was a cool day outside the tower, a scant amount of sunlight slipping through the cloud cover.

"I would like to take you outside the castle if that's all right with you," Kylah said. She had a soft-spoken voice. It was gentle, but powerful.

Apprehension worked its way through me. She wanted to take me outside the safety of these walls . . .

I forced my worry away, reminding myself that Ronan had asked her to do this. Besides, this was likely the only chance I would get to leave again after the tavern incident.

"Milton," she called quietly.

The Head of House appeared, bowing. "How may I be of service, Madam?"

"Fetch my harness and eye mask, would you please?"

"Of course."

He marched off and Kylah unclasped her mantle, carefully draping it over her arm before moving onto her dress. She deftly undid the line of buttons down the back without looking.

I glanced away as she slipped it off her shoulders, concerned she was undressing in the middle of the courtyard, but other than a handful of gawking males, no one blinked at her actions.

"I am still decent." Her voice held a hint of humor.

Casting my gaze back, I saw she had a white bodysuit hidden beneath her dress. The material was glossy, reflecting my face back at me. She bundled her loose curls and looped them under the braid before pinning them flat.

318

"Ah, much better," she said with a smile once she finished. "I hate dresses."

I tilted my head at her. "Then why wear them?"

Her eyes glinted with mischief. "Because I love being underestimated even more."

Milton returned a moment later with the requested item, bowing as he held it out for her. She traded her clothing for the harness.

"Thank you, Milton." She leaned close, whispering conspiratorially. "You're my favorite, but don't tell the others."

Milton was blushing up to his roots when she pulled away. He smiled shyly. The whole interaction had me nearly choking on my spit.

He faced me and his expression hardened. "You're feeling better, I see." He walked off, but not before I caught him mutter. "Maybe I should sleep with the Lord and get the week off."

Color spread across my face. I vaguely remembered Ronan carrying me through the courtyard to his tower. I'm sure more than one person saw us and made up their own version of events.

I darted a look at Kylah. Her expression remained unchanged. Either she hadn't heard, or she was pretending she hadn't.

"This is for you." She offered the harness with a teasing smile. "It's how we fly our children."

I took it with a quiet laugh. I rested my gaze on her face, studying her in a new light. I sensed there was more beneath the pretty veneer.

The harness was a light brown leather with steel buckles to adjust the size and tightness. I stared at it with a quizzical expression before my gaze snapped to her. "Wait, did you say we're *flying*?"

She dipped her head. Then a small, mischievous smile snuck across her lips. "Unless you're afraid."

I maintained eye contact as I stepped into each loop and jerked the harness up to my hips. It was tight but fit me just barely.

A trill of laughter. "I knew I would like you."

Attached to the ends were two long straps that ended in a series of buckles. She took them and secured them to her ankles before offering the eye mask. It was just a strip of cloth with two slits for the eyes.

"You don't need one?" I asked as I tied the ends around my head.

She stared unblinking and I saw a thin membrane briefly slit over her eyes before retreating. "Belenus fae are born with a third eyelid."

"That's handy."

She smiled. "It is."

I peered around, nibbling my lip. No one was paying attention to us, but I still found myself asking, "Won't it be strange for you to take a halfling flying?"

"Not if they think you're sleeping with the Lord." She winked.

My face heated. She had heard Milton. "I swear, it's not true."

She smiled. "I know. Better to let them think it though so no one looks too closely at your glamour."

"But don't they know your mates?"

Discomfort briefly pinched her features. "We're waiting to announce it," she said evasively.

"That doesn't make you uncomfortable?"

She gently shook her head, her smile returning. "I know how much he cares for you."

I mustered a small smile. She was a better person than I was.

"Are you ready?"

"Let's do this."

Her wings stretched to their full size. They flapped and the accompanying wind gust pushed me back a step. She slowly lifted off the ground, and when she was high enough, I rose with her.

My stomach dipped as she carried us higher and higher. The ground became a speck of color and my heart galloped away in my chest. I clutched the straps on either side of my head with a white-knuckled grip.

The mask narrowed my field of view, but kept my eyes relatively protected. The wind was deafening, roaring across the sky. The leather creaked and groaned under the force of it.

"Are you sure this is safe?" I shouted.

"Perfectly. A fall from this height would kill you in an instant."

There was a second of shocked silence before I barked out a laugh. "Funny."

She reminded me a little of Kian, but her mischief was more subtle and unpredictable.

Her powerful wings carried us high into the sky. My heart was in my throat the entire time, but exhilaration was mixed with the fear. As we flew through the cloud cover, I ran a hand through one. They weren't soft like they appeared. They felt like mist.

An awestruck smile took over my face as Kylah slowed to a stop, her wings keeping us suspended above the clouds. Over our heads, the ribbons of lavender and turquoise wove through the blue.

Kylah grinned down at me. "Time for some fun."

That was the only warning before her wings snapped close, and she dived toward the ground. I was suspended in the air for a second before the straps stretched taut. My stomach bottomed out as I fell with her.

We dropped toward the ground with the speed of a bullet. The air pressed in on all sides. My cheeks were near my eyes with my lips flapping open. The leather felt on the verge of tearing in half.

I loved every second of it.

I threw my arms out to my sides, intimating wings. The wind swallowed my shriek of excitement as we barreled toward the sea.

Kylah's wings shot out at the last minute, slowing our descent so she narrowly avoided the water, but I didn't. I hit the sea with a splash, cold saltwater stinging my eyes as I was dragged over the surface.

I whooped loudly, urging her to go faster, and she did, soaring back into the sky, only to dive-bomb again. I screamed with glee as my stomach threatened to detach from the rest of me.

Her wings stopped us at the last second again and I dipped sharply back into the sea.

We rose again, but this time, Kylah veered south over the Fayette Mountains. We stopped to hover over them, and I pushed up my eye mask to take in the view.

The mountain's sharp, snowy peaks bit through the cloud cover.

Blue framed either side, with the Te Sea stretching east and the Reoite Sea to the west. I squinted, trying to see if I could spot the landmass that had been separated during the War of the Gods, but it was either too far, or had been swallowed by the water.

I was floored by the grandness of it all—of the clouds and sky stretching into infinity, of the mountain who had seen the birth of this world and would watch its end, of the miniscule size of the ground and all its problems, of how small I was compared to the vastness of this big, beautiful world.

There was freedom in my insignificance. I existed in a vacuum up here. A quiet, peaceful space where nothing mattered but the wind and the sky. I wished I could stay here forever.

"It's beautiful, isn't it?" Kylah asked.

"Stunning," I breathed.

Far off in the distance, there was a black spot interrupting the clouds. I could just make out the faintest flickers of lightning inside it.

"What's that?" I pointed.

"A perpetual storm. It only exists in the sky. It has never made landfall."

My forehead crinkled. "The Faylands is a strange place."

"It wasn't always," she said with a soft fondness. "It looked quite different before the war." There was a touch of grief in her voice. She was silent for a moment. "Ready for one last bit of fun?" she asked, sounding much more cheerful.

I slid the eye mask back in place. "Absolutely."

Kylah shot sideways into the wind. I held the straps in a death grip as the air currents threw me up and down behind her. She dove, then swept back up in a big loop, sending my stomach tumbling.

She did another loop, and another, and another. My lips were flying back from my teeth the whole time. She jettisoned into a spiral, torpedoing through the air, spinning me as she went.

All the rotating was making me dizzy and a little nauseous, but I was having too much fun to care. The leather straps twisted around one another, sharply turning me one way, then another as they untangled.

I surrendered to the moment, letting the wind and leather move me however they pleased.

After one final barrel roll, Kylah flew straight, parallel to the ground.

Air currents flowed under me. I extended my arms at my sides and felt the wind lifting me.

Holy shit.

I'm flying.

An unstoppable grin cracked across my face.

"I'm flying," I whispered, then I was shouting at the top of my lungs. "I'm flying!"

Kylah glanced back at me with a wide smile.

This, *this* is what freedom felt like. No one could touch me up here. I could go anywhere, do anything.

Much to my disappointment, Kylah only flew us a little longer before angling back toward House Taran. She set me down on a cliff edge before landing nearby.

I couldn't squash my beaming smile as I pulled off the eye mask and undid the harness. My heart was racing.

"You're a natural." Kylah's voice was flush with excitement. "We know what kind of flyers our children will be based on their reactions. The fearless ones are always the strongest. You'll be flying on your own in a couple days."

Every ounce of joy sizzled out. My head whipped toward her.

"Excuse me?" I said, overly harsh. "I didn't agree to that."

Her eyes widened. A delicate hand flitted to her lips. "Oh, my apologies. I thought Ronan had discussed it with you."

"No. He didn't," I gritted out.

He knew damn well I wanted nothing to do with my wings, or anything related to the dragon.

This was part of his agenda to get me to learn how to

control it. He knew I would have said no to him, so he sent his mate instead. The conniving, sneaky bastard.

Did he think one flying session would suddenly convince me that my dragon wasn't a child-murdering-monster? I was pissed at him for not only putting me up to something he knew I wanted no part of, but also for ruining my post-flying buzz. I was fuming.

"He tricked us both." Kylah sounded just as upset about it as I was, which made me feel a little better.

I took a deep breath, reigning in my temper. Ronan deserved it, not her.

"Let's enjoy the fresh air a while longer and then we can return," she suggested.

I jerked my head in agreement and took a seat, dangling my legs over the lip of the cliff. My talons sank into the dirt, anchoring me. Waves crashed against the rocks below. I tipped my head back, temporarily pushing away my anger so I could savor the wind kissing my cheeks.

Rustling had me peeling open an eye.

Kylah gracefully lowered to the ground nearby. Not a single hair was out of place. She looked as fresh as before take-off, meanwhile, my hair had ripped free of my braid and was doing a great imitation of a broberie nest. Her wings sat neatly against her sides, the feathers rippling in the wind.

Flying with her had been amazing; a once in a lifetime experience. It was nothing like the terrifying flight I'd been forced to take in Mayhem. If my wings weren't tied to the dragon, I might have considered learning how to use them.

Neither of us said anything. The squawk of seabirds overhead intermittently broke the silence.

"Not that I condone Ronan's actions," Kylah started, staring out at the sea. "But may I ask why you don't wish to fly? You seemed to rather enjoy it."

Her prying instantly raised my hackles. My head swiveled to her face. "Look, I don't know what Ronan told you, but whatever he did wasn't his to share. I don't know you and you don't know me."

She met my gaze with a perceptive stare. "I know that you are allowing your past to control you."

I reared back at her brazenness. Who the fuck did she think she was? She didn't know the first thing about me. "My past is none of your business," I bit out.

She pressed on, undeterred. "Would you deny yourself the pleasure of flying just to spite the one who gave you wings? How does that serve you? That's akin to setting yourself on fire and expecting the other person to burn."

Her words struck a painful chord.

I popped to my feet, hands clenched at my sides. "You don't know a goddamn thing about me," I gritted out. "Where do you get off on saying something like that?"

I threw the harness near her. "You're beautiful and adored. You couldn't possibly know what it's like to be me."

I stormed off to the castle.

Fuck her. FUCK. HER.

This might have been the first time we had met in person, but I had seen Kylah flitting around the castle with a flock of admirers. She was *loved*. There was only one person who had ever loved me, and she had stolen him.

I crested the hill leading to the castle and charged down it.

Kylah landed in my path.

"Move," I growled, vibrating with anger.

She faced away from me and slipped her bodysuit from her shoulders, exposing her back.

I gaped at the web of white scarring across her skin. Their lighter coloring stood out starkly against her olive skin. The scars looked like tree roots with the way they all branched off from one another.

She met my gaze over her shoulder. "I was not always beautiful and adored."

She jerked the fabric back in place and flew off.

28

VERA

I stormed inside his tower, on a tear.

"RONAN!"

I couldn't believe his gall. He'd sent *his mate* to do his dirty work. I didn't know if I was angrier with him, or her.

The woman had only known me for two seconds and she was making judgments on me and my life. Who the fuck does that?

A halfling armed with linens came down the hall.

"Do you know where Lord Taran is?"

"Try the dungeons," he suggested as he passed.

"Where are those?"

He pointed below.

There had to be an entrance through the training room.

"Thanks."

I marched for the spiraling staircase and charged down it, my fury billowing around me. I threw open the door to the training room and sent it crashing against the stone. Kian jolted at my entrance.

"Woah." He held out his hands as I stormed toward him. "Where's the fire?"

"Where. Is. He?"

I surveyed behind him. There was an unmarked door I hadn't noticed before. I started forward but Kian stepped into my path. "Trouble . . . Ronan's busy right now."

"Move," I growled.

When he didn't, I tried to dart around him, but he was faster. "Godsdamnit, Kian. Move."

"I wish I could, but—"

"Let her through."

Ronan stood in the darkened doorway. Shadows played over the planes of his face. I couldn't read his expression. Terse, hushed voices echoed from the dark corridor behind him. A muffled scream followed.

"What's going on in there?"

Ronan stepped aside. "Assist Finn," he told Kian, who quickly disappeared into the secret area I assumed to be the dungeons.

Ronan shut the door behind him, explaining, "Lord Cern did not send the Saor. I am attempting to find out who did."

He turned to me with a shockingly soft expression. "How are you feeling?"

"Fine," I said quickly, shrugging off the question. I wasn't here for chit chat. I hit him with a fierce glower. "What did you tell Kylah about me?"

He said nothing.

His silence inflamed my frustration. "Tell me," I demanded.

His eyes roved tenderly over my face. Bizarrely, he cracked a smile.

"What are you smiling at?"

It broadened a fraction. "You."

My brows dipped, lips pinching together. "You're acting strange."

"Am I?" he rumbled.

"Yes. You're in a good mood. Why are you in a good mood?"

He chuckled. The rich, masculine sound sent warmth pooling in my belly. "Am I not allowed to be?"

I scrutinized him. Up until yesterday, he had been furious with me about refusing to use my dragon to help, and then he'd been furious with me for poisoning it. Only one reason came to mind for his abrupt shift.

He thought his secret plan with Kylah had worked.

Heavy disappointment flushed through me. He was only being nice because he thought he'd gotten his way. Bitterness, thick and stinging like corth acid, bubbled in my chest.

"I'm not flying," I said hotly and Ronan's face shuttered. "What did you tell her?"

When he didn't answer me for a third time, I'd had enough. "I don't need this." I stormed to the door.

"I told Kylah everything," Ronan called at my back.

I crashed to a halt and whipped around, my voice rising with disbelief. "*Everything*?"

"Everything."

Molten anger licked through my core. I breathed through my nostrils like a pissed off beast, fist clenching and unclenching at my sides. "You had no right!"

His gaze darkened. Flinty eyes locked on mine. "I had every right."

"That's corthshit and you know it. We're nothing to each other."

"You were poisoning yourself." His voice was low and dangerous. "I thought Kylah could help." He crossed his arms over his chest and stared in silent demand.

I wasn't going to apologize for taking gold dust. It was any of his god damn business. I thrust my chin up at him. "You didn't ask her for me. You asked for *you*."

So, I'd save his precious House.

"No," he said firmly.

I searched his gaze. I didn't believe him for a second. "I think it's time for me to leave," I declared. "I won't put you in any danger. I'm going somewhere where I'll be safe. The mortals and king won't be able to find me."

His gaze hardened. "Where is this magical place you think you'll be safe?" he asked arrogantly.

I hesitated to answer but fuck him. This was my life.

I boldly lifted my chin. "I'm going to the Crone."

Shock, complete and utter shock, crossed his face, and then his gaze turned pitch black. He was in my space in four quick strides. "You are *never* going back to her. Do you understand me?" he snarled. "I don't care if I have to throw you in my dungeon, she is never getting near you again."

I blinked at his sudden rage. "You don't control me. And besides, the only reason you care is because you want me to protect your House from the king."

"Is that what you really think?" he asked, hurt flashing across his face.

"I think you have a House and a mate to think about."

His gaze ignited; his chest swelled. "Forget my House. Forget the king. This is about saving your life! If you weren't so determined to throw it away, you would see that."

"There is no saving me," I shouted back. "When are you going to see that!"

Understanding lit his eyes. The black retreated. "I went to see the Crone," he said quietly.

"Excuse me?" I hadn't heard him correctly.

"She said you need to remember your dragon isn't the enemy."

I threw my head back in laughter, the sound saturated in judgment. "Not the enemy? Of course she would say that. She's a glutton for my misery."

"You're your own glutton," he said in a hard tone. "Have

you even tried to remember how and when you were cursed?"

"I've blocked out everything to do with my childhood, and for good reason."

No good had ever come from sifting through my awful upbringing. What little I remembered was fraught with loneliness, pain, and an intense fear of the darkness within.

I had no memories of the dragon, other than sleeping in chains every night to keep it locked away. I didn't know what the darkness was, only the bone deep certainty that if it was ever released into the world, it would do terrible things—and it had.

He stepped toward me. "Why are you so afraid of your dragon?"

"Because it killed children!"

"Why are you afraid of harming children?"

I looked at him like he was demented.

He advanced further until we were toe to toe, enunciating every clipped word. "Explain to me how the woman who fearlessly stared down the Enforcer is so petrified of her own shadow, she would rather poison herself than fight?"

"We're not having this conversation."

"Why, Vera?"

I started backing away, but he caught my arm.

"Tell me."

I wrenched my elbow out of his grip, hissing, "Drop it."

"No."

My blood heated. "It's not any of your goddamn business," I snapped. "When are you going to get that through your thick skull?"

He looked me over, unfathomable disappointment in his gaze. "When did you become such a coward?"

Coward? He had the audacity to call me a *coward*? My anger exploded out of me like dynamite.

"I WOULD RATHER DIE THAN EVER BECOME LIKE HER."

My eyes rounded.

My mouth snapped shut.

I stood frozen in shock.

My chest heaved up and down with the force of my breathing. Time stretched as thoughts raced through my mind, too scattered to seize on any one.

A litany of confusing emotions welled up. Sadness and shame were the most prevalent.

I briefly met Ronan's gaze. There wasn't an ounce of surprise on his face. He had already known and wanted me to see it too.

"How pathetic am I?" I choked out.

A finger hooked under my chin. Gentle eyes touched mine. "You were raised under circumstances that would have broken most, and turned the rest cruel. But despite everything you went through, despite her best intentions, you remain kind and brave," he said softly. "You are remarkable."

Tight fists squeezed my lungs.

"I'm sorry, Ronan," I whispered defeatedly. "I know you need my dragon, but I—I can't become her, not even for you."

"I know. I just want you to be okay." He smoothed his thumb over my cheek. "That's why I sent Kylah. She can draw out your wings with magic. I thought you might enjoy flying."

At my look of apprehension, he added, "You don't have to do anything you don't want to."

"What about the king?"

"He is my problem." He dropped his hand and stepped away. "I should never have put that responsibility on you."

"I would help if I could."

He smiled tightly. "I know."

I sighed. "I'm still upset with you for telling Kylah everything."

His smile loosened and stretched. "Give her a chance. I know it might be difficult given the circumstances, but you two are more alike than you think."

She had survivor scars. A tendril of guilt wormed its way through my stomach. She'd hit a pain point and I had reacted poorly. But she had been out of line too.

"I'll think about it."

"That's all I ask. I've returned my best outpost soldiers to train the men here on beast warfare. I'll be overseeing the lessons, and they will run late. You'll have the chambers to yourself for most of the night."

"Oh," I said, masking my disappointment. I immediately chastised myself for feeling that way. I'd just met his mate. I was sleeping in his room because his presence calmed my dragon. Nothing more. "I'll let you get back to it."

I turned for the door.

"Vera."

"Yes?" I spun slowly, my heart crashing against my ribs.

"I—" His mouth closed. It opened again after a moment. "Get some rest."

This time I didn't try to hide my disappointment. "I will."

29

VERA

I napped on and off for the rest of the day, and briefly heard Ronan return around midnight when one of the adjoining doors quietly shut.

I slipped out of the covers and slunk into the hall. Kylah wasn't going to tolerate me sleeping in her mate's room for long. Despite Ronan's best intentions, he couldn't help me. I *had* to take gold dust.

I'd seen plenty of gold laying around the castle. There had to be some in Ronan's tower as well.

I crept down the hall. All the rooms were exceptionally dark. I chose the fourth door on a whim.

The handle clicked and the door silently swung inwards. Moonlight fought its way through the dense curtains covering the floor to ceiling window. The walls were empty. Patches of different colored paint spotted them from where items had been removed.

I found the same in the other seven rooms. Every piece of gold had vanished. I knew if I searched the rest of the castle, I would find the same.

"Ronan," I hissed under my breath.

I didn't understand why he couldn't let it go. I wasn't his to worry about anymore.

I left the gold dust issue alone for now. I would worry about it when I had to.

I backed up to my room. I had difficulty sleeping for the rest of the night, but thankfully I felt better in the morning, and restless.

I couldn't get Kylah's words out of my head. She'd struck a nerve, even if I didn't agree with what she said. I wasn't setting myself on fire and expecting the Crone to burn. I was setting myself on fire to keep any more children from burning.

A deeper, more reluctant piece of me could admit my reaction had stemmed from jealousy. Kylah seemingly had everything—beauty, power, Ronan—and I . . . I had nothing.

I had enjoyed flying with her, more than I'd enjoyed anything in a long time. Of course, if I was going to fly on my own, it would take substantially more work, but what else was I going to do? Mope around, pining for Ronan until the danger from the king was over?

No.

I'd been bluffing when I said I would leave for the Crone's. My risk of discovery there was low, but on the off chance it happened, and word got back to King Desmond . . . I couldn't do that to Ronan.

If flying didn't involve my dragon, I didn't see the harm.

That settled it.

I bathed, threw on a fresh set of clothes, and went to Kylah's room in the adjacent tower.

Hesitantly, I knocked. When the door opened, she greeted me with a smile that wasn't exactly warm, but it wasn't cold either. "Hello, Vera."

"Hey," I said awkwardly, then fell silent.

She stared intently, and I realized she was waiting for me to speak first, which was fair since I'd come to her.

I cleared my throat. "I'm not proud of the way I reacted yesterday." That was as close to an apology as she would get.

"I was out of line as well. I just — I knew someone like you once, and I wished I had told her what I told you."

I smiled tightly in response, unsure what to say.

An uncomfortable silence enveloped us, filled with the unpleasant circumstances of our situation.

"Look, I know things are a little awkward with you being Ronan's mate, and me being his ex . . ." The word hung in the air as I hunted for the best way to describe our relationship—Lover? Girlfriend? —but nothing seemed to fit. "His ex," I finished. "But it doesn't have to be."

"No, it doesn't," she agreed warmly.

My shoulders fell in relief.

"You know everything about me," I continued. "But I know nothing about you. I feel like I'm at a disadvantage."

"Let's rectify that, shall we?"

I took a step back as she exited her room. She was dressed in a similar outfit as yesterday with her hair styled in an elegant braid.

"Walk with me." She linked her arm with mine, and we moved down the hall together. I had to shorten my steps to stay in sync with hers.

"My father was a hateful man." Her soothing voice took up the silence. "Lightning was his favorite form of punishment."

Horror jolted through me. That's what those scars were from.

"It's why, as part of my powers, I can absorb lightning strikes and wield them as a weapon," she said matter of fact.

We reached the stairs, and she released me to descend first. She didn't say anything else, nor did she ask anything of me. When we arrived at the bottom floor, she joined our arms again, flashing me a smile.

"I was born to House Belenus, but it has not been my home in quite some time." A small undercurrent of grief rode her voice, but it was gone by the time she spoke again. "Those are the most important bits."

I watched her from the corner of my eye as we made our way outside. I envied the open way she spoke, the gentle way she touched, the easy way she smiled. She carried no secrets, or shame. She was vulnerable and soft.

I was sharp smiles and bullets holes. I needed people afraid of hurting me.

I could see why the Gods had chosen her for Ronan. She was everything I wasn't.

We stepped out of the tower into a cloudy day.

Kylah turned toward me, arms outstretched. "We'll need to go somewhere private for our lessons."

"Lesson," I corrected. "We'll go from there."

Her head dipped regally.

I stepped into her arms, and she tightened them around me as her wings slowly lifted us off the ground. We flew to the small island Ronan had originally brought me to, landing near the blackened pile of debris that was once his manor.

The edges of the island sat just above sea level. The elevation climbed further inland, providing a bird's eye view of the sea in every direction. A hot breeze blew in from the east, keeping the island pleasantly warm. Tropical plants flourished in the warmer climate.

I could see why Ronan had chosen the island for his guest house. It was close enough to the castle that he could return quickly if anything urgent arose, but just far enough to feel distant at the same time. I'm sure the scenery didn't hurt either.

"May I?" Kylah's voice broke through my observation.

I blinked at her.

She gestured at my back.

The beautiful surroundings were forgotten as trepidation worked its way through my stomach. "Is this the part where you draw out my wings?" I asked uneasily.

I hadn't thought this all the way through.

I hadn't had any gold dust since the tavern incident, and based on what I'd seen in Ronan's tower, I doubted I'd be able to get my hands on any in the foreseeable future.

The wings were part of the curse, and I was alarmed at the thought of trying to use them without gold dust in my system.

I peered up at the sky. Small slivers of sunlight were fighting through the clouds, but sunset was still several hours away.

I was safe for now.

"I need to be back at the castle well before the sun starts to set."

"No problem."

When I still didn't move, she used a hand to indicate my back again. On a deep breath, I nodded.

She moved behind me and felt around the upper part of my spine. Her fingers dug unexpectedly deep, and a cool sensation spread across my back.

"I'm going to release your wings in three ... two ... one."

I braced.

Wings shot out of my back. I hissed at the burning sensation and almost toppled backwards under their weight.

Kylah caught my shoulders to steady me. "Go slow," she cautioned. "It will take some time to get used to them." She released my arms, but lingered close in case I lost my balance again. "They're beautiful. Have a look."

I didn't move, tensing as I waited to see what the beast would do. I half expected it to lunge for the surface, but all the dragon did was lazily blink at me before lowering its head.

Relief trickled through me.

Craning my neck around, I glanced at my wings for the first time.

A black talon sat at the apex of each wing, similar to the ones on my hands—only these were much larger. Stretched over the bones was a thin membrane of skin covered in the silver scales the Crone liked for her spells.

They were three times the length of my arm and immensely heavy, the ends dragging on the ground. My back ached fiercely from supporting their weight.

"We'll need to build up your back strength," Kylah commented as she watched me struggle to remain upright. "But that will happen gradually the longer you keep them out. Let's start with learning how to move them."

She demonstrated by revealing her wings and expanding and retracting them.

I tried to imitate the movement, but my wings didn't respond the way hers did. I leaned back, thinking that might help. The angle put too much weight on my back, and I fell to the ground.

Pain radiated out my back and down my wings. The sensation in my wings was jarring. I'd never felt pain there before.

Kylah helped me to my feet. "How did that feel?"

"Humiliating."

She smiled. "Did you feel where your wings start and your back ends?"

Surprisingly, I had. "Yeah." I twitched, moving my back one way and my wings the other. "It's hard to describe, but they feel like a shoulder and arms. I can move my back independently, but I can't move my wings without moving my back."

My answer earned me another smile. "That's exactly right. Now, let's try again."

It took an embarrassing number of times for me to simply open and retract my wings without falling on my ass.

The movement required stretching the muscles between my shoulder blade with just enough force to open my wings without going too fast and over stretching the wing muscles. Retracting was the opposite. I had to pinch the muscles together lightly enough that I didn't slam my wings together and injure them.

By the time we broke for the day, I'd barely gotten the hang of it, and my back and wings were on fire.

"Do you want to meet again?" she asked as she used magic to hide the wings back wherever they had come from.

Their weight vanished and I staggered with relief. While the pain in my back muscles remained unchanged, the soreness from my wings had moved from outside to inside. I could feel them throbbing deep in my back, like a newly discovered muscle. It was a strange sensation.

I returned my attention to Kylah's question. I hadn't even gotten to fly yet. I couldn't give up before we'd started. I nodded. "Same time tomorrow."

A routine developed over the next week. Kylah would fly us out to the island and spend the day working with me, and then in the evenings, I would train with Kian. Whispers followed me around the castle, but most accepted my special treatment was due to Ronan's interest.

It took two days for me to be able to mirror the movement Kylah had shown me. My back still hadn't adjusted to carrying the extra weight, but it was beginning to hurt less, and the lessons with Kian were helping too.

I barely saw Ronan in those two days. I'd hear him return in the dead of night, but he'd be gone before I woke.

Day three, we moved on to flapping my wings with the eventual goal of being able to lift off the ground. Birds made it look much easier than it was. The action required complete precision. If the wings weren't flapping at the exact right angle, at the exact right time, there would be no lift.

Mid-afternoon, I thought I had it. I stroked my wings downwards, bringing the tips forward and down. They made a loop at the bottom of the downstroke, and I felt pressure lifting them from beneath. Suddenly, my boots were off the ground.

"Holy shit. Kylah—"

I lost the rhythm and fell flat on my face.

I released a pained groan as dainty feet appeared in my eyeline. A hand stretched out and Kylah helped me to my feet.

"You're learning remarkable fast," she said brightly.

I rubbed my smarting face, grumbling. "Doesn't feel like it."

"Getting off the ground is the most difficult part. Things are easier in the air."

"I hope so."

I lost count of how many times I fell on my face after that. This repeated for the next three days. I was able to get higher each time, but I couldn't maintain the rhythm.

Kylah helped me up each time, encouraging me to keep trying.

We didn't talk much outside the context of flying, but I was still learning a great deal about her. She was incredibly kind and patient but had a quiet strength that came out when needed.

Begrudgingly, I was coming to respect, even like, her. I didn't want to, but it was happening anyway.

On the seventh day, feeling frustrated and impatient with how things were going, I tried to work around the issue and jump and flap my wings at the same time to get airborne. I couldn't manage both and the wings immediately snapped back into a folded position.

I smacked my face onto a sharp rock and pounded my fist on the ground. "Godsdamnit."

Why did the wings work when the dragon was busy burning down a city, but I couldn't use them? I swiped away the blood dripping from my nose and glared over my shoulder at the appendages that refused to cooperate.

Work you, stupid things.

"The wings aren't the issue," Kylah said, coming over to help me up.

"How can the wings—the things that are supposed to make me fly—*not* be the problem?" I asked with annoyance as she hoisted me to my feet.

"If you stopped treating your wings like some grotesque insect you want removed from your back and treated them as an extension of yourself, you might actually fly this century."

My gaze shot to her face. She raised a delicate brow. "Am I wrong? Did I mistake the disgust in your gaze every time you look at your wings for something else?"

There was that quiet strength. She knew just when to coddle me, and when not to.

"Easy for you to say. Your wings are beautiful."

Kylah clucked her tongue, *tsking*. "Your wings are beautiful and powerful. You have twice the wingspan of mine, which means you have twice the speed. Keep trying. We aren't leaving this spot until you can lift yourself off the ground and stay there."

I didn't manage before sunset, but Kylah didn't give me any grief about staying, and we returned the next morning.

I arrived more determined than ever to prove her and Ronan wrong. The Crone didn't hold any power over me. I was going to fly, damnit.

It took until the afternoon, and I didn't go higher than a couple feet off the ground, but I managed to stay there. I stared down at the space between my boots and the dirt with wide eyes as my wings steadily beat at my back.

Holy fuck. I was flying! I couldn't contain the smile stretching from ear to ear.

I remained airborne, getting accustomed to the feel of my back muscles expanding and retracting in tandem with my wings. It still required intense concentration to maintain the correct rhythm. I hoped over time it would become more automatic like walking.

"Uh, Kylah . . . how do I get down?"

She crossed over and stood on a rock to reach my hands. "We haven't gone over landing yet. I'll be here to catch you in case you fall. When you're ready, slow your muscles contractions. Do it gradually. If you do it too quickly, you'll fall."

I followed her instructions as best I could but wasn't progressive enough and I came down swaying and stumbling like a drunk. Kylah caught me and eased me down until my boots touched the ground.

"That was a beautiful landing."

My eyes narrowed.

"It was," she insisted with a laugh.

Getting airborne became easier from then on. Each time, I lifted higher, testing the limits of my wings and gained more confidence in them when I didn't plummet to the ground. I still bumbled the landings. I couldn't get the pacing quite right.

On the tenth day, she suggested we practice over the sea.

We stood at the edge of the island, near Finn's castle.

Now that I was spending my days with Kylah and Kian, the asshole couldn't mess with me anymore. I still owed him for his corthshit with the boot.

Tangles of vines and moss were slowly reclaiming the stone, but it looked remarkably intact.

"What's the story there?" I forked a thumb at it.

Kylah sent it a mournful look. "A great tragedy took House Ogma before it's time." Her tone made it clear she didn't want to discuss it further, and I let it go.

"Ready?" Her voice was much brighter this time. "I want you to really push yourself. The sea will be there to catch you if anything goes wrong."

I nodded then straightened my spine and spread my wings—a task that once seemed impossible. My back muscles still struggled to support the weight of my wings, but the pain was leagues better than at the start.

Her tiny form darted forward and leapt off the cliff. She dove toward the sea. Her wings whipped out at the last minute, and she swooped upward.

"Show off," I muttered, but it lacked any heat. I had taken to knotting my hair into a tight bun. It took hours to untangle otherwise.

I stepped onto the ledge and moved my wings just like we practiced and slowly rose off the ground. My breathing held as I focused solely on maintaining the proper beating of my wings.

As I steadily rose, my heart crawled into my throat. I'd never gone this high before. I angled my wings and carefully maneuvered over the sea, my attention on the constant flexing and retracting of my back muscles.

Kylah met me halfway and I was incredibly grateful for her presence. I was a ball of nerves, hyper focused on not messing up the cadence of my wings.

"Stop thinking so much."

My smile was tight. "I don't want to fall."

She gave me a hard shove.

I lost the rhythm and fell. I somersaulted mid-air, fighting the wind and air pressure as I tried to right myself, but it was no use. I plummeted, spiraling toward the sea.

Suddenly, my wings caught a current and I was horizontal, no longer falling. I was gliding.

I released a startled laugh as I clutched at my pounding heart.

Kylah appeared at my side, a proud smile on her face. "Look at you. You're flying."

I was too excited to be mad at her little trick. It worked after all.

"Flying is as natural for wings as walking is for your legs. Once you're in the air, trust your wings. They know what to do."

It was true, even without my intense focus on the pulse of my wings, they were keeping me in the air.

We spent the rest of the day focusing on air maneuvers —turning, stopping, diving, and rising.

We met in the same spot the next day. This time in the evening so I could fly under the cover of darkness.

Kylah flashed a mischievous smile "Care for a race?"

I grinned. "Absolutely."

"First one to touch the sea and make it back to that hand-shaped cloud wins. We go on three."

"One," we said in unison.

"Two."

"Three."

Kylah leapt off the cliff in a barrel roll, spiraling toward the water. I was much more cautious, gently rising and getting my footing so to speak before I dove after her.

She had a head start, and her wings were lighter than mine and had less wind resistance.

She touched the water, then waited, splashing me when I touched down seconds later, before shooting off.

"Cheater." I laughed as I tapped the surface then put my massive wings to good use. They flapped loudly behind me as I gained on Kylah. I caught up to her and we were neck and neck for several moments until my powerful wings put me precious seconds ahead of her.

"Sucker!" I shouted as I shot right through the hand-shaped cloud. Kylah followed a second behind me.

Elated laughter bubbled up. I pumped a fist in the air, whopping. I won. I couldn't believe it. When I didn't hear Kylah celebrating with me, my eyes darted to her.

She was staring at me with a strange expression. I nudged her playfully. "Oh, come on, don't be a sore loser."

She didn't respond to my cajoling. "Has Ronan spoken to you?"

I frowned at the question. "Spoken to me about what?"

She muttered a sharp word under her breath. "There's something I need to tell you."

"Okay . . ."

Tight, forest green eyes silently roved my face. "Do you know how mates find one another?"

My frown deepened. Neither of us had been willing to broach the awkward subject before, and I really didn't see a reason to change it. Ignoring it almost made it easy to forget.

"Kylah, we don't have to talk about this."

"I'm afraid we do."

My stomach tightened. "Kylah—"

"We can see one another's markings."

Her stare was pointed. She was trying to tell me something, but I wasn't quite sure what.

"That's how you knew Ronan and you were mates?"

She slowly shook her head. "I haven't found my mate."

My heart stopped. "What do you mean . . . You and Ronan . . ."

"No," she whispered.

Ronan's strange question back in Coldwater floated up. *Is there a meaning behind all ink?*

Apprehension dawned.

I lost my concentration and plummeted toward the sea.

My descent was too fast. I couldn't right myself with the wind pressing in on me from all sides. Kylah dropped like a bullet. Her hand grazed mine before latching on, but we were falling too fast, and my wings were too heavy. All she could do was slow our speed.

We crashed into the sea. The icy water swallowed us eagerly, pulling us down into its gullet.

The cold punched the air from my lungs. I couldn't breathe. My massive wings pulled me into the black abyss. They were too heavy. I kicked and kicked but couldn't get anywhere.

Something grabbed me and towed me up. Kylah and I surfaced, sputtering for air, waves lashing around us. Together, we swam to the shore. Kylah hauled herself onto it. She nearly fell back into the sea helping me and my waterlogged wings up.

"Vera, are you okay?"

I ignored the question, stood, and stretched out my wings, flinging off the salt water. Then I launched into the air.

I landed with a loud thump in the training fields. Outpost soldiers were giving instructions to the castle soldiers.

Ronan and Finn stood on the outskirts, their heads bent low in conversation.

Pieces of it drifted over to me.

". . . Has been found."

"You're certain?"

"Kian . . . witnessed."

I stormed across the dirt like a dark angel. Eyes flitted toward me.

Ronan whipped his head around, and grinned when he saw it was me.

You motherfucker. You won't be smiling in a second.

I hid my rage, not wanting him to be on guard.

Just before I reached him, I ripped out the sword of the closest soldier, and spun on him, pressing the tip against his throat.

In a whisper, as cold as death, I said, "Tell me, Lord Taran, how long have you known we're mates?"

30

RONAN

Vera held a blade to my throat, but all I could focus on was how beautiful she was. Her hair was gathered into a bun. Damp tendrils escaped the confines and framed her face. Her cheeks were flush, her pouty lips parted. Wet clothes clung to her feminine curves.

Talon-tipped wings created a vicious silhouette in the moonlight. They were just as stunning as the rest of her.

And her face . . . It was wild with fury.

There was a sketch in the House archives of the First Daughter. Tatharra Taran was the only woman born from a god's flesh. The other Gods all created sons. One of those First Sons envied Tatharra's magic. He saw her as inferior, and undeserving of the power she was given.

When she was pregnant with her first child, and at her most vulnerable, he brought an army to her door at midnight.

She commanded her soldiers to stand down, walked outside, and stood alone against the enemy with a swollen belly, clad in only a nightgown. With a single flick of her hand, she tore the bones from the First Son and used them to neuter his army.

I imagined Tatharra's expression as she faced down those men was the same way Vera was looking at me now. My cock didn't understand the danger I was in.

I sensed movement in my peripheral. My men were edging close. I'd reinforced Vera's glamour the moment I heard her land. The soldiers saw a halfling holding a blade to my throat and were expecting me to harm her. They were closing in to intervene.

"Leave us," I barked.

The warriors slowed but didn't stop.

"Now!"

Reluctantly, they filed off the training fields until it was just Vera, Finn, and I.

Finn was waiting for an answer.

Greer, an escapee of House Dagda nearly a century ago, had apparently not severed ties. He'd confessed to feeding the king information.

"I'll deal with it later," I told Finn. "Throw him in a cell. Have it guarded at all times."

Finn dipped his head and departed.

Vera's lips peeled back. Sharp ivory glinted in the moonlight. "I said." The sword dug deeper. "How long have you known we're mates?"

Dread drenched my insides.

I had made a grave mistake lying to Vera.

She didn't just care for me, she loved me more than I thought it was possible for anyone to love someone like me. I had been biding my time, deliberating the best way to tell her, but the whole truth was dark and complex. I had yet to determine how to navigate it without losing her.

Kylah had beaten me to a portion. If she had told Vera everything, who I really was, Vera would be a million miles away by now. I wanted to be furious with her, but it had been unfair to put Kylah in that position.

"I was going to tell you . . ."

Her wings flared out as the blade broke skin. "Answer the fucking question."

Teeth bore into my cheek. "Since our first night in Coldwater."

Vera snapped me a look fiery enough to set me aflame. "You've been lying this whole time," she ground out.

She tried to slit my throat, but I grabbed the blade, and it sliced open my palm instead. I disabled her with my other hand, knocking the sword away. It clattered to the dirt. I snatched her wrist before she could lunge for it.

"Let me explain."

Her nostrils fattened with rage. "If you don't let me go right this second, I'll burn this castle to the fucking ground."

"Do not threaten my House," I cautioned softly. "Your anger is warranted. Your threat is not."

Her eyes burned white hot. "It's not a threat. It's a promise."

She tried to wrench her wrist away, but I held onto it with a gentle firmness. "Vera . . ."

She stopped fighting, lifting her gaze to me. Anguish etched deep lines around her eyes. "What are you going to do, Ronan? Break my heart?" she whispered, voice cracking. "Too late."

My stomach pitted. I released her.

"I had my reasons," I said carefully as she backed up. I knew the fallout of my lie would be nothing short of catastrophic, but I thought I would have more time to prepare.

Her agonized gaze gripped mine. "Do you wish Kylah was your mate? Is that it?"

"*Of course not.*"

"Then why did you lie?" Her voice broke at the end and hit me square in the chest.

"Because," I started roughly. My breath caught in my throat. "I . . . I believed you kept the iron dust because you never stopped seeing me as a monster. I didn't think you could ever love me the way I loved you."

Watery eyes shifted between mine. "I wanted you to be a monster. I needed you to be, but no matter how hard I tried to convince myself, I couldn't."

I stared imploringly. "Then why did you keep the iron dust?"

"I didn't," she said, looking confused. "After we were intimate, I knew I couldn't do that to you. I took it with me to the kitchen and left it there."

"But you could have poured it out or gotten rid of it."

"Ryder found me. By the time he was gone, I didn't have much time left before I knew you'd come looking for me, and I knew if you found me with it . . ." she trailed off.

Horror washed through me. She hadn't kept it.

She took in my expression and her face fell with despair. "How could you think I didn't love you with my whole being? I gave up everything for you, Ronan. Even after you broke my heart."

"I didn't know," I half choked, half whispered. "I thought it was for the best. I wish I could go back. I would give anything to go back."

She pinned me with a probing stare. "But you knew we were mates before I poisoned you. Why didn't you claim me as soon as you knew?"

My heart tripped in my chest. My breathing became unsteady. If I answered that, if I told her everything, I would never see her again.

"It's . . . complicated."

"It's complicated," she repeated in disbelief, her eyes sharpening. "Then uncomplicate it."

A sickening sensation gripped my throat. I couldn't give

her what she wanted, but I would fix this. I would. I just couldn't think of the right words at the moment. "I can't." My voice bordered on panic. "Not right now, but I will."

The tears finally fell. Her lips sank into a defeated smile. "I was never going to be good enough for you, was I?"

"No," I said viciously. "That was never in question."

"Then why?" Her voice caught.

"I can't answer that."

Her mouth set into an unforgiving angle. She shook her head before she launched into the air. Flying in a swift arc, she landed on the balcony leading to my chambers.

Panic squeezed the air from my lungs as I raced after her.

I skidded to a stop inside. Vera was nowhere to be found, but there was a trail of puddles leading into the bathing chamber.

I paced outside the door, with my heart in my throat, desperately thinking of how to assuage her concerns without revealing too much. When she remained locked inside for over an hour, I began to worry. I pressed an ear against the door. It was dead silent on the other side.

"Vera?" I rapped lightly.

Silence.

I knocked with more urgency. "Vera, I need to know you're okay."

More silence.

My stomach tied into knots. I kicked down the door and rushed inside.

Vera was sitting against the bath. She hadn't changed out of her wet clothes. Her knees were pulled to her chest, her head lying atop.

I froze at her expression.

There wasn't an ounce of anger or pain.

There was nothing.

Horror shook me clear to my bones. I knew that look. I'd worn it for centuries. Something inside Vera had broken. *I'd* broken something.

"I didn't claim you for reasons I cannot explain right now, but I swear to you, they had nothing to do with you," I choked out. "You're perfect. You're everything I ever wanted."

She said nothing.

Her blank gaze was unnerving. Silence dragged for a long, agonizing stretch before she rose and tried to move past me. I blocked her with an arm.

Vera didn't yell.

She didn't threaten.

She didn't fight.

She didn't say a word.

Vera was brash, stubborn, quick-tempered, *but she was never quiet*.

That's when I knew. That's when I really knew. I fucked up. I fucked up bad. I fucked up so badly there might be no coming back.

It felt like the two of us were standing on a cliff's edge and one wrong word would send her careening off, and I'd never see her again. With infinite caution, I stepped out of the way. "Please," I begged softly. "Talk to me."

Mechanically, she moved past, crossing over to the balcony, and launched off.

I didn't think. I backed up and ran full speed, pushing off the railing as I leapt into the air. My arms came around her legs, just a breath away from missing. She dipped at the extra weight, struggling to fly.

Her head snapped down at me, glaring. The spark of anger eased some of the tightness in my bones. I could work with anger.

I tightened my arms as she attempted to shake me off. "I'm not going anywhere."

She smiled sharply. We shifted directions and flew over the sea. She slammed a foot down on my face, and I lost my grip.

My back hit the water with an audible slap. I plunged into the water and quickly swam for the surface. I spun in circles, searching for Vera as waves surged around me. She didn't make me wait long before she was there, shoving me back under.

Water seared my nostrils and lungs, but I didn't fight. I let her purge her rage and pain, drowning me over and over.

She wrenched me up by the hair after several minutes, her eyes glowing with pain.

"Vera, please—"

She dunked me under, holding me there for a long stretch before jerking me up. She did it again and again until her drowning efforts became half-hearted as she tired.

I gently removed her hands and surfaced.

I stared up at where she hovered slightly above, tiredly flapping her wings. I could tell she was about to fly away. In a panic, I grabbed her leg, and yanked her down. She landed with a splash, and popped to the surface, sputtering and glaring.

"Please. Let's discuss this."

"There's nothing to talk about," she whispered, eyes welling with pain. "The one person meant for me doesn't want me just like everyone else in my life."

"Want has never been the issue," I said urgently.

A brittle laugh. "Do you know what *I* want?" Jaw tight, she glanced away, but not before I saw the tears misting her eyes. "I want you to stop hurting me."

A blade sunk into my heart. My mate, the woman I loved

with every fiber of my being, had to *ask* me to stop hurting her.

I was no better than the Crone.

"I'm so sorry, Vera," I said sounding like there was broken glass in my throat. "I am so goddamn sorry."

A gulf opened between us. Waves bobbed us up and down as Vera waited for me to say something—anything—but no words came. My stomach turned leaden as she swam over to an outcrop of rocks.

"Vera, wait!"

She climbed out of the water and glanced over, staring right through me.

A cold sensation seeped like rot through my gut. It took me a moment to place because I had not experienced a feeling like it since I was a boy—*raw terror*.

I'd only ever had two beautiful things in my life. Vera and my mother. My mother had been viciously taken. I'd barely survived it. I wouldn't survive losing Vera.

Beads of sweat broke out over my forehead. The Gods could take anything else; my title, my lands, my power, but not her. Anything but her.

I cut through the water to reach the base of the rocks.

"Please stay." My voice trembled. "Even if it's to hate me. Even if it's to hurt me. Even if it's to drown me, stab me, scream at me, set me on fire. I don't care. Just—*just don't leave.*"

Vera was quiet for so long I thought she might have flown off. "Why didn't you claim me?" Her voice was a feather-light whisper. "Tell me and I'll stay."

With time, I could ease her pain. I could show her how much she meant to me. There was still hope for us, but not if I told her what she wanted. If I told her the truth, the whole truth, Vera could never look me in the eye again.

I gazed up at her with wretched eyes. "I can't."

She stared and stared. Tears spilled down her cheeks, glistening in the moonlight. She turned away. "I don't want to be in love with you anymore," she whispered, and then she was gone.

31

VERA

Tears blurred the night. It felt like a knife was slowly hollowing out my chest cavity, severing every artery, every muscle and tissue until there was nothing left. It was taking all my strength just to keep my wings steady.

Breathing was a struggle. Each breath sawed in and out of my lungs, searingly painful, because every intake of air reminded me that despite the crushing heartache, I was alive. I was dreadfully alive.

'I'm sorry.'

He had torn out my heart a *second* time and that's all he had to say . . . Sorry. Un-fucking believable.

The moonlight guided me through my tears. The wind tugged at my hair and clothes like pleading hands. 'Don't do this,' it said. 'It's not too late to turn back.'

But I was never going back. Not to him. Not ever.

He'd taught me a horrible lesson, but a lesson, none-theless. We were chosen for one another by the Gods. I was his other half, and that still wasn't enough.

I still wasn't enough.

And I never would be.

Devastated laughter tore from my lungs.

What a cruel fucking joke.

I wished Kylah had been his mate.

"FUCK!" The scream ripped from my throat, full of the grief I'd held back when I thought we weren't mates. "FUCK!" I screamed for all the pieces of me I'd given that I could never get back. The screams devolved into uncontrollable sobbing, shuddering through me with the force of an earthquake tearing apart a continent.

"Fuck," I whispered for the great tragedy that was my life.

I reached the fanged peaks biting through the cloud cover, and soared over them, putting the Faylands and every rotten memory of it behind me.

We're almost there.

The kaleidoscope of brilliant colors bled into muted browns and greens. I angled right, dipping toward the stretch of lifeless gray. A strip of blue was visible through the dense tree cover. I followed it south, knowing it would lead to my destination.

Spotting the massive circle of stones between the tree-tops, I dove down and landed.

The canopy blocked most of the moonlight, allowing only a small slice through. Monoliths loomed in the darkness like silent sentinels, watching, waiting.

I crossed through the ring into the meadow. The canopy widened, allowing dappled silver light to spill over the ground like fine bodah silk. Cutting my palm with a talon, I squeezed my hand tight until blood dripped over the white petals and hit the soil with a hiss.

Then I waited. There was none of the familiar fear or anxiety of what lie ahead. There was only relief.

The burden I was carrying, the strangling heartache,

would be compartmentalized and neatly tucked away where I wouldn't have to acknowledge its existence. My days would be filled with pain and survival. There wouldn't be room for anything else.

A shadow crossed overhead, blotting out the moonlight as it passed. I peered through the canopy but couldn't see into the recesses of the night.

Probably just an air beast.

It didn't take long for the vortex to appear.

As I stared at the violent swirl of air, a slither of unease wormed its way through my stomach. There was no going back. The Crone wouldn't let me escape a second time. But that's what I wanted.

I started forward, but halfway there, some unnamable force stalled my feet. I glanced over my shoulder.

A cold patch of moonlight fell on the trunk Ronan and I shared. I could see his disgruntled expression while I pretended he wasn't there, could see him launching the bread in the air, and my resistance bleeding away as he kissed me.

I didn't know it then that I was already falling for him. It was why I had been so upset with him for killing the teenager. I didn't want to be in love with a man who harmed children.

I wished I could go back and shake that woman on the log. I'd tell her to stay away, tell her it all ended in heartache.

Somberly, I turned and continued to the vortex.

When I was just inches away, a dark shape landed in my path.

Kylah was there, her wings flared, her green eyes bright and wild. "I cannot allow you to do this."

I stared hollowly. "It's not your decision. My mind's made up."

She advanced a step. "Vera, you are not thinking clearly. You are in pain."

"I know I'm in fucking pain," I snapped. "Because Ronan lied about us being mates and you helped him."

It wasn't Kylah's fault, but she was here, and he wasn't.

Guilt formed brackets around her delicate mouth, but her voice was confident. "I had no choice. I owed him a debt."

I didn't care why she did it. I only cared about getting to the Crone, about leaving all this agony behind. The wind tunnel flickered, a silent warning to enter or be left.

"You need to move," I said.

Her mouth set into a stubborn line. "No. This will not solve anything."

Another flicker.

My shoulders slumped, partially in exhaustion, partially under the weight of my wings. The little strength I had left was fleeting. I didn't have the energy to argue with her, much less force her to move.

"Kylah, *please*."

Her widening stance was at odds with her soft tone. "No, Vera. I will not allow you to destroy yourself."

The tunnel flickered a third and final time before vanishing.

I sagged, a ball of anguish forming in my throat. It would be easy to call another vortex, but in that moment, it felt like an insurmountable task. It had taken all I had left to fly here and offer my blood.

Without the vortex, without my only means of escape, the breakers keeping everything at bay shattered. Raw, searing grief ripped through my bones. I sank to my knees. "He doesn't want me. He never did."

"Oh, Vera." She rushed to my side and gathered me in her arms.

Tears distorted her face as I lifted my gaze to hers. "Just once, I want to be loved. Just once, I want to be someone's favorite person. Just once, I want to walk into a room and light up someone's face." My desperate eyes clung to hers. "*Just once*, I want to be chosen."

Kylah clutched me tighter and I burrowed my face in her neck as big, ugly cries rocked my frame. We stayed like that for a long time, my sobs filling the forest.

I cried my heart out, until my eyes were swollen, and my chest was raw. Until my shirt collar was soaked through. I cried until there were no more tears left, and a numbness settled over me.

I pulled away. "I can't go back," I said weakly. "I won't."

Kylah gripped my shoulders. "You do not have to go back," she said firmly. "We'll go somewhere safe."

"We?" I asked pathetically. I didn't want to be alone right now, but I also didn't know how to ask her to stay.

A gentle smile. "We."

I wanted to smile back. I wanted to accept her concern for what it was, but I couldn't help the familiar suspicion creeping in.

Kylah and I had bonded during our flying lessons, but we were still practically strangers. "Why are you here?" I asked. "Why are you being so nice to me?" No one was ever this nice to me, not unless they wanted something.

She looked confused. "You're my friend."

I couldn't fathom where it came from, but her words made a tiny smile bloom. "Friend." I rolled the word around on my tongue. "I like the sound of that."

She grinned. "Good because there is no getting ridding of me."

I tried to smile again but it came out as a grimace.

"Are you able to fly?" she asked, standing and offering a hand.

I nodded and let her pull me to my feet. I was tired, but Kylah's presence was returning some of my energy.

She rose into the air with me following close behind. We flew north into the Faylands. Tension tightened my muscles as we approached House Taran, but we flew right over it.

We glided in the night, right below the clouds, before she cut through them and steadily rose higher. When I caught up to her, a bright cluster of lights in the distance caught my eye. No, not lights—lightning. She was leading me into the storm spot.

She glanced back. "Stay close!"

Nervous prickles filled my stomach. I was not an advanced enough flier for this, but I continued, trusting she knew what she was doing. The closer we flew to it, the more severe the weather turned.

Violent, hundred-mile hour winds slammed into us. I threw my hands up to protect my face.

"Keep your wings straight," she instructed. "If you give the wind even an inch, it'll throw you for miles."

I tensed my wings like I would a muscle and forced them to be as straight and solid as possible. They had to flap double time just to keep from being carried away. Every foot forward was a fight.

Kylah was having an easier time, but the gale force still pushed her back with all its strength.

Lightning strikes lit up the dark swirl of clouds every second, one right after the other. They were blinding. The wind was a deafening roar, so loud, I couldn't hear my own thoughts.

We finally reached the black, shifting mass at the center. My stomach pitted as we flew straight into it.

The storm swallowed us and for a moment I couldn't see anything as I was thrown up and down in the turbulent wind with rain hammering me from every direction. A blast of lightning lit up the sky and illuminated a cabin of milky blue stone in the distance.

Kylah stayed at my side the entire time, shooting me glances every couple of seconds to check on me.

My wings beat furiously against the wind. I struggled in the currents, but by some miracle, I was able to make it to the cabin.

Kylah struggled with the door. She wrenched it open, and it nearly flew off the hinges as it slammed into the cabin's exterior. Using its frame, she dragged herself inside.

"Come." She waved me through the door. "You must hurry."

When I was close enough, Kylah grabbed my shoulders and helped me inside.

It took the two of us to tug the door closed. She slid a thick bolt across it to keep it in place. The storm sounds immediately cut off, insulated by the cabin's thick stone, but the flashes of light could still be seen through the windows.

Her silhouette moved off, lighting candles and a small fire at the back. The space flickered to life, cast in a buttery glow. Individual ropes hung from the rafters, placed evenly throughout.

The cabin started to shift under the force of screaming wind too loud to be blocked out by the stone.

Kylah snatched two of the ropes. "Hold on!"

I reached for a pair, just as the cabin tipped at a ninety-degree angle. My feet dangled off the ground as my body was thrown sideways. I was suspended like that for several moments, holding onto the ropes for dear life before the cabin righted itself and my boots touched back down.

Not a single thing had fallen. As far as I could tell, everything was bolted in place.

"One moment. I need to create a seal around the cabin," Kylah said.

Her draoistone flared as her eyes shut in concentration.

I glanced at the cabin walls. They were emitting the same blue glow as her draoistone. I crossed over and pressed my hand against the stone. Power thrummed under my palm. It stopped as soon as Kylah opened her eyes.

"There. We're safe now."

"Is this whole place built with draoistone?"

"It is."

She returned to the door and slid back the bolt before pushing it open. The storm was visible beyond the porch, but only soft rain patter hit the cabin. The deadliest parts had been filtered out.

"That's a neat trick," I commented.

She smiled as she shut the door. "Welcome to my little haven."

I glanced around. There were two beds sitting across from each other, a table, some chairs, and a rocker. The furniture was colorful, and on the older side, but well loved.

On the walls were a series of beautiful oil paintings of storms. The largest one had a bright bolt of lightning set against a dark night with a raging ocean below. The others depicted a hurricane, a tsunami, and a field of fiery ice spears.

"Ronan can't find us here?"

"Oh, he'll find us. He will tear The Lands apart looking for you, but he won't be able to reach us."

That gave me a small measure of relief.

My teeth chattered loudly, the cold finally registering. My skin was icy from the wind and rain. I wrapped my arms around myself. It didn't help that the small space was freezing. The fire's warmth didn't reach far.

Kylah's suit was made of a slick material that repelled water instead of retaining it. Other than her hair, she was perfectly dry.

"Poor thing. You're freezing."

She ushered me into the rocking chair in front of the fire and added more logs before draping a fur over my shoulders. Dry clothes were set on the table beside it. "I'll be back shortly."

I slipped out of my wet clothes and changed into the new ones as Kylah rustled around in the kitchen. They were a little small, but warm and comfortable.

I scooted the chair closer to the flames and held out my shaking arms. The fire was steadily producing more heat as it grew, but it would be a while before it warmed the cabin.

Kylah returned with a steaming mug of tea and pressed it into my hands. The heat of it soaked into my palms and up my arms.

I raised the mug to her in silent thanks, then took a sip, and released a deep sigh at the warmth flooding my veins. I slowly drank the tea, staring into the crackling flames as I rocked back and forth.

We were quiet for a while before I broke the silence. "So, what happens now?"

"You'll stay here for as long as you need."

My gaze drifted down to where she sat. "What if that's forever?"

"Then I suppose we'll get to know each other quite well," she teased.

I didn't have it in me to smile.

Her amusement faded. "You should get some rest. It's been a long day."

I nodded, setting the mug aside.

She pressed a hand to my back and my wings disappeared.

"Choose whichever bed you'd like."

I picked the closest one on the right. Sleep was instant.

When morning came, I couldn't get out of bed. I couldn't

even move. I laid under the covers and cried. Kylah sat at my side. She didn't speak, only laid a gentle hand on my arm, letting me know I wasn't alone.

Eventually, I cried myself back to sleep.

The same thing happened the next day.

The morning after that, the Gods were cruel, and wouldn't let me sleep anymore.

Time passed with agonizing slowness. Each dragging second was spent reliving the horrible circumstances that had trapped me here. Sometimes it made me angry, other times I sobbed uncontrollably.

I felt like a ghost, occupying an alternate plane of existence, not really living, but not dying either.

Some food and tea appeared at intervals. Kylah left me alone other than that. She was the only light in this dark affair.

On the fourth day, she gently perched at the edge of the bed as I stirred. "Would you like to get out of here for a little while? I thought we might resume our flying lessons."

I rolled over with a groan, drawing the covers over my face. "Not today."

She squeezed my shoulder and left. We had the same conversation the next day. On the sixth, her patience had thinned.

She ripped off the covers. "Get up. I can't watch you rot away in this bed any longer."

"No." I flipped on my stomach, using the pillow to block out the light. She took that too.

Twisting sideways, I sighed, rubbing my tired eyes. "I don't want to get up, Kylah. I don't want to do anything." Except maybe cry. I could already feel the tears coming on.

"I've known Ronan—"

I jolted up sharply. "I don't want to hear that name."

"I've known him all my life," she resumed in a softer tone.

A stress headache formed, partly from all the crying and partly from the subject matter. I drew my knees to my chest clutching my head. "Please Kylah. I don't want to talk about this."

I was saved by a soft trilling.

She pursed her lips staring at me a moment before she elegantly rose and picked up a scrying mirror sitting by the fire.

"Hello, Roark." Her lips tipped into a fond smile. "How's my favorite cousin?"

"First of all, I'm your only cousin. And secondly, don't you favorite cousin me, Ky! Your dear friend Lord Taran kidnapped me in the middle of the night and had me at knife point for the last twelve hours building him a gods-damn stone tower!"

The door rattled in its frame. "Vera! I know you're in there."

Kylah and I froze, gazes clashing.

"I'll handle him," Kylah told me, swiftly moving to the door. "Roark, I've got to go. I promise to call soon." Roark was in the middle of shouting something when she ended the connection.

She ripped open the door and I ducked by the side of the bed, out of sight.

"Where's Vera? I need to speak with her."

A whipcord of pain lashed my chest at the sound of his voice. I grimaced at the stinging burn, fighting not to cry.

"She doesn't want to see you," Kylah said calmly.

"She is *my mate*."

The pain quickly left on a rush of rage. How *dare* he try and claim me now.

A gust of wind swept through the room, knocking out all

369

the candles. The air swelled with static electricity like the first warnings of a storm. My skin prickled. The hair on the back of my neck rose.

What was happening?

I peeked over the edge of the bed. The view of Ronan was thankfully blocked by the door frame. Kylah was illuminated in the flashes of lightning levitating off the ground with her hair floating around her like she was underwater. Her eyes glowed an electric blue as her wings flared. Electricity crackled between her fingertips.

Holy shit.

"She is *my guest* and *my friend*. You will leave."

"No."

A window exploded. I crouched, covering my head as shards flew. A lightning strike had shattered the glass. The bolt glanced off the ground and slammed into Kylah. Her hands turned out and a blinding flash of light exploded from her palms.

I heard a grunt of pain a second before I caught a glimpse of a body flying backwards.

Kylah's feet touched down at the same time her hair resettled around her face. She jerked the door closed and threw the bolt before looking at me.

I stared, slack jawed.

"What is it?"

"You're a little scary," I murmured as I came out of my hiding spot.

She laughed softly.

I peered through the window. All that was left was the curtains framing it and the two intersecting pieces of wood that had once connected the panels.

There was an enormous stone pillar outside the cabin. I could just make out Ronan's form amongst the ridges in the flashes of light. I don't know how he could have possibly known it was me standing at the window, but somehow, he did, shifting toward me.

"I'm not going anywhere. You can talk to me, or not, but I'll be here."

I leaned out of the frame, teeth bared. "You could sit out there until your bones turn to dust and I still wouldn't forgive you!"

32

RONAN

A flash of lightning ignited the sky, and I could see her. Those lavender eyes, bright with fury, were the most beautiful thing I'd ever seen. Relief exploded through me. She was okay.

The curtains were wrenched closed a split second later.

I'd spent the last week frantically searching for her, desperate with fear that the Saor had kidnapped her, or worse—the king had learned she was alive.

The castle had been turned upside down, and I'd sent Kian into the local villages to see if he could catch any rumors of her capture, both to no avail.

Finally, I'd gone to Mayhem, to the saloon Vera had brought me to, and met Marty. He had almost taken my ear off with a shotgun, but when I told him Vera was missing, he dropped everything to help search. We checked her old haunts, what remained of them, but found no signs she'd been in the city.

Shortly after I returned home, Milton reported Kylah missing, and I knew where they had gone.

At the passing of her youngest sister, Kylah had unleashed her fury and grief into the heavens and created a storm so powerful it had been feeding off itself for centuries. She'd built a cabin inside, and over the years, it became her sanctuary. She disappeared there for months at a time.

The only way to reach the hideaway was with wings, or something incredibly tall. I'd opted for the latter and kidnapped Kylah's cousin, Roark, in the dead of night from House Anu.

I forced him to grow a column of rock strong enough to withstand the storm and tall enough to reach it with ledges built in for climbing and sitting.

Hunkering under a ledge, I clutched at where Kylah struck me. The scorch mark had disappeared, but the sensation of being hit in the chest with lightning was deeply unpleasant.

The column's ledges offered poor protection from the elements. Rain fell in thick sheets, and I was drenched in seconds. Thunder crashed through the clouds like war drums and shook the rock with its percussive boom.

Another burst of lightning flashed across the sky and illuminated two silhouettes behind the curtains. It was easy to identify Vera's taller frame.

Now that I knew she was safe, I could focus on winning her back.

The first order of business was to have a conversation. All I needed was five minutes, and I was confident I could convince her to return home with me. From there, I could work on repairing the damage.

Rain and wind battered the pillar throughout the night. My clothes were soaked through and frozen, clinging to my skin. I was wet, cold, and miserable. But I wasn't going anywhere. The Gods would have to pry my cold, stiff fingers from this rock.

I stayed awake all night, not wanting to miss Vera. Shortly after dawn, she and Kylah exited the cabin. I lurched forward, clinging to the rope I'd used to secure myself.

"Vera!"

She stiffened, head twitching my way, but she refused to look at me. Kylah's gaze briefly met mine. She shook her head in warning.

I sank back. Patience. I must have patience.

They took off into the sky. Pride filled me at how easily Vera flew. She had much to learn before she could fly at Kylah's level, but she had made extraordinary progress.

Which reminded me . . . Vera hadn't been able to hone her fighting abilities since she learned we were mates. Knowing how important it was, I scried Kian to join me so they could continue their training.

A short time later, his head popped out beneath a ledge. His hair was damp and wind-blown, his lips tinged blue. He pulled himself onto the ledge directly below, cursing the cold.

"It's only going to get worse." I tossed him a rope. "Tie yourself to something."

He caught it, laughter between his lashes.

"What?"

"You must have really pissed her off."

"She knows Kylah is not my mate."

Air hissed between his teeth. "Oh, you are so fucked."

"I'm aware."

Chuckling, he dropped his legs over the ledge, tied himself to it, and tried to get comfortable. "How long are you going to stay up here?"

"As long as it takes. Wake me when they return."

He nodded and I settled back, finally able to rest my eyes now that I knew I wouldn't miss Vera. I hadn't slept long before Kian was prodding my boot.

"Wake up, Boss. They're coming."

I straightened, gaze focusing on the horizon. Two forms were moving through the storm. I quickly untied myself, and stabbed my fingers through my hair, arranging it into some semblance of order before I shuffled out onto the ledge.

Minutes later, they set down on the porch.

"Vera please. I only want five minutes."

She made a crude gesture before opening the door, but paused, doing a double take as she caught sight of the male below.

A smile lit up her face. "Kian?"

My lips flattened. I did not appreciate the way she was looking at him.

He grinned. "The one and only."

She laughed, her smile broadening a moment before it fell. Her icy gaze landed on me. "What's your angle?"

"There's no angle, Trouble," Kian interceded smoothly, saving himself from the violent torture I had planned. "I'm just here to make sure you don't make me look bad during our next brawl."

Her distrustful gaze didn't leave mine. "If you think this is going to get me to talk to you, you're wrong."

I kept from pointing out that it was already working, and nodded I understood.

Her focus shifted back to Kian and another smile bloomed. My hands twitched. She eagerly waved him over and Kian followed. The pair of them disappeared into the cabin while Kylah lingered.

"I'm desperate here," I said pleadingly.

She said nothing before following them inside, however, one of the curtains twitched aside.

I couldn't see much, but my eyes clung to that spot. The view made the miserable conditions more tolerable. I hardly noticed the cold as I watched Kian and Vera spend the afternoon sparring. Every flash of silver hair made my chest tighten.

When evening came, they retired and moved out of sight. I slunk back to my rope and settled in for the night. The next day, Kian and Vera switched their sparring lessons to the morning, and in the afternoon, she came out with Kylah.

"Please talk to me," I begged.

I was ignored as she called out to Kian, "Lock up behind us. No one else is allowed inside."

Fortunately, he didn't take orders from her.

As soon as she took off with Kylah, I untied myself, climbed onto the porch, and banged on the door. It opened and I barged inside. "Tell me everything she said."

I marched over to the fire and dropped in front of it, groaning low at the heat washing over my frigid skin.

Kian took the chair. A low creaking rose as he rocked.

"No."

My gaze cut to him. "I suggest you rethink that answer."

His face was dead sober. It was the expression that gave me pause. I could count the number of times I'd seen Kian that serious on one hand.

"What she told me was in confidence. Do whatever you want to me, but I'm not going to betray her trust."

"You hardly know her," I said incredulously.

"I spent a month watching her. I watched her chatting with her horse like it was a person. I watched her give up all her food to a family in need. I watched her struggle and get back up again. I watched her fight and claw her way back to you, no matter how many times you ignored her."

"You admire her."

He shrugged. "It's hard not to."

My lips twitched into a soft smile. "It is."

We fell silent, watching the flames.

"I don't give you enough credit for your loyalty," I admitted, speaking to more than just Vera.

Kian had come to me as a scrawny teenager wanting to serve, to make amends for his family's crimes. I'd turned him away at least a dozen times, but he was persistent, daring to venture out to the island when no one else would.

Eventually, I agreed. Over the centuries, he had more than atoned for his father's actions, and yet he was still here, faithfully serving me.

"I am grateful Vera can count you as a friend."

His eyes gaped. "I think that's the nicest thing you've ever said to me."

"Don't get used to it," I grunted.

He released a quick laugh before his serious look returned. "Why didn't you claim Vera that day at camp?"

My gaze drifted to the fire, brows constricting. The quiet lull of the flames filled the silence. "I didn't know we were mates then."

"I knew the second I saw you together."

I slanted him a disbelieving look. "You couldn't possibly have known. There hasn't been a mate pairing in five hundred years."

His brows raised in amusement. "You kept yourself isolated on that island for centuries. You brought women back, but they were in and out. Then suddenly you're forcing this woman who you've known for all of five seconds into a bargain."

When he put it that way, it should have been obvious.

"You figured it out at some point," he pressed. "Why didn't you claim her then?"

Kian was a child when the Dark Wars started. He was too young at the time to understand the gravity of what happened after, but he knew who I was, what I had done.

"You know why."

He shrugged, angling his face toward the fire. "If it was my mate, I would have claimed her in a second."

I wished it was that simple.

"Please speak to her for me. She listens to you."

He snapped me a hard look. "You broke her goddamn heart, man, and a woman like that—" he sucked sharply on his teeth "—their hearts don't break easy."

Fiery roots spread through my chest. "I know."

"Then either love her right or let her go."

The idea of the latter sent rage blasting through me. "I'm not letting her go anywhere," I said sharply. "I know I made an egregious error, and I'm going to spend the rest of my life making it up to her."

Kian studied me for a long moment, before jerking his head. "I'll talk to her."

"Thank you."

Neither of us spoke again. We took turns checking the window for Kylah and Vera's return. They didn't reappear until dusk.

I rushed out when Kian spotted them, taking my post on the ledge. Upon their return, I resorted to shameless begging. I would have gotten on my hands and knees and crawled to her if Vera would just look at me.

"*Please*. I'll do anything. Just talk to me."

She spun around, wings flaring out. "Anything?"

I nodded eagerly, chest clenching with hope.

"Swallow iron dust, turn mortal, and nosedive off that ledge."

"Vera . . ."

She dismissed me and went inside.

Kylah hesitated, darting a look at the door before she turned to me. "If you love her, you'll leave," she said, not unkindly.

"If I only loved her, I would," I gritted out. "I would have

378

let her be a long time ago. But I am not just in love, I am *consumed*. She is my sun, my moon, my deity. She is every drop of beauty and goodness in my world. I live for her. I breathe for her. I don't exist without her." I sucked in a sharp breath. "And that was before I knew we were mates."

The ferocity of my confession shocked us both.

Kylah bit her lip, looking torn. She relented with a sigh. "I'll talk to her, but I'm not making any promises."

"That's all I ask."

She reached for the handle, but the door was wrenched open. Vera was there, looking furious, on the verge of tears. "You're such a good liar, Ronan Taran, I almost believed you."

She yanked Kylah inside and slammed the door.

"Fuck!" I beat a fist down before crawling back to my rope with a heavy heart. I was slowly losing hope I could fix things.

Kylah and Kian were my last chance.

I watched the window intensely for the rest of the evening. Late at night, I saw Vera stalk past the slit in the curtains with Kian and Kylah on her heels. Based on the motion of everyone's hands, they were arguing, and it didn't appear Kian and Kylah were winning.

More sparring ensued the following morning. Vera's movements were fast and agitated, and she managed to knock Kian on his ass an hour in.

That's my girl.

The session ended much sooner than the previous one, and she and Kylah appeared outside at mid-morning with Kian lingering in the doorway. I snuck him a questioning look. *Is it done?* He dipped his head before disappearing.

Vera stared me down, jaw clenched. "You want five minutes?"

"Yes," I rushed out. "That's all."

379

"Give the halflings an education. Teach them skills beyond servitude."

"Done." I knew there had to be more. Vera wouldn't acquiesce so easily. "What else?"

"Pick me a bouquet of moon roses and be waiting with them by the time we return in two hours. No cheating. If you don't pick them yourself, I'll know."

She had seen the consequences of one flower. If an entire bouquet didn't kill me, it would come close. She crossed her arms, flashing a mean smirk. She thought she had me. She didn't think I would possibly go through with it for just five minutes of her time.

I started scrambling down the tree.

"Fuck! Wait!"

"Five minutes," I shouted.

As soon as my feet hit the ground, I took off like a mad man, wearing a deranged smile.

Moon roses only grew in one spot in the Enchanted Forest. I took the quickest route, cutting southwest across the Hill Lands, straight through fionain territory. They snapped and bit at my heels as I charged up and down the peaks, but I easily outpaced them.

Once I had the flowers, I wouldn't have long before their dust attacked my system. I had to save as many minutes up front as possible to leave time for the painful journey back.

I'd snuck into House Anu's territory only a few days prior to kidnap Roark, but he lived on the edge of the forest. The flowers grew deep in the woods.

It took thirty minutes of sprinting to reach the threshold.

I entered far from where House Anu made its home amongst the trees, but took slow, measured steps, mimicking the movement of a forest animal. Anu fae could sense ground movements and knew the vibrational pattern of every creature here.

The movements ate up fifteen precious minutes, but I reached the thicket without alerting House Anu.

A cluster of a dozen towering honey locust trees grew inches apart. Decorating their trunks were barbs of thorns and needles. They snagged on my clothes and tore at my flesh as I pressed between their trunks.

All the light cut off once I'd made my way through. At the heart of the thicket was a small meadow of moon roses. The glitter dusting their petals shimmered in the darkness. The roses glowed ethereally from within. They were too beautiful to be made from the natural world like the Goddess Anu had spun them from moonlight.

Removing my shirt, I began collecting the flowers with great care, cutting them at the stem before bundling them up. The fabric would provide a barrier between me and the dust. Once I started running, there would be no stopping its escape, but this would allow me some time.

I had lost another fifteen minutes by the time the flowers were secured in my tunic. I clutched them to my chest as I squeezed between the vicious trees. Twenty Anu fae were waiting for me outside.

I growled under my breath, stalking forward. "I do not have time for this."

I had one hour, fifteen minutes left to make it to Vera. I couldn't be late. She would be looking for any reason to renege on our agreement.

They formed a barrier, blocking my path.

"Stand aside."

I was already trespassing. Attacking their people would not be taken lightly. I did not want to make an enemy of House Anu, but these fae were standing between me and Vera. I'd start a goddamn war if I had to.

Their draoistones started to glow.

War it was.

I set the flowers down and cracked my neck side to side.

I rushed forward. Bodies flew into the air as I razed through them. I left a trail of pained groans in my wake. No one died, but they would be incapacitated for several hours. By the time I exited the forest, I had lost another fifteen minutes.

Only one hour left.

I ran.

Fifty-five minutes.

The first hit of dust tickled my nose. A flush crawled over my skin.

Fifty-three minutes.

The warmth reached my blood.

Forty-nine minutes.

The burning started. The pain was minimal at first, but it steadily increased until my entire body was engulfed in flames.

Forty-four minutes.

Blisters formed over my skin. My muscles stiffened.

Forty minutes.

I lost the use of my hands. They were too swollen to hold the flowers. I bit the stems, continuing my sprint.

Thirty-two minutes.

Ten miles short of my goal, my knees began to shake. I couldn't maintain my speed. I ran until I couldn't, then I walked, and when I could no longer walk, I crawled.

First on my hands and knees, and when that became too painful, I dragged myself forward on my elbows. Sharp, jagged rocks sliced open blisters as I crawled over them. Jarring pain rocked me with each burst.

Twenty-nine minutes.

I reached the fionain's domain. They eagerly latched onto my skin and drank my blood. I didn't have the strength to fight them off. I inched forward, taking them with me.

Twenty-three minutes.

My vision started to go. The world turned gray and distorted.

Twenty minutes.

My throat slowly closed. Every breath became a struggle. It took all my focus to maintain my teeth's grip on the flowers as air wheezed in and out of my steadily failing lungs.

Fifteen minutes.

One mile left. My elbows were shredded to the bone and my muscles were convulsing every second. I didn't know how much blood I had lost to the fionain.

Ten minutes.

I reached the base of the rock column, but there was still a three-hundred-foot vertical climb between me and Vera. The last of my muscles gave out and I collapsed. The air filled with the quiet sucking of the fionain stealing the last of my strength.

Eight minutes.

Vera's face, carved by immeasurable pain and grief, flashed through my mind. 'I want you to stop hurting me.'

No. I would not fail her. Not again.

I was going to make it back to her, even if it was the last thing I did.

By some miracle, I gathered the strength to grab hold of the first ledge and haul myself onto it. Then the next. I focused on one at a time. Ledge by ledge, I painstakingly dragged myself up.

The fionain couldn't maintain their grip the higher I climbed and slowly fell away.

I could feel my organs beginning to shut down. I coughed up blood. But I didn't stop. I pulled and dragged and climbed with a singular focus. The last of my vision went and I blindly continued by memory. When I felt the rope of my ledge, I crawled out, hand hitting the air until it met the porch.

I dragged myself on to it and collapsed.

"Oh, my Gods!" Vera's shriek sounded far away.

I thrust up the bouquet. "Five minutes," I mumbled before the world turned black.

33

VERA

"Are you sure we can't have Lawrence look at him?" I asked for what felt like the hundredth time.

I'd been by Ronan's bedside for three days. Kylah and Kian had assured me endlessly that he would be fine, but it was hard to believe it looking at him.

His face was so bloated and blistered, he could have easily been mistaken for an infected corpse. Boils oozing puss covered his body. His eyes and jaw were swollen shut. Abrasions littered his skin. He was unrecognizable.

"Yes," Kian said patiently from the fire. "Ronan wouldn't want word getting out. His allergy can't leave this room. He has too many enemies."

I padded back and forth, the floorboards creaking under my weight. "I didn't even know high fae could have allergies."

He tossed me a sardonic look. "We don't exactly go around announcing it."

Fair point.

I stopped, returning to Ronan's side. "But it's been three days, and he still looks so much worse than the first time," I complained, my voice tight with fear and guilt.

"Hey." Kian strode over and gripped my shoulders, ducking to meet my gaze. "He's going to be fine. I wouldn't risk the boss man's life."

"Neither would I," Kylah announced behind him.

My eyes shifted between them, and I was struck by an annoying realization. I trusted them. I trusted them with one of the most important things to me—Ronan's life. *Godsdamnit.* They'd gone and grown on me without permission.

"What?" they asked in unison, and I realized I was frowning.

"I think we're friends," I grumbled.

They exchanged twin looks of surprise before they burst into laughter. Bell-like tones mingled with husky ones.

Kylah hooked an arm around my waist, eyes bright with laughter. She pouted her bottom lip. "How awful."

Kian rustled my hair. "Poor, Trouble."

"Oh, fuck off." I swatted them away, but I was smiling.

The lightness of the moment dissolved as my eyes fell to Ronan. "I never thought he'd go through with it," I whispered.

Just a sprinkling of dust from one measly flower had put him in an incredible amount of pain. I never anticipated he'd be willing to touch ten.

I also didn't try very hard to stop him . . .

I thought his pain would ease mine, but there was nothing comforting about seeing him like this. It made me sick.

"He loves you," Kylah said like it explained everything.

She disappeared into the small kitchen and returned, handing me a damp cloth.

I kneeled beside him. "Then why didn't he claim me?" Frustration leaked into my voice as I gently dabbed at his cuts and blisters. "I can't understand why he was willing to risk his life to have a conversation with me, but not tell me we were mates."

I looked at Kylah. She had tried to tell me before, but I hadn't been ready to listen. I was ready now.

She sighed softly, coming to sit at my side and gracefully folded her legs under her. "Ronan has a terrible habit of doing awful things for honorable reasons." The low creak of rocking filled the air. Kian's head was tilted toward us, listening from the fireplace.

"Hunt, Moira, Ronan, and I were all very close growing up—"

"Whose Moira?"

"Hunt's mate."

Her name was tattooed on his knuckles. I had a sinking feeling this story wasn't going to have a happy ending.

"They found out they were mates when they were just teenagers. He *worshipped* her. He was first in line to inherit House Brigid, but abdicated so he could come to House Taran and be with her."

That sinking sensation expanded into a pit.

Hunt was an asshole, but behind every asshole was a tragedy.

Emotion glimmered in her eyes. She struggled with her next words. "Moira died under horrible circumstances when she was just sixteen."

My stomach clenched painfully.

"Hunt tracked down and slaughtered every man involved. One was the nephew of a powerful Lord."

"Doesn't Hunt have a powerful father?" I interrupted.

"He did, but his father never approved of the match. Moira was low fae. He thought she was beneath him." A glimmer of rage flashed across her delicate features. "Lord Brigid can bring people back from the dead. He could have saved her, but he refused."

I shared her anger. What kind of a father would let his son's mate die?

"Lord Belen loved his nephew. Caden could do no wrong. He demanded his nephew's murderer be found and subjected to the Bathad. Are you familiar with it?"

I started to shake my head, then stopped. "Wait, isn't Lord Belen your father?"

"He was," she admitted in quiet disgust. "Bathad is a punishment designed specifically for immortals. They are chained to the bottom of the sea and drown over and over again." She met my gaze in outrage. "It's barbaric. Reserved for the worst offenders. Hunt was just a young fae grieving the loss of his mate."

She took a sharp breath.

"And do you know what Ronan did? He tortured Hunt. He took a magic blade, and he mutilated him, cut him so many times, so deep, many of the scars are still visible today. Hunt begged and pleaded with him to stop, but Ronan didn't. He put him into a coma for months."

Kian and I shared a horrified glance.

I really hoped there was more to the story.

"Ronan knew what I knew; that Hunt was too fragile to endure the Bathad. He had just gone through what no fae should ever have to experience. Losing his mate—it would have felt like his soul was being torn apart. The Bathad would break him."

"I also knew that a high fae can't be subjected to the Bathad if they're gravely injured. I couldn't stomach doing that to Hunt, but Ronan, he could. After being denied the revenge my father craved, he was out for blood. He didn't hesitate to accept Ronan's proposal to take Hunt's place."

She paused, meeting my gaze. "And this was *after* he had gone to the Crone and attempted to trade his life to return Moira."

That's how he knew how to find her . . .

"He spent twenty years drowning in the sea," she finished.

"I didn't know any of that," Kian admitted quietly from his chair.

Kylah's lips bent into a sad smile. "Not many do."

Despite my feelings toward Ronan at the moment, I couldn't help the horror and sadness welling up. Thinking of him going through that made me sick to my stomach.

"Why would he do that?" I whispered.

Kylah met my eyes with a firm gaze. "Because no one else could. That's what Ronan does. He protects the people he loves, no matter what it takes, no matter what it costs him. Even if he has to become a monster."

"You said you owed him." I kept my voice gentle, sensing it was a delicate topic. "What did he do for you?"

She stared for a long moment before explaining, "He protected me when no one else would." A tight swallow. "My father wasn't always a cruel man, but after he lost his mate to childbirth, the grief twisted his mind. He blamed my youngest sister, Ephina, for her death, and she bared the brunt of his anger. I think in a way, she blamed herself too. I tried my best to shield her from his wrath, but I couldn't always protect her. She took her own life when she was just twenty."

A mournful silence fell over the cabin.

Ephina had to be the person Kylah was talking about when she said she'd wished she had told someone what she told me.

Kylah dotted at the tears slipping down her cheeks. I reached out and squeezed her hand. My watery eyes met hers. "I'm so sorry," I whispered.

Kian settled beside her and wrapped Kylah in a big hug. I joined him.

"I'm fine. I'm fine," she insisted. "I just haven't talked about this in a while."

We released her but Kian didn't return to the fire.

She stared fondly at the storm paintings I'd admired when I first arrived. "She was a talented artist."

My eyes touched over each one before finding Kylah again. "She was," I agreed.

That brought out a small smile.

It quickly fell.

"She left a note. She couldn't go on living with the abuse. I showed it to my father. I wanted him to understand." Her eyes flashed like a lightning bolt. "He called her selfish and weak."

"After, I went to my middle sister, Helena—she hated him just as much as I did—to plot his death. We had it all planned out, but on the eve we were supposed to attack, Helena was waiting in my father's chambers with him. She had told him everything and laid all the blame on me. She was made the new heir, and I was cast out. She ensured no other House would touch me, or they would risk their alliance."

Her eyes lifted to mine. A tiny smile lit her features amid the grief.

"Ronan took me in, and when Helena scried to warn him what would happen if he continued to harbor me, he told her she could drown in a river of shit." She clasped a hand over her mouth, laughing. "I can still remember the look on her face. No one had ever spoken to her that way before."

A small note of laughter left me.

Kian released a low chuckle. "Sounds like him."

We fell silent.

Only the crackle of the fire, and the soft rain patter could be heard for a long while as Kylah's story lingered in the air.

Her words from earlier haunted me. *I wasn't always loved and adored.* Guilt pinched my stomach, thinking of the way I'd lashed out. I wormed my fingers between hers. She smiled softly at the reassuring gesture.

"What's your story?" I asked Kian. It was mostly to dispel the somber air, but I was also curious why he always covered his throat.

He gave me a lopsided grin. "Stick around long enough and I might just tell you."

Ronan's breath came out as a strained, rasping breath.

I scrambled to his side and pressed an ear to his mouth. Every inhale was a wheeze. "I think his throat is closing up," I said in a panic. "He's having trouble breathing."

Kian came over and listened. "This is the worst of it," he declared, pulling back. "He should be waking up after this."

"Should be?"

He shrugged. "Best guess."

I looked to Kylah. She didn't have an answer either.

"How can the two of you be so calm about this?"

Kylah took a seat beside me on the bed and wrapped her arms around my shoulders. "Ronan has survived much worse," she said softly. "Some little moon roses won't be his demise."

She said it like she knew what would. "What then?"

"His pride or arrogance."

"My votes on his 'I'm big and strong and you must obey' attitude." Kian puffed out his chest. "Or the fact that he thinks he knows everything."

I huffed out a quiet laugh, my shoulders relaxing slightly. If they weren't worried, then I shouldn't be either. That still didn't mean I was leaving his side.

Kylah boiled some cloths and wrapped them around his throat to help with the swelling. His breathing eventually evened out, and I was able to relax.

I held his hand all day, sitting below the bed, ruminating over what Kylah had said. If she was right, Ronan hadn't told me we were mates because he was trying to protect me, but that didn't make any sense. In fact, the more I thought about it, the less sense it made.

My head started to ache, and I put it out of my mind, focusing on Ronan for the time being.

At night, seizures started.

My mouth filled with vomit as Kian had to hold his head immobile. Eventually, Ronan settled, and I climbed into bed with him, laying my head over him so I could make sure he was breathing. The steady rise and fall of his chest carried me to sleep.

I woke with his arms around me in the early morning. I was startled for a second, and then I was rushing to untangle myself and check him over.

He was virtually healed. There were still red blotches puckering his skin, but he looked world's different than yesterday. His eyes opened and he grinned up at me, rasping, "Good morning."

A dizzying wave of relief swept through me. I lunged forward and wrapped my arms around him. "Thank Gods."

I held him tightly for several seconds.

"Does this mean you forgive me?" he asked when I drew back.

He was only teasing, but the question brought all my pain and rage roaring back. A frown hardened my features. "No." My gaze swept around for Kian and Kylah, but both their sleeping spaces were empty. They must have departed while we were asleep.

I climbed off the bed, and loomed over him, giving him a flat stare. "Five minutes. That's all you get."

He shifted up, and I helped, dropping my hands as soon as he was upright.

He reached for me, but quickly realized his error, and dropped them to his lap, clearing his throat. His gaze was open and earnest as he lifted it to me. "Please come home. We can start over. Put all this pain and heartache behind us."

"House Taran is not my home, and you are not my mate."

Ronan grimaced. "I deserve that. Not telling you the second I knew we were mates was a serious error in judgement. You will never know how sorry I am for that."

I crossed my arms. "What about your other lie? You sorry for that too?"

He tilted his head in confusion.

I scoffed. He didn't even fucking remember. "That whole month I tried summoning you. Where were you?"

He implied he'd been with Kylah, but now I knew that was corthshit.

"You sent Kian to babysit me and then just disappeared." My lips started to tremble when I thought of all the times I'd desperately tried to summon him. How lonely, and hard things had been. I wanted to die, and he couldn't have cared less.

"I would have given *anything* to see you, Ronan, and you—" I got too choked up to speak "—You just ignored me." Somehow, that was worse than being with her. "I needed you," I gritted out. "And you weren't there. You should have never left," I finished, getting to the heart of the issue. I locked my gaze on him. "You should have stayed."

Words exploded from him. "It took everything I had to leave you, Vera. *Everything*. But not a single moment passed when I didn't think of you. Where I didn't desperately wish I could see your smile or hear your laugh. Where I didn't worry incessantly over how you were sleeping, or if you were getting enough to eat. Where I didn't wake and find myself coming to you."

"Why didn't you tell me we were mates? If you had, we would be in a very different place right now."

"I can't answer that."

I wanted to pull my hair out. We were going in circles, not getting anywhere.

I gestured between us. "We're both steel—strong and unyielding, and it's going to get one of us killed."

He lifted his head. "What do you mean?"

"We're locked into this silent battle of wills like two swords clashing. It can only end one of two ways. Either one of us surrenders, or one of us gets cut."

A light came on in his eyes. "You want me to surrender?"

I nodded.

He sprang to his feet and rushed for the door. "Meet me at House Taran in ten minutes."

I watched him clamor down the rock column and heaved a sigh. I had a feeling he'd missed my point entirely.

Reluctantly, I climbed down the rock. I didn't trust my flying abilities in the storm without Kylah, and even if I did, I couldn't push my wings out without her.

Flying was steadily starting to feel more natural, but I was still stumbling and bumbling my way through every flight. Fighting, thankfully, was going better. I was building muscle memory again, and able to progress with each session.

I jogged the couple miles to House Taran. The entire House was gathered in the courtyard, eyes drowsy, still in their sleepwear.

What were they doing up? It was early, even for the halflings. We still had a few hours before sunrise.

"Everyone in the Great Hall," Ronan barked as he moved between structures.

Every soldier and staff member shuffled inside the large building running along the east wall. I caught Kylah and Kian among them. Each threw me a questioning look and I shrugged. I knew as little as they did.

As the courtyard emptied, Ronan found me.

"What's going on?" I asked.

He placed a hand on the small of my back. "You'll see."

When we reached the door, he paused, glancing down. "I wish I could remove your glamour for this, but it's not safe."

I didn't know what *this* was anyway, so it didn't really matter. "It's fine."

Every eye on was on us as we entered.

"I heard she's been sleeping in his bed . . ." someone murmured as we passed.

"Only a halfling could love a man like that," another hissed.

I tried to glare at the gossips but couldn't pick them out among the crowd. They formed a semi-circle around the hall with Ronan and I at the center.

His hand fell away. The sharp grate of unsheathed steel rang through the space and then he abruptly dropped to his knee, presenting his sword—in front of his entire House. "I surrender."

Shock reverberated through me and the crowd.

"If winning means I lose you, then this is the one battle I want to lose," he whispered, staring deeply into my eyes.

My pulse skyrocketed as my bewildered gaze skipped over everyone like they might have some answer for this insane turn of events. My eyes jumped back to Ronan. I could only blink at him.

"Vera," he said under his breath. "I have never surrendered to anyone. Now accept my sword, you stubborn woman."

I did and nearly dropped it. It weighed a ton.

Everyone watched in stunned silence, me included, as Ronan rose and softly kissed me. He held out his hand. Mechanically, I slipped my hand into his, my mind spinning.

We left everyone speechless, staring after us as we exited.

The chilled air helped steady my thoughts, and my anger returned with a fervor. I waited until we were out of sight before slamming the sword into his chest.

"What do you want from me?" he growled, taking it.

"I want you to admit the truth. That you didn't claim me because you were horrified when you learned what I was. A monster."

I'd been doing a lot of thinking over the last week, and that's the answer I kept coming back to. The moment Ronan had learned what I was, his behavior took an abrupt turn.

"You are not the monster," he growled. "I am."

I only stared.

"I'm damned if I don't. Damned if I do." He snarled like a beast and grabbed my hand, towing me behind him.

"Where are we going?"

Ronan didn't answer. I waited to see where he was taking me. He rowed us out to the island I'd woken up on and took me to the abandoned castle.

We reached the entrance and Ronan stopped. His gaze lingered on my face, eyes tracing every inch. He was looking at me like he was about to walk into a battle he wouldn't survive.

My stomach clenched painfully. "Why are you looking at me like that?" I asked in bewilderment, a hint of emotion cracking my voice.

"I'm memorizing the way you're looking at me right now," he said softly.

"*Why*?"

His lips thinned into a sad, hopeless smile. "Because you're never going to look at me like that again."

34

VERA

The heavy doors groaned open against Ronan's forceful push. The silence on the other end was deafening, save for the drip of water echoing from the castle's bowels. He entered and darkness briefly swallowed his form before he returned with two torches and offered one to me.

I stepped inside and the smell of dust and decay hit my face. There was a hint of something else too, something foul like rotting meat, but it was too faint to be certain.

"This way." Ronan plunged into the pitch-black.

Our torch light threw ominous shadows over the walls as the slap of our boots echoed loudly in the quiet. Hair prickled at the back of my neck. I couldn't shake the feeling that we were being watched.

Beyond the entry was a grand staircase in disrepair. It was layered in dust with most of its steps missing. One railing leaned heavily to the side, looking as if a single breath would send it tumbling.

Watery blue light cast the area in somber tones.

I tipped my head back, raising the torch toward the lavish chandelier made of draoistone. Blue light pulsed weakly from the stones as if on their last life.

Everything was in the late stages of decay, from the sunken furniture to the crumbling frescos. None of it was quite living, but not dead either.

Ronan bypassed the staircase, taking a sharp left down an arched, dark corridor, and I trailed closely behind.

The foyer's light didn't reach this area. Thick webbing covered every surface from the light sconces to the framed paintings, casting everything in gray tones. The ceiling was lower as well.

"Five hundred years ago, the Gods disappeared, and the beasts swept through our lands like a plague," Ronan's voice echoed off the stone and carried down the hall.

He stopped at a painting, wiping away the film of dust, and held his torch over a horrific scene. Set against a snowy backdrop, fae and beasts were embroiled in a bloody battle. Dead fae outnumbered the living.

"Half of our population was decimated in a single night."

He continued down the hall without another word. I watched him go, forehead scrunching in confusion and concern.

He had said that with a chilling calm.

My gaze flitted back to the painting. The snow was stained red with all the fallen bodies. All the fallen fae bodies. To have lived through that time must have been awful.

Leaving the painting, I found Ronan several feet ahead, his silhouette outlined against the torch light. Every inch of him was rigid.

My stomach tightened. He'd promised answers, but that didn't mean I was going to like them.

He pivoted and continued down the hall, and I followed a few feet behind.

As I passed a door, curiosity drew me to it. The ancient

wood groaned as I gently pushed it open. A cloud of dust materialized and sent me into a coughing fit. I swiped at the airborne debris until it settled.

The room held ornate, hand carved furniture with personal effects sitting where their owner had left them—a hairbrush on a vanity, a robe draped over a chair, and a dress discarded on the floor right where it'd been taken off. The room was frozen in time.

I quietly shut the door and caught up to Ronan. He was unnervingly quiet. I darted concerned looks at him, which he was oblivious to, lost somewhere in his mind.

I was grateful when he resumed his history lesson.

"Every House battled the beasts on their own. Our division made us weak. Six months into the war, and we were on the brink of losing."

He paused at another painting. "Lord Desmond visited each House and urged us to look beyond our petty feuds with one another. We could either die separated and stubborn or survive united."

"All the fae lords and ladies gathered and agreed to make Lord Desmond our king. Within a month, we had beaten back the beasts. He gathered a slither of power from every fae and used it to create the wall imprisoning them and then another for our magic."

Ronan stepped back so I could take a closer look.

The tone of this scene was much brighter. King Desmond stood triumphantly, holding his foot down on the neck of a bloody failin.

I glanced over my shoulder. Ronan was sharing fae secrets, something he had not been willing to trust me with before. It was a huge step in the right direction. I still needed more, much more, but I appreciated the effort.

My gaze met his in a silent thank you.

For some reason, that made his eyes tighten.

He pulled away and we turned right down a hallway. As we did, a specter of blue light shot past. It took the shape of a person sprinting, fearfully glancing over their shoulder. Their front bowed, and they collapsed to the ground.

"What was that?" I whispered.

"Trapped magic."

My gaze darted to Ronan.

"When a fae dies, it is customary to bury them beneath their House draoi tree so their magic can be absorbed and recycled," he said tonelessly, like he was reciting a book. "Otherwise, their magic lingers with nowhere to go."

I glanced around the dark space, expecting a draoi tree to appear. "Where is theirs?"

"It was cut down and pulled out by the roots," he explained in that emotionless voice.

I was about to ask more when we reached the area where the figure had fallen. A skeleton was on the ground. It was so old that the clothes had rotted away. Only small scraps of fabric remained, clinging to the bones. With the way it was positioned, it looked like the person had been running when they died, just like the phantom. There was a hole in their rib cage.

I glanced up at Ronan. The torch cast shadows over the planes of his face. He looked *haunted*.

"Who is this?" I whispered. "What happened to them?"

Ronan didn't respond, striding down the hall.

I followed . . . Reluctantly. The questions were mounting, and the answers were few, but Ronan was leading me somewhere, and I had to trust he would tell me everything when we arrived.

The further we walked, the more skeletons I saw. The way they were poised, their lives had ended violently.

A warm breath tickled my neck. I spun around, but no one was there.

Something was very wrong with this place. I don't think it was just the magic that was trapped.

We stopped in front of a pair of doors. Ronan gazed at me from his profile, but I couldn't read his expression.

"Why did you bring me here?" I whispered. "What happened to Finn's House?"

"You'll see," he said roughly.

He pulled open the doors.

Rancid air whooshed out. It filled my airways with acid, burning everywhere it touched. I slapped a hand over my nose and mouth, hissing, "What is that smell?"

Ronan glanced at me sideways. So many emotions flitted across his face.

"Death."

He moved inside and lit a series of torches mounted on the walls. When he finished, I gasped.

Skeletons were everywhere. They sat in chairs gathered around a large banquet table. Jewelry and scraps of clothes adorned the bones. Plates with the barest traces of food lined the table and were covered in a thick layer of dust and cobwebs.

They had been struck down as they ate. Some had attempted to flee and died at the edges of the room.

My gaze left the macabre sight, touching over the rest of the dark space. Nearly disintegrated banners hung limply along the walls overlaid with remnants of garland.

"They were celebrating something," I noted aloud.

"The birth of the lord's first-born son."

I jerked at the dark rumble of Ronan's voice. He stood off to the side, his face cloaked in shadows.

"What happened here?" I whispered like the dead might hear me.

A stream of phantom blue light burst through the doors. It arced through the room in a violent pattern, snuffing out all the light. It whooshed past me, blowing back my hair, and my torch light sizzled out. Ronan's went out next, and the room plunged into darkness.

My heart threatened to beat out of my chest. The soft scrape of Ronan's shoes was the only thing keeping a panic attack at bay. Light flared and he appeared nearby, holding a torch. It sent shadows playing over his grave face.

"You asked me once why I had to be the Enforcer," he said roughly.

He had never given me a straight answer, only that someone had to do it.

His hand swept over the gruesome scene. "This is why."

Brows rising, I struggled to follow. My gaze darted to his face. "I—I don't understand."

Heavy eyes touched mine. "I did this, Vera. I murdered two hundred innocent fae—fae I knew and respected. Men, women, and children." He raised his head, staring off into the darkness. "What were some meaningless mortals compared to this? They were nothing."

Horror and understanding settled over me.

Ronan had murdered this House. Finn's House.

My eyes took in the room in a new ghastly light before landing back on him. "Why, Ronan? Why would you do this?"

His jaw set into iron. He refused to look at me. "It doesn't matter."

I strode over to him. "Yes, it does. You wouldn't have done this without a good reason."

He inhaled sharply. "How do you know?" he asked, gaze shifting between mine. He sounded so unlike himself—his voice small and lost.

'*Do you think I'm not* haunted *by all the blood I've spilled? That I don't see each and every one of their faces when I shut my eyes?*'

Ronan had been talking about more than just the mortals that day in the forest. I remembered his night terrors too. Every life he took affected him deeply. He did not take life easily. That's why he killed that teenager but spared that woman and her son.

I didn't want to see it at the time, but Kylah was right.

"You are arrogant, overbearing, take things way too far, and have done some reprehensible things, but—" my voice softened to a whisper "—your heart is always in the right place."

His gaze fastened to mine, and he stared so hard, it felt like he was trying to burrow under my skin.

"You're a good man, Ronan."

Steel eyes shined in the darkness, filled with a thousand different things. Tension vibrated through him. His jaw worked, opening and shutting several times.

I placed a hand on his arm. "Tell me what happened," I urged gently.

His eyes dipped to my fingers, then slowly rose to my face. He stared at me for a long stretch before dragging his gaze away, and admitting quietly, "I don't know where to start."

"At the beginning."

On a deep, forceful drag of air, he confessed, "I killed my father when I was ten."

I kept the shock off my face. He'd talked adoringly of his mother many times, but he'd never mentioned his father before.

"He was one of the most powerful Taranis fae ever born, until me. While other boys my age had been learning to spar one on one, I was taking on our entire army. My father despised me for my abilities. He wanted my magic for himself, but since he couldn't have it, he undermined my legitimacy at every turn. I wasn't his son. I couldn't possibly be. He said it so many times, I think he actually convinced himself it was true."

The hollowness in his voice tightened my chest.

"He wanted another child. One he would know was irrefutably his, one he could control—" his voice thickened "—So, he raped my mother while two of his men forced me to watch."

A nauseating anger churned my stomach. I wanted to rip his father from his grave and tear him into pieces.

"I shifted into my battle-mode for the first time and tore out their throats. I ripped him off her, got my mother to safety, and hunted down iron dust. That night, I forced it down his throat while he slept and dragged him out to the sea. He drowned for hours until he turned mortal and died."

I hid a shudder at the emotionless way he spoke of murdering his father. Not that I judged him. If I had been powerful enough to kill the Crone, I would have felt the same.

"He and my uncle were close. My uncle never looked at me the same after that." This time he sounded distraught, and I recalled the fond way he had spoken of his uncle in the forest.

"My mother made me swear I wouldn't tell a soul what my father had done. It was our secret. Out of that horror came an unbreakable bond. I admitted what I had done to my father's council, leaving out the real reason I killed him. I told them I had done it because I hated him, which was true. Given how powerful I was, they were eager to forgive me and put me on the throne with my mother serving as an advisor."

"My uncle disagreed with their decision. He tried to convince my mother to declare I was unfit to take my father's lordship. She refused. She acted as regent until I came of age. I ruled my House with an iron fist back in those days and viciously defended it from any outside threats, no matter what it took. I committed many horrific acts in the name of peace. My mother spent her whole life defending me, regardless of my actions."

He sucked in a sharp breath, lost in memories.

"When the Dark Wars ended, there were only a quarter of us left. By that time, I had already cemented myself as a cold, merciless killer. King Desmond came to me and told me he had learned who was responsible for the beasts."

"A bridge used to connect our realm with the Gods. Finn's House had grown power hungry. They wanted the Gods' realm for themselves. The Gods never anticipated that their children would turn on them. There were no guards protecting the bridge. Members of House Ogma were able to sneak inside their realm and steal the godstone. They tried to murder the Gods and failed. The beasts were our punishment for their betrayal."

His hand clenched into a tight fist. "Or so I'd been led to believe."

"While serving as one of his generals, I came to admire King Desmond. Respect him. He was sharp and an excellent strategist. We were like-minded in many ways. During the war, he proved himself to be a capable leader who cared deeply about the wellbeing of our people. So, when he came to me, and told me what House Ogma had done, when he ordered me to kill them so they couldn't betray us again, I didn't question it. I trusted him."

He released a strained breath.

"I had watched thousands of good fae die needlessly during the war. They deserved justice, and so did the living. Many of them had lost everything. He stole their powers, and had their food poisoned, and I butchered them in the night."

He said the last line so simply, and I realized to him it

was, just like killing that teenager had been. He wasn't just fiercely protective of his people, but all fae. In his mind, it was either them, or the fae.

"My mother found me as I was standing over Finn's cradle with a knife. I was so lost to the blood lust of my battle-mode, I didn't see a newborn babe, I only saw the enemy. If she hadn't stopped me . . ."

The tightness in his voice made my insides twist.

"I had never seen her look at me that way before." His voice cracked. "*Like I was a monster.*"

Tears brimmed in my eyes. I knew how much his mother meant to him.

He spent a moment gathering his composure before continuing, "Days later we would learn of the second part of the Gods' punishment, about the infertility. Not only had I slaughtered hundreds of innocent fae, but I had erased an entire bloodline. House Ogma could never repopulate."

Infertility . . .

"Is the curse why no one has found their mate since the war?" I asked gently.

"Yes. Only mates can produce fae children, and all females mated prior to the war are now barren."

Oh, my Gods. Suddenly everything clicked into place. It wasn't just the fae's magic that weakened year after year, it was the fae.

"That's why the fae laws exist." My gaze connected with his. "The fae . . . You're dying."

35

VERA

He nodded limply. "Our population is fragile and steadily dwindling with every life lost. We needed the mortals to live in fear of us and keep supplying their gold."

I was dizzy with shock. I stumbled back and tripped over a bone. Ronan caught me, gently steadying me. "I know this is a lot to take in," he said softly as he released me.

A hysterical laugh bubbled in my throat. "You can say that again."

My mind felt caught in a whirlpool, swirling with all the implications. "That's why you allow the Rogues to exist, isn't it? I always wondered why a fae lord would allow their property to run away."

"They aren't property. They're family."

My brows snapped together. "What?"

"Halflings are the offspring of two unmated fae."

My eyes widened. I couldn't believe what I was hearing.

I tabled my thoughts and questions on that momentarily, returning to the bigger revelation—why the fae needed halflings in the first place. If their population was as fragile as Ronan said, the fae would be totally dependent on them.

"You couldn't run your Houses without halflings," I surmised. "You couldn't run your estates, feed yourselves, and create the goods you depend on trading for gold without more hands."

Another nod.

"But they're your family. How could you do that to your own blood?"

Ronan's eyes tightened. "I am not proud of the choices we made, but it was the only way to survive. It was difficult at first. There were many revolts, but the birth of each new halfling planted a seed of resentment and jealousy. We were once a great and powerful race, and with every death, we edged closer to extinction. After a time, we stopped seeing them as family. We saw them only as a reminder of our fragility, of everything we had lost."

That was heartbreaking. Silence swelled. I didn't speak again for several minutes, digesting it all.

"What happened after . . . *this*?" I glanced briefly at the banquet table.

"I was summoned by King Desmond. I arrived believing I was there to be thanked, but it was an ambush. Every House's lord and lady was there. An inquisition was held. They wanted answers." He paused, his face falling with despair. "I had been set-up."

"I knew the king would deny any allegations of his involvement. I told them the truth, that I believed House Ogma was responsible for the Gods' curse, and when they asked what proof I had, I could give them nothing. They took that to mean I was the one responsible for the demise of our people, that I had killed Finn's House to shift the blame. The only reason I walked out of there was because they had no evidence. Everyone turned against me, even my own people. I was banished."

"But the king betrayed you . . ." At his silence, I understood. "You never told anyone."

The scar running through his lips whitened with the hard clench of his jaw. "The king didn't make me swing my sword. The king didn't force me to kill innocent fae," he bit out. "I made a choice and I had to live with it."

He had never told anyone to punish himself. It was the same reason he lived on the island. He would have had to look at Finn's castle, at what he'd done, every day.

My gaze touched between his. "Why did the king want Finn's House killed?"

"It was an elaborate distraction. The fae's hatred toward me overshadowed their need for answers. Everyone was so busy mourning the loss of House Ogma that they forgot why the war had started. I suspect King Desmond was the one who had brought down the Gods' wrath, but I have never been able to find any proof."

"Shortly after, my uncle staged a coup, attempting to take advantage of the situation and overthrow my lordship. I managed to defeat him, but not before he killed my mother, and left with half of my forces."

That's how his mother died.

He was quiet for a long beat. "Do you know what my mother's last words to me were?" His laugh was haunted and sad. *"You're not my son."*

My heart lurched painfully.

"She raised Finn as her own. After she passed, I continued living on the island, letting my generals rule in my stead. When Finn came of age, I made him my steward and turned power over to him."

Neither of us said a word for the next several minutes—the air unsettlingly somber—until Ronan's voice drifted through it.

"You wanted to know why I had to be the Enforcer. That's why. I was the only choice. I happily accepted the assignment, bolstered by the hope that I could do something good for the fae, that it was my chance for redemption. But I quickly realized I was doing exactly what I had done to Finn's family. I called a meeting of all the Houses and the king. I pleaded with them to change the way the fae law was enforced."

"And do you know what they did?" His voice took on a despondent, bitter tone. "They mocked me. *You really expect us to believe you care about mortal lives? You don't have a soul, Butcher.*' They made it clear that if I didn't continue my Enforcer duties, my House would suffer dearly for it. So I did."

He fell silent, signaling the end of the story. His eyes sought mine.

I watched the shadows rippling over his face, at a complete loss for words. There was so much to process, I didn't know where to start, so I stood there quietly like an idiot, and Ronan mistook my silence as judgment.

His gaze dropped to the floor.

"You don't have to stay," he said in a voice so hollow, a whole world could fit inside.

I'll understand if you can't love me.

Every inch of his body was braced, prepared for me to crush him because his friends and family, the ones he had sacrificed so much for, never once questioned why Ronan would have committed such an act.

A volcanic rage shuddered through me. How could they not see Ronan's goodness? How couldn't *I*? As contemptable as some of Ronan's actions were, they were rooted in self-lessness. He'd spent his whole life looking out for everyone else. Who looked out for him?

"Ronan, look at me," I said *quietly, fiercely*.

He did. His expression was helpless. I nearly broke down in tears at that look.

"I'm not going anywhere."

"You're not?"

He sounded like a little boy.

It hurt my fucking heart. I couldn't stand to see him like this. I couldn't stand what he had gone through. All alone. I grabbed his arm and dragged him outside, away from his dark memories and past.

"What are you doing?" His voice was pitched in bewilderment.

"You'll see." I tugged him back to the small boat. "Help me row."

Ronan was puzzled, but he picked up an oar without question. We returned to House Taran and entered the courtyard. Plenty were still lingering in the Great Hall. I marched over to it, dragging him with me.

"Vera?" he tried again.

I held his gaze over my shoulder. "I've got you."

I swept into the hall like a tornado. All the chatter cut off at my entrance, every gaze landing on us.

"Fuck you and you and you." I stabbed a talon at his warriors and halflings. Then I turned it on his so-called 'best friend' Hunt. "And especially fuck you." If his mother had been here, I would have turned it on her next.

Kylah, Kian, and Finn were the only ones spared my fury.

"Fuck your dirty looks and snide whispers. You have no idea what this man has been through. What he's done to protect you, and you all treat him like he's worthless. He is good and wonderful, and you are so lucky to have him." My voice rose with each sentence until I was screaming. "King Desmond set him up. The idea that any of you thought he would do it for any other reason, is *disgusting*." I met Hunt's gaze on the last part, speaking directly to him.

His cool mask didn't slip, but tight lines formed around his mouth.

An audible intake rippled through the room. Shocked murmurs started. I ignored them all, turning toward Ronan.

The Enforcer, the most feared fae in the lands, had tears glimmering in his eyes.

He seized my cheeks and jerked his lips to mine. He kissed me until I was breathless, and the world was spinning. "I love you," he whispered between breaths. "I love you so goddamn much."

I pulled back. "Show me."

He swept me into his arms and carried me out of the hall.

We entered his bedroom, and he kicked the door shut. He set me on my feet, caging me against the wall, and then he was on me, feverishly kissing my neck and tugging at my clothes.

"Ronan," I protested weakly between moans, remembering we had unfinished business. "Ron—" He swallowed my voice with a kiss. My body buzzed like live wire, relishing his touch, his lips.

He angled my head to kiss and suckle on my neck.

I groaned. Did we really need to talk more?

My body said no, but my head said yes. It was too important to put off. He owed me some answers.

It took all my willpower to gently push him away. He tried to grab me, but I fended him off with a hand. "You still haven't answered my question," I said panting. "Why didn't you tell me we were mates the moment you knew?"

The unpleasant topic burst the cloud of lust.

His eyes cooled, and sobered. He turned his face away,

but not before I caught the glint of vulnerability. "Isn't it obvious?"

"No."

His head pivoted back, his brows near his hairline. "I couldn't believe it. You are the most incredible woman I've ever met. Fearless, brash, unyielding in her convictions, with a stubbornness and strength that rivals the Gods." His brows fell sharply. "In what realm, would a woman like you be mated to a man like me?"

It was difficult to breathe for a moment. "And when you were certain?"

His stare was intense. "The Crone never gave you a choice."

My lips quivered. He'd given me the space to choose him, good or bad.

Ribbons of hope and tenderness and every other tingling emotion swirled inside my chest, but he still had to answer for his actions in Mayhem and his lie. His love didn't absolve any of that. It didn't ease my pain.

I steeled my spine and met his gaze head on. "You really hurt me in Mayhem. I know I'm stubborn and I don't listen and—"

"You're perfect."

"—But there were a million other ways you could have protected me that didn't involve breaking my heart," I finished.

He sucked in an agonized breath. "I'm so sorry, Vera. I ran back to you once I realized I couldn't leave you, but you were gone."

My gaze danced between his. A lot of what happened after he left was a haze, but I distinctly remember him running out of the kitchen. Even if he had found me, it wouldn't have changed anything. The damage was done.

"It shouldn't have happened in the first place."

"I know." He took a seat on the bed and patted the spot beside him, adding, "Please," when I didn't accept the invitation.

I sighed. It was hard to deny him when he used that word.

I joined him and he took my hand. "What I am about to tell you doesn't pardon my actions. I simply wish for you to understand."

I consented with a nod.

"I told you my mother died, but not how," he started, staring in earnest. "My uncle had been plotting to take my lordship since the day I killed my father, but he could never win any support with my mother on my side. She was beloved by our people. But my actions at House Ogma had implications beyond anything I could have imagined. Many blamed her in part, believing that if she had not protected me over the years, I would not have been in a position to do what I did. It was the perfect storm."

A dark look stole over his face, and the fingers holding mine flexed.

"My uncle convinced a group of my warriors to turn on us and put him in the lord's seat. They captured my mother as she slept. Her sword arm had been made lame by a beast attack. She couldn't defend herself against fifty men. She was brought to the island, and I was forced to surrender. They poured iron dust down both our throats, but I was only given enough to keep me tame. They shackled us and threw us into the sea."

My stomach dropped. I was glad I was sitting.

"I was forced to watch her lips turn blue, to listen to the sounds of water filling her lungs, feel the reverberations of her screams for help, see the moment she knew she was going to die —" his voice caught "—and I could do nothing but watch."

I squeezed his hand as tears slipped down my cheeks.

"I am so sorry that I hurt you, Vera, but I couldn't watch you die too," he choked out. "When I learned what you were and the danger you were in, I panicked."

Things were so clear now.

"It's not your responsibility to protect everyone. Just because you can, doesn't mean you have to, or should. You have to let people make their own choices, good or bad."

He watched me for a long moment before nodding solemnly. "I am so sorry for hurting you and lying to you."

I squeezed his hand. "Thank you."

We were silent for a long while, the room charged with a melancholy air. So much pain could have been avoided if we had just trusted one another to speak the truth, but that was the problem. We never really trusted each other. We had given up the pieces of ourselves that were convenient, the ones we could recover from.

Ronan had surrendered completely. He had given me the power to break him.

It would be so easy for me to lay all the blame on him, to gloss over my role. I could keep the most important pieces of myself, and not risk getting hurt again. But if I wanted a different ending, I had to make different choices.

I rose and pulled off my shirt.

"Vera, what are you—"

I dropped it in his lap. "My pride."

He stared at the garment with his brows drawn before his gaze darted back up to me.

I shimmied off my pants before the nerves set in and kicked them at his feet. "My stubbornness."

The band around my breasts dropped. "My fear."

Next, my underwear. "My pain."

I stood naked before him, shaking. Cold sweat beaded my forehead, and my heart thudded in my throat. Funny how it was easier to charge into battle than bear my heart to another.

Ronan gathered every piece of discarded clothing and held them gingerly in his lap like they were the most precious gifts. "Vera," he rumbled.

Our gazes clashed—mine was full of trepidation.

Fuck, I'd rather gnaw off my arm then say what I was about to say. I couldn't look at him. I had to pinch my eyes shut as I admitted my greatest fear. "I'm afraid I'm going to fuck this up again." My voice cracked. "I didn't think twice when I poisoned you. You hurt me so I had to hurt you back." I had to pause as my throat closed.

"When I saw you that morning with Kylah, when I saw how happy you looked, a part of me was relieved because I knew I could never make you that happy. I've never had friends, or a mother, or a father." A breath shuddered out of me. "The only thing I know about love is pain."

Silence dragged and I squeezed my eyes tighter as my heart beat in my chest like a frightened rabbit. My heart was at his feet, completely unprotected. All it would take was one hit to deliver a fatal blow.

"So, fuck it up."

My eyes popped open.

Ronan greeted me with a smile so wide and disarming, I startled back.

"What?" I choked. He stalked over to me, and I tried to get away, but he caught me, tilting my chin up to his.

"Break my heart," he whispered. "Break it every day for the rest of our lives."

"I-I don't understand."

"Then perhaps you need to hear the end of my story."

He returned my clothes, and I dressed. He gave me space, but his gaze didn't waver. He stared unerringly.

"After my House was threatened, I continued to kill

unarmed civilians over and over again. Each life took a piece of mine with it." He became choked up and had to look away for a moment. "I used to lie awake at night and pray for death, and when I woke in the morning, I wept. Eventually, I realized the Gods would never grant me such mercy, and I shut down. I lived in my battle-mode. I stopped feeling. At first it was bliss, but to feel is to live. I walked through the lands, dead inside."

"Then a miracle happened." He laughed, surprise lifting his brows. "The Gods answered my prayers, but instead of death, they gave me a reason to live. They gave me you. Kylah wasn't the reason I was smiling that morning in the kitchen. It was you. We were celebrating that you'd opened your eyes."

My smile was so wide it hurt.

"It's always been you. *You* brought me back to life, Little Thief. You stole my heart the moment we met."

Little Thief . . .

"That's why you called me that?"

He nodded, grinning.

"I want the mate bond. I want you."

"Are you certain?" he asked quietly.

"Yes."

"There are multiple ways to bond, but this will suffice for now."

He gestured for my hand and slid on the ring from The Wilds. "You kept it," I said in surprise.

He smiled softly. "Of course I did."

He grabbed my hand and pressed it to his heart.

Heat roared through my veins. It felt like the sun was shining inside me. My skin glowed from within. I stared at my hand, turning it in the air. Bright streaks of light were shooting out between my fingertips.

The light and warmth dissipated as quickly as it arrived,

and then this magnetic, all-consuming force took hold. I needed to touch Ronan at the same fundamental level I needed air. Like I was going to die without the contact. Like I was going to die without him.

I *had* to lay my hand on him. I *had* to touch him. I stretched my hand and laid it on his arm. The change was instant. A tidal wave of relief swept through me. The painful buzzing under my skin shifted to a contented hum, whispering all was right with the world.

"How did you live like this?" Shock strangled my words. "How were you *going* to live like this?"

All that fighting, all that arguing. That must have been excruciating for him. And he'd tolerated it all, every cruel word, every cruel act, for me.

"I was willing to do whatever it took to make your heart whole, even if it meant breaking mine," he said. "I was going to get the godstone and then you'd be safe and free to fall in love."

"And then?" I asked breathlessly.

"I would have watched over you and whatever man was lucky enough to win your heart. I would have watched over your children and their children and their children. I would have loved you until every star fell from the sky and the world turned to dust."

Tears brimmed in my eyes. I started to shake. "I need you. I need you right now, Ronan."

"Fuck."

He grabbed my face and jerked his lips to mine. There was nothing sweet or gentle in the way we kissed. We were ravenous, trying to swallow the other whole. Ronan backed me against the bed, feverishly stripping off his clothes without breaking the kiss before he reached for mine.

I was naked when my back hit the bed.

He was inside me in seconds, hammering away in frenzied movements while I planted sloppy kisses over his face. I clung to him as tears streaked my cheeks. The sex was frantic and clumsy but satisfying in its own way. My heart was full, bursting at the seams with love for him.

We shattered together.

Ronan held his weight off me, staying inside me as we caught our breaths. He was hard again within seconds. This time his thrusts were slow and intentional. He stared deeply into my eyes the whole time.

"Gods, I love you," he breathed. "I love you more than I thought it was possible to love anyone."

More tears fell. I grabbed his bottom and pulled him to me as close as possible. There wasn't an inch of space between us as he lovingly rocked into me. Each thrust was shallow but hit right where I needed it. He made love to me like that for hours. Anytime I was close, he'd pull back and start again.

When I finally climaxed, it rippled through me like shockwaves, stealing my breath. I clung to his biceps as my center squeezed him tight and he followed me with a low groan.

We collapsed against each other.

"I love you, Little Thief."

"I love you, Ronan Taran."

Sleep was immediate.

36

RONAN

I woke well rested for the first time in centuries, my heart full, my chest light. Vera had learned my darkest secret, and she hadn't left. More than that, she'd boldly defended me in front of my House. No one had ever guarded me so fiercely, not even my mother.

I didn't deserve Vera, but *fuck,* I would give everything to keep her.

Last night's coupling, while lovely, wasn't nearly enough. We had much lost time to make up for. I rolled over, desperate for her.

Vera's side of the bed was empty.

A lone note was balanced against her pillow.

Dread drenched my veins as my chest squeezed tight.

I swallowed thickly, reaching for it with a tremoring hand. *Gods, no. Please don't say what I think it's going to say.* I could picture it. Her waking in the dead of night and realizing she'd made a horrible mistake. She would have slipped from bed, hastily scrawling out a goodbye.

'I'm sorry, Ronan. I can't love a monster.'

My hand was shaking so badly, I had to use my other to steady it as I lifted the paper to my face.

Ronan,

I've gone to fuck up some very deserving assholes.

P.S. Kian told me it was you. Thank you.

~~V~~

Your Little Thief

I smiled at the line drawn through the "V" and Little Thief written in its place as immense relief washed through me. Vera hadn't left. She'd gone to deal with the Rogues.

When I learned Vera had lost her fighting ability, I wanted to leave them for her instead of handling them myself.

I rushed to throw on a change of clothes, hoping I wasn't too late. I wanted to see the look on those cowards' faces when my mate delivered their just reward.

I wound down the twisting staircase, my pounding footfalls bouncing off the stone. On the bottom floor, two halflings were dusting. I expected them to scurry off, or cower, as they always did.

Shock rang through me when they greeted me in unison, bowing. "Good morning, Lord Taran."

My brows furrowed at their strange behavior. "Have either of you seen the halfling Vera?"

"No, my Lord," the one on the right answered. "The Head of House is in the courtyard. Perhaps he has."

"Thank you."

They bowed again and returned to their work. I sent them a final lingering glance before making haste outside. A small crowd of halflings and soldiers loitered in between the buildings, whispering among themselves. They were no doubt discussing last night's events.

I'd ensured Vera's glamour was reinforced, and though it was rare, it wasn't unheard of for a fae lord and halfling to be together. Still, it had to be shocking to see a cold-hearted killer surrender his sword for love.

I spotted Milton on the periphery, trying to corral his charges back to work, and cut straight toward him.

A soldier pressed a fist to his heart, murmuring, 'My Lord', as I strode by.

I crashed to a halt, head whipping over my shoulder. My soldiers hadn't bowed to me willingly since the night I earned the name the Butcher. Hiding my surprise, I acknowledged him with a nod, and continued on.

The strange phenomenon repeated with each soldier, deepening my confusion.

"Milton," I said when I reached him.

He jolted at my voice and swept into a deep bow. "Apologies, My Lord. The staff have been distracted this morning. I'll get them to work at once."

He grabbed a nearby halfling and started dragging them.

"It's alright, Milton."

He released his victim, and they scrambled back to their companions.

I cleared my throat, lowering my voice. "The staff and soldiers are behaving strangely." Milton had an ear on all the goings on at the castle.

The Head of House cracked a small smile. It was the first time he'd ever done so at me.

My brows settled low over my eyes. "And now so are you."

He chuckled, breaking his professional act. Another first. Milton valued his position too much to ever display any outright fear or disgust, the way many others had. He had been nothing but polite and professional to my face, but I'd overheard his true feelings when he didn't know I was near.

"I believe it has to do with the tongue lashing we received last night, my Lord."

My gaze scanned the courtyard. I was met with a respectful nod everywhere I looked.

"Vera." My lips formed tenderly around her name. She had done this. She had swayed their minds.

Milton cleared his throat, a soft sincerity taking over his eyes. "I for one am deeply sorry for any untrue rumors I had a hand in propagating."

"Thank you for saying that, Milton."

He bent his head.

"Have you seen Vera?"

"She is on the island with Kian and the others, My Lord."

They'd kept the Rogues there instead of bringing them here. Good. A halfling with Vera's fighting skills would certainly raise eyebrows.

"Thank you." I made to walk off but hesitated.

"Was there something else, My Lord?"

I'd promised Vera I would give the halflings access to valuable skills and an education. Even if it hadn't been part of our agreement, I would have done it anyway. I couldn't introduce Vera as Lady of House Taran until the threat with the king was eliminated, but she was Lady here and her opinion mattered as much as mine.

"Yes, I want our young halflings to start getting an education. See if anyone from the Saor has teaching experience."

Milton retained his professional demeanor, but his eyes betrayed his shock. "Right away, My Lord." He bowed and spun around.

I caught his shoulder. "It can wait. Give everyone the day off, including yourself."

He looked uncertain but didn't question it. "Yes, My lord."

I released him and made my way down to the small beach below the cliffs. I dragged the small boat into the water and rowed to the island.

Familiar voices carried to me as I jogged to where my

manor once stood. The charred remains had been cleared and clusters of stones were laid out to begin the new construction.

Kylah, Kian, Hunt, and Vera stood outside the building site, huddled around something while Finn watched from the sidelines.

I stopped beside him. "What's going on?"

He unfolded a hand from behind his back and gestured at the pit door. "Kian informed the others what those men had done over breakfast. They woke up your mate to join in on the fun."

That explained Hunt's presence. He didn't take kindly to violence against women.

I returned my attention to Finn. "I'm surprised to see you here," I remarked lightly.

"Someone had to supervise."

I laughed and was shocked by how freely the sound came. Laughter and smiles had not come easily in the last five centuries. They had to be dragged, kicking and screaming from my throat.

Finn peered at me out of the corner of his eye. "You can't stop smiling."

I felt my face. I was grinning ear to ear. I hadn't realized. I cleared my throat, and evened out my expression, eliciting a laugh.

"Don't. Happiness looks good on you, my friend."

My gaze drifted to him. Finn's raven hair was down, sitting atop his shoulders. He stood tall and proud with his hands folded behind him, carrying a quiet air of strength and authority. All he was missing was a crown.

There was no trace of the blood-spattered babe my mother had carried home so many years ago, but that part of his past would always linger with him.

My chest clenched at the thought.

When Finn turned eighteen, I took him to his castle like I had with Vera and told him everything. I'd taken a large dose of iron dust before the journey and offered him a sword when we reached the banquet hall.

"Kill me, if it will bring you peace."

Finn had come close. He'd pressed the sword to my heart and pushed it in, but he couldn't bring himself to finish.

Our relationship was rocky for many years after that. I turned control of House Taran over to him when he was twenty, and we kept in contact when issues arose, or he needed advice. Through the following decades, a beautiful, unexpected friendship bloomed.

"Thank you for everything," I told him sincerely. "I would not have made it through the last five hundred years without you."

A small smile broke across his face. "I wish I could have done more." He glanced at Vera and his expression turned begrudgingly impressed. "She managed to do in five minutes what I've been trying to accomplish for centuries." His laugh was part irony, part amusement, part bitterness. "I can't believe I'm saying this, but I was wrong about her."

I smiled softly. "So was I."

Vera *was* my salvation.

She was my whole world.

There were a thousand men more worthy than I. A thousand better men far more deserving. I didn't know what I had done to be given such a precious gift, but I would fight with my dying breath to keep her.

There was a commotion at the center of the huddle, and our eyes cut that way. Kylah had shifted, providing a glimpse inside the circle. One of the Rogues was tied to a post.

Vera tapped her lips, staring at him. "What to do. What to do. So many options."

"I can explode his cock," Hunt grunted.

Vera planted her hands on her hips, mulling it over before sighing. "It would be such a tiny explosion though."

"I can cut it off and shove it down his throat," Kian offered.

"His dick isn't big enough to choke on. Isn't that right, Vincey?" Vera tapped the Rogue's cheek and he tried to flinch away, but he couldn't go anywhere with the bindings.

"Who are you?" he growled.

Vera hunched, peering into his eyes. "Take one guess shithead."

His gaze widened a moment before narrowing.

"There's always electrocution," Kylah said.

Vera snapped her fingers and pointed at her. "Love where your head's at."

She turned and a grin split her face when she saw me. The group parted as she crossed over to me. Smiling like madman, I drew her into my arms and kissed her vulgarly, uncaring that we had an audience.

"There's plenty more where that came from," I whispered as I pulled back. "But first I want you to humiliate those men."

She grinned. "With pleasure."

Her eyes moved to Finn and hardened. She cocked back her leg and kicked him so hard in the groin, I heard bone shatter. He shriveled to the ground, clutching between his legs.

"Vera," I said sharply.

Her gaze didn't move from Finn. "He knows what that was for."

Finn limply raised a hand, rasping, "She's right."

I glanced between the two of them. He was my best friend, and she was my mate. It was time to put an end to their feud.

"There will be no more fighting between you two, is that clear?"

Finn nodded, but Vera didn't respond, shifting her glare to me.

I grinned, reaching out to stroke her cheek. "Please, for me?"

Her teeth ground together. She reared back and kicked him again. Finn moaned in pain.

"Vera," I snapped.

She raised her hands. "I'm done now."

She offered Finn a hand. "Truce?"

After scrutinizing her for a moment, he accepted and she helped him to his feet.

She swiveled back to the group. "As much fun as it would be to torture him, it wouldn't be a fair fight. Untie him. I want to kick his ass."

That's my girl.

I wrapped my elbow around her neck, drawing her back against me to plant a kiss atop her head before nodding at Kian. He moved behind the post and quickly untied the ropes.

Kylah, Hunt, and Kian formed a half ring around the Rogue, with Finn and I standing sentry on the opposite side. Satisfied the coward couldn't run, I released Vera, and she faced off against him.

He was healthy and in prime fighting shape. I'd order Kian to make sure of it after I had given Vera the vial.

She cracked her neck, bouncing on her heels, then struck at him. Her fist slammed into his cheek. There was an audible crack as his head whipped to the side, blood flying from his mouth. He went down hard.

"That's for leaving me in the canyon," Vera hissed over him.

He whimpered.

She punched his face again. "That's for outside the wagon." She raised her fist to hit him another time and he curled into a ball, shaking, shielding his head with his arms. Her hand dropped with a sigh. "You're so pathetic, it's not fun."

She turned away and he relaxed slightly. She pivoted and swung her boot hard for his stomach. He went skidding across the ground, groaning. A smile sprung across her lips. "Nope. That was definitely fun."

She pointed at a large Rogue with a bullish build. "He's next."

Kian released him. The Rogue crossed his arms and stared boldly. "You don't want to do this kid."

Vera laughed loudly. "I've been waiting to punch your smug face since the day we met." She came at him like a nightmare. She moved so quickly, she was almost a blur, her fists and legs flying at the speed of a bullet.

She pummeled him while Kian coached her from the sidelines. Kylah was cheering for her. She even had Hunt doing his version of a smile. It brought a grin to my face to see my friends and my mate together like this.

Even Finn joined, applauding when she jumped into a spinning kick and knocked him down.

"How's our prisoner?" I whispered while keeping my eye on the fight. I'd been too busy winning Vera back to visit the scum who'd betrayed us.

"Safely under guard per your instructions."

I bent my head.

When she knocked the Rogue down again and he didn't get back up, Vera glared at door, panting. "Send them back to Mayhem."

I was far less forgiving. I wanted to rip out their goddamn spines, but Vera wanted them to live, so they would. "Tell Kian to take their hands," I whispered to Finn. "Then they may return."

He inclined his head, then approached the others while I cut straight for Vera and threw her over my shoulder.

"Ronan! Put me down!"

I spanked her bottom. "No."

I brought her to the boat, rowed us to the mainland, and carried her to my room.

I threw her on the bed.

"Take off your clothes."

She froze at my husky voice, gaze darting to me. I freed my cock from the confines of my pants. It was raging hard and swollen. I stroked it from tip to base. Vera wet her lips, eyes dilating. Wordlessly, she rushed to strip off her clothes, then paused, awaiting further orders.

"On your hands and knees," I murmured.

She took the position without question, and I groaned low in my throat. She fought me at every turn outside, but in the bedroom, she surrendered so beautifully. Fisting the root, I brought my swollen cock to her lips. "Open."

Her mouth obeyed and her tongue swirled over the head. I cursed, my body jerking. She laughed huskily, the little witch, and wrapped her lips around it. It was a tight fit. They could barely reach all the way around.

Gaze meeting mine, she slowly swallowed as much of me as she could. My thumb smeared the spit dripping out over her cheek. "That's a good girl. Take all of me."

She started to choke, but kept going, her eyes watering, but determined.

"That's it."

Harsh breaths left her nostrils as she struggled to breathe around me. She had to stop halfway, but the sight of her gagging on my cock was the sexiest fucking thing I'd ever seen. She wrapped her hand around the shaft and worked it as her mouth milked me.

I shallowly pumped into her mouth for several seconds and had to pull away before I came right then. My cock released from her mouth with a wet pop.

I twirled my finger, and she spun around, presenting her ass. The toned, fleshy mounds were just begging to get spanked. I trailed a hand down her spine, then pushed down on her lower back, forcing her to arch, and show me more of that gorgeous ass.

I traced a finger near her delicate, puckered hole. "I want to taste you here," I whispered. It was far too tight to take all of me without preparation, but it could take my tongue just fine.

"Gods yes," she moaned into the sheets, shivering with anticipation.

I cupped her soft cheeks and squeezed hard, then I brought my hand down. The pressure was light—teasing.

"More," she moaned.

I spanked her harder. One smack on each cheek. I traced the accompanying blush, mesmerized, before gently kneading the pain away. I smoothed my hands down her thighs and jerked them apart.

She yelped in surprise.

I dropped to my knees and nosed her center, drawing in a deep breath of her tantalizing scent, and my cock kicked. Black threaded through my gaze, and I shook it off. *Not now.*

Her folds glistened with her excitement. I grinned darkly, spreading it around. "Did my little mate like sucking my cock?"

Her head bobbed.

I slowly eased a finger inside. She threw her head back arching into it with a low moan. I slowly worked it in and out as I leaned forward and sucked on her clit.

"Fuck yes," she groaned.

My cock was heavy, the tip beading with arousal, covered in her spit. I dragged my tongue up her center to her ass. It hovered there as I continued to play between her folds.

"You ready?" My breath fanned over her most intimate place and her whole body tremored.

She nodded.

"I need to hear you say it."

"Yes," she breathed.

My tongue lightly swirled over the sensitive crinkles before licking up. She started to shake, and I paused.

"How did that feel?"

"Strange, but good."

"Do you want me to keep going?"

"Fuck yes," she said.

"Mmm. So dirty for me."

My tongue returned to her puckered hole. I vacillated between pressures and directions, finding which ones made her scream, all the while my finger pumped in and out of her. I ate her ass like it was my sole purpose in life, like I'd been put on this earth just for this.

I groaned lecherously when I felt her pussy clamping around my finger and pulled away. She whipped around with a glare, but it dropped as soon as she saw me lining up my cock with her entrance. I grabbed one hip, using the other hand to drag my cock back and forth between her slippery folds.

"Fuck me," she growled.

I gathered up her hair and wrapped it around my fist, pulling her head taut.

"With pleasure."

I slammed into her. I gripped her hip with a bruising force as I pounded away. She splayed a hand against the wall, pushing against me, forcing me deeper with each thrust.

"Don't stop," she panted. "I'm close."

I lightly pressed my thumb against her asshole as I continued hammering away and she moaned.

I continued my brutal pace until she clenched around me. Her legs shook with her release. A low tingle formed at the base of my spine warning me I was close as well. I pulled out at the last second and it hit the floor.

I collapsed beside her on the bed and pulled her against my chest. We were motionless for some time, our strained breaths filling the silence.

Vera propped up on her elbows, staring intently.

I brushed her hair away from her face with a tender smile. "What is it my little mate?"

"Can I have kids; you know with the curse and all?"

"Yes. I had Lawrence test you after he healed you."

Her eyes narrowed a fraction. "Would have been nice if you asked first."

I stroked her cheek. "You are right. I apologize."

She hid her surprise. "Thank you."

"How do you feel about being able to have children?" I asked softly.

"Being the first fertile, mated female in five centuries is a huge responsibility. We can't save the fae on our own."

"No, of course not, but with us, there's hope."

She laid her chin on my chest, distress pinching her brows. "What are we going to do about the king, Ronan?" she whispered.

Our deadline to deliver the godstone was in seven days.

"I have my best beast fighters here, training the castle soldiers. The outpost soldiers are being trained as well, and the traitor has been apprehended."

That didn't ease her worry. "Will it be enough?"

"Shh. There will be time to worry later. I want to enjoy this moment with you."

I tried to coax her back into my arms, but she was adamant on having this conversation. She propped up on an elbow, staring down at me. "The Crone said I needed to remember. Do you think she was telling the truth?"

"I do."

Her gaze turned distance, lost in thought. When it refocused, it was filled with determination. "I want to remember."

I sat up. "Are you certain?"

She nodded. "I don't want to be afraid anymore."

A smile formed. "I know someone who can help."

37

VERA

The Lord of House Cern was as polished and imposing as the mountain he lived under.

Slightly below Ronan's height, he loomed over me without a single thread, button, or hair out of place. The only inconsistency was the laughter lines framing his saffron eyes. They were deep, blemishing his otherwise perfect skin, and at odds with his stony countenance.

"Vera, meet Lord Cern," Ronan said gruffly.

"Pleasure to make your acquaintance." Lord Cern's voice was deep, but polished, like a well-oiled chain. "You may call me Liam." He held out his hand, and long, elegant fingers wrapped around mine.

Ronan had warned me about him on the ride over. Lord Cern wielded an incredible intellect and was as slippery as a snake, but he had an interest in the wellbeing of House Taran.

"Nice to meet you," I said politely, though that was yet to be determined.

We dropped our hands, and his golden gaze flicked to Ronan. "I take it she's the one you came to me for?"

"Yes."

435

"A halfling. How interesting," he murmured. His eyes breezed over me before settling on Ronan. "Was there an issue with the vial?"

"No. We're here for something else." Ronan looked at me to answer.

I met Lord Cern's startling eyes. They were the color of pure gold and blazingly bright. It was a little like staring into the sun. "I need my childhood memories unblocked."

"I see." He swept out his hand, gesturing for us to follow.

Ronan didn't move. "What's your price?"

Liam's head tilted over his shoulder. "I want to see her."

"No."

"Then we have nothing else to discuss." Lord Cern turned and strode off.

Ronan glanced down at me, looking torn before lifting his gaze back to Liam. "Wait."

Lord Cern paused.

"You have a deal," Ronan bit out.

Liam inclined his head.

Placing a hand on the small of my back, Ronan guided me forward into the dim corridor.

Large mirrors lined the ground, reflecting the light from outside. The stone had smooth, concave markings as if it had been hand carved. I marveled at how much work it would have taken to cut through the Fayette Mountain and create this castle or estate—whatever this place was.

Liam walked ahead of us his hands threaded behind his back as his shoes moved over the ground in a precise cadence. "How are things at House Taran?" The question held a casual air, but the stiffness in his shoulders betrayed his interest.

"Fine," Ronan grunted.

Liam turned, raising a manicured brow. "You're certain?"

"Yes," he growled. "I have it handled."

"I hope so," Liam said lightly, but his tone held a hint of warning.

I snuck Ronan a glance. He shook his head, mouthing, "Later."

We wove up rocky corridor after rocky corridor before the walls transformed into tombs. Long, horizontal openings were cut into the stone. Each space contained a carefully arranged skeleton behind a piece of glass. The deeper we walked, the more bones I saw. There had to be thousands.

"What is this place?" I whispered to Ronan.

Liam was the one to answer. "The Catacombs."

I glanced at him in surprise. "You bury your dead here?"

He broke his pace, eyes dashing around. "These contain the dead of all the fae Houses. They turn over the bones once all the magic has been drained, and their secrets are no longer a threat."

My eyes sought Ronan. He was strangely quiet.

I found him watching Liam with the keen focus of a predator, waiting for any reason to pounce. Their interests might be aligned, but Ronan didn't trust him for a second.

My attention returned to Liam, brows narrowing as I struggled to make sense of his statement. "Why would you bury other fae here?"

"These aren't graves. They're archives. We collect and record memories from the bones." He observed me out of his peripheral with an expression that was somehow as curious as it was disinterested. "How is it a halfling knows so little about the fae?"

I got the sense he didn't care about the answer, but wanted to see how I would react. A test. Ronan didn't intervene, trusting I could handle myself, and it made a smile tease at my lips.

"The fae are secretive bastards," I told Liam. "When they're alive anyway," I added, glancing at the bones.

Ronan caught my gaze and I saw a glimmer of pride.

Liam regarded me with mild surprise, like an owner whose pet finally stopped shitting on the rug. "It is easier to pull secrets from the dead. They have nothing to lose." He resumed his stroll with us pacing behind.

We came to a stop outside a set of double doors so tall, I had to crane my neck back to see all the way to the top. The ashen color reminded me of the trees in the Deadwood Forest. In the middle was the same crest I'd seen carved into the mountain face—a skull encircled in a halo of light. Just beneath was an inscription: 'Death is the ultimate enlightenment.'

Liam faced us. "I'm afraid this is where we leave you," he told Ronan. "Behind these doors are House Cern's secrets and we both know you can't be trusted with those."

Ronan bristled. "I'm not leaving her with you," he growled. "Just give me a vial like last time."

Liam gave a quick head shake. "Unlocking memories takes more finesse than simply throwing magic at them. The mind is incredibly fragile and blocks things as a survival mechanism. Those memories must be reopened with painstaking care, or you risk damaging the mind. I'll need access to my draoi tree inside to ensure it's done properly."

Ronan's troubled gaze met mine. He was leaving the decision up to me, despite how much it pained him. He was trying.

I flashed him a bright smile, mouthing, "Thank you."

I turned to Liam. "Try anything, and I'll end you."

His mouth twitched. "Your threat has been noted."

I blew out a breath, imagining everything that could go wrong on the other side of those doors. As untrustworthy as

438

Liam was, Ronan had said he was the only one powerful enough to help.

If he had any nefarious intentions, they couldn't be any worse than the consequences I was already suffering. I didn't want to die, afraid of my dragon. I glanced at Ronan— my love, my mate, my future.

I wanted to live.

I wanted to fight.

"Lead the way."

Liam stepped up to the doors and they yawned open revealing a cavernous library. It was ten . . . twelve . . . There were too many stories to count.

"Liam . . ."

He halted at Ronan's voice.

"If you reveal anything you see in Vera's memories, I'll tell *her* the truth."

Liam inclined his head before stepping inside.

"I'll be right here," Ronan promised.

The doors started to swing back to close, and I had to rush to clear them. 'I love you,' I mouthed. He froze, eyes brightening just as the doors closed with a reverberating thud.

I lurched forward, hiding a smile.

That felt so good to say.

Polished wood paneling covered the library. There were four massive blocks of wood cut from the bottom floor wall with shelves built in. The cut outs were framed by white, ornately carved pillars with gold gilding. Above them, each story held curved balconies where endless rows of shelving kissed the soaring ceiling.

Suspended from it was a massive skeleton that spanned the length of the entire space. Just its spine had to be ten times longer than I was tall. I couldn't take my eyes off it as I followed Liam to a sitting area.

He gestured for me to take one of the winged back chairs, and I sat, staring up at the monster in wonder. A mug of steaming liquid appeared in my hand, courtesy of one of the halflings bustling about.

"Magnificent creatures, aren't they?"

My gaze jerked to Liam. I hadn't noticed him take the opposite seat. He was perched with a leg balanced on his knee as he watched me with a closed expression.

"What?"

"Dragons."

My eyes shot back to the skeleton. "That's a dragon?" I breathed.

He observed me intently, cocking his head. My reaction sparked his interest, and I had a feeling it wasn't a good thing.

"Indeed," he murmured. "Their kind died off well before you were born."

"My mother used to tell me stories," I said lightly, even as the phrase 'my mother' left an acidic aftertaste. I hoped I could sell my curiosity as childish fancy, which wasn't far off.

Dragons were the thing of legends, mythical beings that roamed the skies with the power to raze entire cities with a single breath. I had never seen or heard about a dragon outside the stories the Crone had told me as a little girl, before I learned dragons were very much real.

I thought she had simply made them up to scare me as she loved to do.

Really, the Crone had been attempting to teach me about myself in her own twisted way. I had no idea why she turned me into one, or how. My eyes dragged over the floating skeleton like it might have an answer.

It had an elongated torso and neck, and a tail, but something was missing. "Where are its wings?" I asked.

440

"They were severed to prevent its escape."

I dragged my gaze back to Liam. "How did it end up here?"

A glass of water had appeared in his hand. He drew slow circles over the rim as his golden gaze appraised me. The strum of his finger over the glass created a soft, lyrical humming. It reminded me of an aibeya playing its harp.

Remembering the mug I had been given, I sniffed it.

"If I was going to kill you, I wouldn't use poison," Liam said mildly.

Still, I set the mug down. I wasn't that reckless, even with Ronan outside.

Relaxing in the chair, I studied the library as I waited for Liam to begin.

Fae flitted between the rows of shelves, armed with books and scrolls. Others sat at one of the many tables lining the wide aisle, flipping through their stacks. Some read, some hastily scribbled notes.

"It was brought here to study," he finally answered. Not once did he stop dragging his finger over the glass. The sound was velvety soft, slipping between my bones, and causing pleasant tingles over my body.

I sank deeper into the seat. "And what did you learn?"

"Curious thing, aren't you?"

Round and round his finger went on the glass. My eyes tracked the movement, mesmerized. Gravity pulled at my eyelids. Keeping my eyes open suddenly took a momentous effort. The sound he was creating was so relaxing.

"I'm willing to make a trade. I will tell you about dragons. In return, you will answer my questions." Liam's voice cut through the tranquility of the music.

I shook my head. "I'm here for my memories."

"And you'll have them."

The last time I traded knowledge for knowledge, I'd

been burned and left defenseless. My tongue felt heavy as I struggled to respond. "No," I rasped and finally allowed my eyes to shut.

"Dragons were the most powerful of their kind," Liam's smooth voice began. I didn't stop him. If he wanted to offer free information, I would gladly listen. "Some would say too powerful. They were the Alphas of the beast world. With them, a horde of unruly, savage animals was able to unite and fight as one. We were on the brink of losing the war before King Desmond brought the Houses together and Ronan hunted down every dragon. The beasts fell into chaos after that."

"Wh—" It was difficult to speak with the lethargy settling into my bones. "Why not just kill them all? Why lock them behind a wall?"

"They can reproduce at an astonishing rate. Their population is triple the size of ours. Killing them all would have taken decades and far too many lives."

Because beasts could kill high fae . . .

Liam remained quiet. The musical notes he created floated up into the air like the softest, most dazzling snowflakes. I wanted to catch one on my tongue.

"How are you feeling?" he asked.

I peeled open an eye, glaring at him for disrupting the blissful quiet.

He stared, swirling his finger around the glass. There was an underlying meaning to his query my foggy brain couldn't make sense of. My brows pulled sluggishly together. "Why are you asking me that?"

Liam took his finger off the glass for half a second and the calm cocooning my senses was ripped away. I bolted upright in the chair as a cold realization crashed into me. He was making that sound on purpose, controlling me.

"Ronan," I screamed at the top of my lungs.

"He can't hear you. I had these walls reinforced after Ronan's little intrusion."

I tried anyway. "Ronan!"

His finger returned to the glass before I could scream a third time, and that soothing melody lulled my body into a false sense of safety.

Round and round his finger went.

My limbs turned syrupy. I felt weightless, suspended in air, unable to move, but this time my mind was aware of what was happening. I couldn't hide the panic in my voice, as I whispered frantically, "What are you doing to me?"

"Shhhh. You will not be harmed. You have my word," he told me. "I am using hypnosis. I am going to put you in a trance, and we will have a friendly conversation."

"Friendly?" I echoed bitterly.

"I am barely using my powers. If you prefer, I can simply rip out the memories I require. I've heard it's quite painful." He paused, then said, "Remember, I did give you a choice."

Idiot. Idiot. Idiot.

"I'll tell you what you want to know," I hurried out. "You don't need to do this."

He clucked his tongue, laughing tonelessly. "Afraid it is too late. You made your choice. We must all live with our choices."

My body sank through the chair. I fell deeper away from the library until I was floating in a black abyss, staring up at the tiny speck that was Liam's face.

"Ronan will kill you for this!" I shouted.

Liam's mocking voice carried down to me. "Good thing you're not going to remember any of it."

The darkness dragged me into its belly.

38

VERA

Faint, dappled moonlight glittered overhead. I was surrounded by the silhouettes of trunks and brush, but it was too dark to make out anything else. A cool breeze blew through sending up a chorus of rustling leaves before the forest fell silent.

A soft, nearly inaudible sound floated through the trees. My ears struggled to identify it.

It sounded again, louder.

Someone was crying . . .

I crawled forward, peering through the vegetation.

A stream of moonlight illuminated a clearing. A girl knelt at its center, her arms trembling. Her face was turned away, but I could tell she was young based on her size. She couldn't have been more than five or six.

"Please, Mama. It hurts."

"Wipe your tears," a sharp reprimand rang out.

The speaker was cloaked in shadows, just outside the ring of moonlight, but the voice was unmistakably the Crone's.

I skittered back.

"The harder you fight, the more painful it will be."

I watched between the foliage as the girl's shoulder dislocated itself with a ghastly snap. More bones popped out of place, rippling and contorting under the skin. The girl screamed with every movement.

"Mama, something's trying to break out of my—" Her shout was interrupted by fangs punching through her gums. Blood dripped from her mouth as she swayed on her hands and knees.

"MAMA, PLEASE! MAKE IT STOP!"

The Crone crouched, tipping up the girl's chin with a sharp nail. "Calm yourself. You have nothing to fear. You are becoming whole."

Her spine cracked, one notch at a time, and reformed longer and stronger.

"I don't want to become whole," she cried. "Please! I'll be good. I swear."

The Crone backed into the shadows, ignoring the little girl's pleas.

I realized three things at once. That little girl was me, this was a memory of my first shift, and I wasn't going to let her—me—go through it alone. I lunged forward, breaking through the brush, and kneeled at her side.

I stretched towards her, but my hands slipped through her like smoke.

Sssssh, Little One, a shadowy voice purred, and I jolted back. *Everything will be alright.*

The girl's whimpering died off. "Who are you?" she asked in a wonderous tone, but I knew she wasn't talking to me.

I am your ssshadow. I am here to protect you.

I couldn't say how I knew, but I understood the voice was coming from inside her mind, and I could hear it too.

It whispered more soothing words to the little girl, comforting her through the shift. She babbled back, her pain and fear bleeding away, despite her body contorting at horrifying angles. When it was done, a baby dragon sat in the clearing.

The memory dissolved and I was wrenched into a new one.

Leaves and branches crunched under the little girl's feet as she held her arms out and sailed between the trees, making zooming sounds. I looked around seven this time.

She stopped at a small, dead bush and blew a breath of flames at it, giggling when it set on fire.

Very good, Little One, the dragon praised.

She raced toward a thick, fallen log. Her little legs couldn't clear it on their own. Wings sprung from her back and lifted her over it, folding away as soon as her feet hit the ground, and she continued running.

Our connection is weakening. It's time to ssshift again.

She slowed to a stop and got down on her hands and knees. The shift was seamless. One minute the little girl was there, and the next a dragon, slightly larger than before. It was growing with her.

The memory faded into black, quickly replaced by another, but this time I was a participant, instead of a voyeur.

I lay curled on a familiar bed, surrounded by four yellow walls. My tail moved in agitated sweeps. A threatening growl issued from my lips at the figure entering the room.

"I saw the scarsss." The guttural, smoky voice came from me, but wasn't mine. "You will not harm her again."

The figure laughed, a light feminine trill. "So protective of our little girl," it murmured. "Very well. Another time then." A slow, wicked smile curled their lips before they glided to the door. "You can't protect her from me forever, dragon."

A new memory began.

I was older, ten maybe, and screaming in pain. "God no. Stop. Please stop."

My spine cracked and grew. I was shaking with terror. "Please. I don't know what you are, but please stop."

You know me, Little One. Calm. You are sssafe.

"No! You're a monster. Just like her. Stay away from me!"

I scuttled back in the leaves, but there was no escaping the shift. Excruciating pain tore through me as I sobbed, my body breaking into a million pieces. Trees bowled over in my wake. I could see over the top of the forest, to the mountain beyond.

My dragon had grown to full size.

I shifted back.

I hate you, I told the darkness. *I hate you, and I never want to see you again*. On a deep breath, I hardened my heart and mind and locked the monster away. *You're never going to hurt me again.*

The memory vanished, but another didn't begin.

I was left suspended in darkness. My terrified, pounding heart clawed its way up my throat. I pinched myself repeatedly trying to wake up, but the pain told me it wasn't a dream.

A giant silhouette lumbered toward me in the inky black. Glittering silver scales glowed from within, illuminating the figure of a creature.

The dragon was the length of a train, and as tall as a giant. Wicked, curved ridges notched its spine, which was layered in a hard plating. The same plating extended to most of its body, like thousands of scales woven tightly together to create an impenetrable armor. Its only soft spot was a patch of skin on its under belly.

Body length talons sliced out of paws and tipped the apex of its leathery wings. Its head was the size of a wagon and was covered in plating with flexible looking spikes jutting out. Between its massive mouth were rows of dagger-like teeth.

As it drew closer, I lurched back in horror.

It paused, sinking down. Its legs folded neatly beneath it like a cat and its wings tucked into its sides. Vibrant amethyst eyes met mine and I was struck by the intelligence in them. I'd never seen that in a beast's gaze before. They were all cold and empty.

"Hello, Little One."

Its mouth didn't move, but its primal voice rang out as clearly as if it had. This was the first time I'd heard it speak to me outside my mind, and its words hit me like a frozen whip, stinging and chilling at once.

An overwhelming sense of peace and comfort flowed into me. I don't know how I knew it was coming from the dragon, but I did. Somehow, I sensed its intentions too. It wasn't there to hurt me. It only wanted to talk.

I didn't move again, feeling trapped in some bizarre dream. The source of all my agony, all my nightmares, was sitting in front of me, wanting to have a conversation.

"How are you here?" I whispered.

I didn't know where here was, or how I'd arrived.

"We are in our mind."

"It's *my* mind," I snapped. "You're just living in it."

The dragon watched, unblinkingly, with those purple ember eyes. *My* eyes, my talons, my wings—it was like looking into a giant fucked-up mirror.

I stared back for a long stretch, at a complete loss for words.

"I saw some of our memories," I eventually confessed, feeling insane for talking with this thing, but something

448

deep inside told me I needed to, that it was important. Heck, it could be the dragon's influence again—there was no way of knowing—but I did know this confrontation was a long time coming.

I'd run from it my whole life and it had gotten me nowhere.

"You called yourself my protector," I started, unsure where I was going, but quickly gained confidence. "You did protect me once, but where were you all the other times? Where were you all the times the Crone threw me in the well? Or all the times she tortured me?"

I didn't know if this creature had a conscious, but I couldn't help the acidic anger bubbling up through every crack. I'd watched it promise that frightened little girl that it would protect her, and she would have clung to that promise.

"Where were you then, oh mighty protector?" My voice was pitched so high, I might as well have been screaming.

I wanted to. I wanted to wail and shriek and howl. How dare it lie to that little girl. How dare it make that pretty pledge so it could use her, the same way everyone else had.

That promise was corthshit. The Crone would have never given me anything to protect myself. She cursed me with the dragon to torment me, and it had.

I wanted it to admit it. I wanted it to feel *something*, which was irrational. Just because this thing could talk, didn't mean it understood compassion, or guilt. At the end of the day, it was just another beast.

"Trapped by you," its ancient voice echoed around me. "You grew to fear me and kept me captive in the darkness for years."

Ice slithered into my veins. It was part shock, part something I didn't want to name. That is exactly what the memories showed. I didn't fear the beast when I was young. I

449

embraced it, but as the years went on, and the dragon got bigger, our relationship changed.

Hazy impressions of memories flitted overhead, projecting their emotional residue. As they rushed by, one by one, I could feel the shift.

It didn't happen overnight. It was a gradual process between the ages of eight and nine, when the Crone's abuse heightened, and I pulled away from the dragon as it became tangled up in my complicated feelings toward the Crone.

She had put the dragon inside of me, and she was an evil witch. Add to that, that all the abuse stemmed from the dragon parts, and it became a monster. I was too young to know how to hate the Crone, so I turned that hate on myself. On the part of me she had created.

The only crime the dragon had committed before I locked it up was simply existing.

A sickening, unwanted guilt wrenched my insides as I remembered the Crone's words. 'Monsters aren't born. They're made in the dark.'

Had I made my dragon into a monster?

No.

The dragon had terrorized me for years. It wasn't innocent in all this.

"You've been trying to seize control of my body for every night as long as I can remember. You forced me to imprison you."

It shook its gargantuan head. "Not take over. Protect."

"What could I possibly need protection from in my sleep?"

"Your dreams. They make you scream."

My breath caught, snagging on the fleshy part of my throat. It felt like a rusted knife had been shoved down my windpipe. Breathing was impossible for the next several seconds until a sharp, burning gasp tore from my lungs.

"You were trying to protect me from my nightmares." My voice was breathless, strained, and horrified all at once. I might have blocked out the Crone's abuse, but my unconscious mind never forgot, replaying it creatively in my dreams.

Its giant head tipped in what could only be described as a nod. "I am your shadow. I am always with you. Will always protect you."

A long, shocked silence followed.

I was dizzy. I had to sit before I fell. My feet folded under me as I collapsed.

A thousand different thoughts and emotions hit me at once. "But you—you killed those children in Mayhem," I whispered, clinging to the conviction I once held as absolute; that the dragon was a bloodthirsty monster, and I, its unwilling host.

"Fire knows no bounds. It does not discriminate between young and old. I saved us."

"You went too far. You could have stopped."

"They would have come for us. I ensured you were safe. I have always ensured you are safe."

I couldn't deny the truth ringing in its words.

A band of pressure squeezed my skull, a stress headache forming. This was all too much, the implications too great. I rocked back and forth, clutching my head as I struggled to wade through this messy, fucked up situation.

The one thing I kept coming back to was what happened in Mayhem. The dragon had killed more children than I wanted to count and left numerous others as orphans. If they had died because the dragon was protecting me, because I'd released it, it meant their blood was on my hands.

It meant the dragon wasn't the monster, I was.

Suddenly, I was falling, flailing through the darkness. I slammed back into consciousness with a strangled gasp.

"Vera, what's wrong?"

Everything.

I wanted to tell Ronan that, but the words wouldn't come. They were stuck in my throat like a hook. My back arched off some foreign smelling sheets, sucking in choked breaths as I fought a tidal wave of tears.

Hands seized my cheeks. Ronan's face swam above mine. My body was a bundle of glass nerves, and his feather light touch was all it took to shatter. A low, keening wail bellowed from my aching lungs. "I did it. I killed those children. Not the dragon. Me."

Wordlessly, Ronan slipped in behind me and pulled me into him. He ran his fingers through my hair as great sobs split the room. I didn't deserve his comfort but clung to it anyway, clung to his solid strength. It was the only thing keeping me from tumbling over the edge.

His calloused palm was warm as it glided over my hair. His presence and gentle touch soothed my jagged edges after a time, and the self-loathing squeezing my lungs in a tight-fisted grip slowly unclenched. I felt like I could breathe again. But just barely.

"Do you wish to talk about it?" Ronan asked in such an uncharacteristically gentle voice, the flood of tears threatened to spill all over again. I really didn't deserve him.

"Not much to say," I said, my voice was hoarse. "Turns out I'm just as awful as the Crone. Maybe worse."

Ronan loomed over me in a flash with a darkly savage expression. "You are *nothing* like the Crone. Don't ever speak about yourself that way again."

"It's true," I croaked. "It's my fault those children are dead. The dragon was protecting me. The dragon has been trying to protect me my whole life."

His fierce expression didn't ease at my whispered confession, but his eyes softened. "Us. The dragon was protecting us. Do you blame me for those children's deaths?"

"No," I rasped.

"Then you can't blame yourself either. Their deaths were tragic. If you want to blame anyone, blame the Nighters."

I turned my head away as tears rushed down my cheeks. "It's not that easy for me."

He gripped my chin and gently forced my gaze back to his. "You are the fiercest, gentlest soul I've ever met. The world has not been kind to you and instead of letting that harden you like so many would, you chose to fight to ensure no child would ever suffer the way you did." He stared deeply into my eyes. "Do you understand the courage it takes to stare down the darkest part of yourself and decide you will not allow any of that blackness, that pain, to spill out?"

More tears leaked down my cheeks. His words were too much on my overwrought system.

"I wish I could. Life would be so much easier."

"Perhaps," he agreed softly. "But then you wouldn't be you. You wouldn't be the woman I am hopelessly in love with."

He'd already told me he loved me numerous times since Finn's castle, but it meant so much more in that moment when my whole world had been turned upside down, and nothing made sense. But he did. He—we—always had, even when it seemed impossible, even when I believed he was fated for another, our connection had felt like the most natural thing.

Despite the wretched knot of emotions squeezing my chest, I found myself smiling through the tears.

He pressed his lips to mine.

The door opened, but Ronan was in no hurry, sipping from me, savoring me like decadent wine.

A throat cleared. We ignored it.

Our mouths moved against one another in slow, sensuous movements. No one else existed in that moment beyond me, him, and our profound love.

"Pardon the intrusion." Liam's voice cut through the intimate moment like a cold knife. "But you need to see this."

Ronan's head whipped toward him, growling, "This better be good."

"It's your House that's under attack," he said coolly. "Not mine."

We rushed to untangle ourselves, and I quickly dried my eyes.

"Why didn't you say something?" Ronan hissed as he shoved on his boots.

"I believe I just did."

Ronan glared as Liam exited into the hall. We quickly followed, and he led us to where the corridor ended in an open arch. I shielded my eyes against the bright day. The coastline was sprawled out before us in brilliant blues and greens.

My gaze drifted east, to where House Taran was a small speck of black in the distance. I could just make out the faint outline of something orange surrounding the castle.

I sucked in a sharp breath. "House Taran is on fire."

Ronan peered over me and tensed before glancing at Liam. "You didn't know about this?"

"No," he said, looking concerned by the fact. "Whoever it is did an exceptional job keeping the attack a secret."

"Do I need to be worried, Lord Taran?" he asked, aiming for an indifferent tone, but he couldn't hide his aggravation. "You said you had it handled."

"I do."

Ronan grabbed my hand and started running.

"For your sake, you better hope that's true," Lord Cern's voice carried to us.

"Why is he so concerned with House Taran?" I asked as I kept pace with Ronan.

"Kylah is his mate."

39

VERA

Everything was in chaos at House Taran. Dark red stained the moat. Flames licked over the castle walls. Screams echoed from the courtyard, blending with the metallic clash of swords.

"The drawbridge is closed," Ronan said quietly, taking in the scene. "How did they get inside?"

I scanned the castle's entrance. There was no sign of a break-in. The walls and barbican were intact. If it wasn't for the bloody moat and fire, I'd have no idea anything was wrong.

"Could they have scaled the walls?"

"No, the archers would have stopped them."

The battlements were empty. They must have been driven from their posts.

"What about the treachna?" It would have devoured anyone who tried to come this way.

"It's only territorial of the moat," he explained. "Which means the assailants must have come from inside. We need to find a way in."

My wings pushed out of my back. "I'll fly us over the wall."

A small grin tugged at Ronan's lips.

"What?" I asked in bewilderment. What could he possibly have to smile about right now? The castle was under attack by Gods knows who and we had no idea who was dead or alive on the other side.

He gestured to my wings, immense pride in his voice as he said, "You drew them out on your own."

I instantly tensed.

Even knowing why the dragon acted the way it did, our conversation wasn't enough to overcome the years of terror it had ingrained in me. I expected the beast to try and seize control at any moment.

When it did nothing but calmly watch from the darkness, I sagged with relief.

Thank you.

You are welcome, Little One.

There was a guttural roar before a body sailed over the wall and splashed into the moat. I rushed forward, but Ronan caught my arm. I glanced up at him. He was vibrating with tension as he leveled the corpse with a murderous stare.

"The Saor are here."

My gaze drifted to the body. It was floating face down but was dressed in the same artic furs I'd seen those men wearing.

He released me and uneasiness spread through my chest. They'd come for me.

"We could be walking into an ambush," Ronan warned. "We can't risk flying in blind. We have the element of surprise. We need to use it."

I nodded, retracting my wings just as easily as I'd released them. Later, I'd marvel at that feat.

Wide rings disrupted the moat's surface as something massive moved under the water. There was a flash of fangs and a dozen eyes right before the body was snatched under.

Ronan marched forward.

"What are you doing?" I hissed as he waded into the murky water.

"There are escape tunnels running under the castle. My ancestors had them dug in the event of a siege."

I stared at him like he was insane. "What about the giant water beast?"

I knew first-hand what would happen if we entered the treachna's domain.

He glanced over his shoulder as he sunk in up to his waist. "We've got a short window while it eats. We just have to be quiet."

Oh, this was a terrible idea. Terrible. But there wasn't a place in the world I wouldn't follow this man. I'd walk right into the Darklands if he asked.

I crept into the bile-colored, foamy water and nearly vomited at the disturbing feel. The moat was overly warm, but there wasn't enough heat to be considered hot. It felt like swimming in a pool of sweat.

Something bumped against my leg—a dismembered arm—and I swallowed a surge of nausea. I was going to have nightmares about this.

I will protect you.

Yeah . . . about that . . . if this is going to work, no more taking over my body without my permission.

Its giant head tipped in a solemn nod.

Gods, that was going to take some getting used to.

I reached Ronan and he grabbed my hand. "Hold your breath on the count of three."

"One, two, th—" We froze as spinal ridges broke the surface, speeding towards us. "Don't. Move," Ronan whispered from the side of his mouth.

"So much for a short window," I breathed back.

My heart beat a feral rhythm as the spines glided through the water, then suddenly disappeared.

"Where'd it go?" I whispered, spinning in a slow circle.

"Doesn't matter. We need to get to the tunnel."

I peered around a final time before nodding.

"Deep breath," he instructed before he dove under, and I quickly followed.

Underwater was just as opaque as the top. Sediment had been kicked up by the treachna and was clouding our visibility as it floated in the muted sunlight.

Ronan expertly cut through the water. I had no idea how he could see where he was going, but it was easy to trail his dark form.

The barbican's rippled reflection swam above us. Just before we reached it, Ronan surfaced for air, and I followed his lead. One deep breath and we were diving back under.

He swam further and further down. The moat was deep, much deeper than it appeared. My lungs started to sting.

We reached a rusted wheel jutting out of a muddy embankment. Ronan gripped it and tried to turn it to the left, but it didn't budge. He made a barbed, gurgled sound like a curse that sent a flood of bubbles toward the surface.

He readjusted his hands and tried again, wrenching it harder. Still nothing.

The sting in my chest morphed into a burning. I tapped him on the shoulder and pointed up, signaling I needed to surface. He gave a lone nod of agreement and released the wheel before pushing off to get ahead of me.

I caught a dark flash in my periphery and tugged on Ronan's ankle, pointing that way. I saw it again, this time in the opposite direction, and spun sharply toward it, but it was gone.

Searing pain gripped my lungs telling me I'd run out of time.

I had to surface. Now.

I started kicking like mad, passing Ronan. He sensed my urgency and swam hard. A quarter of the way there, a large shadow appeared overhead, and we froze mid-stroke. Ronan pressed a finger to his lips.

Fiery hands squeezed my lungs. A strangled gasp flew out my lips before I could stop it. The sound was mostly muffled by the water, but it was enough.

Three heads and dozens of eyes shifted toward us.

Shit.

Our gazes collided for a split second and then we were swimming back to the wheel for all we were worth. I didn't dare glance up, but I could feel the vibrations as the treachna's massive body dove for us.

There were three high-pitched shrieks, one after the other, sounding far too close for comfort.

When we reached the wheel, my lungs on the verge of bursting, I finally braved a look back. The treachna's tentacles were propelling it straight toward us.

"Hurry," I screamed, but it came out as a jumble of bubbles.

I lunged forward and grabbed hold of the wheel, helping Ronan turn it. Nothing happened at first and then the metal moved an inch, groaning, and then another before it started turning just as my vision dotted.

I threw a frantic glance over my shoulder. The treachna was only ten feet away.

It was the stuff of nightmares with three dragon-like heads, each with a dozen purple eyes, and the body of a snake. Hundreds of barbed tentacles jutted out at every angle. The three mouths opened in unison and released a blood curdling screech as it sped toward us.

Ronan peered back and cursed, pulling the wheel with vigor. The door popped open, and he shoved me inside before flinging himself in after me.

Air burst into my lungs. I gasped at the same time I landed hard on my shoulder.

Ronan had better luck, catching onto a rung right below the hatch. Water gushed in, directly on top of me. I threw my hands up, protecting my face, as Ronan struggled with the wheel.

He gave it a final twist, and the water cut off just before the tunnel reverberated from the collision with the treachna. The lights on the walls rattled. Debris and dust rained down. It rammed a second time before it fell silent.

I collapsed back, choking in deep breaths as Ronan jumped down.

"You okay?" He stretched toward me and helped me to my feet as I rubbed at my smarting shoulder.

I had to cough a few times before I could answer. "Yeah, I'm fine."

He allowed me a few moments to recover before he unsheathed his sword and grabbed my hand with his free one. "We need to keep going. Stay alert."

Jarred flames, like the one I'd purchased in the village—only these didn't throw off any heat—were strung along the walls, casting shadows over the slime covered stone. The tunnel was partially flooded and smelled foul. We had to slog through ankle high, putrid water.

As we descended deeper into the dark labyrinth, the cobwebs grew thicker. The temperature dropped, too. Gooseflesh broke out over my skin from the chilled air.

We came across a body floating in the water. There was no blood, or any signs of a wound. The skin was pale gray and leathery, stretched tightly over bone.

Ice filled my stomach. "Are they one of ours?"

"No. The body looks old," Ronan observed, carefully stepping over it. "They probably got lost down here."

My gaze dipped briefly to the poor soul as I maneuvered around.

"How far do these tunnels go?" I asked.

"Miles in each direction."

"Do the Saor know about the tunnels?"

"My uncle does."

That explained how they were able to breach House Taran. They could have used an entrance far from here and entered undetected.

The layer of water thinned as we came upon a row of cells in what I assumed was the dungeon. They were filled with decaying, ancient torture devices. One held a body.

A curse flew off Ronan's tongue. He raced forward, busted the lock, and wrenched open the cell, before checking their pulse. Their head lolled to the side, and I saw the brutal slash across their throat.

"Who is that?" I whispered.

"The traitor," Ronan answered, rising. "The Saor are trying to cover their tracks."

He exited and we continued down the row of cells.

Past them, were a set of crumbling stairs leading up to a wall. Ronan pulled on one of the jars strung over it. A section of the wall split off, revealing a dark corridor. The opening was wide, but low.

"Wait here," Ronan instructed before bending himself in half to fit through the door. He was gone a couple minutes before he reappeared beckoning me to follow.

I ducked through the opening. It led to the ground level of one of the towers, but I couldn't say which. A halfling darted past us, screaming hysterically.

I caught Gisa by the arm. She yelled, thrashing in my grip. "Calm down," I whispered. "It's me." She paused, her chest heaving, her eyes white with terror. Her blouse was covered in soot and blood. "What's going on?" I asked gently.

"They—they came out of nowhere, and—and—" Her words cut off as she started to hyperventilate.

I grabbed her shoulders. "Breathe. You're safe now." I took a deep inhale, waiting for her to do the same. She did and several slow breaths later, her shaking had eased.

"What happened?"

"Th-they came out of nowhere and started attacking!"

"Whose they?" Ronan asked.

We knew the Saor were involved, but didn't know if they had help, or were alone.

"I—I don't know. I've never seen them before."

"That's alright," I told her. "See that opening behind us?"

She nodded limply.

"It's a tunnel. I want you to wait at the entrance and wave people inside. You hide in there until one of us comes for you. Understand?"

"Yes."

I gave her shoulder a final squeeze before releasing her. "It's going to be okay."

Another nod and she started for the tunnel.

A small smile was playing on Ronan's lips when I glanced back. "What?"

"You're going to make a wonderful Lady."

I grinned, my chest filling with warmth.

A scream rented the air, dissolving the tenderness of the moment.

"Come on," he said.

Ronan and I proceeded through the tower. When we reached the exit, the door was broken down and we could hear the battle echoing from the courtyard.

Pressing a finger to his mouth, Ronan gestured for me to

463

hide against the wall, and I did, crouching as he peered around the corner. Whatever he saw had his eyes bleeding black, but he didn't say a word.

I peeked through the window above me and swallowed a gasp.

Taranis soldiers were embroiled in a bloody battle with Saor. Halflings were hiding behind buildings and over-turned carts. Kylah, Kian, and Finn were at the center of it all, going head-to-head with the Saor.

Blue pulsed over the courtyard as each side used their powers. Kylah was throwing lightning bolts, Finn was ordering Saor to attack one another, and Kian was flashing around, cutting Saor at the knees.

"What are they doing?" I whispered.

Despite using their powers, Kylah, Kian, and Finn, were all pulling their punches. So were the soldiers.

"They might be traitors, but they were fellow soldiers once. It is not easy to take the life of a man who you once fought side by side with." Ronan's voice dropped to a dark whisper. "But I have no such compunction."

The color bled from his eyes until they were twin midnight orbs, as dark as a starless night.

His muscles swelled, testing the limits of his skin, and warped his tattoos until they were unrecognizable. Vicious planes sharpened his face, and a snarl twisted his lips.

I couldn't be certain, but he seemed taller too.

Like a seal popping, the full force of his power hit me. It was cloying, like thick smoke. It dug daggers into my skin and ripped the air from my lungs. I gasped, a hand flying to my throat. An invisible force felt wrapped around it.

"Holy shit," I choked.

He stalked past me into the courtyard, and I rushed to follow.

Ronan barreled through the enemy, tearing them into

464

pieces. Limbs and heads flew into the air. When Ronan reached the epicenter, he grabbed the throat of one of the Saor and lifted him into the air.

"Who. Sent. You."

His chilling, gravel voice made me shiver.

"Fuck . . . you . . . Butcher."

He crushed his windpipe and tossed him aside like a doll.

Ronan faced the remaining Saor and raised his hand. "I considered you all brothers once. Now you'll know what it's like to feel my wrath." With a single flick of his fingers, their spines exploded from their bodies.

Guts and blood sprayed everywhere.

Most died instantly, but the more powerful twitched, clinging to life. Another motion of Ronan's hand, and their spinal columns wrapped around their necks, and crushed their throats. They went still.

Shocked silence swelled like a distended body.

I could only stare at the carnage, at the courtyard steadily running with blood. It formed an eddy at my boots as it flowed around.

I'd seen death before, but never this candid, or gruesome. I could see straight into body cavities where a spine once was.

One hundred Saor laid dead.

Halflings and soldiers crouched, making themselves appear as small and unthreatening as possible.

Ronan stood across from me, the sea of corpses between us. His eyes were fathomless and wild. His fingers were stained with blood. Chunks of entrails clung to his hair and clothes. He appeared monstrous, like a nightmare compressed into flesh.

Even though the initial danger had passed, he wasn't calming. He vibrated with violence, looking like he'd rip

465

the head off anyone who approached. Ronan had lost control.

Despite his disturbed state, despite what I had seen Ronan do, I knew he would never hurt me. If there was only one thing I was certain of, it was that.

I darted forward and threw myself into his arms. Every inch of him was hard and tense. He didn't move, as I awkwardly clung to him in an unreciprocated hug.

I jerked Ronan's head toward me and those chilling black eyes pinned me in place. "Stay with me," I whispered.

We stared at each other for what felt like hours but could have only been minutes. Slowly, his arms wound around me. His face dipped to my neck, and he crushed me to his chest, clinging to me. I hugged him just as fiercely.

The tension steadily melted from his muscles.

Just as the black bled from his eyes, a scream ripped through the air, and we jerked apart.

"There's a fearga!" someone yelled.

In the far corner of the courtyard, a giant, furless looking rat stood on two legs. Its head was bald. It had no eyes and two large fangs jutting from a lipless mouth. The beast had a small girl cornered. It was slowly leaching the life out of her.

Time slowed.

Everyone scrambled forward.

But we were all too far away.

My heart beat ferociously in my ears.

She was going to die. If I didn't do something, she was going to die.

Don't make me regret this.

I pinched my eyes shut and let the thin barrier between me and the dragon drop, bursting into beast form.

We lunged across the courtyard in a single bound, our girth crushing a wall beneath us, as we snapped our massive mouth around the fearga's head. It popped in our mouth like a bloody cherry, then we scarfed down the rest.

It all happened in a fraction of a second.

I blinked and I was back in my body, naked, crouched before the girl. I reached for her. She was pale and unconscious but breathing. I slumped in relief, tears pricking my eyes. *Thank you.*

"Vera!" Ronan roared. A stampede of footsteps followed.

He slammed to the ground and pulled his shirt over my head. "We need a healer," I told him.

"Kian, get Lawrence," he bellowed.

"On it!"

Kylah and Finn caught up to us. I waited for the inevitable horror. They knew what I was, but knowing and seeing were two very different things. They stared with awe.

"I see you've found my dragon."

Ice shot into my heart at the sound of King Desmond's voice.

We froze.

The air turned cold. No one moved. No one breathed. You could have heard a bullet drop.

Ronan was the first to shake off his shock. He charged over to the dead Saor and wrenched a cracked scrying mirror from his grip. King Desmond's face stared out at us.

"You sent the Saor," Ronan growled.

"Did you really think that little plan of yours would fool me? I had that pathetic mortal spilling all your secrets right before I snapped her neck, but not even she could confirm what I'd found in my dungeon." The king's eyes drifted to me. "All whispers of a dragon were merely rumors and speculation."

My stomach bottomed out. He'd known what I was all along...

"I couldn't just steal your mate outright. As hated as you

467

are, it would be egregious to break up the first mated pair in five centuries. But a dragon? Now that's something I can sell."

Ronan gripped the mirror so tightly, it was on the verge of snapping.

"The Saor were meant to provoke her into shifting and gain the confirmation I required. Now I have it." Two figures stepped into view. "Lady Belenus and Lord Brigid are my witnesses." The king's smile was sharp. "I'll be seeing you very soon."

His face vanished and Ronan dropped the mirror.

"What happens now?" I asked on a shaky breath.

Ronan's expression was grim. "We prepare for war."

40

RONAN

Liam's irritated face appeared in the scrying mirror. "Do you have any idea what time it is?"

"Be at my House at sunrise," I barked.

"Do I need to remind you—"

"Kylah will be here. You demanded to see her. Now's your chance."

His eyes sparked with excitement, but he quickly covered it. "Fine, but I expect—"

I ended the connection.

He'd be here. Not even death could keep him.

I knew because I felt the same way about the woman in my bed.

I should be with her. Instead, I was in my office, frantically thinking of a way to protect her.

I couldn't sleep. I could barely breathe. With the dread and panic pressing down on my chest, every inhale took a godly amount of effort.

Vera's shift had left us in a dangerous predicament, but I didn't fault her. She already carried so much guilt over Mayhem. She wouldn't have been able to live with herself if she hadn't saved that girl, and thanks to my mate, she was alive, on her way to recovering.

We'd spent the evening putting the castle back together. The fire had badly damaged the southwest tower, the western curtain wall was demolished, and we'd lost seven lives.

I slammed a fist on my desk, then grimaced remembering Vera was asleep in the other room.

I was a godsdamn fool. The king had never stopped hunting her. He'd just been using the Saor to do it discreetly.

But how did he know we were mates?

I pushed the question aside. That was the least of our worries now.

A knock sounded.

"What?" I asked gruffly.

The door cracked. Lawrence was on the other side, clutching a bag. "I've been recalled," he said remorsefully.

He had no reason to be sorry. I understood he had a duty to his House, the same as me. If he ignored his Lord's orders, his loyalty would be questioned, and he would risk alienation from his House.

"Thank you for your service, Lawrence. You will be missed."

He gave a lone nod in farewell, moving to close the door, but paused, meeting my eyes. "Best of luck to you, Lord Taran."

Somberly, I inclined my head and the door shut a moment later.

One healer wouldn't help us win the battle against King Desmond, but the odds seemed to be stacking against us by the minute.

"Fuck!"

I sent everything flying off the desk just as the door

opened again. For a hopeful second, I thought Lawrence might have had a change of heart, but it was Hunt's gruff voice that came through the gap.

"Bad time?"

"More like a bad five hundred years," I said, spearing fingers through my hair as I dropped into my chair.

Hunt entered with two glasses and a jug of poitín. "Knew I'd find your ass brooding in here." He placed the items on the desk before taking the chair across from me.

"What do you want?"

"Kylah told me what happened."

Snatching a glass, I stiffly poured a drink. "I preferred when you left me to brood alone."

He filled his own glass, staring pointedly. "I should."

He was quiet for a long span as his eyes cast around my office, intermittently sipping on the poitín. "I remember the night we got rip roaring drunk in here."

I recalled the time well. I took a drink and savored the burn as I swirled the liquid around. "It was the night before your bonding ceremony."

He'd been a nervous mess. I'd poured poitín down his throat, along with my own, and we'd ended up burning down a village. No one had been harmed, but my mother was furious.

A quick, gruff note of laughter sprang from him. "I didn't know a person's face could get that red."

I chuckled around my glass, smiling as I remembered my mother's fury. "Neither did I."

We'd spent the next year up to our elbows in horse shit, mucking out the stables, but it had been worth it. Hunt and Moira's bonding ceremony was beautiful. They had bonded similarly to Vera and me.

There was an older, more ancient mating ritual, but it

was considered archaic and hadn't been performed since the War of the Gods.

We fell silent, nursing our drinks.

The fond nostalgia of our childhood drifted away, and the familiar weight of our centuries' long animosity returned, settling over the room like a damp cloak.

"Where have you been?" I asked, setting down my glass.

Hunt had been noticeably absent during the attack.

He appraised me over the rim of his glass. "I went to see my father."

My breathing thinned. Hunt's family was our last hope to avoid a war I wasn't sure we could win.

He took a drink before setting it down. "My father wasn't forthcoming at first, but he couldn't resist the rare poitín I brought." His lip curled in disgust.

Lord Brigid was a nasty drunk.

"You're harboring a dragon. He isn't going to back down and neither is House Belenus. They're going to come at you hard with everything they have until she's either dead or captured."

Fury tunneled through my veins like fire. They weren't touching her. I slammed a hand on my desk. "They'll have to get through me and my army first."

I knocked back my drink. The poitín's warmth helped cool some of my ire. I'd been hopeful Hunt could persuade his family to alter their course, but part of me had known it would be a foolish endeavor.

"Thank you for speaking with him."

He didn't acknowledge my statement, staring. "What's the plan?"

"Come back at them, just as hard."

My soldiers had been training for this inevitability. They were as prepared as they were ever going to be.

"What about the girl?" He cocked his head, pursing his lips thoughtfully. "A dragon would be useful."

"No," I said fiercely. "I won't ask her to."

He inclined his head.

"I assume you'll be heading home?"

I'd asked him to talk to his family on my behalf and he had. Our business was concluded.

"Yeah." He tossed back the rest of his drink and slammed the glass on the desk. "The others might have forgiven you, but I don't." His face transformed into a familiar mask of scorn. "A woman murdering piece of shit like you doesn't deserve a mate."

He rapped a knuckle on the desk, glaring down at me before he turned and strode for the door.

"For once, we're in agreement," I called. "I don't deserve her, but I am going to fight like dark to keep her."

He paused, shooting me an unreadable look, before storming through the door.

"He's fun."

Vera stood in the adjoining doorway, haphazardly dressed, with her hair in messy waves around her face.

I gestured her over.

She came to me, and I pulled her into my lap, facing away from me, and dropped a kiss on her shoulder. "I'm sorry. Did we wake you?"

She shook her head. "I couldn't sleep."

We both knew why.

I clutched her as the air turned heavy and somber.

She twisted toward me, her face filled with trepidation. "What are we going to do about the king?" she whispered.

I tucked her hair behind her ear. "What my House does best. We fight."

My words didn't offer her the assurance she was looking

for, but she didn't ask more questions, and I was grateful I didn't have to give more answers I didn't have.

She turned away, settled into my arms, and I spent the next several minutes holding her and stroking her hair, trying to coax her back to sleep.

Abruptly, she bolted up, turning to gaze at me with her brows scrunched together.

"What is it?"

"At House Cern . . . You told me Liam and Kylah are mates, but she told me she hadn't found her mate."

A muscle beat against my clenched jaw.

"After her exile from House Belenus, Kylah lived with me at House Taran for many years before they found one another. She left to live with him, and I received the occasional scry. Then one day, she walked into House Taran like she'd never left. She knew of Liam only as the Lord of House Cern. He'd stolen her memories and wiped any trace of himself as her mate."

Thunderclouds rolled through her gaze. "How could he do that to her?"

"He has his reasons." Reasons I didn't agree with, but they were his reasons all the same. "He will be arriving here shortly."

Vera peered over her shoulder with a displeased expression. "Why?"

"He's our only ally."

Her mouth tightened angrily. "He's not getting near her."

I was delighted she and Kylah had become friends despite the circumstances under which they met. Kylah was dear to me. It pleased me she was dear to my mate as well.

I grinned. "How did I get so lucky?" I whispered, stroking her cheek.

Tight brackets formed around her eyes before she

glanced away. "Your House is about to go to war because of me. I wouldn't call that lucky."

Gently, I tilted her chin toward me and lowered my lips to hers. The kiss was soft, exploratory. I pulled back, still holding her chin as I stared into those stunning eyes. "I *am* lucky."

The luckiest man in The Lands.

She smiled thinly.

I released her and steered us to a safer topic.

"How are you feeling?"

There wasn't much time to discuss what happened before she went to sleep. Shifting into her dragon, even to save that girl, couldn't have been an easy decision for her.

Her forehead pinched pensively for a moment before she lifted her gaze to me. "Shockingly okay."

"Truly?"

"Yes," she said softly, a smile forming. "We've been talking."

My brows lifted in surprise. "You and the dragon?"

I wasn't aware that was possible. It had to be telepathy of some sort.

She nodded. "It's going to be a long journey to heal old wounds, but this feels like a good start."

A smile cracked my cheeks. "I am very happy to hear that."

I tucked her into my side, and we sat in companionable silence, enjoying one another's company until the first rays of dawn snuck through the curtains.

"It's sunrise," she said in a strained whisper.

The gravity of our situation came crashing down. Dread's heavy weight returned to my chest.

It was time to face reality.

"Let's make our way to the War Room."

I'd directed the others to meet us there at dawn.

Vera moved off my lap, and I stood and held out my hand. Her warm palm wrapped around mine and we made our way there together.

Glass stands were positioned around the room with statues interspersed between them. The cases housed the weapons of the fae lords and ladies before me, their accomplishments inscribed on the wood below.

Vera crossed over to one of the stands, eyes widening as she read the description. Inside the glass, a stone spear darkened with blood was displayed.

"Did someone really kill a giant with that thing?"

"Trefor Taran did in the War of Gods. He blinded it, then cut it down. Or so the story goes."

"The War of the Gods . . . You mentioned it before, but I've never heard of that war."

"It happened thousands of years ago. After the godstone was created by my ancestor, some of the more scrupulous Gods wanted it and used the fae to fight their war."

"Wow," she whispered, turning to peer more closely.

Kian and Kylah arrived a minute later, shortly followed by Finn and Liam.

Lord Cern was greeted by hostile gazes. We were all aware what he had done to Kylah, though I was the only one who knew why.

"Pleasure to see you all as well," he said dryly. His golden gaze skimmed over Kylah, and a quick smile bloomed.

Vera glared as she grabbed Kylah's arm and dragged her over to the opposite side of the room to stand with Kian.

Liam watched them quietly for a moment before turning his attention to me. "I presume this is about the attack?"

I nodded. "King Desmond has declared war against us."

Liam's expression sobered. He would have learned of Vera's dragon while he returned her memories. It wasn't hard to guess what King Desmond wanted with her. "How long do you have?"

"House Dagda, House Brigid, and House Belenus are already making battle preparations," Kylah informed us. "We have three days."

"What are our options?" I asked the group.

"We should call in the remaining outpost soldiers," Finn suggested.

"That will provide us with two hundred more men," I said. "It's a good start, but it's not enough."

"We go to him," Kian volunteered. "Take the bastard by surprise."

I shook my head. "His draoi tree is in his castle, just like ours. He is most powerful there."

"Then we burn it down." This came from Kylah.

"That is an act of war, love," Liam interceded before I could.

Kylah frowned at the term of endearment and Vera sent him a scathing look.

"King Desmond declared war the moment he attacked us," Finn pointed out.

"House Anu won't see it that way," I murmured. "They're neutral now, but if they learn we were harboring a dragon, they'll side with the king."

All eyes swung to Liam.

"I can't get involved. My House isn't built for war like yours."

"We don't need you to fight," I explained. "Just give our people safe harbor."

His gaze briefly slipped to Kylah. "Done."

"He'll have House Belenus and House Brigid on his side, and he'll take our powers before we ever reach the battle-field. We're grossly outnumbered and outpowered." My warning washed over everyone, and a grim silence descended.

"We have something he doesn't."

We all looked to Vera.

"And what is that?" Liam asked.

"A dragon."

Her face morphed into a dragon's head, and shock slid over Liam's face. He would have seen the dragon in her memories but witnessing it firsthand was something else entirely.

Kylah, Kian, and I all watched on with pride while Finn watched with begrudging respect.

Smoothly, she shifted back.

My mate was exquisite.

I crossed over to her and lowered my head. "Are you certain?" I asked quietly. "You don't have to do this."

She gave a quick, confident nod before throwing her shoulders back and addressing the group. "Let him come. I'm ready. I can control his beasts."

It was like a weight lifted off everyone's shoulders. With a dragon on our side, we stood a chance.

"Vera, I want you to practice with the treachna. Kylah, I need you in the sky. Finn, prepare the women and children to travel. Kian, I need you to get word to the outposts."

"What's the word?" Kian asked.

I met each one of their faces with a hard, determined gaze.

"Three days from now, we're going into battle."

41

VERA

A fog blanketed the chilly morning as I stood on the bridgeway a few feet above the moat. The water appeared a dark amber under the overcast sky. Wisps of mist reached out over the surface like ghostly fingers, lending an ominous atmosphere to an already dreary morning.

I'd put on my best show in the War Room. But now, standing outside with the fate of Ronan's House hanging in the balance, I didn't feel so confident. The weight of my role, the need to be successful, hung around my neck like a noose.

The pressure was made worse by the fact that I'd never understood my ability to control beasts. It had always just . . . happened, along with the rest of my powers, and now I had three days to figure out how to make it happen on demand.

And if I couldn't?

Everyone I loved was going to die.

With their powers—Ronan, Kylah, and Kian could beat the king's beasts no problem.

But without them . . .

My stomach was a pit of srphies. I wanted to vomit up the small breakfast I'd eaten.

I am here, Little One, the dragon's smoky voice whispered through my mind.

Hysterical laughter bubbled up my throat. I never thought I'd be receiving comfort from my dragon, but I'd been wrong about it in so many ways. It'd been trying to protect me my whole life, including with what happened in Mayhem.

The latter, I was still struggling to come to terms with, that those children had died because of me. I didn't know if I ever could, but I did know it wasn't the dragon's fault.

We stayed up all night talking. I wasn't going to be letting my guard down anytime soon, but we'd come to an understanding. I wouldn't lock it away in the darkness, and it wouldn't take control without permission.

Thank you, I responded.

A light drizzle started to fall. Small ringlets formed in the moat, rippling out across its expanse.

"Are you going to stand there all day, or call it out?" Finn sniped at my back, and I stiffened.

Liam needed to make preparations before he could accept our halflings so they wouldn't be leaving just yet. Unfortunately, that meant Finn had nothing to do, and Ronan thought it would be a good idea for him to assist me with the treachna.

I'd played nice with Finn earlier for Ronan's sake, but Ronan wasn't here, and the kick to the balls I'd delivered didn't make Finn and I even, not even close.

I held up my middle finger, and put him out of my mind, fixing my eyes on the moat.

It was large, like the beast it hid. The idea of controlling something as large and powerful as the treachna for my first time was daunting.

"Well?" Finn called caustically, and anger trundled through me.

"I'll call it up when I'm good and ready. If you have a problem with that, you can *go*. Hopefully, back to whatever primordial ooze you crawled out of."

He lost everyone, Vera. I know he can be difficult, but please try to get along. For me.

Ronan and I discussed Finn on the ride to Liam's yesterday. I'd refused to tell him about Finn's bullying because he cared about Finn a great deal, and Finn cared about Ronan just as much. It was Finn's only redeeming quality and I didn't want to taint their friendship.

Getting along was a stretch, but I didn't need to go out of my way to antagonize him. I sighed, flashing my gaze over my shoulder.

"I've never done this before. I need some time."

To my shock, Finn only nodded. There was no accompanying sneer or biting insult.

A shocked chuckle escaped. "Look at us being reasonable. The sun must have risen in the Darklands."

His lips twitched in an imperceptible smile. "Or we're on the brink of war."

My stomach sunk at the reminder. I twisted back to the moat, plucked up a fallen leaf, and released it into the moat.

The briny breeze carried it swiftly over the water. At the center of the moat, massive ripples formed causing a surge of mini waves that sent water lashing against the edges.

The beast's body formed a dark shadow beneath the surface. Three fins cut through the water and converged on the leaf. One second it was there, and the next it was gone.

So were the fins.

I wouldn't have much time to gain control over it once the dragon and I drew it out.

If we could.

481

A tier four beast was on another level, and the king had plenty of them in his arsenal. But, if we could control it, we could control any of the beasts he brought.

The rain came down harder and I groaned. The weather today was miserable. Too bad Kylah was off doing air reconnaissance. Her weather powers would come in handy.

"Oh, I'm sorry," Finn said in a fake saccharine voice. "Why don't we wait for more convenient weather? Say after the king comes and murders us all?"

I scowled at him. "I get it. You don't have to be such a dick."

Thirty seconds. That's how long our little truce lasted.

Ice crystallized in his gaze. He stalked toward me.

"Do you think this is a game?" he asked in a low hiss. "You aren't just fighting for yourself. You're fighting for *everyone in this House.*"

I bristled at his tone but tamped down the need to snap back at him. He was on edge. We all were. "I understand."

He advanced until we were toe to toe. "No, I don't think you do. The king had my House's food poisoned. And then with a flick of his hand, he stole their powers, rendering them helpless. The king is ruthless, and he has no care for any of us. He will do *whatever* it takes to get what he wants." He stabbed a finger at the abandoned castle in the distance —his castle. "If you fail us, that will be our fate."

Finn's chest was heaving when he finished. I glanced up into his icy blue eyes and was taken back by the stark fear filling them.

He was afraid.

Terrified even because he knew better than anyone what the king was capable of.

He pulled himself together and stepped a few paces away, his cold mask returning. "We must leave nothing to chance."

482

My eyes roved over his face. That was the first raw emotion I'd ever seen from him. Guess there was some warmth in his iceberg heart after all.

"If King Desmond can steal magic, why doesn't he just steal mine?" I asked.

Finn flashed me a condescending look and I realized it was a stupid question. If he could, he would have no need for me, or any of the beasts he'd collected.

"We're on the same side," I reminded him. "Now back the fuck up so I can tear the king a new one when he arrives."

A foreign emotion burst over his face. He quickly hid it, but not before I saw the teeny slither of respect. He knew I had seen it and scowled in response. "You better," he snapped before retreating.

I smiled to myself as I focused on the water. "Concentrate," I whispered.

Closing my eyes, I pictured the treachna, and imagined it coming to me. When no tell-tale splashing followed, I peeked open an eye to see a still moat.

Damnit.

Come on, Vera. You can do this.

I breathed deeply, centering myself, blocking out the rain, the cold, and the worry, and thought back to the time the dragon controlled the beasts in the canyon. Its voice had whispered through my mind, and then suddenly the beasts obeyed.

Can you ... talk to other beasts ... with your mind?

Correction, our mind. Since we shared it. Which was a trippy thought in and of itself, but I didn't let myself dwell on it.

Yes.

How?

I push out my energy and force my way inside their minds.

For the lower tiers, obedience to an alpha is instinctual. The more powerful they are, the harder they are to control.

I was communicating with the dragon the same way it communicated and controlled the beasts.

We need to command the treachna in the moat, I told the dragon.

That will be difficult.

How difficult?

I will need control for a beast this powerful.

I hissed out a breath as the nerves returned in full force.

I'd given up control in the courtyard, but I hadn't put any thought into it at the time. All I was thinking about was saving the little girl. Nothing else mattered.

It clicked.

This wasn't about giving the dragon control. It was about saving House Taran, about protecting my mate.

I imagined Kylah and Kian—the pair that had wormed their way into my heart despite my best intentions. I imagined Ness, my trusty mare who'd saved my life and never left my side. I pictured Ronan's handsome, smiling face. I clung to those images, to the people I loved most.

I couldn't fail them.

Let your love be greater than your fear.

Marty had told me that once when I didn't want to go out on a full moon. He reminded me I wasn't fighting for myself. I was fighting for him, for Ryder, for Boone.

I hadn't really understood what he meant until now.

I sucked in a deep breath for courage and said on a shaky whisper, "You have control."

There was no shift, but I felt the second the dragon seized my mind. My body turned leaden and unresponsive. Without any directive from me, my arms raised, like they were being controlled by invisible strings.

I tried to put them down, but they didn't cooperate.

My heart pounded feverishly in my ears.

You must calm, the dragon hissed. *I cannot focus.*

I took a breath.

Let your love be greater than your fear.

Let your love be greater than your fear.

LET YOUR LOVE BE GREATER THAN YOUR FEAR.

I released the air, pushing out all my concern and worry, and surrendered to the moment.

Very good, Little One.

Power pulsed through my limbs, thumping in time with my pulse. It shot out of my hands like a cannon blast, twirling and intertwining across the water in invisible ribbons. The moat turned choppy.

Come to me, the dragon's voice echoed through my mind. The words were gentle and hypnotic, like a hooked finger beckoning the beast. A gargantuan, dragon-like head appeared across the lake. Two more joined it. They didn't move, staring unblinkingly.

Come to me. The whispered words were more forceful, but still held an air of invitation.

Again, the heads did nothing.

What's going on? I asked.

This creature is strong and willful, the dragon answered, then told the treachna, *Come to me. Now.*

The dragon's tone had lost its honeyed edge. It was a command.

The three heads writhed in unison, emitting a low hissing and clicking. As one, they opened their large mouths, showing rows of razor-sharp teeth.

Uh oh. I don't think it likes being ordered around.

It dove under the water, creating a tidal wave. The treachna's massive form sped toward us underwater.

Stop, the dragon's voice rang out.

The beast didn't listen.

485

It is . . . strong.

I could hear the strain in the dragon's voice. My heart threw itself against my breastbone. Not good. Not good at all.

Panic clawed at my throat as it barreled toward us. More of our power pulsed out. I clutched my head at the onslaught of pain. A band of pressure was squeezing my skull.

"You need to stop it," Finn snapped.

"I'm working on it," I growled.

Finn sniped at me some more, but I tuned him out.

"Focus, Vera," I whispered.

I needed to do this *with* the dragon, like in the courtyard. We were a team.

I opened everything to it— bared my heart, body, and soul. A spike of fear rose, and I shoved it down. I had to trust my shadow.

The treachna reached us and rose from the lake. It was terrifying up close, standing as tall as the castle. Water sluiced off its scales in rivers.

I swallowed thickly. Its three thick necks connected and led down into an even thicker serpentine form. Spiked ridges raised along its spine, flaring with aggression.

STAND DOWN, the dragon and I roared together. More clicks and hisses issued from the treachna's three mouths.

My pulse hammered in my chest.

I cried out as more power poured out of us. My head was on the verge of splitting in half.

Its three maws opened wide and lunged. I tensed, pinching my eyes shut. I didn't want to watch it eat us alive.

NOW!

I braced, waiting to feel its teeth, but instead I felt plumes of hot, rancid breath rushing over my cheeks.

I slit an eye and saw gleaming fangs inches from my

face. The middle head was in front of us with the other two not far behind. They were frozen. The only sound that could be heard was the loud chuffing from their flared nostrils.

It is ours to command.

Holy shit.

I blew out the world's longest breath. *Let's make it take a couple steps back.* I did not like how close those teeth were to our face.

Move back.

The three heads slithered back in unison a foot.

More.

The treachna pushed a safe distance away, and I was able to relax a little.

Tapping my lips, I contemplated what to do next.

Let's make it dance, I told the dragon.

Dance.

The three heads started to gyrate.

"Is this your doing?" Finn choked in a horrified tone.

I nodded, not taking my eyes off the treachna.

"Well, stop before it gives me nightmares."

I laughed. It was a combination of relief, joy, and shock. *Time to send it home.*

The dragon issued the order and the treachna backed away, sinking into the water until it disappeared. I couldn't stop the wide smile springing across my lips. "We did it," I whispered. *What else can we do?*

Whatever you wish.

I imagined whips of fire and they materialized in my hands. I snapped one out, eyes widening at the sharp lashing sound. I pictured them vanishing and they did.

You've been holding out on me.

There was so much I didn't understand about my powers because I'd never wanted to learn, but I did now.

After we beat the king, I want you to teach me everything we can do.

It would be my pleasure, Little One.

I—correction—*we had* controlled a tier four beast. Tier. Four. Exhilaration pounded through my veins. I couldn't believe we'd actually done it. I whooped, punching my fist in the air.

"This is not the time to celebrate," Finn's irritated voice cut through the joy of the moment. "Some measly whips aren't going to stop the king's beasts and you barely controlled the treachna. We'll celebrate once you've done that a hundred more times. With ease."

I glared, but he didn't back down, and I relented with a terse, "Fine."

He was right. I refused to admit it to him but until I could control the treachna flawlessly, I needed more practice.

And so, practice I did.

The dragon and I called the treachna from the depths of the moat over and over again until breaking into its mind was as easy as picking a lock. The more times we did it, the less pain and time it took.

When night fell, we had managed to control the treachna twenty times successfully. As the beast returned to the moat for the final time, I sank to the ground exhausted. My body felt like gelatin.

"Ronan is an optimist," Finn said, hovering over me. "He always has been. I am the opposite. There is a possibility, no matter how strong or prepared you are, things with King Desmond might not go as planned."

I peered up at him, lips twisting sourly. "You mean if I fail."

"Yes."

I studied his face. There wasn't a hint of the animosity I

had grown accustomed to. He wasn't trying to be cruel. He was being realistic.

"What's your point?"

"We need to plan for every contingency."

I understood the unspoken question. If I failed to stop the king's beasts, what choice would I make? No one would force me to surrender myself to King Desmond. Ronan would kill them. Ronan would kill Finn for even suggesting it.

"What would you do in my place?"

"For Ronan? I'd carve out my own heart and offer it to the king on a platter."

No hesitation. No uncertainty.

"You really care about him, don't you?" I murmured.

A strange expression crossed his face. It vanished so quickly, I must have imagined it. "More than I care to."

I turned away, staring out across the moat. I hadn't let myself dwell on the alternative, on what would happen if I failed to stop the king's army. Could I knowingly hand myself over to another monster?

No, I had barely survived the Crone, and all she wanted from the dragon was its magical parts for spells.

I didn't know exactly what King Desmond wanted with my dragon, but I knew whatever it was, it wasn't good. I'd rather die than fall into his clutches.

"I'm not going to fail," I said firmly.

Finn's mouth set into a severe line. "You better hope for all our sake's that is true."

42

RONAN

"Where are we going, and why do I have to wear this?" I paused in the middle of buttoning my overcoat and glanced at Vera. My throat caught.

The dress I had made for her fit perfectly.

It was violet with a dipping neckline that framed the swell of her gorgeous breasts—breasts I had given much attention to the night before.

I had made good use of yesterday evening, keeping Vera under me for hours, but tonight was the last before we faced the king. It had to be special.

The dress cinched at her waist and fanned out into layers, made to look like living flames when she moved. Soft, silver curls spilled down her back, complementing the color beautifully.

A dagger was strapped to her thigh, visible through the slit running up her leg. Gold bands fitted each of her biceps with a dragon head breathing fire.

"What?" she asked self-consciously, and I realized how long I'd been staring.

"You are magnificent," I breathed, crossing over to her. I

lifted her chin. Dark charcoal lined her pale amethyst eyes. Gold glitter dusted her eyelids and blush colored her cheeks. "A living piece of art I want to mount on my wall and stare at forever."

I lowered my head to hers and kissed her gently, careful not to smear the gloss on her lips.

"You didn't answer the question," she murmured against my mouth.

"It's a surprise," I murmured back.

As I drew away, I noticed her hands were covered in lace gloves. Kylah must have given them to her when she assisted with Vera's makeup.

"Remove those," I demanded.

Her chin jutted up belligerently, eyes flashing. "No. They're *my* hands."

Beneath her defiance, I could scent the bitter tang of nerves. I froze, eyes widening, before a quiet smile formed. I could scent her emotions again. The wall between us was gone.

This would be the first time she would meet House Taran without her glamour, and her looks would be judged. She was nervous.

My eyes traced a slow path over her.

Her eyes were bright and glittering like pale purple moonlight casting its startling radiance over the ocean. Her fangs were wickedly sharp, but delicate, and when her lips formed around them in a smile that was so beautiful, so uniquely her, it made my heart stop. No other smile could compare.

Her talons, dark and smooth, were capable of such a gentle warmth when she touched me, or an arousing viciousness when she put me in line.

Every inch of her was perfect. Breathtaking.

I brushed a thumb over her cheek. "I wish I could kill them," I said softly.

"Who?" she breathed, eyes lifting to mine.

"Anyone who ever made you feel like you were less."

Her irritation vanished as an errant tear slipped down her cheek. My thumb was there to wipe it away.

Vera had spent her whole life hiding the inhuman parts of herself, but her dragon was not something to be ashamed of. I wanted her to take pride in who and what she was. I wanted to celebrate every beautiful piece of her.

"Tonight, I want you to step out of the shadows," I whispered. "I want every part of you to burn brightly."

Tender, lavender eyes stared reverently into mine. "It's very hard to deny you when you say things like that."

I fought a smile. "Good." I dropped a soft kiss to her lips before pulling away.

She removed the gloves and discarded them, revealing those wicked talons I had admired from the moment we met.

There was only one thing missing.

I collected my mother's brooch from the armoire. The white ivory had faded to a yellow cream with age, but every line of House Taran's emblem remained sharp. I ran my thumb over it, wishing my mother was here to pass it on.

I turned to Vera. "My mother would want you to have this."

Her eyes darted between the brooch and my face, brows pinching. "Are you sure? I know how much it means to you."

I stepped up to her, briefly meeting her eyes. "The Crone told me it wasn't my most treasured possession anymore, and she was right."

Tears swam in her eyes as I pinned it near her shoulder.

My hand lingered on it, grief squeezing my chest. I never

got to say a proper goodbye, or apology. My mother went to her grave hating her only child.

"She'd forgive you, Ronan."

My eyes lifted to Vera's in surprise.

She covered my hand with hers. "If she was here today, she'd forgive you."

"You think?" I asked hoarsely.

A smile graced her beautiful lips. "I know."

I didn't know if that was true, but I'd like to hope so.

"Thank you." I kissed the top of her head and returned to dressing, not wanting to make this night about me.

I wore my finest black breeches and tunic with a red overcoat adorned with intricate silver embroidery and cuffs. I finished with the last piece—a thin barbed mantle of gold, woven with rubies, placing it atop my head. I rarely ever donned my lord headpiece, but tonight was a worthy occasion.

I offered my arm. "My Lady."

Her eyes dragged over me and her arousal perfumed the air.

"Careful," I purred.

Her eyes widened as a rare blush stole over her cheeks. "Sorry."

She'd always kept her more vulnerable emotions guarded with anger. I'd never seen her embarrassed before. I traced the color, staring down at her fondly. "Don't be. There will be time for that later."

I'd make sure of it.

I offered my arm again and she looped her smaller one through it.

I escorted her to the Great Hall. Bright light glowed through a crack in the curtains over the windows. They'd been covered to keep from ruining the surprise. Low chatter and laughter floated out as we crossed the courtyard.

The two guards at the entrance bowed before opening the doors. A hush fell over the space as Vera and I stepped up to the threshold.

All of House Taran was gathered inside, including the two hundred outpost soldiers who arrived this morning.

I'd greeted them personally, disclosing the secret Vera had stormed in and revealed only a few days prior. That, coupled with the support of the soldiers here, went a long way in diminishing the centuries long disdain they held for me.

Vera sucked in a sharp breath, eyes running over the hall.

It had been transformed into a lavish ballroom. Adorned with cascading ivy, delicate crystal chandeliers, and looping lavender garland, it glimmered with ethereal light. Every corner glowed with the soft luminescence of enchanted flora and twinkling fae lights.

A long table was lined with moon roses protected under glass, ivory candles, and lace. Platters of food had already been served so our entire House could enjoy a meal together.

Soldiers and halflings were dressed in their finest garments, lined in two neat rows to form a narrow path from the door to the throne.

Vera glanced up in shock, a thousand questions in her eyes.

"It's a celebration," I explained.

"For what?"

I grinned broadly. "You."

She didn't react the way I'd hoped, worry crossing her features. "Ronan, this wasn't necessary." She tried to unlink our arms. "We're facing King Desmond tomorrow. Do you really think—"

I put my face close to hers, tightening my elbow, and

494

holding her in place. "Did *you* really think I would miss what might be my only opportunity to show you off? I want the whole world to know you're mine, but I'll settle for my House."

That drew out a smile. "If you insist."

"I do."

Milton was waiting for us just inside the door. I had asked if he would be the one to make the announcement, and he'd excitedly agreed.

He bowed to us, then glanced nervously at Vera. I imagined it was quite a surprise to learn she wasn't a halfling, but my mate. "Do—Do you like the decorations, My Lady?"

"He did them himself," I whispered.

She graced him with a smile. "They're beautiful, Milton."

His shoulders sank with relief. "Thank you, My Lady." He turned to address the crowd. "May I announce Lord and Lady Taran!"

I dropped Vera's glamour.

A short stretch of silence followed, filled with amazement and shock—both at Vera's true identity, and that no lord would ever take a lady that wasn't his mate—before the hall erupted in wild cheering and applause.

I guided Vera to the start of the procession.

"Is it really true?" Alec, one of my youngest warriors, asked. "You're mates?"

Vera stared up at me adoringly, and I soaked up her attention. "We are."

His throat bobbed with nerves as his gaze fixed on Vera. "Please pardon the intrusiveness, My Lady, but-but can you have children?"

Vera took no offense to the question, smiling softly. "What's your name?"

"Alec, my Lady."

"Nice to meet you, Alec. Yes, I can have children."

Alec's eyes brightened. He slammed a fist over his heart as he bowed. "My Lord and Lady."

We continued down the line, greeting halflings and soldiers alike. The same questions of our matehood and Vera's fertility were repeated, and each time we answered, we saw them come alive with hope. Because that's what we represented. A glimmer of hope, a chance at a future for the fae for the first time in five hundred years.

Near the end of the line, closest to the throne, waited our friends. Kylah, Kian, and Finn wore wide smiles. Liam was with them.

"What's he doing here?" Vera hissed as soon as she caught sight of Lord Cern.

"I invited him." He was taking a great risk harboring our people, and if someone tried to keep me from Vera the night before a battle, I'd scorch the Lands to get to her. "Be polite."

She sent me a sharp look but didn't argue.

Liam acknowledged me with a nod. "Congratulations." He reached for Vera's hand and kissed it. "You look ravishing, Lady Taran."

She didn't return his greeting, discreetly jerking her hand out of his grip. "I've got a knife under this dress," she hissed quietly. "If you so much as look at Kylah wrong, I'll use it."

Amusement formed between his lashes. "Noted."

We moved along and I leaned toward her to whisper, "That's not exactly what I had in mind."

"I didn't stab him," she whispered back. "That was very polite."

I chuckled and pressed a kiss to the top of her head. "My protective little mate."

Kian greeted us next. He slammed a fist over his heart, bowing. "Maybe in the next life, Trouble." He winked and dropped a quick kiss on her cheek. I released a warning growl that had him dancing away with a laugh.

Kylah pushed past him to wrap us in a hug. "I am so happy for you two." She squeezed us tightly before stepping back.

Finn came forward. "Congratulations to you both." He shocked me by wrapping me in a tight embrace. Finn wasn't fond of physical touch. He pulled back, and a silent exchange passed between him and my mate. It ended in him bowing to her.

"You managed to win over Finn," I said as we moved along.

"I don't think 'win' is the right word. More like, I forced him to begrudgingly accept I wasn't going anywhere."

I laughed softly.

I expected that to be the end of the procession, but to my shock, Hunt waited for us by the dais.

He bowed to Vera. I held out my hand. He didn't move to reciprocate. A brief, tense moment passed until he clasped my hand, pulling me close. "I'm not here for you," he growled quietly.

He released me and I helped Vera up onto the platform before joining her and clasping her hand. The hall was silent, every face focused on us.

"Tomorrow, we ride into battle." My booming voice echoed throughout the space. "I wanted you to know what you're fighting for. Tomorrow is not just about survival. It's about hope." My gaze met Vera's. "May I introduce Vera, my mate, and Lady of this House."

The hall burst into thunderous applause. The sound was deafening, rattling the weapons on the walls. The whooping calls and whistles went on for several minutes. The noise died down when Finn stepped forward carrying an exact replica of my headpiece. He presented it to me, before he returned to the line.

At that moment, I regretted that I couldn't truly claim Vera, not in the Old Ways. It was too risky. This would have to do for now.

Raising the mantle, I stared down at my mate. "I claim you," I whispered just for her and gently set the crown on her head. Tears misted her eyes, brightening her lovely gaze.

I grabbed her hand and turned us to the crowd. "I give you Lady Taran!"

The hall exploded in applause.

"Bow before your Lady."

The soldiers and halflings fell to their knees, slamming their fists over their hearts. Kylah, Kian, Finn, and Hunt bowed while Lord Cern gave a lone nod of respect.

"You can tell them to rise," I whispered.

Vera's face lit up. "Really?"

I nodded.

She cleared her throat, and said in the most dignified tone possible, "You may rise."

When they did, I could tell she wanted to dance on the spot. Her exuberance was adorable. I pulled my power-hungry mate in for a kiss.

We angled apart, and I escorted her around the table that had been set up on the dais. It was a smaller version of the one below with enough seating for us, Kylah, Kian, Finn, Liam, and Hunt.

Milton must have known Hunt would be joining us.

We stood behind our chairs, gazing out at the crowd. "Would you like to give them another command?"

She nodded eagerly.

"Tell them they can find their seats."

Again, she used her most dignified voice, sounding like a

Lady worthy of my mother's brooch. "You may find your seats."

The Great Hall filled with the sound of scraping chairs while our party joined us on the dais. I leaned close to Vera. "This night is for you, but there is one more thing I need to do."

She gave her assent, and I straightened raising a goblet. "I have one more announcement."

A hush fell over the hall.

"I name Kian Taran Army Commander."

Kian's face went slack with shock.

I lifted my goblet to him. "I can think of no one I trust more to lead our men and women into battle. To you." I took a drink, and the hall rippled with movement as everyone did the same.

A round of congratulations circled our table. Kian accepted each one with his usual humor, but his face was slightly red.

Everyone remained standing until I pulled Vera's chair out for her before taking my own on her left. Finn sat on my left along with Kian and Liam. Kylah took Vera's right and Hunt sat on the end.

"Let us eat!" I bellowed.

Everyone dug into their meals.

Kian darted Vera a glance. "Did she put you up to that?"

"No. You earned it, cousin."

His face brightened before he turned to his food.

Finn leaned toward me. "I'm happy for you, brother."

I clasped him on the shoulder. "Thank you for standing by me all these years."

"Thank you for doing the same."

I squeezed once before dropping my hand.

Light chatter mingled with scraping utensils at our table. As dinner wore on, the goblets of poitin were loosening everyone's smiles and lips. Hunt especially. The man had a vice for vices and was four cups ahead of everyone else.

Vera nudged me, tipping her head toward where Kylah and Hunt were getting cozy at the end of the table. Hunt grunted something that made her laugh, and a metallic crunching filled the air.

I glanced to my left. Liam's fork was bent in half. He hadn't touched his food.

"Lord Cern, your food is getting cold," I noted, a silent warning to mind his business.

Vera turned toward him, followed his eyeline, and scooted her chair up to block Kylah from view. "You lost your chance, Asshole," she muttered under her breath.

She returned to her dinner, missing the calculating glare Liam leveled on Hunt as he drummed his fingers on the table.

I knew that look. It was the same look he'd given Kylah's father the day he discovered the lightning scars. Nothing happened to Lord Belenus that day, but a year later, he mysteriously went missing. His body was never found.

I'd bet good silvers Liam was plotting how he would make Hunt's murder look like an accident ten years from now. That's how he operated, decades ahead of the rest of us.

I caught his gaze and narrowed mine in warning. 'You're a guest here,' I mouthed. 'That can easily be changed.'

'If I watch her smile at him one more time, I'll pour acid into his drink,' he mouthed back.

I rose and clapped my hands. "It's time to dance."

Everyone quickly finished their plates, and the banquet table was dismantled and set along the walls, leaving an open area.

I stretched my palm out toward Vera. "May I have this dance, Lady Taran?"

She rose hesitantly, darting a nervous glance at the dance floor as she placed her hand in mine. I guided her off the dais. The crowd parted, shuffling against the walls.

I placed a hand on the small of her back, jerking her close, and grasped her left hand.

"I don't know how to dance," she whispered, settling her hand near my shoulder. "And I'd rather not make a giant fool of myself in front of our people five seconds after being introduced as their Lady."

It warmed my heart to hear her call them our people.

"Do you trust me?"

Her eyes lifted to mine. She stared intently for a moment before the gentlest of smiles touched her lips. "With every piece of me."

43

VERA

A grin lit up Ronan's face, turning it from intimidating to heart stopping in an instant. His metallic eyes were soft and serene, his smile strikingly white against his tanned face. He looked so handsome, it was hard to breathe.

He looked every inch the fae lord, cutting a commanding figure in his fine clothes and crown.

His broad shoulders filled out the red velvet jacket and cream undershirt nicely. Dark dress pants hugged his muscular legs and ended at glossy boots. He was freshly shaven, his finger-length blond hair styled roguishly to one side with a gold crown perched atop.

Though he was clean and polished, he couldn't erase his wild edge. The dark flames tattooed across his throat peeked out beneath his collar. The slight bend to his nose, and scar cutting through his lips interrupted his otherwise perfect face.

He leaned close, our breaths mingling. "So do I."

An enormous smile seized my lips. My hand smoothed up over his shoulder and neck to rest on his cheek as my eyes shifted between his. My voice was a feather's brush. "I love you, Ronan Taran."

He pressed his forehead to mine. "I love you, Little Thief." His shaky breath tumbled over my lips as a shudder ran through him. "So much it terrifies me."

He pulled back, and I glimpsed fear mingled with adoration in his eyes. Not fear of loving me, fear of losing me.

My hand slid from his cheek to his shoulder as I pinned him with a sharp, resolute look. "Don't let him steal tonight."

He stared for a moment, eyes shifting between mine before he gave a firm nod and clutched me against him. "Ready?"

"As I'll ever be."

He made a gesture.

A low drumbeat started. Kian stepped out and sucked in a deep breath before belting, "Oh, we'd be alright if a knife was at our throats."

The crowd echoed him in unison.

Oh, we'd be alright if a knife was at our throats.

Oh, we'd be alright if a knife was at our throats.

Thump. Thump. Thump. Their feet hit the floor in time with the slow drumbeat.

We didn't move as the hall sang around us.

"What are we waiting for?" I asked in hushed tones.

He grinned, his eyes lighting up. "You'll see."

Hunt took up the next line. "Oh, we'd be alright. If. A. Knife. Was. At. Our. Throats. Because we know the battle's not yet won."

Because the battle's not yet won.

Because the battle's not yet won.

The beat picked up tempo.

Ronan spun me gently before pulling me back in, but we still weren't dancing.

Next, Kylah sang, "And a Taranis fae never runs."

And a Taranis fae never runs.

"We'll fight until our dying breath," came from Finn.

We'll fight until our dying breath.

Until our dying breath!

"Oh, we'd be alright if a knife was at our throats! Ho!" Kian finished off the song and started it over again, the crowd echoing each line, much quicker than before.

Oh, we'd be alright if a knife was at our throats. Because the battle's not yet won. And a Taranis fae never runs. We'll fight until our dying breath.

A fiddle joined in, strumming out a quick, jaunty beat.

"Hold on," Ronan whispered.

That was my only warning before he swept me around the room. We spun in circle after circle, my hair flying out behind me.

Ronan moved me effortlessly, gliding us around the room in large, sweeping circles.

We circled the crowd in a wide loop. They were singing and stomping their feet in tune with the words, cheering us on.

Oh, we'd be alright if a knife was at our throats. Because the battle's not yet won. And a Taranis fae never runs. We'll fight until our dying breath.

He stopped us, flung me out, before spinning me back, and nearly dipped me to the floor.

Applause and whistles rang out as he kissed me deeply.

He jerked me upright, and we skated in wide circles, flying around the floor. Ronan was firmly in command of the dance, as he was in all things, but he scrutinized my face every few seconds to ensure I was enjoying myself and adjusted course if needed.

I was already flushed from the little poitín I'd drunk, and the dancing only intensified the color spreading across my cheeks. I was hot, dizzy, and wonderfully giddy. I couldn't contain my smile as we spun in a never-ending series of circles, my dress fanning out like flames.

The lights and faces blended together in a beautiful swirl. The animated singing was interrupted by the loud cheering of Kylah and Kian every time we passed.

I tipped my head back, laughing, joy swelling in my heart. Never in my wildest dreams could I have imagined this moment—dancing with the love of my life, surrounded by people I loved and cherished, who loved and cherished me back.

With a startled gasp, I realized what I was feeling, and tears pricked my eyes.

"What is it?" Ronan's voice was tight with concern. I could feel him starting to slow us and tightened my hand over his back in silent demand to keep going.

He did.

I took a moment to gather my thoughts.

"I—" I choked on the word and had to stop to clear the lump in my throat. "I'm happy. For the first time in my life, I'm deliriously happy."

The worry in his gaze fell away, replaced by adoration. He stared at me in silence for so long, *I* started to worry.

"What?"

He grazed a thumb across my cheek, his touch achingly light, as if he feared anything stronger and I would vanish. "You're everything I prayed for in my darkest hour."

Tears slipped down my cheeks, but for once I was crying with happiness. Ronan's rough fingers were there to wipe them away.

The lively song ended. A soft, moving tune took its place as the fiddle slowed and a flute joined it.

Ronan stopped us, lowering his hands to my hips. I threaded my arms around his neck, and we swayed intimately to the music.

As I stared into his soft silver eyes spotted with emerald flecks, the rest of the room fell away. It was just Ronan and I, moving in time with the beautiful melody.

I glided my hand up his neck and played with the hair at his nape. "Thank you for tonight," I whispered.

He pressed a soft kiss to my temple. "I'm only sorry I didn't do it sooner."

I rested my head against his shoulder, and let Ronan move us to the music, content just to be in his arms. Everything was so perfect, I wished I could stop time, and stay in this moment forever. I wished tomorrow didn't have to come.

When the song ended, disappointment wormed its way through me.

"Please join us," Ronan announced, and people flooded the dance floor as a more upbeat tune began.

Ronan and I danced to another song before a throat cleared behind us. "Can an old man cut in?"

I whipped around. Marty was there, holding a bouquet of flowers.

"Marty!" I lunged toward him so quickly, my crown clattered to the ground. I wrapped him in a hug, squeezing tight. "How did you get here? How long have you been here? How did you even—"

"We met while I was looking for you," Ronan said, voice low. "I had Kian run him here."

I turned and threw myself at him. The heady scent of vanilla and amber wood flooded my nostrils. "Thank you," I mumbled into his jacket.

He banded an arm around my back, dipping us to collect my fallen headpiece. "You're welcome." He gently placed the crown atop my head.

"One dance," Ronan warned Marty as he released me. "Then I'll be returning for my mate."

"One dance," Marty agreed.

Ronan kissed me again before he strode off and approached Liam. The latter was glaring at Hunt and Kylah dancing together. Beside them, Finn and Gisa were dancing intimately.

I faced Marty with a huge smile. "I can't believe you're here."

His eyes crinkled. "You look beautiful, Darlin'." He shook out the flowers I'd squished during our hug. "These are for you."

"Thank you." I accepted them and set them aside on a table. "May I have this dance?"

He chuckled. "You may."

I hadn't heard his dry, rasping laugh in ages and it instantly brought a smile to my face.

We clasped hands and stepped back and forth in time with the music.

My eyes ran over his face as we danced. There was no inkling of resentment for me not responding to his note—technically, I had, but he'd never received my message—but I still felt like I needed to clear the air.

"I'm sorry I didn't respond to your letter," I said as we swayed. "I wasn't sure . . ." My sentence trailed off. I was uncertain how to phrase it.

"I wasn't double crossing you like all those other Rogue bastards," he finished. "I understand, Darlin'."

I smiled softly, relief washing through me.

I was so grateful for Marty, and I regretted that I hadn't always treated him right.

The Crone had taught me to read and write, but there were still huge gaps in my education when I arrived at the Rogues. I used to sneak out to Mayhem's school house in between practice, watching and listening through a window.

Marty had caught me reading one of the books I'd stolen

and offered to help. I was so embarrassed, I threw the book at his face and ran.

He tracked me down at the Rogues' compound and whacked me over the head with it. *Consider us even, Darlin'. Be at my saloon in an hour.*

We spent every day of the next three years together. I'd hang out in his saloon, and he'd teach me everything he knew. He even offered to talk to Boone about getting me a vest multiple times, but I declined. It didn't feel right asking him to do more than he already was.

Once the lessons were finished, we saw less of each other. I was too busy with the Rogues, and Marty's kindness made me uncomfortable. He never asked for anything in return. In my messed-up mind, that made him untrustworthy.

Knowing what I know now—that he had seen me as a daughter—I wish I had gone back more.

"Thank you for everything you've done for me," I said sincerely. "It might not have seemed like it at times, but you were the only good thing in my life for a long time."

He pulled me in for a hug. "It was my pleasure, Darlin'," he whispered. He flashed a glance at Ronan as he pulled back. "You've got a lot of good in your life now. You don't need an old man like me."

I shook my head. Wavy tendrils tickled my cheek with the motion. "I'll always need you."

He smiled.

"How's Esma?" I asked, wanting to lighten the mood.

Marty's grin took up his whole face. "We're expecting."

"Marty!" I shrieked, a smile cracking my face. I yanked him into a hug. "Congratulations! I'm so happy for you."

We pulled back and I saw the faint glimmer of tears in his eyes. He quickly turned away and dried them. "Yeah—" his voice caught. "Yeah, we're both real excited."

"I can't wait to meet them." I was going to spoil their kid rotten.

His face grew unexpectedly sober. "You will," he said firmly.

My forehead crinkled. "Will what?"

"*Meet them.*"

Tension coiled in my stomach. "Ronan told you about King Desmond."

The lines around his eyes grew strained. "I wish there was something I could do to help."

"You're doing a lot just being here."

The song died off. In my peripheral, I saw Ronan had finished his conversation with Liam, and was watching us.

Marty leaned in to whisper, "You beat that bastard king's ass, Darlin'. You hear me? You beat him good."

"I will," I said, sounding far more confident than I felt.

I dropped my hands and drew him into a tight hug as worry wormed its way through my chest. "Go home," I said quietly. "As much as I love seeing you, I need to know you're safe."

He nodded as I stepped back and hunted for Kian amongst the crowd. Our eyes met. 'Please take him home', I mouthed.

Kian's face turned mock serious. He did a curtsy Milton would approve of. 'I will at once, My Lady,' he mouthed.

I laughed. He was an idiot, but he was my idiot.

He winked before gesturing Marty over.

I hugged Marty a final time. "Thank you, Old Man."

He grabbed my shoulders, staring fiercely. "This ain't goodbye, Darlin'. You thank me another time."

I forced a smile and nodded.

"That's my girl." He jerked me in for another hug before making his way over to Kian.

As soon as his back was turned, my smile fell.

He wasn't any safer at home than he was here. As long as the Nighters had the godstone, Marty, Esma, and their baby —they were all in danger. The entire Mortal Lands was.

One problem at a time. Beat the king, then you can worry about the Nighters.

I nodded to myself and pushed out a forceful breath.

Ronan started toward me, but Hunt interceded before he could reach me, lazily extending a hand. "Care to dance, dragon?" The slight slur to his words was at odds with the sharpness in his pink-orange eyes.

I peered around him. Ronan's gaze was narrowed on Hunt, but he wasn't approaching.

Hunt had been there for the Rogues, but we hadn't spoken since the tavern. Kian said he'd asked after me. Curious what he wanted, I mouthed 'I'll be quick' to Ronan before slapping my hand in Hunt's.

He intertwined our fingers and moved us to the music while keeping a respectful distance.

His movements were sure and steady. I studied him beneath my lashes. "You're not actually drunk, are you?"

"Unfortunately, not," he said gruffly. His eyes were focused elsewhere as we danced.

I followed his stare and found him watching Kylah. "You like her."

He scowled, copper gaze slicing to me. He jerked his chin at Liam. "I don't like *him*."

Ah. Hunt wasn't interested in Kylah romantically. He was protective of her and was using the guise of being drunk to keep her away from Liam without losing a limb. Smart.

"So, what are you doing with me?"

We weren't exactly friends.

He cocked his head to the side. "I never had a chance to thank you. As fucking stupid, and unnecessary as it was, you took a lightning bolt for me."

I squinted at him. "Ronan did a lot more for you than that," I pointed out. He was the only one who wouldn't forgive Ronan and I couldn't figure out why.

"That's between me and Ronan. Anyway," he drawled. "I owe you a debt. Anything you need, name it."

"Forgive Ronan."

His eyes slitted.

"Fine," I huffed, glancing at my mate on the sidelines. He and Liam were in a heated argument. I refocused on Hunt. "There is one thing." I leaned close and whispered my request.

He sent me a long glance before he jerked his head.

We danced for another minute before the song ended, and we stepped apart.

I searched the crowd for Ronan, but he was gone.

There was a tap on my shoulder. I spun to find Milton. He bowed. "My Lady, Lord Taran wishes to inform you that he had an unruly guest to attend to but will return to your side at once."

I glanced at the sidelines. Lord Cern was missing too.

"Thank you, Milton. Let him know to meet me at the beach below the cliffs. Kian, too, when he returns."

He inclined his head. "Of course, My Lady."

I didn't know what was going to happen tomorrow, but I did know if this was my last night in these lands, I wanted to spend what remained of it with the people I loved.

I pressed through the crowd and found Kylah dancing with a soldier. She was resplendent in a pink chiffon dress, embroidered with silver petals. It was sleeveless on one side. The other draped to the ground.

"Mind if I steal her?"

He pressed a fist over his heart. "She is all yours, My Lady."

I thanked him, grabbed Kylah, and towed her behind me to the small beach below the cliffs.

The moon was high, and the sea was calm. Waves gently rolled in before retreating. Off in the distance, a storm brewed, lightning flashing across the sky, but it was leagues away.

I kicked off my shoes, hiked up my dress, and stepped into the water. It was icy, but I didn't care, wading up to my knees.

"Vera, what are you doing?" Kylah called from shore. "You're going to ruin your dress!"

I turned and floated on my back, letting the sea carry my weight as my dress billowed out around me.

"Are you telling me the great Kylah who can wield lightning to strike down her enemies is afraid of a little sea water?"

There was a beat of silence. "Of course she's not." A feminine shriek sounded, and I lifted my head to see Kian carrying Kylah in his arms toward the water.

He walked into the sea with Kylah scrambling up his chest. "Kian, don't you dare!"

She screeched as he plunged them under. I chuckled softly, enjoying the waves gently rocking me.

Fingers wrapped around my ankle and yanked me under. Icy sea water doused my face and undid all Kylah's hard work on my hair. I popped to the surface to see Kylah's pleased face.

"What was that for?"

Kian appeared, grinning like a mad man. "For being our friend."

He grabbed me by the waist, and together, the two of them hauled me underwater.

I rose up, laughing, my heart happily thumping away in

my chest. Arms spread wide, I threw myself forward, and bowled them over. We landed with a great splash, our laughter filling the night.

A great clap of thunder shook the sky. The storm was still a way off, but it was growing closer.

We ended up on our backs, arms linked, floating in a circle. We stayed like that for a long while, chatting, joking, and laughing like we'd known each other all our lives. Eventually the conversation died off and we fell into a companionable silence, letting the waves rock us up and down.

Dark clouds started to speed toward us. The looming storm was an unwelcome reminder of what we were up against.

"What do you think is going to happen tomorrow?" I whispered.

"We're going to send King Desmond scampering back to his House, wishing he'd never messed with us," Kian said confidently.

Bright lightning streaked across the horizon as I tilted my head toward Kylah.

"I don't know," she said quietly. "But I do know, he'll have to get through this whole House to get to you, and I'll be first in line."

"We'll both be first," Kian chimed in.

Warm ribbons threaded through my chest and tangled around my ribs. I unlinked my arms, stood, and leapt on top of them, mumbling, "I love you guys."

"Love you too," they echoed as we sank under.

When we surfaced, it was much darker than before with thunder rumbling overhead. The wind had picked up, whipping the sea into a turbulent frenzy, and sent my hair lashing against my cheeks. I glanced to the shore, debating if it was time to leave.

A burst of lightning illuminated it.

Ronan stood there, vibrating with tension. He pinned me with a stare so intense, I felt like a rabbit caught in a snare.

"We should go," Kylah murmured to Kian.

As they turned to leave, I lunged forward and wrapped them in a hug. "No matter what happens tomorrow, I'm so grateful we met."

They squeezed me back, telling me not to worry, that everything would be fine.

I watched them make their way to shore, a heaviness growing in my heart. I hoped to Gods they were right.

Ronan stalked into the water. He didn't seem to notice the waves lashing around his legs, or the stormy sky.

My stomach sharpened at the shadows in his eyes. "Ronan, what happened? Is everything—"

He seized my face and pressed his lips to mine. His mouth moved against me, frantic and uncontrolled, his hands holding my cheeks with bruising force.

"Ronan," I said sharply, pushing him away. "What's gotten into you?"

His hands clenched at his sides as black flickered in and out of his gaze. The sea raged around us, as powerful and turbulent as his expression.

I cleared the damp hair the wind was whipping into my eyes. "What's wrong?"

Another flash of lightning, and I saw the strain creating deep trenches around his eyes. His shoulders rose and fell sharply with the force of his breathing.

"Ronan."

"I can't lose you."

You won't, I was going to say, but I never got the chance.

Ronan hauled me against him and crushed his lips to mine.

His hands were exceedingly gentle, tangling in the crazed mess the salt and wind had made of my hair while his mouth was unrelenting, skimming and brushing and teasing. Fire ignited in my belly, and I melted against him, matching his urgent pace.

The powerful sea current tugged at my legs and unbalanced me.

Ronan caught me by the shoulders and broke the kiss long enough to growl, "Wrap your legs around me."

He helped me hike one leg around his hips, and then the other, bringing his steely arousal to press tightly against my most intimate parts. He propped a hand under my bottom to support my weight and carried us deeper into the sea.

The hand in my hair tightened, bending my neck to deepen the kiss. Ronan's hot tongue thrust in, tangling and twisting with mine in tantalizing sweeps.

I moaned as the fire in my stomach pushed lower.

Ronan pulled back and pressed scalding kisses across my jaw and down my throat, biting and suckling the fragile skin as the first droplets of rain fell. The cold water stung against my fevered skin.

The hand supporting my weight tightened on my ass as the other trailed down to lightly pinch my nipple through my dress. I gasped. The rough palm continued over my flank and across my thigh to slip beneath my dress.

The pad of a finger lightly circled my cloth covered slit as Ronan's mouth continued its tortuous movements over my neck.

My body was engulfed in an inferno. Panting, I tipped my head back, seeking relief in the icy rain. Cold water splattered my flushed cheeks. Ronan lips followed, painting a fiery trail down my throat and collarbone before latching onto a breast.

I cried out as his warm lips closed around my nipple

through the soaked dress. The sound was drowned out by the roar of the sea and thunder echoing around us. The rain intensified along with the pace of the finger stroking my center.

I panted, grinding against it, against the hard length pressing into my stomach, in a desperate bid for relief.

"Ronan, I need you." My voice was just above a whine, but I was too consumed with need to care.

When he didn't respond, my head snapped up and blazing silver eyes slammed into mine. His eyes were glowing with something far more dangerous than hunger. He took himself out one handed, then used both hands to grip my ass and position my entrance over the blunt tip of his scalding member.

He stopped there, his fingers digging into my hips.

"Ronan!"

He held my gaze, eyes glinting with a savage light. Waves surged violently around us as lightning split open the sky. "You will not give yourself up to the king tomorrow, no matter what."

My jaw twitched, fighting the urge to sink my teeth into him. "Ronan . . ."

His fingers dug in harder. "Promise me."

I stared at him as rain sluiced down our faces and sea spray hit us from every direction. He was doing his best to hide it, but beneath his desire, I could see he was terrified.

"I promise I won't go with the king," I vowed softly. "No matter what." I meant it with my whole heart.

A careful hope glowed in his eyes.

Thunder roared overhead.

He snapped his hips and buried himself to the hilt.

"Yes! Again!"

He withdrew and plunged back in with a single, powerful thrust.

I moaned at the top of my lungs, pulsing around him. He grabbed my hips and began hammering into me with a merciless force. I screamed in pleasure with each clap of thunder.

His thrusts were as rough and powerful as the waves lashing us, his expression as savage and wild as the sea.

Pressure mounted and coiled low in my belly until a bright flash of light exploded behind my eyes. My orgasm detonated through me like dynamite. Ronan's teeth gnashed. He released a thunderous roar that rivaled the storm and then he followed me into release.

I collapsed against him, freezing and soaked to the bone, but my insides were humming with delight. "Mmmmm," I mumbled happily into his shoulder. He pulled out and tucked himself away before shifting me higher and carrying me out of the sea.

He brought me back to our chambers, cleaned me up, and dried me off while I floated in a cloud of bliss. When he finished, he lowered me into our bed, got behind me, and tucked me into his chest.

He clung to me in a tight embrace, his shaky breaths gusting against my temple.

"What is it?"

"Did you mean what you said? That you won't go with him?"

I frowned, reaching up to stroke his face. "Everything is going to be fine, Ronan. I told you how well it went the last two days with the treachna."

Dread filled eyes shifted between mine.

I knew what was behind this. I cupped his jaw, forcing his gaze on mine. "I haven't taken gold dust since you burned my pouch. I want to live. I want to spend the rest of my life with you, and have little blond tyrants running around, barking orders at everyone."

He lifted a brow at 'tyrant', but he was smiling again.

"I solemnly swear to you, Ronan Taran, that no matter what happens tomorrow, I will not go with King Desmond."

The rest of his tension melted away. "Thank you." His hand slid up my hip. "Come here." He jerked me close, raising my nightgown. "I'm not through with you yet."

44

VERA

A horn bellowed through the quiet dawn. Grim-faced warriors filed out through the drawbridge as Ronan and I watched from the battlements. One by one, they formed into ranks.

"How many is that?" I asked, glancing at Ronan.

He was dressed in black armor with a red wolf's head emblazoned across the chest. A silver cape was attached to the shoulders.

He opened his mouth, but a litany of failin howls cut him off, echoing up from the Hill Lands. I counted ten before the noise subsided. King Desmond wanted us to know he and his beasts were coming.

"Three hundred." The corded ropes of Ronan's arms popped with strain as he gripped the top of an arrow slit. His troubled gaze linked with mine. "It might not be enough."

Srphies had been writhing in my stomach since I'd woken. I didn't know if any of it would be enough, but I needed to be strong for Ronan, for our people.

I captured his hand. "Stop worrying. You said it yourself, one of your soldiers is worth ten of theirs."

"One of *our* soldiers," he corrected, dropping a kiss to my knuckle.

It was easy to put the gravity of our situation out of my mind when it was just the two of us.

Last night had been magical. Ronan and I had made love for hours. I'd gotten to say a proper goodbye to Marty, and had Kian run him enough gold to feed him, Esma, and their baby for years. I'd also sent Ness to him.

It was too risky keeping her here, but there were no tears this time. I'd promised her we would see each other again, and I intended on keeping that promise.

"Ours," I said, leaning in with a playful grin.

I managed to drag a smile out of Ronan, but it was short-lived, his lips setting into a grim line. "Our warriors are worth ten of theirs when they have their powers."

"King Desmond hasn't taken them yet," I said in a hopeful tone, trying my best to stay optimistic, but it was growing increasingly difficult.

He turned away, bracing both hands on the dark stone as he took in the scene below. "He will."

The coils in my stomach tightened. "We have archers to fend off any air attacks by House Belenus, and House Brigid will only be there to heal, right?"

"House Belenus' army outnumbers us four to one and House Brigid will be there to heal their low fae instanta-neously. They will not tire or weaken like our soldiers."

The reality of our situation was grimmer than I antici-pated. We had my dragon, but there was only one of me, and a thousand of them.

We fell into an uneasy silence, observing the assembling army.

They were outfitted in black, studded armor with blood red capes affixed to their shoulders; helmets carved with wolves covered most of their faces; matching shields laid at their feet. Each had their choice of weapon.

Standing a few inches taller, Kian was easy to pick out as he moved among the soldiers, checking their armor. He was dressed like Ronan, but his plating extended to his neck.

The final soldier filed out, dressed in all black. Hunt.

He turned, peering up at us. A silent exchange passed between him and Ronan. It ended with Hunt giving him a solemn nod, and Ronan returning it. He joined Kian, helping him check on the soldiers.

"Where's Finn and Kylah?" I surveyed the faces below but couldn't find them.

"Finn is escorting the halflings to House Cern. He'll join us soon." His head swiveled around, searching. "I am not certain about Kylah. I haven't seen her since last night."

"Neither have I, but I'm sure she'll be here soon."

She wouldn't miss this.

His head inclined fractionally.

My attention returned to the soldiers and one of the srphies writhing in my stomach crawled into my throat. They were all depending on me. I hid the nervous tremor in my hands. What if I—

"You won't fail them," Ronan said with that unnerving ability to know just what I was thinking at times.

I peered at him. "You sure mates can't read each other's minds?"

His eyes softened for a moment as he tucked a stray hair behind my ear. "Positive." As soon as his hand fell away, his hard expression returned. "You won't fail them," he repeated, saying it with such conviction, it almost made me believe him.

I laughed, going for playful, but it came out awkward, betraying my nerves. "How can you possibly know that?"

"Beasts are dangerous, not only because of their powers, but because they are mindless predators, subject to their baser instincts. Not only do you possess all the faculties and reasoning skills of a higher being *and* the power of a beast, but you can control all other beasts." He turned toward the army. "You are the most powerful creature alive," he finished simply.

He said it like it was inevitable, like an outcome where I didn't defeat the king's beasts wasn't a possibility.

Controlling one tier four beast on its own didn't mean I could control a whole army. I'd controlled the horde in the canyon, but the highest tiered beast that night had been a failin. The king had countless threes and fours.

My brows pulled low. "But you just said you weren't sure if we'd have enough men."

His face canted my way. "My men and I have had the privilege of our magic all our lives. We have never faced a battle without them. It is our skills I doubt. Not yours."

A smile graced my lips. Ronan's confidence emboldened me with my own. I could do this. I would do this. *We are ready, Little One*, the dragon affirmed.

Kian and Hunt signaled they were finished.

A mask fell over Ronan's face. He became the general, the battle-hardened fae who had led thousands in the Dark Wars. His hyper focused gaze touched mine. "Are you ready?"

I gave a lone, confident nod.

I had to be.

There was no other choice.

He stepped up onto the ledge and dropped off. The walls shook from his landing. I pinched my shoulder blades together, drew out my wings, and followed.

Three hundred eyes were on me when I rose from my crouch. These men and women were all here, risking their lives for me. Tendrils of apprehension snaked through my stomach. I had no words for them, no guarantees of success.

Before my thoughts could spiral further, Ronan was there, holding out his hand. "My Lady."

I took it.

His palm was steady and strong against mine. It chased away the lingering fear and doubt. I would defeat the king's beasts because it was either that, or give up my mate, and that simply wasn't an option.

I grinned up at him. "My mate."

A thread of tenderness briefly slipped through his mask before it snapped back into place. "Shall we?"

"Let's do this."

We made our way over to the soldiers. Hunt and Kian stood at the helm. Armor clanked as every soldier dropped to their knees and slammed a fist over their heart.

I kneeled and laid my fist over my chest.

"Vera, you are their Lady. You do not bow," Ronan informed me.

I lifted my head and met the gazes of the troops. "These men and women are putting their lives on the line for me. It's the least I can do."

There was a brief bout of silence followed by a thud. In my peripheral, I saw Ronan on his knees, pressing a fist to his heart. Our gazes met. His eyes glittered with admiration and respect.

The soldiers, Ronan, and I rose as one.

We watched each other in silence.

"Are they waiting for something?" I whispered out the side of my mouth.

Ronan dipped his head to my ear. "For their Lady to address them."

"*Me?*"

I felt him smile against my skin. "You."

I'd never given a speech before, let alone one right before a battle. I'd been there for one of Marty's though. Boone had become ill hours before a full moon, and Marty had stepped in and rallied us before we charged into the desert. He was a spectacular leader. It was a shame he'd retired.

Throwing my shoulders back, I tried to emulate Ronan's confidence.

"I won't lie to you. The odds are against us. King Desmond is marching toward us with eight hundred Belenus soldiers, two hundred healers, and a hundred beasts, all armed with magic. Soon the king will take yours and we will be outnumbered and outpowered, but we have something they don't." I paused, taking in everyone's face.

Let's give them a show, I told the dragon.

Yessss.

"We have a dragon."

I backed up several feet and let the dragon take control. The shift was seamless. My body melded with the dragon instantly. We reared back on our hind legs and blasted a jet of fire into the air, slamming our front paws down when we finished.

That's good for now.

The dragon relinquished control and the shift back was just as painless.

I was grateful for my suit of armored scales Kylah had made for me. Every inch of me was covered in them except my face. They could shift with me, and back, without leaving me naked.

The army was momentarily stunned. Not all of them had been there to see my shift in the courtyard.

"We've got a motherfucking dragon on our side!" Kian shouted.

Hunt whooped loudly, creating a cascading effect down the line of soldiers. The army broke out into cheers and whistles. I returned to Ronan, and he tucked me into his side, grinning with pride.

Finn came bolting out the castle. "I need a word," he said urgently.

Ronan nodded curtly, and the three of us stepped away.

"Liam has Kylah," Finn rushed out. "He kidnapped her last night during the ball."

Ronan went still, rage sharpening his face.

"How do you want it handled?" Finn asked.

"Are the halflings safe?"

He jerked his head.

"Do nothing. We don't have the luxury of time and she'll punish him plenty."

I smiled inwardly. That she would.

"Move out," Ronan roared.

The last line of soldiers did an about-face and started north. The line directly behind them did the same and so did the next until the entire army was turned around and heading into the hills.

I fell in step on Ronan's right with Finn on his left.

Kian and Hunt took up the shanty from last night. At the same time, two soldiers peeled away and flanked the army with drums.

Oh, we'd be alright if a knife was at our throats.

Because the battle's not yet won.

And a Taranis fae never runs

We'll fight until our dying breath.

Until our dying breath! Ho!

Our army rose and fell with the landscape like a wave, the shanty droning on in the background.

We'd crest one hill, to march down to the bottom of another. Some were small and could be seen over, but others loomed large and high, blocking everything from view.

Ronan called for Kian to halt the army at a base.

Kian and Hunt waited below with our troops while Ronan, Finn, and I scaled the top. He'd chosen one of the tallest hills, and we could see clear across the Hill Lands.

Despite the still morning, a breeze swept over us. It had a dry, unnatural feel to it like pressurized air blowing out of a freshly opened tomb. Disquiet bloomed over every face. The soldiers below stirred restlessly.

"What just happened?" I whispered, with a note of panic.

"Our powers are gone," Ronan informed me.

I relaxed slightly. "We expected that."

"Yes," he started in a tight voice. "But I imagine it feels the way it did when the Eye stole your fighting knowledge."

My gaze swept over everyone. There was an air of deep discomfort, of loss. I knew exactly what that felt like. They weren't helpless, even if it seemed that way.

"The king has stolen your powers." My voice washed over them. "But he can't take your experience. Your bodies know what to do. Trust them."

My words discharged some of the nervous tension, but not all.

Movement in the distance caught my eye. Thick fog crept over the hilltops, stretching toward us like ghostly fingers. It shrouded everything in its path.

"Ronan, look." I pointed.

His face turned grim. "They're coming," he said quietly.

Dark clouds rolled in, casting a shadow on everything below. Between the fog and the clouds, it was impossible to see anything beneath us.

A streak of red lightning lit up the sky.

"Shields!" Kian bellowed.

Clanking sounded. A floor of shields appeared, each soldier holding one over their head.

A litany of bolts struck the surrounding hilltops; an incessant, loud buzzing filled the air like a swarm of insects.

Finn and I dropped into fighting stances.

"Kian!" Ronan roared.

"Archers take your positions," he shouted. "Fire on my command." Twenty men and women broke away and scaled the surrounding hilltops.

"Everyone else, hold steady," Ronan ordered. "We have the advantage on the ground. We need to draw them to us."

The buzzing grew louder until it was deafening.

"Archers, hold steady," Kian bellowed.

The first set of wings appeared between the dark clouds.

"Keep holding!"

Hundreds of figures became visible. Everyone braced. Time slowed as we waited with bated breath for them to reach us. Finally, the buzzing reached a crescendo as they appeared overhead.

They flew right over us without firing a single shot.

My jaw gaped as I watched them dive down behind us and disappear into the fog.

"What are they doing?" I whispered to Ronan.

Trepidation filled his face. "I don't know."

I heard movement below us, to the north. I wheeled around and peered through the dense fog. Dark shapes were creeping through it, but they didn't look like bodies. I couldn't tell what they were.

"Ronan," I said uneasily.

He followed my line of sight and released a sharp curse. "We're being surrounded."

The air turned eerily silent.

Nothing happened for an uncomfortably long stretch until a dark shadow walked through the wisps of fog on the hilltop directly across from us.

As they drew close, it coalesced into the figure of a man. I tensed, waiting for King Desmond to make an appearance.

But it wasn't him.

"Finn?"

Ronan's question echoed my shock and confusion as I did a double take between the man standing beside us and the one on the other hill.

They were identical.

Our Finn waved a hand over his face, and it melted into a stranger's. Wings extended from his back. He sent us a two-fingered salute before he leapt into the air.

Glamour.

Ronan and I had a split second to exchange looks of horror before the other Finn, the real Finn, gave us a smile so blisteringly cold it froze my blood. He stepped aside, revealing King Desmond.

Dread plunged my stomach.

Murmurs of confusion rippled below. The soldiers couldn't see what was going on, but they could hear.

Kian and Hunt called to us. When we didn't answer, they scaled the hillside, and froze at the sight of Finn standing with the king.

Ronan's brows knitted tightly together as his eyes shifted between Finn and King Desmond. He couldn't reconcile the image of his closest friend—his champion, his confidant—standing beside his enemy. "Finn . . .What are you doing?"

"Come now, Enforcer. You're cleverer than that." King Desmond smiled sharply. "Who do you think gave me the poster?"

Shock slapped Ronan's face. He stared at his best friend in utter disbelief as the pieces fell into place. "The poster . . .

528

the Saor . . . the door . . ." Intense hurt flared before his expression devolved into fury. "It was all you. *You're the traitor.*"

Finn let the accusation hang in the air for a moment. "At last, you see what's right in front of you." An icy smile wormed over his lips. "The Saor were too incompetent to stop your quest, so I took matters into my own hands. The king was perceptive enough to collect your blood during your visit. I used it to track Vera's brand and steal the candle. It took more compulsion than I expected, but it obeyed all the same."

He had sent the storm and destroyed the door.

"But I heard Greer confess."

My gaze shot to Kian. His features were drawn into a tight frown.

Finn's lips twisted mockingly. "You've never been the brightest, have you? I compelled his confession before he was ever brought in for questioning."

I had no doubt now it was Finn who slit Greer's throat.

"Why?" Rage strangled Ronan's question.

Beneath the anger, I could see his anguish. He had already been betrayed once by someone he trusted, and to have it happen again by his closest friend . . . Ronan was *gutted.*

My heart cracked open.

"*Why?*" Finn's eyes flashed with hate. "What a stupid question. You took everything from me."

"We were like brothers," Ronan gritted out.

His voice carried a thread of desperation. He was trying to reach the Finn he knew.

The fissure in my heart grew.

Finn's mouth twitched in revulsion. "We were *never* brothers."

Ronan flinched.

"I made you think we were. I can even admit, I had myself convinced at times because it was the only way to edge the truth, but deep down, I never forgot who you were, or what you had done."

"If this was your plan all along, why didn't you just kill me that day on the island?" Ronan hissed. "I gave you your chance for revenge. You should have taken it. There was no need for any of this."

A cruel snarl lifted Finn's upper lip. "Death was too light a punishment." The rage lingered for a moment before his cool mask fell into place. "I purported to be your biggest advocate, preaching your praises to anyone who listened, but secretly, I loved every second you suffered. Your misery was enough for me, but then you had to find your mate." His stinging gaze sliced to me. "No one was less deserving."

A horrifying realization hit me. "You knew we were mates in Coldwater, didn't you? That's why you said those awful things."

He hadn't been trying to protect Ronan. He'd been trying to *hurt* him, to break us up.

"You made it so easy," Finn gloated.

Fury like I'd never seen lit Ronan's eyes as he realized the version of Finn he knew had never existed.

"I gave you everything," he growled. "Control over my House, my people's love, my money, my unwavering loyalty and support." Ronan's rage grew with every word. "What more did you want?" he bellowed. "I would have given you anything you asked!"

Finn tutted, tilting his head. "What I want can't be given, Butcher. It must be taken. Thank you for keeping my House's magic for me. It's the only useful thing you ever did."

He signaled to the king.

King Desmond raised his hand. A shimmering pink

ribbon arced out of what was once House Ogma. It flowed across the sea and ebbed around the hills before slamming into Finn. His eyes glowed unnaturally bright as his body convulsed.

The last of the magic emptied into him. Finn was washed in a white glow, his dark hair floating around him. He was overflowing with his House's magic. It popped and crackled at his fingertips, spitting sparks like fire.

The king snapped his fingers, and Ronan's body jerked.

Frantically, I lurched toward him, skidding to a stop when I saw his draoistone flare brightly. The king had returned his powers.

Why?

I didn't understand what was happening, but Ronan did. Every ounce of color drained from his face. He released a guttural cry, terrified eyes slamming into mine. "Run!"

In the same breath, Kian and Hunt turned to the army, bellowing, "RETREAT!"

The soldiers erupted into a run but were blocked by a wall of Belenus soldiers appearing out of the mist from the south.

More joined them from the east and west, encircling our soldiers in a crescent ring. They braced their shields, holding out spears to form an impenetrable wall. A sheet of rain fell in front of them, protecting them from my fire.

The fog cleared to the north, to the valley lying in between Finn and King Desmond's hill and ours. A hundred beasts laid in wait, each held by a handler.

There was nowhere to go.

We were surrounded.

I noticed House Brigid's absence. This wasn't meant to be a battle. It was meant to be a massacre.

"Don't do this," Ronan begged. "Your fight is with me, not our people."

Finn's electric blue eyes cut to him, and a burning smile formed. "I won't be doing anything."

He sucked in a deep breath, and a swirling mass of magic coalesced around him so bright and powerful, I could feel it from here. "Ronan Taran, slaughter your House."

45

VERA

Everything happened at once.

The mass of magic slammed into Ronan. Kian and Hunt dove for him. Our forces collided with the king's. I screamed.

Rage poured from me as I ran toward the edge of the hill, the dragon bursting out of me. I only had eyes for Finn.

We would tear out his goddamn throat.

We were airborne for only a moment before a spray of arrows let loose.

Pain sliced through our wings. We glanced back to see dozens of golden barbed arrowheads imbedded in the soft membrane, tied with wire. We felt a peppering of tugs seconds before the arrows were yanked free, tearing our wings apart.

Searing pain ripped through us.

We tried to move our wings, but they wouldn't respond. We could hear the sickening flap of the ruined tissue right before we crashed into the earth.

Pain was everywhere. It felt like our blood was on fire. We couldn't maintain our dragon form anymore and had to shift back.

The agonized throbbing moved from outside to deep inside my back. I curled in on myself, in too much misery to do anything but lay there.

The sounds of battle raged around me. Clashing steel mingled with strained cries. Below the high-pitched sounds were the deeper baritones of vicious growls and snapping teeth.

I don't know how long I laid there before I gained enough strength to twitch my head around and take in my surroundings. I laid in a shallow crater made by the fall. Over the rim was a sea of monsters.

We'd landed in the valley with the beasts.

We must move Little One. Our mate needs us.

Ours? I asked.

Oursss. He protects you when I cannot. Now we must protect him.

Purpose and determination flooded my veins with energy. I staggered to my feet, swaying. The movement caused a fresh surge of pain, but I managed to stay upright by sheer force.

When will we be able to fly again?

I didn't know anything about the healing time for beasts. The ones I injured on a full moon either died or ran off.

Not for some time, Little One.

Strained grunts and meaty thunks drew my eyes to the hilltop behind me where three figures grappled. Hunt had Ronan in a headlock while Kian held his arms. They were trying to bring him to the ground and pin him there, but he was too strong.

He threw Hunt over his shoulder, and slammed him so hard into the ground, his spine snapped. He swung out at Kian with a powerful kick and sent him sailing off the hill, landing nearby.

Ronan tore off his armor with a roar. His eyes were

darker than I'd ever seen them, black as night in the Darklands. A chill raced down my spine.

Kian got to his feet, glancing at me. "You, okay?" he asked.

"Yeah. You?"

His lips quirked. "Fresh as a daisy." His humor died as he glanced up at the hill where Hunt was clamoring back to his feet. They nodded at one another.

"Kill Finn," Kian shouted as he raced up the hill. "It's the only way to break the compulsion. We'll hold Ronan off for as long as we can."

I spun toward Finn and King Desmond. They hadn't moved. They stood on their hill, wearing smug, gloating smiles like they'd already won.

One hundred beasts separated us. There were sloaughs, callitechs, feargas, kelpas, fets, even an abieya. They were all tier three and four beasts. King Desmond had brought the most powerful of his arsenal to kill us.

My stomach bottomed out.

Each one was chained with a gold collar and muzzle, overseen by a guard.

Some of our soldiers were on this side, fighting the beasts, but most were engaged with House Belenus.

I twitched my wings and fire blasted over my back. I wasn't going to reach them by flying. I needed to create a path.

I opened my mouth, imagining the horde of beasts engulfed in flames. Fire shot from my mouth in a spiraling column. It was met with a wall of ice from a callitech. The fire glanced off the thick sheet before dissipating.

I tried three more times with the same result.

I cursed. I'd never regretted not learning what the dragon was capable of more than in that moment.

I needed to control a beast from here. I scanned the

hoard. It would take too long to control them all. I just needed one strong enough to kill King Desmond and Finn.

I spotted a fomoire near the base of their hill. A shiver skittered down my spine at the dark purple, bordering on pitch-black, gaze set in a skeletal face. It had no nose or mouth.

I had seen a fomoire in action once before, a hundred feet in the sky, its black shroud rippling in the wind as it plagued twenty Rogues at once with their worst fears, turning reality into nightmare. It was death incarnate.

"Free the beasts," King Desmond ordered. "And bring me my dragon!"

A cacophony of rattling chains sounded as the beasts' muzzles and collars were removed.

I shut my eyes. *We need to gain control of the fomoire. Now.*

The dragon nodded.

I order you to stand down beast, the dragon's command reverberated through my mind.

The fomoire didn't move or give any indication it heard.

Try again.

Fomoire—

A sharp crack sounded. Something cold and hard whipped around my throat. My eyes flew wide to see a spinal column around my neck. Before I could react, a powerful yank sent me sprawling to the ground.

Rough earth scraped my skin as I was dragged backwards, fingers clawing at the bone in a desperate attempt to loosen it. Through the haze of panic and dust, I saw a dullah on the other end.

I shot a burst of flames at it. The callitech blocked the attack.

An axe arced through the air. The spinal column split in half. Alec, the young soldier I'd met the night before, offered me a hand up as another charged the dullah.

"Soldiers, on Lady Taran!"

Six warriors formed a circle around me, shields at the ready as the beasts prowled forward.

"I just need enough time to gain control of the fomoire."

They nodded.

Alec turned to me. "It will be an honor to protect you to the end, My Lady."

I smiled grimly. "Let's hope it doesn't come to that."

They struck out in unison, brandishing their weapons.

Let's get control of that fucking fomoire.

FOMOIRE, STAND DOWN.

Its eyes flicked to us. The emptiness I saw there was chilling. Beasts were wild, savage monsters, but there was a spark of life in their eyes like any living thing. This fomoire had none.

No, a foreign voice blasted through our mind.

STAND DOWN!

Nothing.

Dragon! What's going on?

It's mind . . . There is a block that shouldn't be there—a solid wall of rock I cannot break through.

The fomoire opened its mouth and a chill so cold it burned crashed into me.

The valley disappeared.

Scorched earth surrounded me. Everything was blackened and dead, smoke rising from the carcasses of grass and trees. I stood at the center of a ring of burnt skeletons. There were hundreds, and they were all child sized.

A dragon roared in the distance.

Sickening guilt wrenched my stomach in a hundred different directions. I fell to my knees and reached out to cradle an infant's rib cage. It disintegrated in my hands.

My brows furrowed as I watched the ash pour through my fingers. This wasn't right. The dragon and I had a long road to mending our past, but I knew with bone deep certainty that it wouldn't have done this, not unless I asked, and I would *never* ask for this.

For all my faults—and there were many—I wasn't the Crone.

I gasped, slapping a hand over my mouth.

I *wasn't* the Crone, and I'd die before I let that change.

I rose, dusting off my hands.

"Is that the best you've got?" I screamed at the sky.

I was jolted back into the battlefield. It was eerily silent.

The valley was filled with beast carcasses and the bodies of slain soldiers. Broberies chirped, hopping between bodies to peck at their flesh. I ran at them, scaring them off the Taranis soldiers. They took flight and landed several feet away, waiting.

My eyes drifted over the bodies, then swept over the valley and hilltops. Everyone was gone. Cold shock froze my blood.

The battle had already ended.

No, no, no.

I couldn't have been under the fomoire's influence for that long. Could I have?

Heart thumping in my ears, my gaze crawled over the surrounding carnage. Only a dozen beasts lay dead while at least a hundred Taranis soldiers had perished. We hadn't won. A sickening sensation started in my stomach and spread throughout my body.

My eyes stopped on four cloth covered bodies laid out in a neat row. "No," I whispered. "This can't be real."

I *couldn't* have missed the battle.

I pulled back the first cloth and saw Kian with his throat ripped open. Maggots writhed in the wound. I shrank back, dropping the sheet with a gag.

I took a measured breath, then slowly reached for the

cloth again, desperately hoping for a different result, but the image remained unchanged. My happy, joking, chaos-loving Kian stared listlessly into the sky, the pungent scent of rotting flesh emanating from him. He'd been dead for days.

Tears pricked my eyes as my stomach heaved. I bent over and emptied all its contents on the ground.

It couldn't be true. Kian couldn't be dead.

Blood rushed to my head. I felt dizzy and unbalanced, a coldness spilling into my veins. I sank to my knees.

There were still three cloths left.

Bile and horror clogged my throat as I reached for the next one with a shaking hand.

Kylah's perfect porcelain face stared back at me, but it was missing its scalp.

I released the cloth with a choked, horrified yelp.

How had she ended up here? Had she escaped Liam to join the battle, or had King Desmond gone after her?

An eyeless Hunt lay under the next cloth. His eyes had been gouged right out of their sockets.

It took several breaths before I gained the courage to pull back the fourth and final cloth. I already knew who it would be but couldn't stop myself from looking. Ronan's face had a gray pallor, and the skin was stretched tightly over the bone. There was a depression in his chest where his heart had been ripped out.

I slapped a hand over my mouth, tears brimming in my eyes as a scream built at the back of my throat.

"*No.*"

The word was a threadbare whisper against my palm.

Everyone I loved was dead.

Reality came stomping down on me like a giant's foot. I could feel my bones breaking beneath its crushing weight. I was breathless, numb. I sat back in absolute shock.

None of this is real, Little One.

I was weightless, floating in some alternate dimension.

This is the fomoire's doing. You must fight. I cannot pull you from its clutches.

My talons scrabbled desperately in the dirt, trying to pull myself back to earth, but I couldn't. I was paralyzed.

Help me, I begged.

My body moved on its own volition, turning away from the bodies. I didn't fight the dragon's control.

Look at the sky, Little One.

My head tilted back, staring at the stretch of blue. My brows furrowed. There were no ribbons. My head came back to the bodies. They glitched, blinking in and out of sight.

This isn't real.

That's right, the dragon coaxed. *Our mate is still alive, and he needs us.*

Steely eyes and a devilish smile flashed through my mind.

A surge of energy chased away the numbness.

I stood, fists clenched at my side. This wasn't real, but it would be if I didn't get out of the fomoire's grip.

I hunted for the fomoire's presence in my mind. There was an icy trail beneath the smoke and power of the dragon.

There's only one beast allowed in my head, and it's not you! I untangled the two and shoved the fomoire's presence so hard from my mind, sharp pain cracked through my skull.

The nightmare dissolved.

I opened my eyes to see I was in the valley. I checked the sky and saw the ribbons threading through it.

Ringing steel and battle cries reached my ears. Alec and two soldiers were furiously battling the beasts. The other three had fallen. My stomach twisted sharply at the sight of their slack faces. They'd given their lives for me and I didn't even know their names.

"You couldn't control my beast, could you?"

My head snapped up. King Desmond watched me with mocking eyes. Bastard thought he was untouchable because of his pets.

Control one of the other beasts, I told the dragon.

STAND DOWN, the dragon's order reverberated like a shock wave across the minds of the other beasts. It felt like a lifetime passed as the dragon attempted to pry into their minds, press its will into theirs.

I cannot, the dragon panted. *All their minds are blocked by the same impenetrable wall.*

My gaze cut to the king. "What. Did. You. Do?"

A coy smile lifted his lips. "Ensured they served one master and one master only," he said. "Me."

No, it wasn't possible. The only thing that could control a beast was a more powerful one.

"You need some proof, I see. Fomoire, kill that failin."

The fomoire locked eyes on a nearby failin. It whimpered and released a shrill howl before going shock still and collapsing to the ground.

The treachna, I said in a panic. *Try to call our treachna.* It would be unaffected by whatever King Desmond had done to these beasts. We weren't far from House Taran. It could get here quickly.

The dragon's magic reached out.

I do not sense it.

What do you mean?

It's gone.

"Don't bother calling the treachna." Finn's hoarse voice was barely above a whisper but was easily carried by the wind. "It's dead."

King Desmond's lips formed a pitying smile. "You lost this battle before it ever begun."

"No," I whispered. This couldn't be how it ended.

I turned and started fighting my way back to Ronan, but a thrush of beasts blocked me.

"Let her go," the king ordered. "She needs to see for herself."

I watched in shock as the beasts parted, forming a narrow path. He really did control them.

But he didn't control me, and he never would.

I raced back up the other hill.

The sight below made my stomach drop.

Kian and Hunt's bodies were discarded at the base. Their heads had been torn off and placed a few feet away so their healing couldn't bring them back.

The wall of Belenus soldiers remained unbroken, trapping our warriors between them and a rampaging Butcher. He was mowing through our soldiers like butter. Half of our forces were dead.

As my eyes ran over the living, my brows slammed together. I'd seen what Ronan was capable of in the courtyard. He could have killed them all with a flick of his hand.

A fragile hope unfurled in my chest. Ronan was in there somewhere, fighting.

I skidded down the hill and returned Kian and Hunt's heads to their bodies. Threads of muscle and tissue immediately leapt between the two parts, but it would be some time before everything was woven back together again.

Ronan was engaged with five soldiers, their swords clashing loudly as the others attempted to break through the wall of shields.

My mate looked monstrous. His muscles were swollen to gigantic portions. His legs no longer fit the confines of his pants. The fabric hung in tatters off his massive thighs. Feral edges warped his face into a mask of rage and savagery.

And his eyes . . .

They were bottomless pits reflecting the violence he was

unleashing on his own men. Gooseflesh broke out over my body, but I forced myself to move.

The soldiers battling Ronan saw me as I rounded his back and halted their assault. Ronan tensed to lunge at them, and I threw myself between them. He froze, sword held over his head, muscles bulging and coiled in lethal brutality.

With a roar, he swung towards my neck.

There was only time to shut my eyes.

When my head remained attached to my body, I opened them to find the sword centimeters from my throat. It was so close, the delicate skin kissed the blade with every breath.

My eyes rose from the sword to Ronan. His nostrils were flared sharply, his ribs rising and falling with his labored breaths. Gray flickered in and out of his gaze, battling the black. The arm holding the sword shook.

"Ronan, it's me."

Gray overtook the black for a moment. It vanished a second later and Ronan snapped his teeth at me and released a growl so menacing the hair along my arms rose.

I'd interacted with him in his battle-mode before, but this was different. It was like Finn's magic had stripped away everything that made Ronan Ronan. All that was left was a vicious predator intent on seeing all blood spilt.

My pulse leapt frantically against the blade. "Ronan, I know you're in there. *Please*, you have to fight. I can't stop the king's beasts."

Recognition returned to Ronan's eyes as gray overpowered the black. He strained against the magic, forcing him to hold the blade at my throat, taking in the devastation around us.

Tears welled in his eyes. "Forgive me."

Black slammed down over his eyes. He pulled back the sword.

A scalding flash of pain flared in my stomach. I glanced down to see a blade sticking out of it. I staggered back, lips parted in shock. My hand came to the wound as I stumbled back and fell.

Blood pumped through my fingers at an alarming rate. I put more pressure, screaming at the accompanying blast of pain. Soldiers tried to rush to my side, but Ronan cut them down, one by one.

Two figures surrounded me as I collapsed on my back, a deluge of sharp curses flying off their tongues. Hunt and Kian's faces swam above me in the haze of pain. Hands brushed aside mine and pressed to my stomach. I cried out.

"Heal her!"

"I can't! Just slow the bleeding until her healing kicks in!"

The rending of fabric sounded far away. More pressure came to my wound.

"Stay with us, Trouble."

There was a great roar, and my helpers disappeared.

I touched my hand to my stomach, feeling the blood leaking under my palm. I knew this couldn't kill me, but it sure felt like I was dying. Sharp spikes of pain shot through my stomach as the flesh began to knit together.

A sound drew my attention up. King Desmond and Finn loomed on the hill above me.

With the little energy I could muster, I raised a shaking hand to shoot a torrent of flames at them.

"I wouldn't do that if I were you," King Desmond warned. "I've given the beasts a kill command. I die and every beast in my arsenal will reign darkness on this House and all its people."

My stomach plummeted.

"You're lying," I hissed.

Except he couldn't.

I turned my hand on Ronan, wincing as a barrage of flames shot toward him. I didn't want to hurt him, but I didn't know what else to do. Without looking, Ronan whirled his sword behind his back. The steel shielded him from the attack.

My hand fell limply to my side.

Time seemed to slow as I took in the scene around me. The heavy tang of blood hung in the air. The cries of the dying echoed all around. Our people were falling left and right to Ronan's sword.

Kian was unconscious. Hunt was slipping in a pool of his own blood as he tried to get to his feet. His right arm hung off his shoulder, connected by only a few bits of sinew.

As Ronan spun, slicing out his sword, I saw the glint of tears on his cheeks. Ronan was in there, watching as he slaughtered his House one by one.

Killing Finn's House had devastated him. This . . . there was no coming back from this.

A heavy weight wrapped around my heart as my hand slipped to the dagger hidden in my boot. It took a few tries to get to my feet, but I managed. The dagger felt impossibly heavy in my hand. I tightened my fingers on the hilt.

Hunt's eyes locked on the weapon before sliding to my face. Pain tightened his features. He knew what I intended. He'd been the one to give it to me. It was the favor I had asked of him —a dagger made of pure gold.

I promised Ronan I wouldn't go with the king, and I'd meant it at the time. The dagger had been a back-up plan. If King Desmond won, he wasn't going to take me alive.

But things had changed.

Hunt said nothing.

My gaze found Ronan. He didn't notice me. He didn't see the tears streaming down my face or me raising the knife to my chest. "I love you and I'm sorry," I mouthed.

Gripping the dagger with two hands, I poised it right over my heart, and faced King Desmond.

"I want to make a bargain."

Vera and Ronan's story continues in...
Nights of Gold and Gods

Pre-Order on Amazon

ACKNOWLEDGMENTS

Ya'll, this book and I have been through the wringer. I had what I thought was a great draft waiting for me when I published Nights of Iron and Ink. While I was working through the last round of edits before it went to betas, my mom was diagnosed with cancer for a second time. The proceeding couple months were a scary time (don't worry she's doing great now).

In addition to high anxiety about my mom's health, I was hit with the worst seasonal depression of my life. Just getting through the day was a struggle. At the same time, I realized I *hated* the draft of Nights of Steel and Shadow I had spent months writing and editing.

I was devastated.

With a release date looming, I made the incredibly difficult decision to scrap the whole draft and start over. The rewrite was hard. It took *eight months*. I spent most of the time writing it questioning if I had made the right call, or if maybe I just wasn't as good of a writer as I thought I was.

But, I'm just as stubborn as Vera and Ronan, and I refused to quit. I had faith and kept showing up, and it paid off. Out of that hardship, this beautiful story was born, and I love it as much as Vera and Ronan love each other, and as you know, that's a hell of a lot.

First and foremost, I have to thank M.H. You were my rock and sounding board through this whole experience. Thank you for all the omelets when I was plugging away at the keyboard. Thank you for all the understanding and support when I had to say no to things so I could work on this story. Thank you for all the little things you did to make my life easier. This book wouldn't exist without you. BIG LOVE.

Thank you to my bestie Jennifer for taking all my calls and listening to me every time I needed love, support, or guidance for this book. You got me through some very dark times.

Lastly, thank you to all my readers who stuck with me while I struggled to get this book out. You have no idea what your continued love and support meant to me.

Made in the USA
Las Vegas, NV
22 November 2024